COCOA
CARA MIA

COCOA
CARA MIA

R. T. EPLING

XULON PRESS

Xulon Press
2301 Lucien Way #415
Maitland, FL 32751
407.339.4217
www.xulonpress.com

Paperback ISBN-13: 978-1-66284-937-4
Ebook ISBN-13: 978-1-66284-938-1

Fibbies – FBI agents.

Benjamin Silverman – Mossad agent.

Sean – Irish hitman.

Daniel Colzani – Owner of the Black Tulip restaurant. Daughter Tanya.

Bernie – Homeless guy on King Street. Sleeps under Hubert Humphrey Bridge.

Billy Paine – Teenager works at the boat rental dock on the Indian River.

PROLOGUE

Cocoa, Florida Funeral Home

HER EYES ARE so startling. They enchant like the blue of an iris, its first bloom in spring.

Her name is Iris Anne Silverman. Honestly, her hair is the color of honey wheat. Soft skin is porcelain. Beneath the Roman nose, those lips still had a blush of pink youth even in death.

His call: COME FORTH
Was not for me –
His voice: VENGENCE IS MINE
I will repay –
"Let's go Rock. Visiting hour is starting."

Toby "Rock" Tyler listened as in a trance. The night sweats and shaking were absent. This was not a nightmare or reoccurring reflection; this was real time mental rage. What kind of a man could do this to an innocent child, and what would a man do to him if he could confront this monster alone? This thought, like so many others lingered and still no answer came. He had acted out several possible scenarios over the years in subconscious sleep.

None of them lined up now with the sermons of the previous three funeral services. The first one for his wife, Natasha, last year for two little black girls, and now a white girl from a wealthy family has been found—all along King Street, Cocoa, Florida. A press release named the man, King Street Killer, in headlines after the second girl was found along the section of King Street that extended west of Cocoa. Funeral sermons for the past two murdered children called for a restraint in emotions and peaceful non-violence in Cocoa by their mothers and so far, there has been peace.

A fury within a small vocal group had been raised then and charges made that the authorities were not committed to the mutilated little girls because they were black. One year later, today's headline reopened those old wounds.

A sense of foreboding now hangs over our town. Out historic spot in central Florida's east coast along the Indian River is fearful. Gone are the carefree days filled with fun in the sun. Outside influences threaten our peace and tranquility. Illegal drugs, race baiting, politics, and murder have invaded our paradise.

SUNSHINE NEWS ~ COCOA Monday, November 18, 2013
Rowena Simpson
KING STREET KILLER - STRIKES AGAIN!!

This time an FBI profiler is brought in.

Last Year – not one; but two little girls were, sexually assaulted, and brutally murdered on the west side of Cocoa. Their funerals were well attended by West Side Community

Church. Our county sheriff, mayor, city police chief, and a few other east side citizens attended.

Reverend Jerimiah of the West Side Community Church preached and called for peace and calm in our community. Both children were remembered and their mother's wishes were carried out for Serena "Rene" Jones and Sabrina Moore. No disrespect was shown toward the officials.

Perhaps a society that condones and, in many cases, supports the use of street drugs and the abuse of young girls in real life as well as in all forms of entertainment has come to Cocoa.

Human trafficking for sexual abuse and cheap labor is here in our backyard. This goes unreported in most cases because there are large sums of money to be made by the wealthy among citizens of Cocoa.

We have been ignorant. After learning of the crimes, we have been willing to look the other way in denial. Excuses of unemployment, uneducated youth, and breakdown of families has lulled us to sleep. Especially in the predominant African American west side of Cocoa, we watched and waited as the problems increased. Pressure has been building and is ready to explode.

It may take another September 11, 2001, attack to bring the sleepy citizens of Cocoa back from their drug and alcohol induced slumber. There are rumors similar plans are in the works from outside. Many within America believe the country has gone to the dark side of civilization, never to return.

Politicians and their lawyers skirt the constitution with reckless abandon, all for political advantage. Is there any wonder that the overthrow of the government is seriously debated among the citizens? The support for radical change is heard every day. Can revolution in America be far away? Most believe there is no political solution to our self-inflicted mortal wounds. The self-indulgent political leadership is in large part the reason for the moral decline of America. The capitalistic/socialistic experiment has failed.

A clarion call for return to moral restraints and family-oriented rule has sounded loud and clear. There are small groups in every country that are rebelling against the greed and corruption of their suppressive governments. They long for the dignity and honor of a moral family as the center of their society. Some have resorted to violence. What other choice did their leaders give them?

Today, another girl is laid to rest in Cocoa. The funeral service is expected to draw large crowds. She too suffered at the hands of the King Street Killer according to unnamed sources. There are many similarities to the first two murders. A major difference exists though: her daddy is rich, and she is white.

CHAPTER 1

An early morning fog rose Ghost like above the Indian River Lagoon as I, Toby Rockwell Tyler, leaned on the railing of the River Front Park gazebo. My forlorn glances matched the miserable cry from the floating sea gull I called Jonathan. The yellow DO NOT CROSS police ribbon no longer restricted the gazebo I considered my outside office. Authorities had assured me my life was no longer threatened. However, last night's call confirmed one or more wanted me dead.

Zany Adam's call said she had some important information and would bring it along with breakfast within the hour. She worked as a private investigator out of her small upstairs office nearby in the historic Porcher House south of the park. Brevard County Sheriff John B. Woodall introduced us when I applied for my own P.I. license two years earlier. Though unlike in every way imaginable, we hit it off and became close friends.

Ms. Adams insisted I work under her license until mine was issued. She even provided a small desk for me in Zany Adams Investigations office. She also refused to call me any name other than "Rock." Mr. Tyler was too formal and Toby too soft for a hard-nosed former Chatham County Georgia Sheriff's detective she insisted. "Rock" is solid man! The feisty little red head introduced me to her many girl friends as "My Rock."

Few things disturb any homicide detective to the point of despair more than the murder of a child with crime scene evidence being slim to none. Water has a tendency to contaminate if not destroy vital evidence. This was the third girl to be murdered and found along King Street in Cocoa. Rain, ditch water, and the Indian River contributed to the despair in each case.

The killer in all three had left similar mutilations and the murders had been designated the work of a serial killer after the second murder. The FBI was brought in, and the turf wars and political posturing was in full force once the press was informed.

Due to my past performance in child abduction and murder cases in Georgia, Brevard County Sheriff Woodall asked me to be a consultant in the first case. There was trouble inside and outside the various law enforcement departments, so Sheriff Woodall secretly swore me in as a deputy to work undercover.

As I listened to the river, small white caps rolled atop wave after wave as they lapped against the wall below the gazebo. Mist from the fog clung to everything. Suddenly, I was startled to see a body rising up from the depths. The old panic rose up from within my chest followed by a cold sweat and a shiver that shook my whole frame.

A distant metal click caused me to turn toward the parking lot and away from the grizzly "vision" in the water below me. It took longer than it should have to recognize Zany as the face of my wife and then the third girl fished from this very spot in recent days slowly receded from my mind. I turned back and stared down at a long piece of white sail as it unfurled and drifted back down below the undulating surface. The Ghost seemed so real.

Fear of failure to find the killers of my wife and the children settled back into the corner in my mind. I had made peace with this fear. It motivated me. Fear can sharpen the senses and produce automatic trained reflexes.

"Breakfast is served, Monsieur," Zany announced as she approached the gazebo.

Zany did a little bow and placed two cushions on the wrap around benches inside the gazebo. She unfolded a TV tray and placed a large white paper bag in the middle of the table. Main Street French Bakery napkins followed with steaming Styrofoam cups of coffee from Ossorio's holding them down. Lastly, she added a tray of mixed croissants and Danish.

My face probably reflected the gloom I felt as I followed the rocking motion of the river below my feet where the vision had disappeared. Most murder cases that are closed have good evidence and witnesses are rounded up within forty-eight hours of the crime. That was not the circumstances in all three child murders. All were tortured, murdered, and moved to positions along King Street. A year between this case and the second child's murder left so many unanswered questions. Serial killers usually escalate and seek attention.

"What, no *merci beau coupé?*" Zany asked, pouting.

Zany patted the cushion next to her, crossed her eyes, and looked down her nose from her lifted head. Her eyes were squinted, and the small mouth pouted. At a distance, she would be mistaken for a large child rather than a small woman.

"Sorry, Zany. My *office* has become a crime scene and I haven't adjusted very well," I responded. "The breakfast is a nice gesture. I assume the prune Danish is for me."

A slight smile appeared on what many had described as my stone face as the smell of French Roast coffee drifted up to draw me to it. I lifted the napkin wrapped cup and took a long sip.

That was followed by a bite of the pastry and an appreciative, "Um, this is good, a senior citizen delight on a foggy morning."

As if on cue, the sun peeked out from the horizon, and the wooden banister along the boardwalk sparkled. There was strength in the sunlight and the fog would soon burn away. We sipped, chewed, and watched a large sailboat emerge from under the Hubert Humphrey Bridge.

It cut south in the rising fog. Jonathan seagull was joined by three others as they hovered at the stern and shrieked their disappointment of no food offering.

"When I was a kid, this river meant everything to me," I quietly explained. "I caught stringers full of trout, snapper, sheepshead, and drum out of her. I swam through her, and later water-skied on her, all in the dead of winter. Zany, this was a child's paradise."

She wiped a few crumbs from the corner of her mouth and asked, "What is it now that you are grown man?"

"The river weeps, and Cocoa is an angry city. This morning I turned on my signal to turn right. An attractive woman waiting on a one way out started to pull in front of me before I could turn past her into the one-way entrance to the library. She blew her horn and screamed at me," I explained sadly.

I finished the Danish, wiped my mouth, and placed the napkin into the empty bag.

"Children are afraid to play here in the park," I continued. " When I walk over here from my paying job at the *Village Voice*, the women with toddlers gather them together until I walk through Taylor Park to here."

"Georgia on my mind" started playing on my smart phone, a gift from Zany. I was still learning how to operate and remember to carry with me. I punched the right button and heard a voice like hers say, "You have mail." When I touched the screen, a message appeared:

> "Terrorists continue to attack outside and inside our country, while the two-party system and political analysis holds us hostage with paralysis. The recent capture of a good old boy from Georgia charged with bombing the lawyers who represented an Islamic terrorist is much in the news. The ACLU refuses to defend him even though a death penalty is possible, which prompted a bomb threat against the ACLU." Fox news reports. The sender was General Lee from Georgia, known only as a historic person to me.

Then the theme from the movie *"The Good, the Bad, and the Ugly"* chimed from Zany's chartreuse tote bag.

She slipped it out and said, "Ah, our county Mounty."

"Morning Zany," the sheriff's gravelly voice came over speaker phone amid office chatter.

"Morning handsome, I hope your wife is with you, or has your office been bugged?" she teased.

"Better than that, Mona Lisa has a built-in radar and more informants that this whole department put together," he laughed.

After a pause and some background chatter, the sheriff continued, "There has been a bombing in Georgia. Could be connected to a terrorist's cell in Florida. Might be some work for you through mutual friends. Ask your friend to call me when you see him."

Zany smiled as I held out my smart phone to let her see my message from Georgia.

"I might," she said.

After a dramatic pause, she said, "Okay, I'm on it like white on rice."

"I love it when you talk dirty to me. Hope to see you soon," the sheriff laughed.

Zany did her New Orleans' voice impression saying, "That would be dirty rice for you, sugar. See me?"

"Not if I see you first," he laughed.

Her high-pitched laughter rolled across the river from the River Front Park. She clicked the off button and dropped the flamingo pink phone back into her bright chartreuse bag, picked up her second pastry, and nibbled thoughtfully.

A sea gull circled the gazebo and then perched on the gazebo rail. His head swiveled, his long neck stretched skyward, and he shrieked a mournful cry as his black eyes pleaded for a meal. The expression struck me like I am the worst abuser of wounded waterfowl in the history of mankind. Marked by a missing toe on the right foot and part of his yellow beak, my private eye river assistant squawk made sure everyone knew Jonathan Livingston Sea Gull was back on the job.

A dilemma was now present. I fingered the second prune Danish wrapped in a napkin inside my shiny white hooded windbreaker pocket. I was hoping Zany didn't notice. It was a present for my boss Gus at the *Village Voice*.

I picked up the breakfast bag. While the trash could be secured, nonetheless, I slid it slightly off, opened the bag's top, and set most of it into the opening exposing a tip of the Danish treat.

"Gus has the store open by now. I better walk over there and act like I want to write my column today," I told Zany. "Gus can be grumpy if I don't get it in on time."

"I didn't give you the information I said I had," Zany said as she picked up her things. "We have a new client. He is the father of the last victim."

"Iris' father called you?" I asked her as I turned back from the trash can, my poker face on.

Iris' father was the wealthiest lawyer and major landlord in Cocoa.

Zany giggled, "No."

She hooked her arm through mine and walked with me toward her candy-apple with white trim vintage corvette convertible.

"A discrete and always accurate source from the Cocoa PD told me," Zany said, smiling mysteriously.

"I didn't know you had any sources in the CPD who could be discrete or accurate," I commented sarcastically.

"Now Rock, be nice," Zany chided him. "Most of the blue are true blue in our fair city."

She hooked her right arm through my left again and squeezed it against her as we walked toward her corvette like a happy child.

"What should we do with the sheriff's information about the father of the last victim, our wealthy new client?" Zany asked. "As well as possibly work on a home-grown terrorist case?"

I turned back toward the trash can. Jonathan had the prune Danish on the table and was refusing to share any remaining crumbs with his noisy relatives. It reminded me of how the various law enforcement agencies withheld goodies from each other.

"It's your call, Zany," I told her.

"Let me handle the wealthy client and you work with the sheriff and the Georgia boys for free, okay?" Zany asked, though she was barely holding her laughter at bay.

She nearly bent over with laughter like a preteen. Her freckled face, crinkled nose, and squinted eyes completed her disguise as a kid masquerading as an adult.

"I'll go make our favorite editor happy and write another Ghostly story about our dearly departed Ethel Allen, and maybe get us front row seats for the play rerun," I told her almost seriously.

Zany crossed her eyes, looked up while looking down her still crinkled nose, and opened the door to her corvette.

Then she put on her pouty face, and said, "Okay, I'll let you in on the big case."

I had to smile. She is so darned cute. The car door clicked shut and purred to life when she turned the key. The designer sunglasses and scarf in place, my Parisian waitress was soon lost in traffic toward Brevard Avenue looking to the entire world like a kid on a joy ride.

I followed her on foot to the French Bakery and bought Gus a prune Danish and a takeout cup of French roast coffee. At the corner of Brevard and King Street near the Black Tulip Restaurant, I watched Gus open the office door to *The Cocoa Village Voice*. It would be interesting to observe the old newspaper man pretend to miss the not-so-subtle intended reference to his age when he received my prune laced breakfast gift.

Gus was the first person to befriend me when I returned to Cocoa. We met at Murdock's Restaurant while having lunch. I saw their sign on I95. Our mutual interest in writing led to an invitation to visit his weekly paper and our friendship and my employment was immediate. That was my first day back in my old hometown, a great new start.

CHAPTER 2

One Year Earlier

Cocoa, Florida November 20, 2012

THE FLORIDA HISTORICAL Society is housed in the old post office building located on Brevard Avenue on the east side of Cocoa near the Indian River lagoon. This historic section is filled with shops, restaurants, a live theater, and two small waterfront parks. One building dates back to 1888. Early families still have relatives here.

The **Territory of Florida** was an organized incorporated territory of the United States that existed from March 30, 1822, until March 3, 1845. Florida was admitted to the Union as a **State** after being a political pawn between Spain and Great Britain.

"So, your name is Jack Frost," an elderly lady (later identified as the one the library had been named after) asked as she glanced at the sign in sheet that showed the name as J. Frost/ Research.

"No. That is my *colder* brother, I'm Jim. The J stands for James, but I go by Jim," I told her with a smile.

"So *warmer* Jim, how can we help you?" The lady had a twinkle in her eye as she looked toward another greeter, an amicable man (later identified as the Founder and President of Mosquito Beaters) who was as warm and as pleasant as herself.

"I'm writing an article about a play for *The Cocoa Village Voice* called *The Ghost of Ethel Allen* which begins next month here in the Village Playhouse. I want to research the real Ethel Allen of the 1930s and her death. Any help you can give me will be greatly appreciated," I told her. "Also, I want to write about the people, places, and things of interest from 1930 forward."

Directed to a desk in the far-right corner where I stated my name and reason for being there. This man informed me that he loved research. He was big, gruff, raw boned, and wore a pepper gray mustache. His attire was made up of safari shirt, matching cut off trousers, and high-top canvas sneakers. He stood up from his blinking computer and marched left toward the first of several long floor to ceiling bookshelves. I followed.

After showing me the section on Brevard County he said, "Go back to the table behind my desk, and I will bring you the appropriate reference books on the history of Florida," he offered.

Having learned from my early education to follow library instructions, I returned and pulled a folding metal chair up to the folding table and sat down with folded hands. After three or four trips, my library expedition leader had piled books of every historic description literally head high on my table.

He stood briefly at the swaying table's left almost at attention. I knew not whether to tip or stand and salute.

"Thank you," I said politely. "I will jot down all the titles and authors. I do not have time to read them right now."

Even my best smile did not bring a sense of humor from Jungle Jim. He did, however, direct me to the Cocoa library for information on Ethel Allen which proved to be very helpful. The 1934 Cocoa Tribune report came from the library's microfilm. The unsolved murder of my Natasha has very little information in Florida Today newspaper.

I did my jotting, gave thanks again to my Alma Clyde Field Historical Library greeters, walked out and down the concrete steps. I headed south on Brevard Ave to Murdock's for my usual gourmet gorgonzola bacon cheeseburger with onion rings and coffee. Today, I would add key lime pie.

Two well dressed women sat at a table outside eating salads, were sipping white wine, and discussing the disappearance of a second little girl from west Cocoa.

One whispered, "You could not pay me to live in west Cocoa."

The other replied, "Someone should go over there and ask Solomon to tell them what is going on. If anyone knows, it's the west side wise man."

Inside, served by an attractive young waitress, I was soon savoring every morsel of my meal and trying to fight off the memory demon of child murders.

The really interesting thing about Murdock's is that it is another historic building that includes windows from the original Brevard Hotel (1926) on the Indian River Lagoon. Other parts of the old hotel are incorporated within Murdock's or hanging from the high ceilings. The bar is made from the

Brevard Hotel doors. Today, the bar tender is "Cranky," a new addition.

A new habit has developed since I began my part time reporting job with *The Cocoa Village Voice*. The boss insists I give him a receipt for my expenses while on assignment. This is a royal pain since I have been a cash and carry man from age ten. I offered to pay my own expenses rather than go through the hassle of a debit card. That caused such a ruckus I finally relented. The Chase Bank across the street from the Bank of America in the Village now handles James (aka Jim/Jack) Frost's high finances and knows more about me than all the alphabet agencies of all the countries in the world. Frost is a pseudonym, still they know, I know.

My bill paid, I left a generous tip for my beautiful young waitress and pocketed the receipt. A T & T began to vibrate in the front pocket of my light shiny white windbreaker.

"Hello Boss," I answered.

"How many times do I have to tell you? Don't call me Boss," Gus asked in his grumpy voice.

There was a long pause, then, "Where are you?"

"Leaving Murdock's, you want something?" I asked.

"Yes. No, not anything to eat," Gus answered, "Just stop by Chase and pick up two hundred in $10 bills."

"Ah, you shouldn't have. My Christmas bonus early, but I'll take it," I responded, then the cell went dead.

A young black man with a navy-blue hoodie was at the ATM making the machine sound like a Vegas slot machine, so I went inside. The second teller had finished with an elderly woman. I stepped up and made my request.

I swiped my card, she hit a few buttons, and handed me the cash through the little Plexiglas slot.

Going inside was the right choice because the same guy was still working the ATM outside with bells bonging.

Fifteen minutes later, I handed the two hundred dollars, plus the required debit card receipt for lunch to Gus and he handed me two fifties and a hundred-dollar bill. I breathed gorgonzola, medium rare, chopped steak, and onions on him.

"How do I know this is not funny money boss, err...Gus?" I asked him with a smirk on my face.

He looked at me in utter disbelief, muttered under his breath, and shook his head while putting the $10 bills and receipt into the cash register. Gus can be a bear. I love him like the father I never knew.

Blue lights began to flash on the wall behind Gus' antique solid black walnut desk. A black and white CPD cruiser with all lights flashing screeched to a halt in front of *The Cocoa Village Voice* office. Two officers, one a lieutenant and the other a sergeant rushed in with pistols pointing at me.

"Face the wall and spread those legs!" the lieutenant demanded as he shoved me tight against the wall with his open left hand and holstered his weapon.

His first pat down missed my 1911 Colt belly holster. He found the two hundred plus in my front pocket money clip, and finally my P I identification. Then, he found the Colt and realized I could have drawn my weapon while his was holstered.

"Put your hands up against the wall!" he demanded angrily.

He handed my Colt to the sergeant who ejected the clip.

I nodded toward Gus when he asked, "Where did you get this kind of money?"

He took a step backward and then pulled handcuffs from a shiny cuff case that matched his wide black belt, twelve-inch MAG-LITE, patent leather shoes, and holster.

"You have been identified as the one who robbed the Chase bank fifteen minutes ago. I'm placing you under arrest. You have the right to remain silent. Anything you say can be used against you in a court of law. If you cannot afford an attorney, one will be appointed for you. Do you understand your rights?" he asked, following police protocol.

Before I could answer his shoulder radio called him.

"Lt. Gillard," he answered.

"The Chief wants you to call him on a land line ASAP," the dispatcher said.

"Tell the Chief I have arrested the armed robber from the Chase bank. Man calls himself a P I by the name of Toby R. Tyler. We will be there in ten minutes, out."

The Lieutenant took my hands one at a time and clicked the cuffs tight against my wrists behind my back.

"Put that weapon, clip, billfold, P I identification, and money in a sealed bag," he instructed the sergeant. "Move that crowd away, Sergeant, and open the back cruiser door."

He turned me toward the newspaper office front door and drew his weapon ready to meet the press and his fifteen minutes of fame.

"LT," the dispatcher called in an excited voice. "Hold everything. The Chief will be there in two minutes."

Not to be denied his fifteen minutes of fame, Lieutenant Gillard opened the door and pushed his captive outside.

"Say again. Did you tell him I'm coming in with the man who robber the Chase bank?" the Lieutenant asked.

"I told him LT, and his orders are for you to stand down," the dispatched replied.

A man held a video camera on his shoulder while the sergeant pushed him and others back from the open cruiser door, no doubt believing him to be the news media.

The lieutenant's vicious smile vanished as his neck and face turned red with anger. He holstered the pistol. Traffic was stopped on east bound King Street (Route 520) in front of the office.

Another cruiser arrived on the scene and two officers began moving pedestrians out of the street. They drove them across the street toward a large crowd gathered around the Black Tulip restaurant on Brevard Avenue.

Lieutenant Gillard had a firm grip on my right arm while we stood in the open door of the office.

Neither Gus nor I had said a word during this whole show. The cuffs were cutting into my wrists and my arms ached from the upward pressure that was being applied by the overzealous lieutenant.

Cocoa Police Chief John Brody walked casually up the sidewalk and led me back into our office. He motioned for the sergeant to join the four of us inside.

As soon as the officer was inside, the Chief closed the door, turned his key, and removed the cuffs. He frowned slightly when he saw the fresh cut marks over old scars on my wrists pinched by the cuffs.

"Our apologies to you, Mr. Tyler, this is a simple case of mis-identification," Chief Brody explained. "The perpetrator from the Chase bank robbery is in custody. He wore similar clothing."

The Chief looked at the bag the sergeant held and said, "Return Mr. Tyler's personal property."

Lieutenant Gillard took the bag from the sergeant. He held it out and then dropped the bag to the floor as I reached to take it from him.

"Sorry," the officer said.

"Yes, you are," I replied and retrieved the bag,

Pocketing my money clip, billfold, and P. I. identification, I inserted the clip in the Colt 1911, chambered a round, and clicked the safety on. It was completed quickly in one smooth motion while my eyes were locked on the lieutenant's red face and bloodshot eyes.

"Chief Brody, we will be reporting this robbery in *The Cocoa Village Voice*. We would appreciate it if you would supply us with all the details," Gus spoke for the first time.

It was not a threat, but the tough old editor was expecting full cooperation. Gus was respected far and wide in the newspaper business. Officials in Florida and especially Brevard County valued his views. What he said carried a lot of weight with the Mayor, City Manager, and Chief of police and the Sheriff.

His editorial on the invasion of citizen privacy had struck a nerve with federal, state, and local law enforcement agencies and departments. The public had backed Gus and let the various agencies know they had better stop breaking the laws they were sworn to uphold and enforce.

Lt. Gillard and I were still in a staring contest.

"Gus, in your report you can add that the robber was a young *black* man and that he looked a lot like your old *white* reporter," I said angrily. "And his *navy-blue* hoodie was exactly like my *shiny white* windbreaker."

Lt. Gillard's face and neck had never lost their redness. They darkened and he took a step toward me and then seemed to realize that I still held a loaded 45 and showed no alarm.

To all their amazement the man with the camcorder was still filming through the window. I lifted my jacket front and returned the pistol to the custom-made belly holster. Noticing the angry stare from each officer, the cameraman closed down and ran up King Street west toward U S 1.

Chief Brody had his hands full with the disappearance of a second child, Sabrina Moore, also age thirteen from another neighborhood playground, and now this armed robbery. The senior officers under his command were acting like loose cannons.

The fact that both girls were barely into their teens and black was starting to stir up trouble. Racism that had been under control since hiring several black officers. The former chief of police, and the mayor, who had been a local athlete, were both well-respected by the citizens of Cocoa.

I had empathy for Chief Brody, but I had no respect for his brash Lieutenant and Sergeant.

I also supported the freedom of the press and the ruling Gus had cited for his editorial.

Gus had quoted from Justice Louis Brandeis: "The makers of our Constitution undertook to secure conditions favorable to the pursuit of happiness. They recognized the significance of man's spiritual nature, of his feelings, and of his intellect. They knew that only a part of the pain, pleasure and satisfactions of life are to be found in material things. They sought to protect Americans in their beliefs, their thoughts, and their emotions and their sensations. They conferred, as against the government, the right to be let alone—the most comprehensive of rights and the right most valued by civilized men."

"The right to be let alone" and not harassed in a showboat false arrest by the Cocoa Police Department was weighing heavy on my civilized mind at the present time. My dark side was saying, *you can snap him like a green bean*…my better self was overruling with, *control your anger. You have the right to ovoid escalation of violence.*

Pastor Jerimiah had become good friends with me through Gus, who attended West Side Community Church on King Street occasionally. He had grief counseled the "cub reporter" as Gus affectionately referred to me, his free-lance writer, and ex-deputy sheriff from Georgia.

The counseling stabilized and compartmentalized my life. I'm now able to separate the real from the unreal, and to make imagined and dreamed issues lose control of my mind and actions.

Unfortunately for our mutual friend, Pastor Jerimiah was also the Pastor of the two young girls who were murdered. So, Pastor Jerimiah recommended me to another counselor.

My new counselor, a woman, vaguely reminds me of someone, though I can't remember who. We have made the transition from male to female better than I expected. It worked for Tony in *The Sopranos*. Being partially disabled and in the grips of grief after losing my wife had brought about a neurosis close to clinical depression, but nothing official was put in my record. The final verdict is still out as far as all are concerned, especially me. However, when it became apparent I was not making sound judgment decisions even in my routine duties as a detective, I had taken a medical retirement from Chatham County Sheriff's Office (CCSO). The medical evidence was public and documented.

We made great progress until that 2 A. M. call which brought about what Dr. Beverly Sinclair calls a "downer."

For an example, she used an airplane, "When a person is normal, he flies straight, level. He maintains altitude and attitude. The return of old habits can be deceptive and cause their victim to be in a nosedive before he sees the ground rushing up."

I call them night sweats and dreamed in minute detail waking up trembling, often in a rage and soaking wet.

The recent 2 A.M. caller that brought on this "downer" talked in a garbled voice but had sounded like he knew me. I had memorized the call from start to finish and was able to share it with Dr. Sinclair during our next appointment.

"Hello, Jack. What are you doing this fine morning?" the caller asked.

"Who is this? Its 2 A.M. I'm sleeping," I said angrily. "What do you want? You sound garbled. Speak up."

"Oh, I'm sorry you are having trouble hearing me. It is not what do I want, Jack. It is who do I have and what am I doing, Jack. I have a girl. That is one too many. You should know. I am murdering her. I'll let you get back to sleep now, Jack," he said and the line went dead.

The man had called me Jack. He had called the number under the *Village Voice* byline James Frost. He had repeatedly said Jack not James or Jim.

I had grabbed a steno pad and pen from the nightstand. I wrote down word for word what the caller said and taped it. The conversation still continues in my nightmares.

There was no answer at the CPD, so I left a message to call me back. I called the BCSO and repeated the call word-for-word to the night dispatcher.

Lightning flashed so bright it looked like daylight down on Brevard Avenue. Then the wind came and rattled the fire escape door. The sky opened and rain came down like it was shooting from a fireman's hose.

The dispatcher asked for my number and what time the call came. She asked if there were any demands or requests. I assured her there was nothing more than what I gave her. She said she would pass it on and someone would be in touch.

As usual, adrenalin kicked in and I focused on the conversation as written. A detailed report was submitted and I kept a note card of the essential information I needed to carry as an unneeded reminder. The bullet card was a lingering habit.

- Time of call 0200 exactly.
- Male voice garbled – scramble phone – satellite?
- Normal conversational tone. Acted like he knew me. Repeated Jack for James.
- Made statement he was holding a girl. One too many. Was murdering her.

My cell phone rang. I was keeping the land line open in case the caller called again.

"Hello. Yes, this is Tyler speaking," I said.

The man identifying himself as Lt. Robinson, night shift commander BCSO, asked if the caller had called on my cell phone.

"No, he called on the land line," I told him.

The Lt. repeated the conversation exactly as it was given.

"Yes, that is correct and complete," I told him. "Yes, I called CPD first. I got their answering machine and left a message to call me back. No, no call back yet. Yes, I gave them this number. I'm keeping the land phone line open all night Lieutenant. Thank you, good night."

This conversation also written out and taped.

The following night, the deluge came around midnight. Lt. Robinson had brought me up to date on his CPD contact. The phone system had malfunctioned the night before. They were installing new equipment. He said a Lt. Gillard was acting night shift commander if the caller called again or if I needed to contact his counterpart at CPD, *fat chance of that.*

There was a rattling of the escape ladder outside followed by breaking glass woke me from my restless sleep. I grabbed the Colt, entered the hall in a low crouch, checking the hall, and then the narrow room. Moving quickly to the broken window, I moved the flapping curtain back slowly, and peeked outside at the fire escape. No one was there or on Oleander Street below. Heavy rain continued running down the street like a small river onto Brevard Avenue. A brick shaped object heavily wrapped in thick clear plastic, waves at me from the floor, surrounded by shattered glass and rainwater. Gusts of wind billow out the French ruffled curtain as additional rainwater splashes onto the carpet in torrents.

Prudence, our elderly housekeeper, will be more than a little disturbed when she views the damage to her decoration contribution. Securing the window with all-purpose duct tape, I then attack the glass and water damage, hoping to save the beautiful jade green carpeted room.

I put on rubber gloves and then open the plastic baggie that contained a note. "*Stay out of this or you are DEAD - BLOODY*

BLACK Jack!*" The individual words appeared to be cut from a newspaper and fastened to a single sheet of lined notebook paper under a strip of clear tape.

Once done, I sat down at the kitchen table. I must admit I was tempted to return to the mindset that brought me back to Cocoa. However, after losing my wife and later my employment as a deputy sheriff in Georgia, I was determined to forget my past. My few real friends were distant or dead. The past that haunted me belonged in the sea of forgetfulness. I told myself, the present is all that matters, *"Live and let live."*

However, a serial killer's presence does something to a city. Friendly faces begin to cast suspicious looks even toward known associates. My old Atlanta nightmares were returning in full force. Another monster is out there I am sure. Unless he can be found, another innocent child will be robbed of any chance to experience a meaningful life.

My romantic memory of Cocoa being like Thornton Wilder's play *"OUR TOWN,"* about a nice life, in a normal town was beginning to fade. In a city known for its pristine mansions like the (1916) Porcher House or our oldest surviving wooden building (1888) known as Miss Julia Robert's sewing shop, Spanish moss gently waving from majestic old tall sprawling live oak trees, and quirky, southern charm, our Cocoa was about to be griped with modern big city fear. I hated to see this happening in my hometown, my city of refuge, Cocoa Cara Mia, *Cocoa my beloved.*

Immediately, a story comes to mind from my research in *The FLORIDA Historical Quarterly,* the old fall 1997 issue was still on my desk. Cities of refuge were built along the Florida coast for ship wreck survivors in late 1800. Men who manned the cities were called Keepers.

June 15, 1903: Keeper is getting worse with diarrhea and fever. I sent Herman, keeper's son, to the post office with his transcript, and also with letter to Dr. Hughlett of Cocoa about the sickness. (It took two days for the doctor to arrive at city of refuge a distance of 55 miles to give Ludwig H. Hovelsrud, his wife, and seven children medicine for dysentery. Bad drinking water from a rotten wood tank was found to be the culprit.) June 23, 1903: Keeper went to Heaven this morning at half past seven. "Peace to his ashes."

Before I went to the office of the *Voice*, I turned the note over to the BCSO without explanation. If Chief Brody wants to complain about jurisdiction and a crime being committed on his new night shift commander's watch, that's his call. My mind was made up, I refuse to be involved in any way with CPD. Let the entire department know bad blood exists between us. After the false arrest and bullying, professional courtesy has ended.

When I got to the office, I debated with Gus concerning publishing my piece in the *Voice* about the upcoming play *The Ghost of Ethel Allen* in light of the missing girl and the threat on my life. Gus had the final say and the article appeared on Thursday.

That same afternoon, a call came into the office. Gus took it and then he handed me the phone with a frown and shrug of the shoulders.

It was Chief Brody. He asked about the vandalism of my apartment, why I didn't report it to his department, and asked if I would come in and discuss it with him. He held on in a long silence.

After my one-word reply, "No," he said he was disappointed, "I thought we were friends."

After another long silence, he said he did not have time for this kind of game and that he could require me to come in. The pause continued between us.

I finally replied, "I'll bring my lawyer and we will discuss false arrest, and strong-armed tactics."

He hung up. In all my superior training and counseling, I have not learned how to handle threats in an adult manner. I freely admit turning the other cheek has been slow to develop.

Walking around in front of Gus's desk and killing the urge to thrown the cordless against the wall like I had after Natasha's murder showed no real progress, I carefully replaced the portable telephone back in its charging holder. Not wanting to discuss the call with my editor, I slipped on my old shiny, windbreaker and headed for the door.

Sometimes, concealed anger is not my best suit. The calm can be very evident before the storm. Also, it pays to acknowledge the internal alarm when it rings to cover one's behind.

"No need to go far out, Santiago," Gus remarked with a terrible attempt to sound Spanish.

I should have appreciated his effort to take the edge off, but I couldn't. I didn't appreciate the reference to my favorite novella being connected to the CPD. In fact, in my mind's eye, I could see myself stabbing a long knife attached to a boat oar deep into the ugly blood red face of Lt. Gillard as he rolled up out of the blue Caribbean Sea.

Now, that I thought of it, he had the wide face, glassy eyes, and ugly mouth of a hammerhead shark.

My better self-whispered then shouted, *"Better get out of Dodge."*

As I sat on a bench in the gazebo by the river trying to calm the rage within, I looked at the new journal I started a couple days ago as suggested by my new shrink. I shouldn't call her that. She is really a nice lady. It just goes to show what a lousy mood I was in.

MY JOURNAL
November 18, 2013

Cocoa Village
Cocoa, Florida

I am Toby Rockwell Tyler, Rock or Rocky to my childhood friends, then others.

My pseudonym and byline in *The Cocoa Village Voice* is headed: James (a.k.a. Jim) Frost. This is the anniversary of two murders.

Sunday, November 18, 1934, a lively Ethel Allen, age nineteen, was brutally murdered and tossed into our beautiful Indian River Lagoon. Loss of life is always tragic for those who love and are left behind. Of this, I am presently, personally, and painfully aware.

A day that will live in infamy, November 18, 2011, is the tenth anniversary of my precious wife Natasha's death. Natasha was taken from me by murderers yet unknown. Someone knows and I have vowed to find them. I love you Tasha...

Those who counsel me have asked me to talk it out. It is wise counsel I know. Tomorrow I will start to write about the history of Cocoa and the people, places, and things I have loved. "Write a piece about the upcoming play," my editor Gus advised.

"Maybe it will help." I will never give up the search. They took my Natasha. God help me.

The trick is to relive the event in order to solve the crime. A danger of allowing the past to gain access to my mind and begin to control my actions is a present reality. There have been times when I was incapacitated by obsessive thoughts that led to almost total compulsions. Military and law enforcement careers and the necessity of taking the life of others brought fear of wrongfully bringing harm to others or me. Yet, extreme caution can be fatal to oneself.

All the senses are engaged in a homicide investigation. The mind photographs the crime scene and those pictures are permanent. Constantly looking for the motive, means, and opportunity, you walk through the murder in your mind over and over after sifting through all the evidence and "what ifs." You are warned to not take it personally, get too close, and lose your objectivity, but *good luck with that*! Above all, do not take the law into your own hands.

I was assigned to write about the play concerning the Allen girl's death. Like "Father Knows Best," in my case it's Editor Gus who more than knows best. "The Ghost of Ethel Allen" will be performed at our historic Village Playhouse here in Cocoa Village next month. The people, places, and things of Cocoa, from the beginning until now will be pure pleasurable research.

I have fond memories of Cocoa from my youth in spite of my personal tragedy. I have no regrets serving in the military or the Chatham County Sheriff's Department. The move here was a good one and I enjoy Cocoa, though none of my close family or friends remain here.

Gus told me my former watch commander in Georgia told him I was a moral man living in an amoral complex world. That sounds a little too literary even for book worm like me.

I believe I will start with some research at the Florida Historical Society mid-way up Brevard Avenue across from our weekly newspaper office Tuesday.

*PERSONAL NOTE:

Sheriff Woodall notified me that a middle-aged black male, street name Gimp, was found executed, gang style, near Canaveral Groves west of Interstate 95. He was shot in the mouth and both eyes and ears at approximately twenty feet by a small caliber gun using jacketed hollow-point bullets. He was believed to be a pimp. Several shallow razor-like cuts marked his face. It was likely a professional hit. Someone was sending a message to everyone to keep quiet about what they see and hear in the hood.

Exact details of the homicide were not released to the press, yet a full report was in SUNSHINE NEWS the following day. Gentleman Johnny B. (J. B. Woodall) is not a happy camper.

I attended the Serena Jones Funeral.

"I want my life to count for something worthwhile. I want to be somebody, Momma. Serena 'Rene' Jones loved to sing and dance. She was a delight. Everyone loved her."

Those were some of the quotes from Serena's mother that Pastor Jerimiah used in the funeral message. The pain and suffering of loss drew you in while the helplessness pushed you away from this grieving mother. How do you give comfort to one who lost her thirteen-year-old daughter, her only child who had been sexually abused repeatedly? She had no husband. No woman had ever looked more broken than this mother.

There were several people who spoke briefly in memory of the little girl that everyone loved. Out of respect for the family, they were asked to encourage and make their comments short.

A young girl read a poem entitled "*Purple*" to Serena. "This is from everyone," she said, holding the large poster board paper over her head so all could see. Each sixth grader had signed, some drew hearts and pictures. One drew the child walking with her mother holding her hand. Her family and friends all wore something colored purple. There was even a rare public appearance of the ancient silent Solomon, although he was hidden from the congregation.

I stood near Pastor Jerimiah outside the West Side Community Church on King Street. The preacher was shaking hands with those who filed by. None making eye contact with me. The child's small coffin was carefully loaded into a spotless black Buick ambulance. Four very angry young men served as pallbearers. The most notable pallbearer is a handsome muscular teenager named John Henry. He is a former Cocoa High School all state athlete. John Henry played a large part in the school bringing home three consecutive state football championships. He is a well-known and deserving Cocoa hero.

City officials sat together during the funeral and now file out one behind the other with the new Mayor in the lead. Racial prejudice is still present in the city as it is everywhere there are different ethnic groups assembled. For the most part, harmony prevails between the races in Cocoa. There is resentment in all races against outsiders.

Cocoa resents being under a federal court consent decree dating back to 1999 that stemmed from a lawsuit claiming the city did not provide for adequate political representation for African Americans. City officials were forced to change voting district lines to ensure one district had over 51 percent of its population as African Americans. Many point to this as unnecessary federal interference and gerrymandering as the past Mayor was a popular African American and elected by a City-wide vote.

John Henry turned to face the Pastor, "If there was a God, He would have to be the Devil to let this happen to Rene. The men who did this are dead men."

His eyes were slits and the muscles in his powerful neck coiled and alternated side by side. His arms hung loosely while his oversized hands continued to straighten and then clench into massive fists. He dropped a paper coffee cup into the bucket for cigarette butts. This nineteen-year-old, covered in an expensive Hart Schaffner Marx power suit, stood out amongst the mostly modest clothes worn by the close friends and family procession.

John Henry had come from humble beginnings as everyone in Cocoa knew. He excelled in sports and was an average student. He stayed away from the gangs and drugs that were running rampant in his west Cocoa community. Something happened in his senior year, and he slowly began to change. He lost interest in offered football and basketball scholarships to several colleges. John Henry became a private young man with no close friends. He had expensive clothes, drove a new black Lexus, and he and his half-sister owned a condo with no apparent employment. Criminal activity was suspected, but there was no record of John Henry on file in any law enforcement agency.

It is said that Native American Indian women turned aside from the march of the main body to deliver their babies alone. When they were able, they caught up. The mothers presented their newborn with pride to the traveling village, especially if it was a strong man child. There was often a celebration of life in the joyful ceremony.

Such was not the case with the baby boy born to a mother who gave her name as "Rosa Lane Henry," though listing no name for the father. "Rosa" was not seen by anyone in the hospital or around Cocoa after the day he was born.

Chief Brody nodded to me as he shook hands with Pastor Jerimiah. We were still on the outs since his covering for his loose cannon officers. He was the only officer in the Cocoa Police Department who knew some of my background. Uncle Rob had been friends with him before he became Chief, and they had visited each other's homes occasionally before he died.

He knew I was a Cocoa High graduate, had a full athletic scholarship to Florida State College, was a newspaper sportswriter, Special Ops in the military, and a detective in the sheriff's office in Georgia.

My Uncle Rob willed us his condo on the beautiful Indian River Lagoon to me as a wedding present. Natasha loved Rob, his condo, and the river. All ancient history now as the condo is gone. It was sold early on in an effort to erase the pain of the past.

I went through the sheriff's office in Titusville when I applied for the concealed permit and my private investigators license. The license comes through the Department of Agriculture in Tallahassee, the state capitol. I had made it a point to meet the Chief and introduce myself. Chief Brody had given his condolences concerning the loss of my wife and congratulated me for the work on the children murder cases in the Atlanta and Savannah area when he welcomed me to Cocoa.

The heart of Cocoa is not all darkness. The city is centrally located in Brevard County which is on the east coast of central Florida. However, there are 179 registered sex offenders living in Cocoa. The crime index of Cocoa continues to be the highest of any town its size in Brevard County year after year. Most of the murders and home invasions are drug related and occur west of U S 1 in low-income neighborhoods where West Side Community Church is centrally located.

These crimes are common and not very newsworthy. They are of extreme interest to the detectives who catch the cases and do not close them. Unclosed cases are thorns in the mind of case officers even when they go cold.

Therefore, the duty CPD detectives were pleased to have the body leaning against the sign on the county side, facing west on King Street, even though Serena was across the street from the city police station. There were no known witnesses who saw the abduction from the playground, or the body posed a week later at night by the Welcome to Cocoa sign.

The BCSO, Brevard County Sheriff's Office, had jurisdiction and had taken responsibility for the investigation of this child's death believed to be by homicide. The ME had not ruled it as such pending a complete autopsy. Sheriff John, J. B. Woodall and two of his homicide detectives who had caught Serena's case had also attended the funeral and were present at the burial. An all-out effort was to keep the clues away from the press until any leads were fully developed and one or more suspects found. There is always the possibility of a guilt-ridden confession from the one who has taken the life of another. The two case detectives joined Sheriff John B. Woodall as they observed the people attending. The sheriff motioned for me to come over.

No one came blubbering to confess to this homicide of a child. There were a number of known criminals present and at least four individuals that had done time for murder according to the detectives. In conference with the three officers by invitation, I had not liked any attendee for the murder by observation. The normal gallows humor was missing. An innocent child was dead.

My work on the Atlanta and Savannah cases was mentioned as well as me being a detective with a respected sheriff's department in Chatham County Georgia. The open cold case of my wife's murder was not mentioned, but Woodall had expressed his condolences and frustration of no new leads when I had applied for the P.I. license.

Her murder had fallen to his department also due to being just across the Cocoa/County jurisdiction line. The crime scene being almost the identical spot where my wife's life ended and the best part of me departed. They were openly pleased when I assured them I would assist them in any way possible, we shook hands. Then, I went to rejoin my friends, Pastor Jerimiah, and Gus.

They had been asked to come back to the Church for some light refreshments. I noticed that even though the mother had no husband, she had her Church for support. She had a big family and the Church family was well represented.

There was food and drinks left over after more than three hundred people filed through the fellowship hall and into the parking lot. They all seemed to know each other. They were shy toward me because I was not known to them. I was accepted as a friend of their Pastor. I drew some comfort from them as they shared support for the mother from their almost universal and equal poverty. Together they were strong and that meant something real and lasting. Most of her neighbors were poor, but they were happy to share such as they had with the member who had lost her pride and joy. I am bothered by the lack of non-Church people.

I researched a case from a *Florida Today* newspaper of a recent Orange Park, Florida murder of a young girl. James Harper pleaded guilty to kidnapping, raping. and murdering seven-year-old Summer Fern Thomas, who was dumped in a trash bin and later found in a landfill. In a deal sparing, Harper avoided the death penalty. The twenty-one-year-old Harper was sentenced to life in prison without the possibility of parole.

The discovery of Summer Fern's body touched off an outpouring of support in northwest Florida and southwest Georgia for the Thomas family. Days of vigils and fundraisers were held so Summer Fern's mom could financially afford to stay home with her other children. A mountain of stuffed animals, balloons, and notes to the family sprang up near a tree across from the little girl's home.

Like most little girls, Summer Fern loved to dance, play dress up, draw, and color. Like Serena, her favorite color was purple.

At Summer Fern's funeral, hundreds of purple balloons had been released into the sky, purple flowers adorned her small wooden casket, and her family wore purple ribbons.

Summer Fern Thomas had her brown hair in a ponytail with a red bow when she went missing. She was carrying a lunch box and wearing an old Hannah Montana backpack. It was purple.

There was no Cocoa community outpouring. The burden of finding the killer of this little girl Serena attached itself to the ongoing one of finding the killers who took my Natasha.

The TDD

Stepping away from the crowd, I dialed (703) 482-0623. The voice activated switchboard put me through to an extension and a man named Richard Lawson. To my knowledge there is no employee by that name who works for the C I A. Nevertheless, I left a coded message (Life Preserver) on Richard's answering machine. TDD (The Dirty Dozen) had called him Dick.

Although I have never worked directly for what I laughingly call *Christians IN Action* (CIA), I am well connected from past military missions that included the Agency and D.I.A. "Dick" was the only agent from my past that I can call a friend, if he has friends. I also have distant relatives who were with those organizations.

While I trained at Quantico with Dick and others from the "Company," a bond was formed with them as essential members of our team. There is life and death trust in others like no other group I have ever been associated with and believed impossible. It is difficult to explain in words. It is more like a thought process that connects intentions.

The mind games in school become life or death actions on the mission. Every member of the team has a specialty, but each can do every other member's skill. The essential thing in every case is we all think the same things and all work as one body, twelve men in one body, all in one accord, working our plan. We formed a private society and took an oath to always look out for each other. We called ourselves the (Dirty Dozen Team) or DDT...a *weed killer.*

There are no poor members from the team in this DDT society. Due to the nature of our work and possible short life expectancy, the members have a stash of wealth from short term investments, brought to maturity by friends of "Dick." So, when a member throws out a call for a life preserver, it will reach one or more wealth preservers who can make things happen in high places. A chain reaction within DDT begins immediately.

Stop, Look, and Listen

After I left the funeral, I walked back to my '"outdoor office" by the River. I remembered reading that on June 6, 1967, William Hall was beaten to death on north Merritt Island in Brevard County. Since then, there have been over forty more unsolved homicides. There is great determination for all of us that Serena will not become forty plus.

"*Stop, Look, and Listen, Work the clues, Means, Motive, Opportunity,*" my mind went to work.

"Stop, Look, and Listen," I said out loud to myself.

Those three words had been taught in Cocoa Elementary by the crossing guard teacher (before you cross any street), at Quantico by the special ops chief (before you cross any body of water), and at the Police academy by the Chief of Detectives (before you cross off any possibility).

So, I'm talking out loud to myself, but I'm not *crying out loud* like a hopeless basket case, thank God. I'm recalling training and not hearing voices. I am reminding myself: I will stop letting personal issues interfere, I will look at all the evidence, and I will listen with a trained ear.

With pencil in hand, I made note of past training and trainers, and started a To Do List.

STOP:

- Stop trying to connect *everything* to solving Natasha's murder.
- Stop letting the actions of others distract from searching for Serena Jones' killer.
- Stop pretending I am retired from the human race. (I will not be a recluse!)
- Stop living in the past. (Where eating and drinking myself into an early grave prevailed.)

LOOK:

I must see every person, place, and thing that is there and especially what or who is not.

- See connections and know there are no coincidences.
- See and recognize the fatal flaw in believing everything depends upon me.
- See the weaknesses in myself and others. (Do not expect the impossible).
- See all the evidence that is offered and hidden as it becomes available.

LISTEN:

I must hear what is relevant and what is missing.

- Hear witnesses completely. Especially what their body language says and doesn't.
- Hear what the Indian River and City of Cocoa has to say.
- Hear other trained homicide people—past and present.
- Hear and act on what is known to be true.

I look at this list of things and vow to review it each morning before doing anything. A person can get bogged down in the details or careless by acting on instinct alone. This one thing I know is I am driven to use my training to find this killer of the innocent. Peace reigns now. There is no raging inside me to seek and destroy like before. Fear is mostly gone, thankfully.

There is a day I look back on now and know there is an honorable internal fear previously unknown. The fear of what I might do to another human being has passed, it humbles me every day, and I am grateful. To be honest, I have not forgiven these murdering people, but I have accepted they are human and I will not kill them provided they do not threaten others.

As a trained law enforcement professional, my job is to find the convicting evidence, then locate these evil doers, and turn them over to the judge, jury, and executioner. As a private investigator, I am sworn to submit any criminal evidence to an officer of the court. In these cases, my agreement is with "Gentleman Johnny," J. B. Woodall to control unauthorized leaks to the press.

The sheriff has not admitted even privately that there are bad apples in Brevard County law enforcement and the Cocoa Police Department. Past records show there has been corruption and disciplinary actions taken. Several sworn officers and other employees have been fired and a few are serving jail terms.

The majority of officers are no doubt good, but the few make it impossible to trust any. Therefore, "Gentleman Johnny"

(Uncle Ted's pet name for his friend, also his scotch – J.B. Rare or Johnny Walker) and I are keeping our relationship private. It would be humorous if the work we are doing wasn't so deadly serious the way we sneak around like junior G-men.

Recently, I woke up in a different world. For the first time in a long time, there had been no bam of a shotgun, or dat–dat–dat cry of machine guns, spat of my service 45, nor even the occasional fading smile of my Natasha.

The smell of oriental soup and instrumental music wafts through my two-inch cracked window facing Brevard Avenue. Viewing my large live oak doing her Spanish moss sprightly dance, I listen to my substitute rooster, the wild and crazy mockingbird practicing one of her purloined songs, and all seems right with this window of the world, as crazy as it is.

Today, the aroma of my Brazilian special roast coffee, complements of my friends at the Black Tulip, is mingling with the egg drop soup from next door.

My suspicious mind wonders if the signature offering was headed to Tai ~ Tai Restaurant or had it found its way home with its part-time chef. Our occasional across balcony visits were limited to respectful bows.

Two toasted egg bagels smothered with cream cheese join my coffee, tape recorder, notes, and yesterday's *Village Voice* on the small desktop by the window overlooking Brevard Avenue.

Somehow, I have managed to misplace my smart phone. Zany had been quick to lend me one of her extras. A flamingo pink job and she pretends not to notice my frown. All her ring tones are the same: *The Good, the Bad, and the Ugly*.

"Hello Zany," I answered. "No, you didn't wake me. I'm having bagels and coffee with some light reading."

She laughed her I know better laugh and said, "Knowing you, it is week-old bagels with 'War and Peace.'"

"Nah, two-days old and *The Village Voice* from yesterday," I told her.

After a long pause, she asked, "You going to be busy later today? We have been invited to go sailing around two. It would be after Church."

"Not going to Church today," I responded. "Yes, I would like to join you. Where at two?"

"The Cocoa Marina," she said. "I'll see you there. Bye."

There is a little girl excitement in Zany's voice even when she is being dead serious. This call sounded like she was going on her first high school date and couldn't wait to hang up and call her very best friend. It's enough to give a fellow pause and consider what he has gotten himself into.

The bird has hushed her singing, if you can call what a mockingbird does as singing. The gentle breeze continues to sway the Spanish moss as I munch the slightly stale bread and sip the fresh coffee from my old, much stained 12-cup Mr. Coffee pot.

How I would love to share this moment out on the balcony with my lovely Natasha this morning. She taught me to appreciate the simpler things in life.

I hesitate to disrupt the nostalgia by going over the material of *The Voice* and the murder of innocence.

CHAPTER 3

THE TRAINED MIND is a constant hunter even while the body sleeps. I came out of a shallow sleep, reading what my ears had heard, over and over, on the tapes, reading left to right in my mind. The same as if it was written in a case book. Even before Zany's call. *How does that work?* I wondered.

I played the BCSO tapes over and over in my window room overlooking Brevard Avenue, reading and rereading my Atlanta and Savannah notes. I even read my old *Village Voice* articles and any reader's comments that remotely mentioned children.

The latest tape was a live recording unlike my first BCSO incident report recorded. Hearing the killer's voice said almost as much as the words he spoke.

START tape: "*We're going to kill another thirteen-year-old girl. There is nothing you can do about it Jack,*" STOP: the caller bragged or was there a cry in that voice? START tape: "*Next one, I'll call her Sara. I am not scared, Jack. I am not alone, and we are not confused, or sick, jump back, Jack, or you're dead. I cannot escape. Better run again while you can. My intent is to get even then die. Hope this helps you (pause) you are no longer far out man."* *STOP* tape.

"*We.*" There is more than one person or multiple personalities involved as *"they"* confessed to murder, threaten to commit another, and kill me if I don't "*jump back or run again.*"

It implies I am the batter and he (they) are the pitcher (in complete control). When have I ever run away? He (they) know personal things about me. (*I am no longer far out* is a Hemingway term that Gus uses or an old hippy term).

I had waited for the caller to go on hoping maybe this time the sadistic murderer would make a mistake. The FBI profiler had been able to paint the picture of a man who looked normal, but was in fact one who was sadistic, driven by pleasure of being cruel for sexual gratification, possibly being impotent. Water was involved positive or negative. The body of Serena had been sexually molested. She had been posed on a night it rained. The mutilation did not appear to be gang or cult related. There was no connection to the families of the two girls or any known arguments or threats. Neither was named Sara.

The calls and crime scene gave some evidence, but none of it had brought the detectives any closer to the identity of this child killer.

He was very familiar with police procedures and investigative techniques. The body had been washed before being placed at the Cocoa Welcome sign. There were no footprints, fingerprints, or under fingernail scrapings. It had rained.

START tape: "*You are one sick bastard,*" I had stated just above a whisper. The Sheriff's office detectives who had jurisdiction had tapped my apartment phone after that first 2 A.M. call.

The discovery of a young African American girl's nude and displayed body. Her back against the Welcome to Cocoa sign facing west across from the CPD office complex on King Street, (Hwy 520) was still vivid in my mind.

"*It is not our fault.*" The altered voice was steady, although it was a familiar cocky casualness. ("*We did not do it.*"), echoed in my mind, then I remembered the first call.

"What is not your fault? Sadistically abducting two young girls and murdering an innocent child, who is not at fault, and degrading her by exposing her nude body for all to see? Let Sabrina go."

"*That is not the name we gave you, Jack.*" STOP: The last part was more of a soft whisper. That could be a female or the machine reducing the voice characteristics or a demon. At this point in the investigation, nothing or no one without a solid alibi was ruled in our out.

START: "*Listen you moron!*" The casualness and controlled whisper was replaced by a deep rage and a new voice. "*It is not our fault.*" *We did not make ourselves sick either. Who murdered the innocent in our country? Meet Sarallah!*" The line went dead.

Sarallah was later identified as Islamic for God's Revenge. *I must remember everything from Iran.* There may or may not be a connection to my past—Iran, Atlanta, Natasha, Cocoa.

I had picked up the cell phone on the first ring. Caller I D flashed BCSO. I moved the window curtain enough to see no cars parked or people on Brevard Avenue. Like the other call at 2 A. M. there was no trace. The caller had used an offshore scramble phone.

With the words still bouncing around in my mind like that morning, I sat in the shade by the now closed upstairs window curtain, placing the clues and suspicions in their place. The Brevard County Sheriff's Office was withholding information. That was a given. Me, an ex-Georgia Sheriff's detective, I am a civilian now and not privy to official information to open ongoing homicide investigations. *Supposedly only the sheriff and I know I'm on the force.*

Having a better relationship with BCSO than with the CPD and knowing a scramble phone is being used in connection with the commission of this crime, I was certain of increased FBI involvement. Any day now they would move in and attempt to take over. It was simply a matter of time until the turf wars would begin in earnest and political posturing would run rampant. The blame game would start, and politics was close on its heels in this upcoming mid-term election year. This case has race card written all over it to muddy the water. Fibbies do not share their toys. Even john q. public shared police departments mistrust of the Fed after all the political pressure applied to influence recent elections. Federal creditability is at an all-time low, yet TDD lives.

Still, the tried-and-true method of sorting out my thoughts and feelings are at work. Like a medical doctor, detectives are trained to keep all the diagnostic possibilities in mind until they are ruled out by hard cold facts. A logical reason for this murderer(s) to involve me in these crimes is there. As usual, I had all the early suspicions, but unlike a certain Cocoa police lieutenant who jumped to conclusions, I would not let these suspicions rule or even slightly influence my search for this killer(s). I'm going to sweat the details. Work the clues. It is time to call out the cavalry.

I caught a restless four hours of sleep. Most nights, this was becoming a habit. Waiting for the 2 A.M. call and wracking my overworked brain for enemies past or present who would want to torment me.

The killer said, "*My intent is to get even—better run again Jack.*"

After a McDonald's big breakfast, the bagels didn't cut it, I drove out to Pilot Travel Center near I95, an old Starving Marvin service station, where one of Brevard's unsolved murders had taken place in the men's bathroom back in '93. There is still a large billboard facing west on 520 with the young man's photo and a reward offered through CRIMELINE 1-(800)-423-TIPS.

West Cocoa is still a dangerous place. I hear heavy gunfire faintly to the south even now. The Sheriff's work farm and East Coast Florida College have a shooting range there. The neighbors, mostly black, complain that they can't tell if a crime is being committed or the police are practicing. Both happen on a regular basis. The range is open 7:30 A.M. until 10 P.M. weekdays and 6 P.M. on Sunday.

One man told the Sheriff, "They robbed a woman the other day. Shot her right out in the street. We heard it and thought it was the gun range. It was at our neighbor's house."

Sitting on an empty soda crate outside the Center was a young lad who looked like he had no particular place to go. We negotiated a business arrangement after serious discussion. I offered the young African American boy five dollars, after union-management style agreement, to read a message after I dialed the number. His call was from the outside pay phone to Langley, Va.

"Hey! Yo. There's a cracker man here in Cocoa, Florida calls his self Jack Frost. He is mixed in offing kids. Sup with that?" He read like we rehearsed and exactly like I wrote it, handed the phone back, and snatched the extortion waged fiver. I took the note.

I hung up. Behind I heard, "Man, no black man going to talk like that these days," the young linguist protested.

He looked at the ground around his bare dirty feet and shook his head in disgust. Then he held the five up and started walking toward the store.

"You won't fool *anybody*, man," he said as he rolled his eyes, giggled, and offered, "Add another fiver and I say it good."

I turned away to see a gangbanger wanna-a-be strolling toward us. Had to look twice to make sure I saw the face clearly. The young man had a lacerated long slanted face like a cow, vacant dilated eyes, rolled back thick lips, and a navy-blue baseball cap pulled tight on gridlocks. He wore a dirty dark tank top tee, and his red cutoff cargo pants hung low around his butt. No shoes.

"Sup, Gator?" the boy who had made my call stepped back as the man snatched the five-dollar bill out of his hand and dashed into the store with surprising quickness.

"Give it back. Give it back big mouth gator," the kid screamed at the closing door.

He squinted at me and held out his hand for another five. The demonic cow looked out the window.

"What's the matter with that guy?" I asked as I peeled off another five and placed it in the outstretched grimy little hand. "You know him?"

He looked at the five in his hand then made a face by pulling the corners of his mouth and sticking out his tongue toward the staring figure in the service station window.

"Everybody knows Gator. Granny says he is possessed. He does Voodoo under the humped bridge," he explained

He stuck the five into the front pocket of his cut off bibbed overalls. Only one strap across his slim shoulder held the denim up. The silver button on the other side was missing and that strap hung down behind.

"Gator, he creeps folk out when he dances," the kid said.

Possession by demons is an area I have compartmentalized. Considering my mind as a filing cabinet, I file the spirit world under *weird*. One case had fallen to me because the body was discovered across the city line of Savannah. Witchcraft belongs to Savannah, and they are welcome to retain their heritage, a real *Midnight in the Garden of Good and Evil*.

The nude body had looked like a porcupine with all those sharp sticks protruding, a Voodoo doll corpse. Oh yeah, another wonderful memory to place among my many souvenirs. Homicide detective dreams are made of these memorable experiences.

The human mind can be like a camcorder and the past becomes the present in living color. I still give the usual involuntary shudder as I pass Natasha's unsolved homicide site on the other side of the median. Michael Capponi's large billboard moves me. There is no statute of limitation on murder. Our cases may be cold, but they are never closed. The billboard sign with the young man dressed for his high school prom haunts me as he smiles down on me driving east on 520. Like all the other cold case homicides, there were witnesses who knew, but would not come forward to testify for love nor money. Fear and apathy overrule love and money. West Cocoa has been called little Viet Nam back in the day. Old-timers still called it that much to youngster's dismay.

Brevard County Sheriff's Office has this description with Photos: CRIMELINE 1-(800)-423-TIPS on their web site.

"Unsolved Homicide of Michael Capponi:

On July 9, 1993, at approximately 11:55 p.m., the victim was located in the bathroom at the Starving Marvin's convenience store, located at 4455 West King Street, Cocoa. Witnesses observed at least two black males running from the scene after the shots were heard.

The black male shown in the composite was seen leaving the bathroom in the company of another black male after the shooting occurred. He is described as eighteen years of age at the time of the incident, 6'0 tall, 130-140 pounds, wearing a dark colored tank top and red knee length shorts. The second male was shorter and heavy set. Both were last seen on foot eastbound from the store. Provide information for a reward up to $5,000.00." One thing for sure, the composite was not Gator. No one could forget that mug shot.

My new pink cell phone started playing Eastwood's theme song from *The Good the Bad and the Ugly* as I passed the Cocoa Police station. My mind reminded me, *there are no coincidences.* The combination was too much. The laughter was deep and refreshing.

"Mind, I needed that," I said as I thought out loud, "*The Good Chief – Bad Sergeant – Ugly Lieutenant, is very true in our case.*"

The text message was brief and labeled unknown, "Missed your call, will be in touch. Uncle Richard."

I returned to the apartment and opened my journal to *that* November in 2001. The day is still too early to meet Zany. I have agreed to share some past journaling with my counselor. We agree it might help with getting control of the violent flash-backs that still occur with some regularity.

My life has been threatened. We always take that seriously. Those in my old outfit have agreed to drop a dime anytime our life is threatened. Two of our dozen lost their lives in the operation that Jack and I was captured. Three others are dead and there is no public record available concerning their deaths. Covert operations are off the books so to speak. The telephone call cost a little more since my military days. There are other numbers available if needed.

Back to making a copy of my November journal entry: Revised.

Cocoa Village Cocoa, Florida
November 18, 2001

My Journal:

"Toby, according to this COCOA: A Living History, Cocoa celebrated its centennial in 1995.

'On Wednesday evening, October 1, 1895, shortly after dinner, residents began to gather at a storefront building owned by J. F. Wooten.'" Natasha read while I rowed our rented boat along the Indian River Lagoon near Cocoa Village.

I couldn't stop smiling at her bowed head as she read to me like I was one of her students. I was so happy to be in the presence of my beautiful wife of ten years. Small beads of perspiration had formed on my upper lip even though it was a cool November day. My old fishing grounds slipped by as I glanced at the top of her naturally curly blond hair held in place by a red ribbon that matched her modest red, white, and blue sun suit. Occasionally, I caught the wild strawberry scent of her shampoo and glint of golden hair. I searched 360 in 15-degree scans.

She looked up from the open Cocoa history she was holding on her lap and smiled that schoolteacher expression.

"Aren't you interested in the history of your hometown?" she gently chided me. "Your Uncle Rob Tyler willed us his condo on February 6, 1991, for our wedding present. It's still home. You are always talking about how much fun you and your friends had learning sailing, fishing, skiing, and then camping out on these very Indian River islands."

The book cover faced me as she held it up to screen her eyes from the bright sun reflecting off the smooth yellow-green water. Funny how she slyly mentioned our wedding anniversary often in seemingly unrelated subjects. Like I was likely to forget that most wonderful day she completed my life. Uncle Rob Tyler had filled in for my family who were unable to attend our wedding. My mother had passed five years earlier. Dad was AWOL, presumed on another drunken "trip."

A mullet jumped, turned slightly midair, and landed back in the river with a splash behind her. As her oarsman, I checked my diver's watch and noticed that we had about used up our rental time. I nodded agreement and turned the rowboat toward shore. The prevailing afternoon wind was from the southeast. This was as I remembered from sailing years ago. The bow was pointed just astern of the Indian River Queen docked at the marina.

I lined up Natasha's head with a clump of palmetto palms on the other side of the river to keep my rowing straight. Palmetto palms, red mangrove, and gigantic sprawling live oaks covered with hanging Spanish moss brought back a flood of childhood memories. Those were the best of times and the best years of my life.

Football was great, but it was this river that held everything together for our little band of river rats. Watching a hot-dogging friend go flying up on the beach still on my waterskies, we all rushed to him in concern. We laughed with him afterwards. Stories like this were worthwhile history.

"I love the more recent history, my love," I told her with a smile. "Do you have a suit like the bathing beauty on the cover of your history book?"

Putting my arms and shoulders into the rowing in earnest now, the little skiff was leaving a nice wake behind. Perspiration outlined my abs through the recently acquired Cocoa high school orange V-neck tee. I attempted a mischievous pirate's grin across my wind burned face. No long black hair or earring, though, and my hair was still cut military style.

Natasha turned the book around and scanned the waving woman in a one piece raised high up on her thighs.

She looked up accusingly like a mother that has caught her teenage son reading something they both knew he was not supposed to be reading.

"Just row the boat ashore Toby Rockwell Tyler," she said.

Her porcelain face showed a slight blush and her full pink lips displayed the pout that I loved. The merriment in the bright blue eyes gave her away along with the tapping of her right foot. The book was turned over in her lap showing a sky-blue back cover.

"Toby, watch out!" she yelled.

I lifted the oars and looked in the direction she was pointing. A large blackish grey back submerged as the boat passed by. We watched as a mature female manatee drifted by about three feet from us. The flesh was flayed from fresh propeller marks across her back in two separate injuries.

"Oh, Toby look, it's trying to swim. Poor thing, we have to help it," Natasha said sadly.

"We'll notify the Fish and Wildlife Service. Maybe they can get a rescue team out from Sea World," I told her.

I slipped the boat into the slot that matched the number on the boat, tied it up and helped Natasha step up on the dock. We walked to the office, signed our rowboat back in, and turned in the tag.

"Thank you for getting back on time," said the young teenage boy who had checked us out. "On a nice day like today, some people forget to come back, and some don't care. We got a no wake zone around the dock. They don't care. Come roaring in and bounce off the dock fenders."

"There is a wounded manatee drifting about thirty feet south of the dock. Could you call the Fish and Wildlife Service and get a rescue team to help?" I asked him.

We watched as the kid looked up the number in the yellow pages. I took the slip of paper with the written number.

"The phone is on the other side by the outside bar," the kid said. "Watch out for the kid with the blond ponytail. He's got a gator mouth and a bad attitude problem. He's the one bouncing that mahogany speed boat. Dad's a lawyer and owns half the buildings in the Village."

Two children armed with play fishing rods and reels, a small tackle box, and a cellophane bag labeled Savannah Candy Store shuffle by under the protective arm of an older boy. Their guide soon had a bobber and plastic minnow attached to the lines. The little boy and girl sat on a piece of canvas with their legs hanging over the side from the knees down.

"You told me your name was Billy earlier. What's the last name?" Toby asked.

"Paine. Our family has been here since 1885. Alfred Ossing Paine, Captain U.S. Navy, was one of Cocoa's founding fathers. That's what my dad said anyway. I laughed when he told me. Ossing is a funny name," he told me as a toothy smile stretched across his freckled face.

"Thanks for the history and the number Billy," I said as I smiled back.

I turned to see Natasha watching the children on the dock near the river's edge. Her smile was better than Mona Lisa's and she was much prettier. We had discussed adoption, but had not made a decision. Children had been a desire for both of us before and during our marriage. No pregnancy, though before I deployed.

"Let's go make that call Natasha," I said.

Her eyes were twinkling when she turned toward me with that million-dollar face.

The little girl had laid her fishing pole down and was kicking her feet up and down. She held the candy bag close to her chest. The boy was holding his pole in one hand while watching his index finger on the other. Stuck to the finger was a yellow wrapper from a bit-o-honey flapping in the gentle southeast breeze. Both chewed contentedly while the older boy watched, arms folded across his chest and sighed from visible boredom.

"You go ahead, Toby," she said. "I'll try to keep the manatee in sight as long as I can and wait for you on the end of the dock."

Her face was full of concern like the time a dog and a deer had run in front of our deputy sheriff's pickup that night and was crippled. The game warden was called from the truck's radio. There was nothing we could do but wait and watch the doe suffer in the ditch.

I remembered how I held her tight, when she cried and whispered, "She's trying to get up, maybe she has fawns."

The officer had to put the animal down and loaded the dead blue tic hound along with the deer into his truck. He turned it in as a vehicular accident out on highway 21 near Rincon, GA. The owner of the hound had been running after the dog and swore at me. He told the officer he would swear in court I had purposely swerved to hit the deer and his blue tic. Skid marks where I tried to stop punched a huge hole in his eyewitness account.

Finding the phone, the kid at the boat rental place had directed me to, it took several attempts before I was able to talk with a Sea World rescue team member. I identified myself as a deputy from Chatom County Georgia. I assured the team member, Carol we would keep the animal in sight until her team could arrive at the marina dock in Cocoa.

"Oink," a cough like voice came from the round table near the wall phone. It was followed by other similar throat clearings and coughs.

I turned away from the table, but out of the corner of my eye, I took detailed mug shots of the two boys and two girls seated near him. Both girls were sitting very close to the blond-haired boy with a red sweat band and a foot long ponytail. They all were underage, but the boy held a can wrapped in a brown paper bag in his right fist. The other boy held a can of ginger ale. Five cans still in their plastic holder perspired on the table. Each youngster was tanned even though it was November. The blond wore Marine red swim trunks that matched his sweat band, and his partner wore camouflage cutoffs, neither wore shirts. The girls wore itsy teeny bikinis and smiled constantly.

"My position, Jim, I did not do it," said the voice behind my back had been lowered but it was the same as oinker.

Interesting; that same phrase was used by our murder suspect years later.

I signed out our rowboat again. The children were still on the dock. Neither held their play fishing poles. The older boy leaned on the rail and stared into the shallow water, bored out of his skull while the Savannah Candy from the bag had taken the younger two completely under its spell.

They faced each other wide-eyed, open-mouthed, and exaggerated shark like chomping motions on their sticky salt-water taffy.

The wind from the southeast had picked up and there was an occasional small white cap on the dark blue water channel. A large gray thunder head cloud had drifted in from the west and hid the sun. Natasha chose to remain on the dock as lookout while I rowed hard toward her last sighting.

Southeast wind and swimming in a circle had brought the manatee back near the dock according to Natasha's last directions. I drifted with the wind.

Teenage laughter and remarks came over the water in bits and pieces from the dock. I turned in time to see the blond pony-tail take a deep bow from the waist toward Natasha, say something, and then step down into the driver's seat of a speed boat.

"Look, Toby, over there!" Natasha pointed and shouted.

I heard the speed boat come to life and then saw it headed straight toward the surfaced manatee. I placed the boat between the wounded animal and the speed boat. All four in the speed-boat gave a one finger salute as they roared by less than a foot from collision.

Journal entry made while waiting for the Sea World Team to arrive.

Postscript: Team arrived and found the manatee. She was dead.

PP SCRIPT!

TODAY IN COCOA, MY NATASHA WAS TAKEN FROM ME BY MURDERERS. I AM DEVISTATED AND NO LONGER

DESIRE TO LIVE. THAT IS THE TRUTH SO HELP ME GOD!

To the best of my recollection, this is exactly what happened on November 18, 2001, before my Natasha was taken from me on King Street here in Cocoa, Florida.

The counselor was correct. Reliving in my mind and writing out the events of that day has helped me deal with the pain. I decided to follow her advice and replace the pain with fond memories of our times together.

As Detective Tyler, I relive all events searching for clues and murderers. There are a bunch of bad, mean, evil people in this world. The character traits are often spotted in the very young. This young man from the bar was headed for trouble unless somewhere along his way of life a major change is brought about. The other three were followers who often become scapegoats when the realities of life catch up.

As I continue to search everything I can remember of that fateful day in detail, I see the day darkly some days and nights. At other times I see, hear, and think in extremely clear reality. It is at those times my mind rebels as having been subjected to too much.

A running diary of significant thoughts helps me cope with the never-ending search for those who took my Natasha in the prime of our lives.

Realizing it was time for a sail with Zany, I put the journal I'll share with my counsellor back in the case book of homicides. It is the old-fashioned way of keeping everything together. To my knowledge, everyone who does homicide investigations now does so by modern technologies. I'll stick with the tried-and-true method.

CHAPTER 4

THE SAILING TURNED out to be more like cruising down the river on a Sunday afternoon. There was no wind for our sails and the trip was cut short. I returned to find a visitor on the way to my apartment.

As I watched from the balcony of my apartment, my old friend Jack Frost crosses Brevard Avenue with the grace of a ballet dancer. He weaves between crowds of pedestrians that are pouring out of the Cocoa Village Playhouse. The former CIA agent has both elbows locked at his sides, forearms fully extended, navy-blue cap pulled over his eyes, and his head down. My old platoon called him *Ghost*. He is like a vapor and a viper.

I'm remembering times when Jack's extended fists held blazing Colt 45 pistols. We were simply amazed by the man's ability to hit multiple moving targets. His record still holds on the FBI wall of fame in Quantico, Virginia. The FBI Academy, where we trained, is located on 385 wooded acres on a Marine Corps base about 36 miles outside Washington, D.C. Accurate rapid fire was a much-appreciated skill on our ill-fated covert operation in Iran years ago that left me beaten unconscious, nailed to a tree, and left for dead. Jack was severely tortured before his escape. Like others, we had formed a lifelong friendship at Quantico. It was Lee Marvin's Navy equivalent of the *Dirty Dozen* without the criminal record.

A slight smile formed as my mind returned to the present. Today, this friend was blending in, and no one would be able to describe the man who passed by holding two large paper cups filled with Ossorio's double espresso coffee. Jack has the ability to look ordinary. Ordinary would be the last word anyone who had been involved with Jack Frost in any capacity would use to describe this most dangerous man.

I waited by the door for the squeak that always comes from the top step. Instead, a light knock on the door sounded my guest's arrival. I opened the door and looked into cold black eyes where no light lives anymore.

"Hope this java is as good as you say it is. I had to run a gauntlet as chattering monkeys attacked from all sides," he said. "But of course, you observed all that from your sailor's lofty crow's nest.

"Why've you purloined and published under my name, left tenant?" the English brogue was in perfect contempt.

The accusation caught me off guard and brought a smile, "My rank at retirement was Lieutenant Commander as you are well aware."

I took the steaming double espressos from the outstretched hands.

"Never knew your rank or branch of service as it changed with ever assignment. Your orders: SEAL platoon as needed," he replied.

Opening the small refrigerator I asked, "Milk or Irish Cream?"

"Irish Cream if you please, sire," Jack's smile had become half-way cruel.

We sat down near the window with the small folding table between us, sipping our strong Italian coffee through the perforation in the hot coffee to-go plastic lids.

"It is good, Rock. The espresso satisfies. The bitter is better than in Cocoa," he said.

His reflection in the window showed the years of service. Excellent training could not stop the aging.

"There are two reasons for the theft of your name. At first, I needed a strong pseudonym. James is close. Second, and most important is the fact I want to keep you close to my heart. Seriously, Jack, I am being framed by unknown people, and now my life has been threatened."

"I never left you in Iran, Rock," he told me.

"I know *that* Jack," I assured him. "How could you? Neither of us was ever there."

"Jack, I need your help. I am trying to find the ones who murdered my wife. When I came back from our disastrous mission, I knew my life was worthwhile only because I made her smile," I explained. "Natasha was very fond of you, and she was a great judge of character."

Then, I filled Jack in on all that had happened in Cocoa. Natasha's murder, the tapes, undercover, and my recent false arrest. Now, three people knew I was a sworn deputy under deep cover. He never spoke, only nodded. When I finished, we moved to the balcony and sat in silence for several minutes.

"What think ye?" I asked.

"I have come to realize there are many more bastards born into legitimate families than illegitimate. There are times for flight and times for fight," Jack replied. "Iran is still the west's public enemy number one. Our little caper is far from over. The enemy is within."

We continued sipping for several minutes watching the cars and pedestrians move slowly along Brevard Avenue. Jack had declined the offer of dinner at the Black Tulip or Cara Mia Riverside Grill. The theater crowd had mingled and moved on. A flow of tourists trickled by beneath, couples gazed into the many shop windows as the men tried to look excited.

Jack stood in one quick fluid motion.

"Natasha, despite her Christian religion, was the only woman I ever really cared about," he declared abruptly.

After a long pause, his English brogue broke through again, "That includes my bloody mum."

He carefully set the empty espresso cup on the window sill.

A lethal man faced me and nodded his head once in the affirmative, held up his empty right hand cupped in a mock toast and said, "To Christ's Crusaders, I'm in."

That spoke volumes. He, like me, remembered Iran.

There was no doubt that every resource available to this hunter of men would be put into practice. People in every branch of several governments and most private agencies would be happy to assist this man who had touched them or someone close. Many owed their very lives to him, including me. He could have escaped in Iran, but let himself be discovered. Jack Frost was the most feared man among us because he was virtually unlimited by red tape or conscience. The west is blessed to have Jack Frost as a friend and not as a foe.

It was the latter that worried those who knew him well. There was no prosecutable evidence that Jack sometimes broke the law and became judge, jury, and executioner.

The United States government had trained him well to be their assassin. He had more enemies than friends both inside and outside his native land. Jack was believed to hold dual citizenship, here and Ireland.

My face showed gratitude I'm sure. I took the outstretched band of steel that served as a calloused karate right hand. Jack turned the door handle behind and silently exited. Again, I listened for the stairway squeak and smiled when no sound came. Walking to the window overlooking the street, I knew we would not see each other again anytime soon unless the need arose. There was no Frost on Brevard Avenue. He had simply vanished as a vapor.

Two souls, who walk a common path, yet we are as separate as the poles. Silent sadness caught me in the shower. Hot water cascaded over me as I fought off recollection tears. Natasha, Jack, and I were so full of life once. We were invincible, certain to make a difference in the world.

Odd that Jack should mention Christ's Crusaders, the recent group formed as Al Qaida in reverse. Like Al Qaida, they shouted Allah, but then Christos before blowing up a mosque.

Dressing for dinner brought new and improved lines of thought. A cool evening called for an outside meal on a side veranda or sidewalk table at the very least.

Waving branches from the three live oaks suggested tweed sports coat, over quilted navy-blue pullover and gray slacks. The appetite for something special would not leave me alone. Memory serving me well at this point directed me to Brevard Avenue and my nose indicated a left turn. After a careful look across the avenue, and then right, I determined there was no one who did not belong. Military, law enforcement, and private investigation training robs one of the innocent carefree enjoyment of one's surroundings. Real threats on my life reinforce caution.

The cell phone buzzed while I was sampling my fresh bread sticks and seasoned olive oil outside the Black Tulip.

Kind of late for Gus to be calling. One of my many irritants that endeared me to this old editor–in–chief. In more ways than one, he had become like a father to me. Mr. Tyler, my biological father, had abandoned me and my mother after one year to the day of marriage having chosen a bottle over his wife and son.

"Good evening, Gus," I answered as I tried to sound like it was every night that my editor called to wish me well.

"Remember the guy that was filming that fiasco with the CPD in our office?" he asked and waited for my acknowledgment. "Well, he says he just passed a black and white with a naked man handcuffed to the bumper on King Street. Swears it is Lt. Gillard and he has a photo to prove it. He wanted to know if I would buy the photo and the office film from him."

"He might want to offer it to the CPD public information officer first, Gus. She could out bid you I'm sure," I suggested.

We were both laughing so hard we couldn't hear each other's goodbyes.

Daniel Colzani, the owner drifted by and smiled widely. A Brazilian gentleman to the core, he asked if everything was to my satisfaction. Daniel Colzani is a restaurateur who knows how to make his guest feel special and relaxed in his landmark restaurant, the Black Tulip. The menu still carries their famous twice Roasted Duckling, now headed to this very table.

"Ah, the Roast Duckling, the late Walter Cronkite of CBS News dined here often. He ordered it each time he dined," Daniel said, obviously pleased I had ordered it. "The double-roasted duck, topped with our apple and cashew sauce. The cashews are from Brazil, enjoy."

The first taste of the duckling almost brought tears to my eyes. It rates superb. I gave up drinking when I married Natasha. She had not asked me to, but I wanted to do it because I knew she was very much against alcohol. Drinking had devastated her family and mine.

Jack's visit had been a cause for celebration. A gentle breeze moved across the covered patio and rustled some of the dried hibiscus and oleander. This would have been a perfect night for the three of us. Natasha, Jack, and I enjoyed our times together while I trained first for the military and then together for our missions to parts unknown.

"Natasha is the rose between two thorns," Jack would say.

"She is the yellow rose of Texas," I would reply.

Natasha would do her *Gone with the Wind* impression of Scarlet. "Why Toby, honey, that can't be. I'm from West Virginia."

Hot tears trickled down my cheeks and I didn't care. I found myself dabbing at them absently with a dinner napkin. *Laughing one minute and crying the next. I've got to...*

"Are you alright, Mr. Frost?" Daniel's beautiful daughter Tanya was standing before me dressed in a lovely black strapless dress.

Real concern showed on her face. For a moment, I'm not sure if she or Natasha stands there and who is speaking to me. I blinked back tears.

"Yes, I'm quite alright, thank you," my reply sounded far away.

"Let me refresh your water," she offered and took the glass away.

She reappeared with a fresh glass of water and a new twist of lime.

There is hidden knowledge, deep down like a sixth sense. It speaks to a person in a way that cannot be denied. A feeling of survival at all costs, like a cub reporter knows to run when he hears dogs barking closer and closer even when there has been no adult editor to instruct.

I can understand this grieving when a memory like these triggers it, but it is beyond me why I cry from the depths of my soul for no apparent reason. Then I'm so empty afterward. My entire soul parched. I can't think, I can't feel, and there are no more tears to give. The despair is like taking a test, you know the answer, but you cannot remember it.

Enemies are beginning to assemble. There is a sense of foreboding in the air. A dreadful thought concerning the fate of the second child is playing just below the surface. Why did no one see two children being abducted in broad daylight from their neighborhood? Granted, the living conditions in that hood are poor and no stranger to drugs, prostitution, home invasions, murder, and every type of violence known to man. *The feeling of dread is creeping into my soul again.*

Adult homicide usually comes from family, friends, acquaintances, competitors, or ex-lovers. Child murder is family, friends, acquaintances, rivals, perverts, or predators.

How am I connected to this murderer or am I his convenient source of communication? So many questions. None of this nightmare is what I expected to find when I returned. There was no human trafficking in Cocoa even five years ago, and no one has the answers.

Is this a trance? I look across Brevard Avenue and I see it as it was ten years ago. My mind and emotions revert back to happy times. Yet, I am of all men most miserable. It has been ten years and the promised healing has not come. The craving of alcohol and nicotine has passed. That drawing to self-destruction to end the internal pain and mental anguish is not strong now. There are a few true friends sticking with me. There's a lot to be thankful for, that I know. Yet, there are parts of every day where a large hole in my soul appears, and I blank everything and everyone out.

It is a coping mechanism. Identified as such by my able and astute counselors, I have named it my internal black hole. I sat here once and joined a large group who mourned the loss of a sweet allergic child who was taken from the Village suddenly by accidently ingesting chocolate covered peanuts.

Cocoa Village has a heart. That day she wept together with villagers. The Indian River understands the longings of young children's hearts, too. After the memorial gathering at the Black Tulip, I went to Indian River and she wept with me. Tears flowed into her.

We had mourned the loss of the children in Atlanta and Savannah. Together with the Atlanta children and this lost child and the Village and the Indian River we all mourned together for Natasha.

Is it possible to love a river? Is it possible to love a village? Is it possible for the River and the Village to love you back? Yes, and tears are unspoken words.

I know an old man who has derived his total living from shell fishing this Indian River Lagoon. He would say she loves me. We agree she has been abused and all she ever wanted to do was give of her substance and reproduce. It is amazing how she continues to bounce back time after time when men have been foolish, abusive, and greedy.

Will we destroy the Village, when we borrow money and then print more money to pay the debt interest only? Propping up stocks for short term political gains leads to ruin. The suffering has begun all around the world. The federal government's wealth distribution experiment has failed. Is it time to pay the piper?

Trillions of dollars in debt that the second generation from now will still not be able to pay even if we started to reduce the debt now. Inflation is eating away at our dollar's value. It takes more dollars to buy less food, clothing, and shelter. People are becoming desperate.

We may not burn down our beautiful historic village like the rioters did in Watts and Greece, but there is a meltdown coming to Main Street that cannot be stopped. The die is cast.

Through the Federal Reserve, our government has propped up the economy like they did with the housing market with loans that could not be repaid. They have bought up Treasury bond debt and printed massive amounts of money to stimulate the economy for the short term.

Tension is so tight you can almost feel the citizens bracing for the storm. No one wanted to believe the housing market could collapse. Buy and hold the experts said. The value of a house goes up 100 percent and wages to buy those houses remains the same. Debt goes up by trillions and the payers are unemployed, yet no one wants to believe a meltdown is near. My advisers are wise. They saw it all and moved my inherited assets out of harm's way.

Here I sit in my old hometown. The weather is tropical, and the dinner was excellent. The past brings me times of great joy even with the tragic events that have nearly devastated me. The present is comfortable and that is the problem. We will not believe in pending trouble until something bad happens to us. Cocoa is in its comfort zone. Even the abduction of children and one murder is "over there" in west Cocoa, so the attitude is, it is not my problem.

There goes Bernie, one of our homeless guys, he waves to me from his bicycle.

Bernie is an honest alcoholic, so he says. "Mr. Frost, they try to get me to drink wine. I say no! I am an honest alcoholic, I only drink Mr. G."

He always slips out a pint bottle from his worn backpack with a Gordon's Gin label to show. He goes through the same routine each time we meet.

Sometimes I buy him a sandwich. He likes tuna salad or egg salad from the deli. I cannot bring myself to give him money because I know he is killing himself. He knows how I feel, but that does not keep him from asking for a couple bucks every time we meet. He is a regular at the karaoke sing along.

One cold night, I told Bernie it was going to get below freezing and asked if he was he going to a shelter?

He became indignant and said, "I have ten wool blankets; five for the bottom and five for the top. I don't get cold."

I told him he has to be careful these days and asked if he was staying with some others. Safety in numbers I warned, evil people taking advantage of the elderly and children.

"There is this other guy. He has his bush and I have mine. Another guy is under the bridge," he told me.

I know a lady who takes them sandwiches every day or so. They choose to be alone and have refused the city's shelter even on freezing and rainy nights.

On another of those cold nights, I found Bernie wrapped up in his blankets in the Riverfront Park gazebo. He was sleeping on one of the wraparound wooden benches. I decided to let him sleep and do my heavy thinking in the other office, *The Village Voice* across from the park.

"Where you'll go Mr. Frosty?" Bernie's garbled voice came through a narrow fold in his top five blankets. "Want a sip of Mr. G?"

"No thanks Bernie. I'm going to the *Village Voice* office. Come with me. You can sleep there."

"No can do, a bunch want to tear down this place and build a big hotel. They touch our park, I break they face," he declared firmly.

"I didn't know you were Italian, Bernie," I joked.

"I ain't. Can you spare a couple bucks?" he asked.

The after dinner Brazilian coffee and mints are memorable. We sat here so many wonderful nights sipping in Cocoa Village's sweetness, a history so much like Savannah. I like to think of Cocoa Village as Savannah on a smaller scale. A stretch I know. It's gentle on my mind.

Mr. Gypsy is another character who I can hear playing and singing from the square up the street. He was born in Arlington, Virginia to strict parents. His father owned restaurants and was seldom home. He was forced to work in the places of business and actually learned to enjoy cooking. No problem picking up kitchen work anywhere. Playing music was his mother's gift to him. She is an entertainer and singer.

"Do you ever see your mother?" I once asked, but received no answer.

He believes there is an overthrow of the government coming and he will be in the middle of it. He has been in the major "Occupy City Movements." He is waiting for warmer weather to go to Atlanta and then on to Washington, D.C. for the big one. He dresses like a protester with a ponytail hanging down shoulder length. He lives with a like-minded girl in each city he travels to occupy.

It has been thirty years since Natasha and I sat on this very spot on our honeymoon. In a word, wonderful was our time. We had each other. Indian River and the Cocoa Village were at our feet. Our condo had a view of both. We were completely in love with each other and this town.

I motioned for the waiter who was always within sight from a distance and paid my bill. Time to leave the Black Tulip and memory lane for now, but I will not run from threats or my civic duty to help the sheriff.

A round of applause for the village occupier met me as I came to the square. A nod to me as I made a contribution in the beat-up Maxwell coffee can containing tips, he doffed his black beret to the crowd, and entered a waiting Toyota with Georgia tags and a raven-haired beauty as chauffer.

As the old song goes, "The times – they are a changing."

My apartment building door swung open and slammed back against the wall knocking yellow stucco chips to the pavement. A body hurled out into Oleander Street, rolled twice, and came up running like the hounds of Hell were after him. He held what looked like a switchblade knife in his left hand as the body clothed in black sweats and hoodie disappeared.

The Colt had been in my hand, safety off since the first sound from the door. I entered to find the stairwell dark. Sliding my back along the wall, I reached the top step and flipped on the light switch. It was still dark. I turned the bulb in the socket and the light came on. The door to the fire escape was open. The hall was vacant, and my apartment was locked. A quick check showed that all my intruder indicators installed after my smart phone went missing were disturbed.

Someone had been in the apartment, but someone with a knife had been waiting for me in the dark. My call to Uncle Richard was paying off. Had Jack stuck around or was there more than one friendly Dirty Dozen member now in the game?

Jack's visit brought some relief to my overcrowded mind. There is certainly some truth to there being *more safety in numbers*. No doubt Jack was the avenger connected with the disrobing and cuffing of a leading member of the CPD. The swiftness raises some question, however. Did he already know about my false arrest and the present location of the officer, or was his connection such that he could identify and locate anyone in a matter of minutes?

His reference to "Iran's caper not being over" and the west's new terrorist group *Christ's Crusaders* opens my train of thought. Then the "Vapor" appears and evaporates leaving me to wonder what he is all about.

My visitor is still concerned about our blown mission in the Islamic Iran. It is less important to me as time passes, yet it will always be in our memory bank. Today's visitors to my apartment are another and more urgent matter entirely. A young man armed with a knife standing in the dark of my stairwell had less than honorable intentions toward my person. A knife at close range is more lethal than a pistol when used by someone who knows how to use it properly.

Someone is more interested in my murder than trying to threaten or scare me off. The only thing I am involved with is investigating the abduction and murder of children. Could that have been the murderer? Doubtful. Our guy is more skillful and cautious.

I'll be on full alert, nevertheless. *The Village Voice* calls. I have a full schedule through Wednesday. Zany has requested a little help on one of her investigations and more of Kay's Q.

CHAPTER 5

THURSDAY 2 P.M. every other week finds me in Dr. Beverly Sinclair's office. Today, she stood leaning forward facing her obedient client with palms flat on her small orderly solid oak desk. She had something hauntingly familiar about her that puzzled me.

"Mr. Tyler have you finished dealing with your past?" she asked, sounding like a teacher asking for you to turn in your homework.

"I am Doctor. I'm finished dealing with and dwelling on dreams, events, and people from my past," I told her. "But they are still dealing with me."

I gave her my winning smile and added, "They often deal from the bottom of the deck in nightmares and flashbacks, though."

No need to bring her in on one or more persons trying to kill me yesterday. That's present.

Thirty-minute sessions have been a great help. There was no longer a fear of slipping into clinical depression or worse, schizophrenia. Pastor Jerimiah and Dr. Sinclair do not believe in labeling people according to symptoms, though the terms are still used to describe medical conditions.

I miss my old comrades from the military and law enforcement sometimes. Many of them, like me, had to submit to a shrink at one time or another. It is required after duty requires the taking of another person's life.

I know Jack has spent years in government and private counseling sessions after the Iranian Revolutionary Guard rendered him impotent and turned him into a modern-day Jake Barnes from Hemingway's *The Sun Also Rises*. The same event may have caused Natasha and me to be childless. I had been beaten unconscious, nailed to a tree, and left for dead. Tests were inconclusive as to why we were childless. We both desired children as part of our marriage.

In earlier days, I had to check my articles to make sure there were no plagiarisms from the works of my literary hero, Ernest Hemingway. I can quote from all his writings and most of the scholars who have published journals. The dialogue between Santiago and Manolin is a classic favorite.

The Old Man and the Sea is practically committed to memory. There is no worry about plagiarism now, Gus the editor and employer is a Hemingway aficionado.

Truth is becoming stranger than fiction and some days the sleepy little town of Cocoa is a three-ring circus with every kind of performer attempting to outdo the other. However, we are not alone in the madness. Other towns are starting to form and hold protest marches. Home foreclosures, unemployment, race injustice, and escalating crime are all marching toward a boiling point. Even the police and politicians are calling for a long hot summer.

Counseling sessions are going faster now than when we first started. As I headed home, I began reviewing my schedule for the day. When I reached the bottom stairs to my apartment, a voice called to me from a wooden bench up the street.

I hooked my hands together under my jacket placing my right hand on the Colt 1911, thumb flicked the safety off. All that political correctness has not educated me to the point of walking unarmed up to a muscle-bound African American whose face was hidden by a hoodie with his hands out of sight.

He repeated his question.

"You Frost the *Voice* writer?" he asked as he looked me up and down.

He stopped where my hands disappeared. His large hands came out of his pockets empty.

"Yes, I'm Frost," I answered.

"Hear you're working on Rene's murder, and hear you keep names to yourself if you like what you hear," he said. "You worked the children's murders in Atlanta and Savannah, too, right?"

"I had a lot of help from the communities in Atlanta and a little less in Savannah. I told the Sheriff I would assist in any way I could to find the murderer of Serena and try to rescue Sabrina. We have to work fast, and yes I keep my sources confidential," I answered.

"You need to talk to Straight. He knows about you, too. Straight fought the law and the law won. He'll contact you, but he hates certain blue bellies in this town. He says you and he may have that in common. Straight says the children in Atlanta were black. That helps. Straight knows about all the murders on King Street. Information will cost you," he explained. "There is going to be war in America. The Occupy has groups and the brothers have groups. It will spill over here, too. No one wants the outside crazies to win. The brothers are preparing to defend themselves and there is talk of another Watts. You want to deal?"

I thought about where this was leading.

"I have to report anything that may harm someone, even the person who tells me," I said as I brought my hands out from my jacket. "Is this Straight a straight shooter? I mean can I trust him?"

There was a slight smile as he looked at my hands never making eye contact. Only his mouth showed under the hoodie.

"Straight don't shoot anymore. He is clean shaver. He is still crooked like most bros and he is not gay, but bent don't you know," he answered. "He sells portable pot vaporizers called 'vapes' or pocket hookahs and crack pipes. He is quick with his straight. You can't trust anyone, man."

"How do I get in touch with this Straight?" I asked.

"You don't, he contacts you. He sent you an invitation. Contact kicked from your door before he could deliver. You know me?" he asked.

"How could I, I haven't seen your face," he said.

"Later," I answered.

That trace smile reappeared as he stood. He put his hands back in his pockets, his broad shoulders rolling as he walked toward west Cocoa also known as Little Vietnam or Nam from bygone days. Some names stick no matter how hard a city tries to live it down. John Henry looked back to see my hands still under my jacket and gave an approved nod. The young knifer's I. D. is in.

My research had convinced me that John Henry was fathered by a mixed-race man from the Melungan, pronounced (meh-LUN-jun) clan along the Tennessee – Virginia border. It also convinced me that the Agency files were up-to-date and my access was still available. DNA from John Henry collected by and known only to me at Serena's funeral had been be useful.

The sheriff had texted that a small baby girl from the park had said, "Mokey picked Rene up."

No one interviewed knew anyone by that nickname.

I opened the door and walked up the landing. Inside my apartment I leaned against the wall and said, "Wow!" This could be the break we were hoping, and yes, *praying* for. Straight and a possible lead.

The community across the tracks is more informed than City Hall, CPD, and the BCSO put together on the criminal element. My mind was racing. A book title, "*A Man Called the Straight* came to mind. This Straight could be the key to finding our killer before he struck again.

There seems to be an escalation of violence all over the world. For example, in the United States today, the *New York Times* shows a picture of policemen beating up a defenseless protestor, in Chicago and comes with the caption: "In the Tradition of the Chicago 8, & a Knock-Out Game."

There were pictures of the "Occupy whatever" from days gone by with all the election slogans, Arab Spring, government defaults, Greece burning, Obamacare, and who hates who groups worldwide. I scanned through the papers on my end table and sipped a diet coke.

Brevard County was no exception. Yesterday, dozens of police maintained a late-night guard around City Hall in Cocoa following daylong protests that resulted in thirty arrests. A Cocoa teenager had been shot and killed by a night watchman. The male teenager was an African American and the captain an elderly Hispanic man. This being a political year brought all the race cards out.

National self-appointed spokesmen seeking attention were running over each other to catch a newspaper notice or TV camera with a light on. The little town of Cocoa has become a prime-time target of every kook with or without a cause.

Research articles were reprinted to try to determine the causes of youth unrest in America and around the world. A *Florida Today* article restated one cause:

> "State Department-designated sponsoring agencies team with foreign partners to recruit students. Then helps them obtain visas and match them with employees. Participants and their employers are exempt from Social Security, Medicare, and federal unemployment taxes, according to Jerry Kammer, a senior research fellow at the Center for Immigration Studies. Unfortunately, as the program has boomed—from about 20,000 in 1996 to a peak of 153,000 in 2008—it has denied a place in the workforce for many American young people, who are now suffering record levels of unemployment. Many are third world immigrants. Fraud abounds."

I decided on pizza for a late lunch. The papers could wait. I headed for Ryan's near Taylor Park. The TV in Ryan's Pizza on the corner near my apartment ran sound bites from today in D. C.

Most of the politicians had learned from earlier mistakes. The Occupiers Whatever had turned on them when they tried to blame the "prosperous employed" as the economy culprits, believing the protesters would not think of them as the 1 percent along with their Wall Street, Obamacare exempt banker supporters. They seemed surprised that these young people could think. There were more than hurt feelings as the politicians ran from the marchers who were in hot pursuit.

Some protesters carrying or swinging signs, "President and Congress are at fault – BUTTS – no one is to blame!" A beautiful young woman dressed in a cheerleader uniform chanted through a bullhorn, "Got me a P – Got me an H – Got me a PHD – BUTTS I still need a J-O-B!"

To go pepperoni and sausage pizza with sweet tea and lemon arrived at the corner seat by the bar as Gus walked in. He spotted me, walked over, and took the seat next to me.

The pink cell phone chimed in my jacket pocket. I turned so no one could see my sexy phone or hear me repeat.

"Hello. That's right, this is Frost," I answered quietly.

"Contact will be wearing red and carrying a rolled-up Florida Today newspaper in front of the Play House in thirty minutes," the message said.

"Yeah, I got it," I answered.

My editor–in–chief was watching me separate the pieces of pizza. He had that hungry, hang dog look and took a piece when I insisted. After one bite, I lost my appetite. We nodded and smiled as we sipped and he devoured four pieces. Frank Sinatra started singing *You Make me Feel so Young.* Suddenly, there was Natasha sitting by the window with her back to me.

"You alright, Toby," Gus had his hand on my arm and was gently shaking it.

"Sure," I answered as the memory flooded over me like it was yesterday.

Natasha once said after we listened to that song, "I love you, Toby. Not for the way you make me feel or for what you do for me, but for who you are inside. That makes me secure."

I could hear her soft voice in my thoughts and smell the perfume. Gus still looked at me with doubt.

He didn't ask any questions as I paid the bill and told him I would call him later. I picked up half of the uneaten pieces in their Styrofoam box to go and headed across the street for my River Front Park office and Jonathan Livingston Seagull. My appetite had vanished, but my seagull was there. He made no sound as the bird sized pieces of pizza rapidly disappeared down his long-stretched neck.

I often thought of a chocolate lab from my past, but Jonathan was easier to maintain in that he often skimmed fingerling mullet from our river for himself. He was low maintenance as a dependent and worked for minimum wage as my assistant counselor.

I made it back to my apartment and closed the door before the shakes started. My mind whirled from the false sighting of Natasha in Ryan's by the window. *Guilt or Innocence!* There it was again; a clue that scares me even while I'm awake, just below the surface.

It is a force. It is a truth that is struggling to come to life as a fetus desperate to be born. I slip down with my back to the apartment door. In my mind, like in my nightmares, I have my hands around the neck of the clue and I am squeezing with all my might to get the truth out. I am shaking uncontrollably. The sweat is soaking through my shirt.

"Tell me!" I shout.

She was innocent. I am guilty.

"Guilty of what?" I ask.

There is a fear of the truth that grips my heart. I can feel it pounding in my chest like a trip hammer. This is a truth that I have feared to face. It could bring a psychotic break. It could lead me to suicide.

I am guilty that I am alive, and Natasha is not. There. It's finally out. My heart slowed and I opened my eyes. They immediately filled with hot tears, ran down my face, and mingled with my sweat soaked shirt. Perhaps, now disgust can replace self-loathing.

His call was not for me!

T. S. Elliot said it long ago in *The Waste Land*, "April is the cruelest month." The big picture is the coming back to life of that which was buried and covered in the snow of forgetfulness. That April in Iraq where it all began was to be a simple covert rescue operation. A one day in and out. Turned out to be one day in, sold out (they knew we were coming and brought family members to watch the superior Iranian Guard destroy the Great Satan). We were fortunate to get out alive.

At midnight under the bridge, Straight talks from the dark. I can't see him. He offers to give me the killer of my wife if I let him watch me take the killer down. Gator is there; half in light from the overhead lights and half in darkness under the bridge. The right side of his elongated face is swollen with a fresh shallow razor cut down the side of his face. He is smoking a crack pipe.

Straight said, "Big mouth Gator has found just another way to live in his private Hell."

Suddenly, a muzzle flashes from the other side of the bridge. I rolled right before I heard the sound. A pistol shot rang out and I rolled near the restroom wall. A chunk of cinderblock flew past after the bullet hit the building near my head. I rolled again behind the corner near the river. Someone was playing for keeps. No shot for me. I holstered the Colt. The sea wall was a welcome feel as I slipped over the edge into my river. I swam underwater until the cement ramp for launching boats blocked my progress. The air was welcome to my burning lungs as I let my mouth open just above the water, gasping for air. My age was showing. Even with body armor this swim should have been easy.

The city had passed an ordinance that small boats were not allowed to tie up to the boardwalk. Someone had taken a chance that no patrol would spot a very small rubber raft in the darkness of midnight. It was like old times as I soon towed it silently out between two anchored sail boats.

I peeked around the stern of the sailboat most distant from shore. Blue lights were flashing on two city cruisers and four flashlights were searching under the bridge and along the river's sea wall. A search light began a slow back and forth across the river and the moored sailboats.

The search continued for an hour and then the cruisers killed their blue lights and followed the street by Ryan's Pizza. I gave it another hour, tied the borrowed raft to the railing of my borrowed sailboat cover and swam a mile down river to shore behind Zany's office. I climbed up beside a dock, slipped out of my clothes wrung them reasonably dry, and put them back on. I used my key to open the back door and entered our office. I changed into the dry clothes I kept there for meetings Zany insisted I attend with clients on occasion.

I took a towel and dried the steps up to our office, put the wet clothes in a bag, set the alarm for 6 A.M. and slept the sleep of the dead in Davie Jones's Locker. 6:30 A.M. found me in my apartment safe and sound.

The telephone had a red light flashing. I pushed the answer button. "In general, I would say the grief is burdensome and oppressive. At midnight, you can hear the river's grievous cry." The line went dead. They have great Intel.

If there had been any doubt about one or more persons wanting me out of the game, there can be no question now. John Henry brought me to Straight and he brought my hopes alive that Natasha's cold case could be closer to a closure. Our conversation had been cut short. A genuine meeting or was it a set up to ambush me?

Work the scene. Who was shooting and who was hit? I was the target if Straight and/or Gator were not hit. They were a lot closer to the shooter than me. Although the flash was a considerable distance north of the ridge. Night scope and any average sniper could have taken all three of us with ease. The first shot was definitely from a rifle and the second from a pistol. There were at least two shooters. Unless the rifle round passed through a body before it zipped past me, I was the sole target.

I walked into the "opportunity" by exposing myself instead of hugging the park's outhouse. Of course, a well-trained sniper can take down a person from half a mile or more even in the dark. The "means" was intended death by rifle and/or small arms fire. "Motive" is still questionable as searching for killers, be they for Natasha, Sabrina, or both is more than enough. It comes with the territory. Killers for the most part attempt to stay free forever, while homicide investigators do everything within our power to determine if the taking of a life was justified according to the law.

I came close to a self-defense shooting when Straight's messenger shot out of the downstairs apartment door with an open switchblade pointed at me. Then, there are premediated murderers who take the life of innocent people for a wide variety of reasons or none at all.

Those who taunt law enforcement like one or more are doing by using me as a channel are usually determined to kill until we stop them. In every case, we long to stop them before they kill again.

All this excitement is starting to take its toll on me. The roll in the park and the swim in the river have left me sore and feeling weak. Maybe Gus the Grump will approve a much-needed vacation for me when he returns from his. I find myself watching the office door during his absences. I would never tell him, but he has filled a large part of what was missing in my faith in my fellow man. Gus the man knows I believe. Gus the Editor–In–Chief of Cocoa's *The Village Voice* would never admit to restoring his "cub reporter's" ability to think and write effectively.

CHAPTER 6

I TOOK CARE of *The Village Voice* by answering the telephone and leaving the correspondence in the IN BOX for Gus. The two days passed and no word from my grump the Boss. There had been no report of shots fired under Hubert Humphrey Bridge reported to me by the sheriff or leaked to the press. Zany would have mentioned it if her secret squirrel inside Cocoa PD leaked.

It is as though I have the bubonic plague. None of my acquaintances bother to come by or even call. Jonathan has abandoned me as well. Zany is working overtime on new cases. I have my meals delivered from nearby Thai-Thais for the ease of take out and take-home leftovers. The oriental food seems to agree with me and I am starting to regain some energy. No home cooking for me.

I am actually looking forward to my shrink session today, moved up from Thursday. Gus will be in to open up tomorrow and I plan to become a hermit in my man cave apartment, with lots of leftovers in the Frig.

I have never taken a human life unlawfully. Kuwait, Iran, Iraq, and Georgia are distant memories. Honesty has always been a strong suit in my character. I know it is my sole responsibility to search for and express the truth. Lately, I have begun to question the difference between good and evil in myself. *It is not good that man should live alone. Thou shalt not kill.* God help me. I do not want to hate those who killed my wife.

Some days, I wonder if I am losing my mind. I smell her wild strawberry shampoo and weep sometimes when no one is around. Straight's offer should not still be on my mind. There is still a strong *vengeance is my pull.*

There are nights I wake up in a cold sweat. I sit on the edge of the bed and can see myself taking the shotgun from the shooter. It is loaded with double ought buckshot. I scream and shoot the shooter and the van until nothing is left to shoot.

Those who counsel me have asked me to talk it out. It is wise counsel I know, but I cannot. I'm attempting to write about the history of Cocoa and the people, places, and things I love. Like Gus says, maybe, just maybe it will help. I'm ready for anything. Without counseling, I would have spent the rest of my life enraged, bitter, and angry, and would have tried to get even.

I will never give up the search for those who took my Natasha from me. Her words haunt me. Memory of her is all I have of her. I thought I saw her in Ryan's at a table and again after I left Ryan's in Taylor Park yesterday. She was with a child that looked familiar on the merry-go-around.

My mind tells me, *"Write your memory out. You are a writer, write. Be creative but accurate."*

At my appointment, Dr. Beverly Sinclair begins our session by saying in her professional manner, "Mr. Tyler, let me read back to you what you wrote for me about yourself and an event that occurred several years ago. I asked you to write in third person."

From my memory of that fateful day, I submitted the events of my last day with Natasha as I recorded them in my journal, but this time in the third person.

"You have a remarkable memory for detail Mr. Tyler," Dr. Sinclair said after concluding her reading. "You step outside of yourself and write. Third person is perfect for our purpose. Do you dream in color with those details?"

"Yes, sometimes. I see the highway where it happened, near the CPD station, as a long black ribbon, the van is white, and the blood is bright red. Natasha never says anything. She is leaning left in her seatbelt, smiling, and looking straight ahead but down at the van side door. It is like she recognizes something."

She smiled and I knew what had been just below the surface of my recollection. Beverly had the smile of Natasha.

"Beverly," I whispered, scarcely knowing I had said her name.

Her smile widened as she sat down. The slight frown was gone. For the first time, I noticed her as a woman instead of a counselor who was there to help me.

"That is nice of you to call me by my name. I prefer it to Doctor or Doc, though Mr. Tyler," she responded.

"Then you must call me Toby, all my real friends call me Toby," I said.

I had not told anyone about my near brush with death. I am armed to the teeth, however.

Later that afternoon, I sat in a gazebo by the water's edge, after minding the office for Gus. The southeast breeze brought small waves to the seawall. As usual, the crust from my Ryan's pizza slice was being fed to the small fingerling mullet and sailors' choice.

I was running over the facts of the child murder, in the news reports, and a little inside information the sheriff had passed on to me. Still no mention of midnight shooting from any of my usual sources.

Why was there no eyewitness to the abduction of a girl in broad daylight?

Chief Brody and Sheriff Woodall had pooled all their information. Both were puzzled by the lack of witnesses to the abduction. Every law enforcement officer ever been connected with a homicide investigation believes deep down in their heart of hearts there has to be somebody who saw, heard, and knows something relevant to the case.

I pitched another piece of crust into the small circle of waiting minnows. None moved but instead backed away. The bait bobbed up and down on the surface. There was no Jonathan to scoop up all the bounty today. No danger from above. Wait a minute!

That's it! They know it's there, but they are afraid for themselves. There is a larger fish close. Thank you, Indian River, you've done it again. Who is the *big fish* that is keeping the smaller fish who know something about this murder away?

What happened and when did you learn of Serena's abduction?

Where is known. Serena was abducted from the West Side Playground.

Where murdered?

Why is still questioned.

How is known. The Medical Examiner gives the cause of death: "after multiple sexual assaults and physical torture, this little girl simply gave up her will to live."

The *law of the jungle* and the *fear of the known* rules.

In this day and age of distrust and disgust with all who have sworn falsely to uphold their office and the Constitution, ***SERVE and PROTECT*** have become meaningless words. This is especially true in the neighborhood in which Serena lived and died.

How can we find one honest serving man?

Cocoa Police Department, Brevard County Sheriff Office and the Federal Bureau of Investigation all have good officers. Kidnapping is a Federal offense. Murder outside of city limits is a County Capital crime. Abduction of a child and human trafficking should be a **community** outrage!

If witnesses continue to withhold vital information in this murder, **others will follow!**

CHAPTER 7

THE CALL CAME into the BCSO at 3:30 P.M., January, Friday 13, 2012. This time the sheriff himself called me. This would be another unforgettable Friday the thirteenth. It had been relatively quiet up until now. No calls, no contacts, nothing.

"You are home, good. I've got another child homicide," the sheriff said.

He relayed the hysterical call, "My little daughter has been murdered! She is in a ditch like garbage out on 520, other side I 95! Oh, my God! What am I going to do? Oh, my God!"

"I'm in your neighborhood. I will meet up with you in your parking lot, then you can follow me west on 520 past the Interstate. It's 5:30 now," his said, his voice was full of dread.

Nothing gets to an officer like the murder of a child.

U S 520 east of Interstate 95 becomes King Street in Cocoa and continues across the Indian River Lagoon on to Merritt Island and then dead ends on A1A by the Atlantic Ocean and Ron-Jon's in Cocoa Beach. This is the route the Cocoa Beach Cocoa Chamber of Commerce wants the snowbirds to take when they fly south for fun in the sun. Ron-Jon's Surf Shop being a major attraction and advertised for miles all along I-95.

I remember the same advertised Copper Tan billboards with a black dog pulling on the back of a tanned little girl's white bikini bottom and the mileage remaining to Cocoa Beach long before Ron-Jon existed on Cocoa Beach.

On the other hand, U S 520 west of I-95 soon becomes a straight strip of black asphalt cutting through a seemingly endless tangle of brush and occasional unpaved roads. This area is home to many unjustified homicide crime scenes where the bodies have been dumped.

I looked at my watch on the stand by the bed. A promise to meet Zany Adams for dinner at Kay's Bar B Q on King Street west at 6 P.M. would be delayed. The cold shower had been refreshing and the new blue Old Navy shirt looked right with the tan cargo pants. Now, for a splash of English Leather aftershave to keep me dated. The look reminded me of Indian River sail boating days from years ago.

I met Zany at a Christmas party. Gus, a member of the Florida Historical Society, insisted I go as his guest to their party. The owners of the Parrish Grove Inn gave me the grand tour of the old home that had been ferried across the Indian River from Merritt Island. Zany Adams latched on to Gus and added colorful comment about historical events and period pieces of china and magnificent furniture in the Parrish B&B.

Zany is the daughter of a homicide detective with the Orange County Sheriff's Office. She completed her college degree as a criminal investigator. Her heart's desire was to follow her father into law enforcement. Graduating top in her class should have opened the door into the Sheriff's office as a deputy. Her problem was not brains, it was her lack of bulk.

Samantha Ann Adams stands five feet in a stretch, blond haired, sky-blue eyes, and weighs ninety pounds soaking wet. She still wears absurd articles of clothing occasionally to suit her whims and to retain her childhood name.

Zany loves to eat the pulled pork sandwich, sweet potato fries, baked beans, and sweet tea at Kay's BBQ on highway 520 west of Cocoa.

Never failing to stand up and peer over the wooden backed booths, she says in a loud voice, "This Bar B Q will give you a fat *CAN* and *THEN* you *CAN* become a sheriff's deputy."

She stands there, looking around until she makes eye contact with every law enforcement person in the restaurant. This does much to delight of the large crowd of city and county officers present. Anywhere, anytime officers gathered off duty, Zany is invited as "one of the guys."

I fumbled to get my billfold out to retrieve Zany's number. *Why didn't you enter the number into the cell big guy,* Natasha's voice and then her sweet laugh chide me.

The investigator's business card: sea foam white with a large orange letter **Z** and the writing forms a crescent over the letter stating:

WHEN X COMES TO THE END – Y: CALLS ME – Z!
<u>*ZANY*</u> Adams INVESTIGATIONS
       COCOA...1 800 632 0007

"Zany, this is Jack...," I said.

I was about to leave her a message when her answering service spoke.

"Zany Adams Investigations, this is her service," a well-groomed female voice announced.

"Please tell Miss Adams that I've been delayed and ask her to call Jack Frost. She has my cell number," I told the voice.

Turning the phone off, I slipped the Colt into its side holster, checked to make sure my private investigator's ID is in the navy-blue blazer before slipping it on. I dropped the cell phone into the pocket. Made sure to lock the apartment door and hurried down the back stairs. Backing out of the reserved parking space behind my apartment building, I stopped as the BCSO unmarked car pulled alongside my car carrying the sheriff and a familiar FBI agent with a cruiser close behind.

I buzzed the window down.

"Follow me," a sheriff's deputy shouted through the window.

The cruiser lights and siren came to life as I followed the deputy and sheriff at a high rate of speed on U S 520 West. A CPD cruiser was slow to yield the passing lane to the sheriff's unmarked car. It finally moved to the right to let the three cars pass as they came to the CPD headquarters entrance.

I glanced at the driver. The angry face belonged to the sergeant who had been with the lieutenant that had arrested me falsely. His eyes widened in recognition. The CPD lights began to flash, and the siren wailed as the sergeant pulled behind and followed us to the crime scene about two miles west of I-95.

My windows remained up with the a/c running full blast on an unusually hot afternoon. The angry Cocoa police sergeant was still slapping hard on my window as our Sheriff walked back to join him.

I killed the a/c and tapped down the driver's side window about one inch, and with a straight face, I nodded my head, and said, "Sheriff."

The angered CPD sergeant was hot under his collar, staring into the ice-cold eyes of the top law enforcement officer of Brevard County.

"Detective Tyler is travelling with me at my request to assist in a homicide investigation," the Sheriff said and motioned for the sergeant to step behind my car.

The scene from the rear-view mirror showed an attitude adjustment from angry revenge to pleading with outstretched hands to submission and nodding of the head.

After dealing with the city sergeant privately, Sheriff Johnny B exclaimed as we walked around the deputy car, his unmarked car, and the coroner's van, "God, I really hate this guy, Toby. I thought I was over this rage that runs from the soles of my feet to the top of my head."

I'm not sure which guy the sheriff hates until we walk under the crime scene tape and see the little girl in two parts. She is nude from the waist up, her arms stretched out in front like she was balancing herself face down. The lower part of her body was dressed in a red bikini bathing suit with her feet nailed evenly spaced on a surfboard in the canal's water.

My cell phone vibrated in my front pants pocket, brought another unwanted distraction.

Turning away from the medical examiner and crime photo people, I said, "Hi Zany. I'm with our sheriff right now. I'll meet you at Kay's within the hour. Thanks."

Turning back around, the child's upper torso has been rolled for the medical examiner, sheriff, and sheriff's detectives. A long portion of the backbone and the lowest ribs were exposed. Some insects, birds, and other animals have been at work on the child's corpse. Florida buzzards perched atop palmetto palms on the horizon. Heat promotes decay and releases an unmistakable odor.

Generous dabs of Vicks VapoRub to each nostril, a required preparation by all but the examiner a seasoned doctor or a good actor. I dabbed the Vicks handed to me from the sheriff.

"That backbone been sawed, Doc?" one of the sheriff's detectives asked.

"No," he answered. "The jagged edges are fractures. A sharp-edged instrument was used in a chopping motion, or a large knife was hit with significant force."

The ME was checking the fingers and arms. He waved the back of his gloved left hand and instructed his assistant to hand him bags and wraps for the little girl's hands.

"She was murdered somewhere else and placed here. Same as Serena," he told us. "We will be able to determine the time from the insects and small animals we collected. The stomach is unmolested because she was face down. The lab will tell us the balance."

There was an edge to the sheriff's voice as he asked, "How soon will it tell us the balance, Doc?"

The ME looked up with an angry frown. Their eyes locked. Then they gave way to understanding.

"We will work all night, Sheriff. As soon as we know, we will pass it on," the ME assured him.

"Sorry to snap, Doc. I know you will be working around the clock," Sheriff John said as he struggled to keep the frustration out of his voice.

"As long as it takes, John," the ME responded, knowing how much the Sheriff wanted to catch this sadistic killer of children.

The sheriff nodded to the two detectives and then walked me back to our cars.

"I know there is bad blood between you and the Cocoa PD. Chief Brady filled me in and promised to cooperate with the investigations in every way possible. Still, watch your six," he warned me.

"You don't know anything about a certain officer being stripped naked and cuffed to his Cruiser, I'm sure?" the Sheriff asked, knowing I probably did.

We shook hands and nodded a solemn oath to each other as we returned to our cars. The pressure of finding this human trafficker and the killer of children was shared between us. No words were necessary. We both understood how the chief law enforcement officer and an experienced private investigator with connections can be a powerful team.

A creature of habit, I sit with my back to the outside brick wall nearest the front door of Kay's BBQ. I feel a smile playing with the corners of my mouth as I watch Zany spring from her candy apple red and white corvette. Her short, spiked hair is chartreuse today. Her earrings are tiny blood-red drops. Long black lashes bat constantly over pale blue-green eyes.

A vivid green scarf wraps around her porcelain white neck. She is wearing a black t-shirt with wavy vertical green lines. A tiny black purse swings from her left shoulder on long thin strings.

A pair of black satin skintight pants with glow green skeleton arms and fingers reaching down and across her inner thin thighs completes her uniquely styled outfit. Her steps are short in shiny black leather pumps that give her a bobbing appearance. She uses both hands and leans back to open the large glass door.

The place was packed like sardines and the waitresses were buzzing around delivering orders in orderly fashion. An ample supply of city and county officers were mixed with civilian dinner guests. Zany spots me and skips her usual acknowledgment.

Kay is visiting tables, exchanging pleasantries, and assisting where needed. She nods to Zany and returns her smile as her most loyal customer and friend zips by like a ruby-throated hummingbird.

I stand and pull out a chair for her, and then return to my seat by the wall. The mood is unusually somber as news of the second child to lose their life had spread throughout the county.

"Thank you for having dinner with me, Zany," I said. "Sorry for the delay."

We both notice a man turns his chair so that his hearing aid is pointed toward our table.

"No problem my new-found friend, thank you for inviting me to my favorite place for Q," she said as she scribbles a note and passes it over to me with the small pen.

I read, "P.I. nearby with big ear." She scooted her chair over before sitting down. The eavesdropper's line of sight and hearing was now blocked by her back.

She wrote another note: Criminal Psychologist says killer exudes "narcissistic, anti-social, behavior, he/she sees self as being incredibly beautiful/ handsome."

"Thank you," I say with a slight smile. "Let's take a walk in Riverfront Park after we eat."

I scribbled back. *Someone in the Sheriff's office, maybe the man himself, supplied you with that tip?*

We both ordered the sliced BBQ sandwiches, sweet potato fries, baked beans, and sweet tea.

"Lisa, this is my date," Zany tells our waitress. "Warn the other girls to give my handsome sugar daddy here the bill."

Her look was like the cat that ate the canary. Lisa laughed and hurried away.

I have a loss of appetite lately and don't feel up to par. My workouts and jogging tire me out much sooner than they did even a month ago. These murders are getting to me.

The gazebo in front of the water park was empty except for Zany. She did not look at me as I walked to the other side of the enclosure. She was rereading my note from Kay's: "The feds are involved and there has been some work in the Trapwire area."

I checked for bugs and any unusual wires. There had been one, but it was now gone. Zany knew we were being watched and probably monitored by one or more agencies. The FBI and HS were looking for terrorists and there was no doubt that my smart phone calls had been intercepted by NSA. They were not all as sloppy as the P.I. at Kay's.

"I miss my old friends, Gus and Jonathan," I told her as I sat down.

Zany looked at me but made no comment. We both were well aware of the issues with the Trapwire which is a part of the international face recognition program put in place by the FBI, MI 5, and others.

In February, Stratfor CEO and founder George Friedman addressed the hack credited to Anonymous, saying, "Some of the emails may be forged or altered to include inaccuracies, some may be authentic. We will not validate either, or will we explain the thinking that went into them. Having had our property stolen, we will not be victimized twice by submitting to questions about them," Friedman said.[1]

---

[1] Report in news media 12 August 2012, http://rt.com/usa/news/trapwire-stratfor-email-burton-786/

CHAPTER 8

"TASHA WAS THE first and only person I allowed myself to adore," I told my counselor. "I learned to cherish through her by learning to believe in hope for the human race again. She existed, therefore others might. She was the one who showed me how to nourish a relationship in order to strengthen it, and to make it grow into something other than material value."

"I had become completely selfish as a result of self-preservation," I continued. "First, there was the loss of my mother in her divorce after divorce after divorce. She never had time for me and allowed my aunt and uncle, who raised her, to raise me as their unofficial adopted child. She was confused on what a mother and wife should be after being raised without natural parents. My girlfriend in college rejected me when I joined the Navy after graduation to become a (S.E.A.L.). We had planned to be married. After that, women became objects. I was surprised to learn women saw me in the same way, a boy toy, many having been rejected also somewhere along the highway of life."

I caught my breath as I paused to look my counselor in the eye. I seemed to sink back into the overstuffed recliner as tension ran out.

"It's funny, Beverly, I never in my wildest dreams thought I would be telling this to anyone," I told her. "Even Natasha was kept in the dark about my painful past. About wild dreams, I've had my share and I was not always asleep. You asked if I ever dreamed in color. Yes, all the colors of the rainbow, and sometimes black, gray, and white, the blood is always red to increase the drama."

Beverly Sinclair waited for me to continue. She was professional. I had to give her credit for doing her job well.

I closed my eyes and tried to be honest with her, "I have reoccurring dreams. Sometimes, the lyrics of a song will become a dream. 'Walk a Crooked Mile' for example, leads me to dream of an African American, or Asian mother pacing up and down the crooked street of San Francisco with children's hungry eyes following them constantly. Sometimes, the 'crooked mile' is switched back to the jungle trails or goat trails up the sides of Iranian mountains."

With my eyes still closed, I tell her what I have experienced, "There are times when I wake up in a cold sweat. I have watched different children floating along a river toward Niagara Falls. They are so innocent. Their smiling faces watch me, they wave to me as I run along the bank trying to warn them, but they keep smiling, waving, and drifting toward destruction. They go over still smiling and waving as I shout, 'God save them!' It's like that now, Beverly. I am helpless to save the children. It is Savannah and Atlanta all over again. I was not able to save Natasha, my own wife."

I do not know if my counselor left my file out on purpose, but it made interesting reading while she answered her telephone in the outer office room. Dr. Beverly Sinclair wrote in her notes:

Mr. Tyler's eyes blinked rapidly when he said Natasha, relived painful experiences, and closed his eyes when describing a dream or past pleasant event. He always smiles when he recalls taking a mental color photograph of the Indian River from the steps of his Eau Gallie, Florida elementary school. Today, he recalled that scene and didn't smile.

His eyes are shut now. A tear slipped down each side of his face as he takes a deep sigh. He was trying to use the coping mechanism of replacement of bad thoughts with pleasant.

Iranian Revolutionary Guard agents still haunted his mind. It was a reoccurring nightmare he said, and it seems to be connected with traumatic present events.

He became still and did not answer for several minutes after being asked, "Are you reading the assignments?" The same movements of his head and closed eyelids were there as when he first told the story from his covert operation in Iran. Perspiration formed on his upper lip as it tightened over clinched teeth. No doubt, his body and mind had reacted that way through the tormenting it received that day so long ago. The body had healed. The soul had not.

"Yes, I have read the assignments," I responded. "Pastor Jerimiah covered forgiveness with me when we met for counseling, and he has preached on the subject since the murders. I have explained to the pastor and to others that I understand I must forgive because I have been forgiven and my psychic healing depends on forgiving everyone that harmed me. Understanding alone does not bring the cure, but I do not want to appear ungrateful. I understand that forgiveness is necessary for healing of my mind."

"Do you remember someone from your school days that wronged you?" she asked. "Are you still troubled by that thought sometimes?"

"My best friend did something that shocked me," I said. "Then it hurt me that he would do something like that to embarrass me."

"When you think of it now, does it cause you mental anguish like it did then?" she asked.

"No, I got over it. We went on being best friends through high school," I told her.

"What caused you to 'get over it'?" she asked.

"He apologized and said it was a stupid thing for him to do. Said he didn't know what made him do it. It was just an impulse," I remembered.

"You forgave him?" she asked.

There was a long pause. The room was quiet. In my mind there was something trying to be expressed. It had been there a long time. Always just out of reach but wanting to come to life. *To be understood.* That was the key that would unlock the mystery and the misery was almost available to grasp.

"Yes, I forgave him," I explained. "He forgave me, too, because I had slapped him hard across the face, and we both agreed that we had acted out of impulse."

I did not tell her that my friend had pulled my jock strap and let it snap hard across my back. We were in the junior high locker room after football practice. Years later, I related it to an earlier assault attempt.

"Do you believe that the dreams and current events are connected?" Beverly asked. "In our minds everything is related to something else. We are a collection of our individual parts. We think, we act, and we feel according to stimuli and trained response."

"There is a big difference between me forgiving my friend who acted on impulse and apologized, and those who tortured me and premeditated the murder of my wife and innocent children," I reasoned out loud. "They have not apologized."

"Toby, it does not matter what others do for you to forgive," she explained. "There are people who do not have guilt or remorse. They do not have the capacity to forgive or sincerely apologize. Forgiveness must occur within you before your mind and emotions can heal. You forgive for you."

"I believe I may be in their category. I have read the assignments. I have understood the counsel and preaching and have sincerely tried to forgive everybody that has wronged me," I said, shaking my head. "Yet, the nightmares continue. Sometimes, they overwhelm me while I'm awake. I get so angry and frustrated."

"Are you angry and frustrated now as you are recalling the pain you suffered and being unable to forgive, forget, and save children, and our Indian River?" Beverly asked.

"No, I do not suffer pain from the past. It's the pain of the present," I responded as I noticed a slight twitching of my left hand.

My counselor didn't seem to see me grip my left knee as I raised my voice, "I have no answers as to how I am involved in these murders or why I can't get passed my past. All the preaching, counseling, reading, and praying have not made any difference!"

Dr. Beverly was watching me with a serious expression. Her eyebrows arched, the to my surprise a slight smile crossed her ample lips. I had practically shouted at her. She put her pen down on her notebook and folded her hands on her desk. There was a brief knock on the glass door to her office. She glanced up and shook her head from side to side.

"I'm sorry, Doctor, I didn't mean any disrespect," I apologized. "I can be such an idiot at times. How can events from so long ago and people I don't even know be causing me this pain?"

"Because you are allowing them access to your inner self," she explained. "Your inner self is in control of your life. You have expressed that you feel helpless to prevent the murder of children. You feel guilty about allowing your wife to be murdered. Your frustration was very evident now by a demonstration of anger and hostility."

"I can usually control my hostility," I said quietly.

"You mean suppress or displace the hostility," she calmly corrected. "The coping methods are faulty as you are experiencing. The thoughts come, you apply a patch, and the thoughts find another way. Isn't that the case?"

She waited for me to answer. The silence was deafening again. It was almost supernatural. There were no outside sounds. The normal automobile traffic with an occasional horn blow was absent. The whole world was waiting expectantly. I began to shake. There was a fear that I had never experienced before.

"Yes, that is true. I have tried everything," I admitted.

"Can you forgive those who murdered the children?" she asked pointedly.

There was an evil swelling up from the very depths of my being. The shaking stopped and I became calmer than I could ever remember feeling.

In a voice I barely recognized as my own, I replied, "No, never."

"When you find them, what will you do?" Dr. Beverly asked in her trained voice.

The answer came immediately to my mind. A white sheet dropped between us, and I saw her no more.

"Mr. Tyler, I see you are awake. You are in the hospital," a female voice pierced through my consciousness. "I am the nurse's aide; I'll get your nurse."

A few minutes passed until a female version of my old drill instructor marched in and picked up the metal tablet holding my chart. She stared at me, grunted, and jotted down a note.

"Mr. Toby Rockwell Tyler, you blacked out in your counselor's office and were brought to Wuesthoff Medical Center Rockledge ER by ambulance. The Doctor who treated you is here and will be in to see you," she said briskly, then her auto-practiced hand pulled the wrap around curtain back behind her as she departed.

An elderly man wearing all white except a pale green skull cap and a stethoscope arrived and asked how I was feeling, and we exchanged pleasantries. My throat was raw and dry.

Then he said, "You are recovering well for a man who has been poisoned. I expect you to be taking solid food in a couple days and you should be headed home the day after."

"Poisoned? What kind of poison?" I asked.

"We are waiting for a toxicology report to determine the exact mixture. Your symptoms were very pronounced when our EMT called them in from the ambulance. Unfortunately, we have had similar cases before, usually with children, but more recently with two young women. The base was found to be that found in common rat poisoning. We were able to flush your system immediately. Like I said, you are a fortunate man. We got to you in time, and you should recover quickly. Mr. Tyler you are in excellent physical shape otherwise."

"The poison is what caused me to blackout? I mean did you find any other symptoms?" I asked.

My raw throat must have come from the tube they used to pump my stomach.

"Was the poison in my drink or food?" I asked.

"That is to be determined, but we believe you have been receiving low doses over a period of time, may be months, two or three more than likely. You can rule out an accident. Rats bleed to death internally from anticoagulants. We took a small, microscopic sample from your stomach and liver to be sure. There were intermittent blood spots in your stool," he explained and then picked up the chart, scribbled on it, and then let it hang down on its string. "I'll be back to check on you. In the meantime, be sure to obey Nurse Ratchet and take your medicine."

Was that an attempt at humor or was he alluding to my blacking out in a psychiatrist's office in reference to *"One Flew over the Cuckoo's Nest"*?

I raised my head and almost cried out. It was like getting stabbed in the throat and my stomach at the same time. A sip of ice water went down with a painful swallow. After several attempts, I was able to sit up and duck walk to the closet. My clothes were hanging there, but my Colt 1911 was AWOL. I moved crab-like, rolling my IV drip stand to the door, and quietly opened it a crack to see a large, uniformed deputy sheriff sitting to the right with his back to the wall.

My cute young nurse's aide came in and informed me I had a choice of chocolate, vanilla, or butter scotch pudding for dinner. There was only lime or cherry Jell-O for dessert, though. I ordered double of chocolate and cherry. She thanked me and hurried out.

After dinner, nurse Ratchet came in accompanied by the sheriff. She made notes on my chart after I swallowed a hand full of pills with more than a little difficulty. She departed without a word. Sheriff Woodall closed the door behind her with a loud click.

"I should ask, how are you feeling, but I know better," he said. "You are a stoic S E A L."

I didn't say anything. Sometimes, it is best to wait for an explanation. He paced back and forth from the window to the door a couple times. Frowned and repeated the process. Then, he pulled up a chair real close to my elevated head. I could tell he was conflicted.

"Gus is dead. He was poisoned most likely the same as you," he said, "I'm sorry."

His face showed he shared my sorrow. I let it all sink in and laid there for a long time without saying a word. Both of us have seen death many times. Some have been very personal.

"You are on our watch as a victim of attempted murder. Why didn't you tell me people took a shot at you under the Hubert Humphrey Bridge, Rock? Are you flying solo now?" he asked almost angrily.

I didn't say anything. He shook his head slowly from side to side like a big angry bear. Pursed his lips and looked up at the ceiling where I was looking.

"Your source, Gator is missing."

"Are we sharing all information now?" I asked him. "Both CPD and your good office are leaking like a sieve. I was waiting for you to contact me. I do not trust anyone enough to make a call."

"There have been some enquires concerning you and the children's homicides," he said. "Evidence has been submitted connecting you to both murder scenes, and a witness will testify they saw you near the West Side Park on the day one child went missing."

"Who were the food handlers, and the shooters under the bridge, sheriff, or is that classified on a need-to-know-basis by the Cocoa Police Department?" I asked angrily.

He stood up, scooted the chair back, started to say something, and then changed his mind. My tray arrived. The lock clicked, the door opened, and closed silently as both visitors departed.

Dr. Beverly and Zany were my only visitors over the next three days. I had a lot of time on my hands, so I put it to good use. I liked to ask myself questions and then answer them. Another sign I am an excellent candidate for the Cuckoo Nest.

Question: *Who wants to kill me?* Answer: Several people.

Can I name them? Answer: Yes, and I can give motive, means, and opportunity over the last few months.

Foreign: All military connected. Those who were arrested, have served their terms, or escaped along with their families and acquaintances, not forgetting family or friends of those who were killed in the line of duty.

This month, the United States along with other western countries, restored relations with the Iranians who still hold political and religious prisoners in their subhuman jails, maybe we should shout, "Allah Akbar" before we chant "Death to America – the Great Satan!"

Domestic: Those who have been arrested and served their time. CCSO keeps me informed of those who are out for any reason. Families of those who had someone killed in the line of duty. With word out that someone knows who murdered my wife and possibly the children. The creeping dread feeling is giving way to the dreadful.

The motives for the foreign foes are revenge, domestic bad guys run the gambit of revenge, money, keep from getting caught, protecting someone, jealousy, cover-ups, and the sport of killing a cop.

The means should narrow the field considerably and the opportunities even more so as most are in other countries or states. A few phone calls should clear the list and leave suspects.

The hospital released me right on time and my assigned deputy accompanied me back to my apartment. Zany had tidied up the place and even stocked the refrigerator and shelves with wholesome foods. My leftovers had been confiscated and found poison free. My trusty Colt 1911 was cleaned and oiled, its bath in the river having no adverse effects.

I was informed by the sheriff's office I was free to move about, but to inform them if I planned to leave Brevard County. Also, I was invited to a big law enforcement powwow. Evidently, their "evidence" was not strong enough to arrest me for the murder of children.

After several attempts to return to normal life, I am eating in and receiving no visitors because the murder of my close friend and boss, Gus keeps coming up. Police work tends to promote paranoia in the best of times. False arrest, shot at, poisoned, and accused of murdering children may play a small part in my promotion.

My answering machine recorded several calls. All unanswered. I have added privacy to my paranoia.

The FBI will be leading a closed meeting with all law enforcement officers connected with the King Street murders. Sheriff Woodall's call informed me I would appear as his "special" consultant.

Chief Brody's call reminded me I was a "person of interest" in ongoing investigations.

Zany and Beverly called with condolences on the loss of Gus and offered to help in any way.

The Mayor of Cocoa invited me to his Cocoa Conference on Crime meeting at the Cocoa Civic Center. He is a good guy. I am almost tempted to return that call. I overcame that temptation.

Somewhere in our fair city some continue plotting my demise. Soon, I will know why. Then who.

Evidence points to more than one source determined to eliminate me. Same goal–different plot.

CHAPTER 9

WE ARE GATHERED with standing room only in the auditorium of the Brevard Community College Cocoa campus on Clear Lake Road. For the second time of my life, I see Lewis L. Lawson in person. This is Mister G-man of the F B I, the big kahuna, up close, and personal. He had come to Savannah and taken Natasha and I to dinner after the child murder cases in Atlanta had been closed. He had been Deputy Director at that time, and he had offered me a position in the agency after a five-star evening.

The turf wars became a problem between law enforcement in the seemingly never-ending serial *King Street Killer* homicides and was reported by *Florida Today*. A local firestorm broke out after the national news media began to carry some confidential case-sensitive leaks, supposedly from city, county, and Federal press access causing a lot of finger-pointing. As rumor becomes fact, Cocoa Police Department reports the newest special agent in the FBI was assigned to the Brevard task force and he brought all the arrogance of a federal newbie FIBBIE with him.

It had become very evident tension had been building in every area of the investigation. In most homicides, the murderers and victims were jerks. Drug dealer pops a mule, or a pimp strangles a prostitute in everyday low-life living. Turf wars of this kind were expected and handled in a routine manner and information exchanged between agencies is frictionless in most cases.

As we gather for this closed, invitation only meeting, there were city, county, and federal security officers stationed at each door, and every person is checked by all three before being allowed to attend this meeting. There are no politicians or news media in the room. Everyone attending has met each other while working the cases with the exception of Director Lawson.

Lt. Gillard has requested to meet privately with Director Lawson before the meeting on a serious matter concerning these cases. He indicates he has uncovered recent evidence that might involve Toby Rockwell Tyler in the murders and insisted I be removed from the cases and not be allowed to attend this meeting. All duly reported to me before the meeting.

The Director had an aide bring in Sheriff Woodall and asked Lt. Gillard to turn over the evidence to the sheriff who had jurisdiction on the murders. Lt. Gillard agreed to do that and then insisted again that Toby Tyler was a suspect and not an active law enforcement officer and should be excluded from all meetings if not arrested.

The Sheriff listened. The Director then brought me in and shared the charges, "evidence," and the content found on my missing smart phone. A very familiar Sergeant stood with his Lieutenant and suggested I may have poisoned Gus for the *Voice*.

I walked out at that point. Given a set of headphones, I listened to the meeting outside the room. After the meeting, Director Lawson met with me and the sheriff in my private room. It was cordial but strained. They wanted my take on the homicide cases thus far and any recommendations.

I was forthcoming on all that I had been given access to and asked if there were any other agencies involved since my little adventure with undigested food. They indicated there may have been some contact with mutual friends. One in particular had supplied enough real evidence to keep me from being arrested. It appeared I had been under surveillance the whole time, much of it on film. Then the Director asked the sheriff if he had any further questions for me. He said he didn't and was glad to see me back in action. He didn't offer to shake hands before he departed.

"Now, how are you really, Rock?" Director Lawson asked with a genuine smile on his face.

He stuck out his hand and we shook a warm greeting.

"This has been hard on a lot of people, Rock," he said. "The sheriff is bearing the brunt of the burden and the leaks are tearing him apart. He has been in your corner the whole way. There are ongoing investigations that we would love to have you involved in but cannot legally. The sheriff especially needs your help, Rock."

"*What* can you tell me?" I asked.

"Your friend Jack is suspected of firing a shot in the dark recently and could have been one of the others. We have had a little trouble keeping up with your old friends as usual," he smiled. "His shot caused the shooter to miss you and take out an outhouse near the boat ramp."

"What about Gus?" I asked.

"He checked himself into an ER after passing blood and experiencing severe stomach cramps. His immune system and age were against him," he shook his head sadly. "They were able to determine he had no small doses like you, but the big one was ingested in a pizza. He told them he called and warned you."

"I killed Jonathan," I told him.

Director Lawson looked at me like I was crazy.

"I received a call about someone who could identify the person that murdered Natasha. The source was to be kept confidential," I told the Director. "I lost my appetite and Gus ate the pizza in Ryan's. I had thirty minutes before I was to meet my contact, so I took the rest of the pizza and fed it to Jonathan, a sea-gull near where I go to think by the river."

"The source agreed to meet you under the bridge at midnight?" Lawson asked.

"Yes, the source was a black man with the street name of Straight," I told him. "When I got there, I stood close to the restroom building for possible cover. Another black man, street name Gator, was standing part in light and part in the darkness under the bridge. I saw a muzzle flash and rolled for cover. You know the rest."

"Why do you think someone is trying to kill you?" he asked.

"I'm getting close to finding out who killed Natasha and the children, so they want me dead," I answered.

I watched the eyes of the Director and saw that he agreed with me, but there was more.

"The Bureau has been keeping tabs on you and your friends as close as we could because there is an Iranian on the loose here in the states. The DOD will not confirm that any of you had anything to do with Iran, but a friend has suggested that we keep an eye on you. NSA has all your phone records, and we share with them concerning terrorism. The lost smart phone has been busy providing bogus but amateur attempts to frame you."

"That how the sheriff knows I could not be involved in the murders?" I asked.

"That and he believes you for what you are," Lawson answered firmly.

"You know anything about certain officers in the Cocoa Police Department?" I asked.

He smiled and then went cold like a dead fish. That was good enough for me.

"Director, tell me what you want me to do that will help you. I have the files and profiles from Atlanta and CCSO," I asked him.

"I want you and your friends to drop out of sight and give these cases all you've got. That includes the one that is very personal to you and to me. You have the full support of the FBI," he instructed me.

"We will need a secure location that has contact with all the principals. I will get the rest from other sources," I told him. "Natasha and I had not wanted to go national. We were more comfortable with local folk."

The Man was visible again. There was no doubt in my mind he was concerned for others and not his career only like a lot who had gone before him.

"You two made the right decision," he assured me.

He stood and I stood. We shook hands and he strode out as my assigned deputy came in. After a few minutes, the sheriff returned with a special agent.

"Looks like we will be working together again after all," he said with a smile. "Director Lawson has cleared you and assigned you to a special unit."

He asked the other men to step outside for a minute. When the door clicked, he turned and held out his hand in friendship. His smile genuine.

"The Director is in a position to tell you more than I can legally. His special agent will escort you out of the building and place you in their SUV to look like you are under Federal arrest. You will disappear out of county and city jurisdiction, and surveillance," he explained.

They made it look good as only the FBI can. The witness protection program makes them experts at misdirection of look at this not that. From the corner of my eye, I saw a Cocoa PD cruiser that had a very familiar number. The sergeant from my false arrest had his cell phone to his ear. The serpentine smile on his face told me his lieutenant was a pleased man.

The special agent without a name introduced me to another special agent with no name who was dressed like he had been or was planning a fishing trip. There was no talking. I occasionally glanced at the CPD cruiser that had fallen behind on I95 until the SUV took the Orlando exit.

State route 528 called the BEE LINE by Brevard County natives is a straight shot to the Orlando International Airport. Because of the high rate of speed enjoyed by some tourist who loves to test the drag strip qualities, the BCSO helicopter patrols it religiously with excellent results. One of Brevard's finest was above and slightly ahead of our shiny black SUV. It broke off where all west bound drivers have to decide if they want to continue west to Orlando, or east to Port Canaveral. A call was answered, and the driver acknowledged. We turned east, headed for the Atlantic Ocean. I turned to my new best friend and admired his fishing get up, nodded my approval, but received the silent treatment. Perhaps, we were going on a cruise.

My vision of a state cabin with all you can eat buffet was soon crushed as we turned toward the Space Center. Surely, they were not going to blast off with me to the moon, I thought. Then I remembered stories from Cape workers about the great fishing in federal government restricted waters around Kennedy Space Center. My vision of early childhood catches with my relatives from Titusville and Cocoa returned. The famous Mosquito Lagoon was called the speckled trout capital of the world.

We pulled off the main road and followed a narrow sandy path with palm fronds sliding along the sides of our high-end federal government ride. My mind was uncontrollable at times like these. It should have been on the business at hand, instead it said, "*nice place to film a jungle movie.*"

The trail ended with enough space to turn around. At the edge of a swamp, an ordinary canoe with battery operated troll motor attached greeted us on the shore. My first special agent opened the front door and stepped out with a suit bag and my backpack. I stepped out and took them from his outstretched arms.

If they were waiting for this deputy sheriff to break the silence, they had a very long wait. Interagency cooperation could not be proven by me. They had their fingers in every pie, had me under constant surveillance, and had used me as *bait*. Their "bigger picture" of one sacrificed for the greater good, had cost me the loss of my best friend Gus, and nearly gotten me killed under the bridge, now they wanted a "thank you"? Forget it.

Sunsets on the Indian River Lagoon are always good, even on overcast days. Today, a few cumulous clouds dot the sky, and the view is quite breathtaking, as our canoe glides silently by mangrove thickets on each side. Schools of red drum cause swirls ahead on the surface and the occasional alligator or snake sinks or eases into the water lilies and sea grass.

Using my military training to keep track of the turns and bends in the narrow water way, I see many openings. However, our journey soon ends near a mound maybe built by some of the first Indians to inhabit the area as they consumed tons of shellfish and piled up the shells.

We did not pass anyone along the way and there were occasional beeps on a devise my special agent tour guide held on his belt along with other necessary equipment for fishing. A landing of sorts was constructed of driftwood material. I grabbed my gear and stepped carefully out of the canoe. The steps ended at a moss-covered hatch much like a submarine opening. I turned the circular handle and lifted the manhole cover up until it leaned back. When I turned around my guides back showed toward me and I watched the wake until it disappeared around a bend.

The ladder steps are exactly like those on a submarine our S E A L team used many times in practice and then on covert operations. The U.S. Navy along with the Secret Service are charged with the protection of the President in the White House. Their construction footprint is present everywhere in this temporary combination Oval Office and captain's quarters. I place my clothes and backpack on one of the wall bunks, climb the ladder to close, and then batten down the hatch preventing unwanted guests. I hit the bulkhead level light switch.

The room measures approximately twenty feet by sixty with an eight-foot ceiling that holds recessed lighting and a ventilation system. One wall is all electronics. The desk is an old military surplus made of wood with a matching in and out box.

It even holds a red telephone. I lifted it, no signal. Read cell messages. I look for a camera and motion detectors, but cannot locate them if they are present.

My clothes' bag contains my street clothes, along with other cell phones, and military surveillance equipment. The rubber boots might come in handy if my FBI "friends" expect me to walk home. A little surprised to find my Colt 1911, unloaded but with holster and extra loaded clips of ACP full metal jacket rounds of ammo in my backpack. All toilet articles were present except my turtle shell hairbrush. Someone forgot the mosquito spray and under arm deodorant–stinking Feds!

I called Zany to let her know I would be out of the loop for a few days, out of cell phone roaming. Her voice mail answered. I asked her if she could contact a client that her County friend was meeting in the big O today.

"A new client interview would be very helpful," I confided. "The sheriff doesn't know I know."

Considering my location, I was not surprised at the signal strength.

My stomach, still healing from the damage done but my throat no longer sore, I investigate the Presidential galley to learn the absence of soul food or caviar. However, an ample supply of MRE packets and a case of bottled water occupy the Goat Locker or frig for land lubbers. More latched up wall attached bunks and a propane gas three burner stove complete my room. I choose the steak and potato in gravy MRE and fire up the grill on low. Immediately, an overhead fan whirrs with a red eye blink.

While my meal heats, I search the other compartments looking for hidden devices and other things mere civilians are not supposed to know existed. In a small closet, I find a modern form of vertical telescope. I flipped the cap off the eye piece and pushed the button, but nothing happened. No "Up Periscope" or other Navy excitement. According to my dive watch that the Navy failed to request back when I return to civilian life, it was seventeen hundred hours (5 P.M.) and darkness would soon be settling over my new billet. I visit the head (toilet), munching MRE, and soon humming "*Anchors Aweigh*" between bites and adjusting to lonely shore duty. My real regret is missing the funeral of my friend Gus. Zany was sure to attend, but it would not be like showing my respects and watching all who attended. I'm sure she will find some way to gain access to the eighteen-year-old being held in Orlando.

My body recovered like the doc said it would because they caught the poison in time. Unfortunately, Gus had caught the full dose on his slices and Jonathan caught the rest.

I stripped to my boxers, did some pushups and then crunches until a sweat formed. Then I hit the shower and let the hot water cascade over me. A rough toweling brings me back to almost human in body and soul. I wrapped the towel around me, slipped on my shower flip flops, walked around the corner, and there Jack sat at the table eating a warmed up can of Wolf Brand Chili and oyster crackers. He watched me closely as he ate. He could have been sitting around a campfire out on the range in Texas except for the clothes he is wearing. He is dressed in battle dress swamp gear. I know what the familiar matching waterproof covert bag at his feet contains. Jack is as they say, "Loaded for bear."

"There was no officer of the deck to pipe me aboard," he pouts.

Only one other person knows I'm here.

He holds up a gadget similar to the one the silent special agent wore that brought me to this dance.

"Nice digs, Rock," he says. "I didn't know a sailor of your rank rated the Captain's Quarters."

"Welcome aboard the U. S. S. *Gilligan's Island*," I said laughing.

"We need to make a trip," he announces. "Better suit up unless you go into battle in your birthday suit these days."

I hurried into my military gear, Navy Spec Ops issue, holstered old 1911, and joined the swamp man. He clicks a few buttons on his gismo gadget and everything in the compound shuts down. All like when I arrived except a blinking green light by the ladder to topside.

A small pen light held up to his face showed me the zipped sign for silence. Jack closed the hatch and gave the circular wheel a turn. He must have touched the gismo again because a small running light appeared on the bow of a black inflatable raft that we are both experienced with.

He in the back near the tiller and troll motor and I balance the vessel by sitting slightly forward as we approach small green lights that go dark as we pass. Plenty of red eyes of various sizes greet us in the cannel when the pen light does an occasional sweep. I did not have to see his face to know the cruel smile was there. Jack is in his element.

It took longer to get back than it had to go in by fifteen minutes. The difference soon apparent. Not in the same place and my car barely visible being covered in fresh cut palm fans. I step on dry ground as the last green light shuts down. Jack secures the raft on a low mangrove branch.

Inside my car, Jack finally broke the silence and told me what was going on in country. The Cocoa Police Department knew they had one or more bad cops and a sting operation had been in place for over a year using the latest equipment from the Department of Justice. The word had been put out that I was being held in an undisclosed location pending further investigation concerning the murders of the girls in Cocoa. Chief Brody tried to go to bat for me, but was overruled by the sheriff's department. Sheriff Woodall also had a problem with one or more leakers. So, it was the old *good* cop, *bad* cop routine between agencies.

"Where does that leave us, Jack?" I asked.

"It leaves me here and you attending your friend's funeral," he said. "But first I want to show you something."

While I drove along a better road in the national wildlife preserve, Jack shared that he had visited my apartment and noticed he was not the first to do so. There were movement pads under the carpet outside the door and a video camera hidden inside a hall fixture. Good stuff which looked to be FBI grade. Consequently, he could not get me a suit for the funeral.

The road soon dumped us out just east of Titusville. Playalinda Beach near the launch area to the west was closed at dark. What few Cape workers there were left after the shuttle program shut down still used the north end gate road mostly early mornings. We crossed over the bridge as shrimp lamps were starting to come on under it and out from the Cracker Jack's pier restaurant. We turned south on Washington Avenue and pulled into the Riverside Motel. It was relatively dark in the parking lot and Jack had the foresight to have turned the bulb enough over his end room to give us entrance in our military dress to kill clothing. The room was nothing to write home about.

Inside, we pushed the two beds together. Jack quickly spread a large topographical map of the Saint John's River west of Titusville nearly covering the beds.

There are two main roads crossing the river west of Titusville and Mims to the north. U.S. Route 50 from Titusville crosses the river that runs north to Jacksonville before emptying into the Atlantic there.

"Yesterday, a 'friend' from Iran tripped a BOLO flag when he passed through a facial recognition scanner leaving Orlando International Airport. Most law enforcement agencies do not know it is there," Jack said with that hunter smile playing around his mouth. "Our man in Orlando was able to tail the man he picked up in a rental car to the Brevard County line. They switched cars and drove to I95 and then north to U. S. 50 then back west to the river. There is a fishing camp that rents and charters air boats where the highway crosses the river. They boarded an air boat and headed north toward U.S. 46 out of Mims."

"We are positive that it is our Iranian Colonel?" I asked.

Like Jack, I am moved to be so close to the man who killed our friends and tortured Jack and me.

"The photo I was able to send back was grainy back then, but they are able to overcome that with the new facial recognition advancements," he explained. "We are sure within 96 percent accuracy."

Impressive may be too small a word to express the outpouring of respect and condolences for the funeral of beloved Gus, the newspaper man. There were people from all walks of life that gave emotional eulogies, and the sense of loss could be witnessed the whole day. I met his only living relative at the inquest. She was relieved her Uncle Gus had left me *The Village Voice* and said he had bragged on his "cub reporter" as only he could do, then she gave me a tearful hug.

CHAPTER 10

A DISTINGUISHED ELDERLY gentleman dressed in a conservative navy-blue suit with a white shirt and solid silk grey tie, opened a hand delivered memorandum. His office was on the sixth floor of the CIA building in Langley, Virginia. He placed his reading glassed on his nose and began to read.

"The federal government has a long history about building secret places for reasons known only to them and unknown to taxpayers. They are called undisclosed locations. Because there was a terrorist threat against Toby "Rock" Tyler and perhaps others, federal agents and resources were assigned to assist and protect him recently. A small underground site was made available. It was more underwater than underground. The nondescript mound was accessible only by boat and through restricted electronic guarded grids. Artificial plants covered the cellar entrance and some electronic devices. Real alligators and snakes make their home there. Mosquito Lagoon was well named, the blood suckers' rule, and said facility exists nearby. Even the Brevard County Sheriff does not know the existence of this facility. Secret Service is tight because it is designed to protect the President of the United States in case of attack while visiting the Kennedy Space Center if air evacuation is not possible." {Click R-then #}

The man who had the most to lose if a "doomsday" cache of highly classified NSA material downloaded by Edward Snowden became public, closed his eyes in deep thought. Attempts both legal and otherwise had failed to expunge the unintended connection to agents inside Iran during the failed mission involving Lt Commander Tyler and his team. All survivors are loose ends.

Sheriff Woodall made arrangements for a secure location. Ironically, it too is designated "Undisclosed" by gentleman J.B. Tyler and assigned deputies will work there.

"The pieces are beginning to fit together," Jack mused to me.

"Don't say that Jack!" I thump the thick file down on the table so hard it bounces open.

Pictures of a mutilated child's posed body slid out, "Sorry, Jack. I didn't mean to snap."

I picked up the BCSO, Atlanta FBI, and CCSO file again. I looked at the timelines and pictures on the push pin board. Too much unconnected information and not enough connected stared back at me.

Two black children, last seen in two separate playgrounds, in full daylight photographs looking down showing surrounding vegetation, streets, and buildings within one mile looked back at me. There were no witnesses, no suspect (s), and no trace of the murder location with incriminating evidence.

The two of us, stay up all night putting together possible patterns and where their killer(s) were most likely to strike. We placed ourselves inside the mind of this manic murderer of innocent children. We memorized all the known facts: dates, times, places, and the few interviews.

I acted out the actual abductions from the case files and assumed the killer's psychological profile. Our efforts were productive. The two of us came up with new possibilities.

Could we prevent another child being lost?

Could we identify who wanted to kill me?

Another danger that neither of us mentioned, but both of us have experienced concerned the acting out of another personality so well that you come to believe the profile as your own. A psychotic break nearly brought Jack to a mental state of schizophrenia when his internal and external threshold of pain was surpassed beyond description in Iran, and he was forced to relive it in the CIA debriefing.

I still have days when my past comes roaring back to almost drive me to despair. We have seen others who suffer with schizophrenia and know both Jack and I are fortunate to have escaped. Now, here we are underwater, living in a bunker, under stress that has broken many professionals better trained than either of us. I sat reviewing the files and looking for something we have missed.

The Profiler File: Childhood schizophrenia: It includes hallucinations, delusions, irrational behavior and thinking, and problems carrying out routine daily tasks, such as bathing.

Witness Statements: "The guy smelled like he had never had a bath."

"He was weird man. Like the dude wore dirty marine red trunks and a matching sweat band like old Rambo man. They didn't even fit. Yeah, and dirty old Nikes."

"Did I see the homeless guy? Sure, nothing special. Army raincoat, kind of shuffled along in sneaks, you know, how they do. He was right down by the river, near the bridge. Dude had long dirty blond hair hanging down, shoulder length."

My new scramble phone vibrated in my jacket pocket. I fished it out and flipped the lip open. The sheriff of Brevard flashed urgent!

"Hello," I answered.

"Where are you?" the voice, excited which is unusual in itself.

"Undisclosed," I responded

"We caught a break. A traffic camera in Orlando spotted an old white van and the driver. I'm headed there now. I've got a new crime scene for you, later," the phone went dead.

"Orlando traffic cam caught old white van and picture of driver. Sheriff is in route," came the message from "caller Unknown" on one of my throwaway prepaid cell phones confirmed the information. I suspected the caller was well connected and well known to me. In fact, seated nearby.

In Orlando, home of Disney World, appears the first example of revenue-generating tourist trapping. Orlando was one of the first adopters of red-light cameras. OPD installed many before it was legal to do so. They have forty-one legal cameras installed in the city now. Still money makers.

CHAPTER 11

A SHORT TIME later, I stand studying the writings pasted to the wall with one of the sheriff's child homicide case deputies. It appears to be the former office room, part of an old, abandoned orange packing shed along the railroad south of Cocoa. There are plenty of fingerprints, no doubt, along with old blankets, used needles, condoms, and sandal tracks. Several empty bottles and takeout food containers had been collected and run through the FBI lab. DNA samples had been taken from an old mattress and insect repellant cans. There were no matches from the files. Interpol has not returned their report.

> *"Infidel, come. Here am I!* The vision awaits, somewhere in the great somewhere, a haunting warm smile mocks me. The face that is never totally absent from my subconscious, the yellow rose that I crushed, no, that I shot with double ought buckshot. The virgins await but I have failed."

Graffiti of all kinds covered the walls and there was a partial red chalk pentagram on the floor.

"Kill Jack - the Great Satan's devil dog!"

"On the name of Allah, blessed be his name, we took the oath."

"Why did they use quotation marks under the heading Mr. Tyler, that is our question? Also, do you have reason to believe that the remarks are directed toward you?" asked one of the deputies.

"I believe different people used this site and passed on information to each other. Yes, the messages are directed toward me and others that served with me in the past," I answered.

"Our sheriff wants to know if you have one or more suspects in mind, and if so would you be willing to share that information. It would be held within the department," the deputy asked me.

"Tell him I do not have any solid leads at this time that he is not aware of, and that I will keep him informed. This could be domestic criminals trying to throw us off by using radical Islam slogans," I speculated.

"He has a secure place for you to work when the need arises. Make sure you tell him I told you that when you talk with him. Also, he believes the child homicides and the loss of your wife are two separate cases. We believe this crime site has to do with your wife," the deputy told me as I walked outside.

I carefully stepped between the yellow DO NOT CROSS tapes. It is a crime scene. Gator had been found here; his throat cut from ear to ear. Another deputy waves to us as we get into our patrol car. I wondered why the sheriff had not told his case officer that I am already working from the secure place and using his personal scramble phone. He trusted him with our undisclosed location info, but nothing else.

The answer came immediately when I answered the sheriff's new scramble phone.

We concurred on the site information and then the sheriff said, "I'm in the neighborhood."

He said he also has a new friend in high places and that he and I were the only two authorized to use the borrowed scramble phone. He does not know who my phone lending friends are and has no desire to meet them.

The strong possibility that the work of a "straight" razor is the murder weapon and the one with the best opportunity to use it is in little doubt. Gator's habit required cash or other product to barter to fill his pipe. Gator failed. There is a lot of truth in the saying, *the fear of failure.*"

Back at a very well-known restaurant location, *Cracker Jacks* of Titusville on the Indian River, my assigned Deputy drops me off near my car parked under the bridge.

I like this deputy. He is all business. On the drive back from the new crime scene, he asked no questions and volunteered very little conversation. We shook hands and said goodbye.

"Two orders of sea bass and fries to go," I told the waitress at the take-out window.

"Coming right up," the waitress said as she calls back from the take-out window.

Small whitecaps chase each other toward the Titusville Marina. Cold gusts of ten to fifteen knot winds out of the southeast whip against my white hoodie and evening showers are expected, with possible lightning. A dead palm frond rides up and then slides down with each small wave. It is headed north toward the old railroad bridge and one of my new "undisclosed" locations. Brine water laps against the concrete pilings of the new shrimping/fishing pier and mixes with the aroma of frying fish from the open take-out window.

I must admit I'm more than a little disappointed that there has been no sighting of any wildlife on or in the paradise river from my youth while I wait. Gone are the days when ducks of all species literally covered the mile wide Indian River Lagoon in winter. Formations of brown and white Florida pelicans broke rank and dived into the water for their meals. Pods of dolphin fins breaking the surface while they took a breath and a break from chasing their food and each other.

"That will be $19.95 please," the waitress at the window said, breaking into my reminiscing.

I peel off a twenty and a five. From under the bill of my navy-blue cap I see her smile. My "thank you" receives a "THANK YOU."

The window closes as a rain cloud moves over the bridge bringing almost complete darkness. Outside lights come on from the restaurant and the bridge as I carry Jack and my dinners toward the car. I did not recognize anyone or detect any reason for alarm, but I have that sixth sense that all is not right. I walk passed my car toward a motor home also parked under the bridge.

An elderly man and woman sit across from each other playing cards in their home on wheels. No one was bucking the wind except me as I unlock the car, get in, and start to drive.

Why am I not surprised out of my wits to see a hand from the back seat?

"One for me?" he asked.

CHAPTER 12

"*The executioner's face is always well hidden,*" Bob Dylan's words keep coming to my mind. The man who shot Natasha wore a black ski mask.

"*What else did he have, Toby?*" It was like a shout to my mind. "*Think hard!*"

Now, I'm talking to myself. My head is throbbing like a migraine. I close my eyes and drop to my knees.

The dream is there again. The white van is slowing down in front of our pickup just past the CPD on route 520 west bound. The side door on the driver's side opens slowly and a lone seat-belted figure leans out. He points a shotgun at me. I am swerving left… "NO, I scream!"

I do not want to look at Natasha again. I'll lose my mind if I have to see her again in that position. She is as beautiful in death as when she was alive. The seat belt holding her; she looks at her killer's feet. My hands cover my eyes and receive their tears. Deep sobs wrack my chest with pain. Cold sweat soaks me. I'm going to pass out.

"That's it, see the Nike sneakers, Toby!"

"Natasha? Is that you honey?" She is looking at the sneakers on a boat dock. A young man bows toward her. He has a long blond ponytail tied back.

He is mocking Natasha. "Much obliged madam bovine." His voice and the girl's giggles drift across the water to me in the rented rowboat bobbing on the Indian River. I look for the wounded sea cow and see Natasha turn at the rail.

The speed boat starts with a roar, and I hear, "Toby. Look out!"

Now, she is not alone. There is a man there and young Billy is running up to her and she is pointing at the speeding boat. I row to put myself between the speeding boat and the manatee. They miss us by a foot and the wake causes the floating animal and my rental to rise up.

Lying in front of the driver, under the seat, I see military clothing, a shotgun, and a *black ski mask and the man in Nikes on the dock.*

"ROCK, WAKE UP. Rock, you are scaring the alligators," Jack's face comes into view above me.

He is almost smiling that cruel little knowing one. I hear the air conditioning being forced in from a secure venting system. My mouth is dry and tastes like something has crawled inside and died. I can smell it and feel myself shaking with the old familiar cold sweat on my shirt and face. As I swing my feet over the Army style bunk and sit up, Jack hands me a towel and a bottle of water. I wipe my face and rinse my mouth. There is the scent of salt water, fish, and cheese. There on the folding table we use for meals are two large pizzas to go boxes from Ryan's Pizza. A slice is missing from each box.

We have been working around the clock for a week since my new crime scene visit.

"Who would have believed Ryan's Pizza would deliver way out here?" I said sarcastically.

He held up a large espresso cup to go from Ossorio's and said, "Bloody decent of them to feed the chaps on the front. I took the liberty of testing your food while you fought the good fight in your sleep."

I was having a battle with the damaged taste buds and part of my brain that remembers my love of Ryan's pizza. Also, the warning to lay off the poison that killed Gus was overruled by my growling stomach. Pepperoni and Italian sausage pizza never tasted better.

"Good news and bad, which first?" Jack asked between sips of espresso.

I swallowed another oversized bite of pie and said, "Good first, we could use lots."

"Sheriff Woodall called your scramble phone. They caught the man in Orlando. He was a homeless man wearing old Marine surplus clothes, old Nike tennis shoes. A crack rock, and a Mossberg twelve gauge shot gun were hidden in the back of the old white van. There was no identification on him and no driver's license," Jack said.

"All of that fits the description I gave the Cocoa Police Department detectives the day Natasha was murdered. That *is* good news," I said.

"The bad news is he cannot be the shooter," Jack said, shaking his head.

"What? Why not, everything fits?" I asked.

"That driver can't be over eighteen years old now. That would put him about five years old back then," Jack explained.

I stood up from our dining table, grabbed a change of clothes, and headed for the bathroom facilities. Simple in design but adequate for a President in hiding, I let the hot water stream on my face as much as I could stand, soaped up, and finished an executive shower in the swamp.

CHAPTER 13

"I CANNOT BEAR this cross! My God, my God why have you forsaken me?"

"Humph," came the familiar sound of the RPG as it flew overhead and struck a nearby palm. Shouts in Arabic followed.

Jack and I listened to the one-way conversation from across the clearing that surrounded the abandoned fisherman's thatched hut. Jack signed that he was going to take a position in front to prevent the man's escape through the swamp or Saint John's River by his airboat.

Reference to our crucifixions in Iran confirmed his identity and ours to the Colonel.

The shack was more like a military bunker when viewed through the scope of my sniper rifle. Earlier demonstration of the RPG fired into the palm completed the war-like situation. Ais Indians never dreamed of such weapons, and I wished I had not experienced them.

The Sheriff is on the way with a MRAP and should arrive at this location in fifteen minutes in response to the RPG presence.

The military surplus vehicle was bomb proof and pedal to the metal at 65 miles per hour from the Cape. Built for $500,000 at the height of the wars in Iraq and Afghanistan, the vehicle was the latest and heaviest piece of equipment acquired by the Brevard County sheriff, free as surplus. The local ACLU protested that the armor protected behemoth, weighing in at 18 tons only escalated violence.

Looking for the sheriff was not ideal as there were many things that could not be discussed. Like how I knew who this man was and where he was located as soon as he stepped off the American Air Lines plane from Chicago in Orlando, Florida. Jack's man in D.C. could reach around the world in a matter of seconds after scanning any face that was in his agencies database. He could do that without a trace within or without the agency. A hacker I assumed, knowing Jack, *the man from U N C L E* Richard. The Iranian Colonel as hunter was now the hunted.

As far as the public knows, facial recognition is on a trial basis in a few selected locations. Facial recognition is a computer-based system that automatically identifies a person based on a digital image or video source which is then matched to information stored in a database.

The photograph sent from Jack's satellite phone of the man in charge of the Iranian Guard that captured us was in that database. A BOLO (Be on Look Out) for the man who ordered the death and torture of Jack and me had gone out the day I called to report my life had been threatened.

I parted the grass enough to see the airboat was adrift on the river and moving toward the sniper's nest across the river from the palm fan covered hut.

An arm reached out and was immediately followed by a sniper body being dragged under the black water. There was a swirl and the boat drifted back to the edge by the hut.

Explaining Jack's presence and sharing the information obtained from one or more of his friends, let alone Jack's actions when their tormentor was captured, were not viable options. Neither the BCSO nor the local FBI rookie knew Jack or that we had been using the federal "undisclosed" location. The Director had been misinformed about Jack's "random shot in the dark" under the bridge. When I asked him, Jack simply said, "Ask me no questions."

The two fingers below his eyes flashed the Spec Ops signals. Jack could see another tango, armed with a sniper rifle, two in the bunker, the bunker was booby trapped with the Russian equivalent to C-4. I acknowledged and relayed the message from the sheriff and added ETA nine minutes. Then the *Ghost* disappeared under the water near the second sniper's nest.

First, the sheriff's department had called on my pink cell and said, "Wait for back up. Do not engage the suspects alone. Repeat, hold your fire until the sheriff arrives."

Then sheriff Woodall called on our special phone, "Rock, I'm on Route 50, ETA your 20 in five. Do not return fire. We need the terrorist suspects alive. Acknowledge, over."

Neither call was acknowledged. What to do about Jack was heavy on my mind.

Flamingo pink buzzed. I answered in a low voice.

"You got a cold, Rock, I can barely hear you?" Zany asked. "I got in to question my friend's client. You won't believe what I learned."

There was a long pause and then a shot ripped through the weeds an inch from my head. I killed the cell and slither back a few feet in the black muck where no weeds grow. The chop of rotor blades sounds in the distance. A speck follows the river from the north. Visual must have been made because a Blackhawk turned and lifted toward the west across a line of tall palms. I used the distraction to relocate and find better cover behind an old log.

"Rock, we are on the Brevard side of the river. MRAP is too heavy for the bridge. I can see your airboat and will join you shortly. Out."

I backtracked and met the sheriff at our boat, his river patrol boat tied up to my airboat as I slog up like the monster from the tar pit. Accompanied by two armed to the teeth deputies and the local "rook" special agent FBI in charge, it's all they can do to keep from laughing. Before anyone spoke, a tremendous explosion rolls over us.

The sheriff and special agent fall flat. Sheriff's detective deputies are on their phones trying to learn what happened. I wash off as much muck as was possible and climbed back on my boat. The FBI phone crackles, instructing the Blackhawk to investigate. They found a large hole filling with river and partial remains of two men, fish, and alligators. I look back, two more tar pit monsters stare at me.

Back at the fish camp an excited owner repeated, "Si, two men rent boats."

I returned ours. I find an old piece of corroborated card box that soon becomes my cushion and backrest to protect the cloth lining of the rental car from wet swamp smell. An hour later finds me free and the rental returned with me back in my car headed toward the I95 520 exit and Cocoa. My disappearing act was over with every agency reporting the excitement on the Saint John's River.

CHAPTER 14

"IN RESPONSE TO the shooting at Fort Hood, Army Chief of Staff Gen. George W. Casey Jr. said: "As horrific as this tragedy was, if our diversity becomes a casualty, I think that's worse."

On "Fox News Sunday" this week, former CIA director Gen. Michael Hayden said of the Boston bombing suspects, "We welcome these kinds of folks coming to the United States who want to be contributing American citizens."

Luther scanned the microfilm newspaper clips. He found comfort in the articles that twisted the stories to favor a point of view instead of the fact of murder. The work of terrorists reported as "workplace tragedy" and Benghazi a "protest against a video."

Mr. Luther Law, a collector of people who hold such views and "interviews" them in the comfort of his own especially selected dungeons. Much of the material he uses comes from his guests themselves, often recorded without their knowledge. He delights in placing individuals in extreme circumstances to test their compassion for terrorists.

The psychotic break came for Luther on September 11, 2001. Two of the bodies caught on film plunging from the top of the Twin Towers belonged to his wife and daughter. He collected everything he could, every source on that "tragic day" as reported and photographed by excited reporters of every stripe.

"The September 11 attacks (also referred to as September 11, September 11th, or 9/11 were a series of four coordinated terrorist attacks launched by the Islamic terrorist group al-Qaeda upon the United States in New York City and the Washington, D.C. area on September 11, 2001" No mention of those who lost their lives in Pennsylvania. Luther lost a brother there. In fact, "Let's Roll" came to mind, and is repeated each time he interviews one of his "collection."

A deep moan echoes today's interviewee when he hears the steel door close and the words, "let's roll." A naked, well-known defense attorney sat leaning forward, arms and legs bound to the metal captain's chair that was bolted to the concrete floor. This unhappy condition brought about when the fully clothed attorney broke his right to remain silent earlier today in this very court.

"Remain seated counselor, no need to rise," said the voice piped into the "cell."

"Court is in session. We need to redeem those terrible Islamic murders of the innocent by meeting fire with fire. We need to engage in serious soul-searching.

We must not only redeem ourselves, but we must also make the victims of 9/11 meaningful so that their lives will not have perished in vain. We will teach you the law of an eye for an eye, most honorable Attorney."

Mr. Law's "guest" was found in contempt of court again. He protested being forced to watch his reported so called "tragedy" of people leaping to their death rather than burn in flames. A tape recording of his famous interview on TV stating that he had sympathy for the Saudi pilots who gave their lives for something they believed in so deeply; played over and over again.

Between showing the film of people weeping and jumping on September 11, 2001, from the Twin Towers, the attorney showed no remorse only grief from his physical discomfort.

When he saw his tormentor's wife, daughter, and son standing atop a burning building he became sick and threw up his Saudi salad with dates.

"Did you find this film disagreeable, counselor? I must apologize for not following my deep belief in having your wife and children jump to their deaths from a burning building. It is your fault for being unmarried without children. This is the best I can do with a man who only has feelings for himself."

He was provided with a quick cold-water shower by a water hose technique some called water boarding, but his soiled white robe and Saudi sandals were torched along with defiled undergarments.

Now, a day later, part two of the attorney/host interview began again with the audio from Pennsylvania last words, "Let's roll." It was entered into evidence, by the CIA, that the Muslim, peace-loving lawyer failed to be converted to an infidel and was left beheaded in an abandoned NYC warehouse. Attorney Luther Law's video tape showed no remorse for this Islamic attorney's moaning or practiced pleadings for his life before his white hooded judge.

There were other guests to engage for interviews. David, aka Luther had a collection of P's as he called them, "five peas remain in my pod."

A presswoman, politician, policeman, preacher, and a pedo-phile filled out his guest list. He was delighted to find all of them in Brevard County, Florida, all members of an Islamic cell.

David (N) Dawson, dubbed Double D because he had no middle name, was dead to the world. Like so many others his body was never found and was declared unrecoverable in the 9/11 terrorists attack on the Twin Towers. His wife, son, and daughter were found after they plunged from the building the family that fateful day. David was outside their car locating the camera his daughter had forgotten when the first plane struck. He was pre-vented from entering the building by security while firefighters and paramedics rushed inside. David knew how to become anyone he wanted to be and disappear without a trace. Langley graduates came with life altering skills. Mr. Dawson became Mr. Law.

It was during his interview of the Muslim pedophile that he learned an old acquaintance from the farm was working with the police to find a serial killer of children.

That was not believable because the man he knew as Jack Frost would not work with any law enforcement department on any case after the Dirty Dozen's Iran double cross.

The man had become a lone wolf. David was about to send this lover of young boys to meet seventy boy virgins when he mentioned Toby Rockwell Tyler, a.k.a. James "Jack" Frost.

———

My drop out of sight ended at the swamp. I and my burner phone from Jack are back to abnormal life. Drug pushers and pimps use cheap pay per minute phones a few hours and then get rid of them. Looking out the window over a slice of Ryan's pepperoni pizza, I saw another mirage. I first thought the vision my overworked and unappreciated mind flashed was that I was having another mistaken identity like the day I saw my deceased wife. The profile of two men unlikely to be seen together; old spies were sitting on a park bench.

The second look confirmed and removed all doubt. They are real. These two were oil and water, Irish and the Israeli, with known enmity within the agencies.

One pretended to be reading a *Florida Today* newspaper while the other pitched breadcrumbs to a gathering gang of squirrels and assorted birds that thought him a benevolent gentle giant.

I gulped down the rest of my lunch and flashed a ten-dollar bill at my pretty waitress. She nodded and smiled as I tucked it partially under the side of my teacup. Stepping between empty white cast iron outside chairs to either side, I turned south toward Zany's office in the Porcher Mansion. The Israeli laid his newspaper on the bench, stood up, glanced across the street at me, and sauntered along the winding concrete trail of Taylor Park toward the adjoining River Front Park. I turned back and crossed the street to Thai-Thai's Restaurant. We seemed to be alone.

Crossing to the opposite street corner, I used the windows on the old Bad Bird's Art building to check on the still seated former IRA enforcer known to me only by the single name Sean.

Benjamin Silverman, the notorious Nazi hunter and believed to be an unofficial Mossad agent, circled around the statue of Benet along the memorial bricks toward my unofficial gazebo. Sean stood and followed the path taken by the Israeli, trailed by circling squirrels and hopping birds.

The impromptu meeting started when Sean finally circled the jets of water shooting up in the small children's water park.

"Lo Yank," he did not try to disguise himself in any way.

His face had the map of Ireland stamped on it for all to see as his clothes cried Dublin. His smile reminded one of a great white shark and the glassy eyes were cold as the Arctic. Tough men had been known to wet their skivvies at the sight of him and hoped he would shoot them in one kneecap only, a signature mark of an IRA visit to one who crossed the wrong friend as a warning.

"I see we are having a reunion of old spies today. Question is, why meet in an old, retired military man's office?" I asked as I bumped Israeli Ben's scarred fist held out to him top and then the bottom.

Both were no doubt remembering our trip to Iran especially. He was the go-between on our transportation.

"Nice to see you, too, Rocky," without hesitation Ben continued. "This is neutral territory for allies in a search for a common enemy."

Nodding to Sean, "We are sharing intelligence for mutual benefit."

"A rag head has escaped to your neighborhood. My employers desire to question him before the Jews extract their pound of flesh or your countrymen read him his rights," the Irishman said as he spit into the gentle water as it licked the piling below.

"Is this truth what I read in your paper?" Sean handed me a faded and much wrinkled piece of newsprint.

Chicago Residents Stunned!!!

Police in Chicago south side report the discovery of an arms cache of 300 semi-automatic rifles with 50,000 rounds of ammunition, five tons of cocaine, and twenty-five prostitutes in building behind the library. The Community Organizer spokesman exclaimed – We are all shocked, we never knew there was a library in that community."

I know this is Sean's way of telling us that America is not lily white when it comes to violence in the name of political correctness or legal operations. I broke a long silence as we three stood with hands on the gazebo railing looking into my beautiful Indian River.

"Does this search have anything to do with the attempts to kill me?" I asked.

"Getting narcissist in your old age, Rock?" Ben smiled and shook his head. "It has everything to do with your demise as well as that of your wife."

He studied his old friend for a few seconds before he continued, "We got that much out of a young Islamist before our friend here terminated our relationship."

He did not hide his contempt toward Sean.

"I was merely following directions," the enforcer face was in complete denial. "The young lad was in a room with a black bag over his rag head. The Israelis were behind the soundproof glass listening and looking whilst I completed our friendly discussion. I removed the bag and looked through the glass. A high Israeli official drew his right hand across his neck."

Ben broke in, "Whereupon our Irish friend here withdrew one of your famous Bowie knives and gave our only reliable source a new smile from ear to ear!"

Ben regained his composure after a deep sigh, "The international sign for terminate the interview terminated our only witness."

The knuckles on both fists turned white as he griped the railing and stared into the river.

I stood between the two men and could feel the heat waves from them on both sides of my face. Try as I might, I could not stop my upper body from shaking. Tears started to roll down my cheeks and birds flew in fright as my laughter boomed from under the gazebo roof.

Just as I recovered enough to offer my apologies, Sean said in a still quite brogue, "Talk about your classic spy craft misdirection."

His face was still deadpan, but that remark doubled me over with uncontrollable fits of mirth. Even Ben was forced to smile. Putting a right arm around my old Mossad friend's broad shoulders, I turned him toward the children being splashed by the alternating up jets of cold water. Sean had his eyes locked on a sailboat with bikini clad captain being swept north by a gentle southeast breeze. Four deadly, long scared fingers on each hand drummed on the top of the railing.

We walked over to a high-backed bench and sat down, watching a well-known Steven seagull steal a little girl's French fry bag while her slightly bigger brother walked her over a water hole that was due to gush upward.

The water shot up nearly knocking the little girl down. She scrambled to her feet flapping her arms and screaming at her betrayer. Her mother laughed and held her in a beach towel, while her older of the two brothers were Kung Fu fighting with another blasting water geyser.

"Why would God create a man like Sean, Rock?" Ben still had a dazed look on his face.

"Let's get back to the reason for your visit. Why are so many people interested in the Iranian that you and I remember from our well-known blown covert operation?" I asked.

"Our lads learned that the man whose wife, our other Irish-American friend blasted by accident on that ill-fated op, is behind one or more plots against Ireland, Israel, and the U.S." Ben said as looked around me to see what Sean was doing.

Another bag of breadcrumbs appeared, and the brute was chumming small fish, no doubt scheming to slaughter larger ones later with minnows.

"They have even produced a double agent believed to be in the U.S. How is our old Ghost?" he asked.

"Jack comes and goes like the wind. He is involved here. Works only with me and has sworn me to secrecy. Terrorist plots? Funny, I'm sure he would know. He is solo, but well-connected," I answered.

"How much have you discovered about Natasha's murder?" Ben noticed the immediate stiffness in my body and frowned like he wished he had never asked. "I'm sorry, Rock, I really am."

"It's okay, Ben. The Sheriff was a friend of Uncle Rob, and he has treated me kindly. His office is keeping it open and not treating it as a cold case. The clues are scarce. It is being treated as a random shooting. Two unsolved murders in nearby Titusville are in the same category," I explained.

"I don't want to raise your hopes on hearsay, Rock. Word is the Iranian put out a contract on your wife because he confused you with Jack because of your pseudonym at the Cocoa paper," he told me. "He received information that Jack Frost, the Irishman, came from Georgia and is writing for a paper in Cocoa, Florida. He is connected to some serious money through arms deals and terrorists all over the Middle East, even in the U.S. He went rogue after the death of his wife."

For several seconds, I could not respond, then asked, "How reliable is your hearsay?"

"Our Mossad, MI6, the Irish, your CIA, and FBI have been briefed on the possibility that he is here and wants to kill Jack himself. He also is believed to be a chief over several sleeper cells here and in England," Ben nodded toward Sean. "Hard telling what is to happen if that weasel gets to him first. His only love is Ireland and killing. Who knows what Jack Frost would do?"

The big Irishman turned to face his two companions and ambled toward us. He walked on the balls of his feet like a large cat. His head turned as he walked like he was exercising his muscular neck rather than taking in a complete surveillance of his surroundings. He stopped in front of us, right foot back, and left hand in his windbreaker, leaning slightly forward.

"What is your employer's interest in locating our mutual Islamist?" I asked

I looked out of the corner of my eye. There was a slight squint and a long delay before an answer came from Sean.

"He lost a dear friend to this butcher in our homeland. In a homily on hate, the priest stressed, 'one is not to hate the other two religions or its people. The Jewish teachings have our God, while jihad is a creation of Satan. Yet, we Catholics are to refrain from violence against ordinary Islamists.' For that saying, my employer's friend was crucified on the Church cross one midnight as the bell rung to summons the people. It was in Belfast this was done," he explained.

"What will you do when you find him?" I asked.

We watched and waited for his answer.

"Because there is reliable intelligence that our three countries are to suffer terrorist's attacks and your loss and threat is known, I am to let a representative hear us during our discussions. The recordings with copies will be made available to selected authorities. This is why I'm here," he told us quietly.

A Cocoa police cruiser drove past Ryan's Pizza and turned east on the street toward us. Ben walked through the trees in Taylor Park by the time it parked, and Sean followed the river walk to the bridge parking lot in the opposite direction. Neither man looked suspicious; men, women, and children moving with them leaving the parks while others entered.

Seated watching the mother and towel wrapped children leave, I spied Chief Brody and his assistant ease out of their car and walk across the grass toward me. The burner phone buzzed.

I withdrew it from my coat pocket and saw the text: "Woodall headed your way. Has info–get it, wants help–no way–you were alone in the swamp–I have two guests–J. I stared amazed to watch the message disappear letter by letter in reverse.

Is there anything a hack cannot do these days? I lifted my chin in acknowledgment to the arrival of the sheriff and a Lieutenant as they exited the Sheriff's unmarked car. The phone in silent mode started to vibrate. I let it go to message in pocket.

"Mr. Toby Rockwell Tyler, I have a warrant to search your personal property and for your arrest on suspicion of murder. You have the right to remain silent, anything you say can be used against you in a court of law, you have the right to an attorney, and if you cannot afford an attorney one will be appointed for you. Do you understand your rights?"

I decided to exercise my right to remain silent.

Chief Brody removed a recorder from his pocket and said, "The suspect has acknowledged his rights by nodding his head isn't that correct, Lieutenant"

His lieutenant said, "Yes, Mr. Tyler has acknowledged his rights."

They made no move to show me a warrant or arrest me. I see over their shoulders and watched as Sheriff Woodall and his detective deputy driver park beside the CPD cruiser. Mr. J, my nonexistent swamp buddy, again well informed. It's a pity I am the last one to receive the knowledge that I have been a target of an Islamist terrorist. An Iranian confused with Mr. J, who had indeed killed one of his wives in Iran years ago. How much of this information the departments and agencies knew and have shared is anyone's guess. Pity they have not shared it with me. I was in Iran and witnessed the whole operation. It was *my* operation. *Or was it...*

The sheriff arrived and shook hands with the three of us and was quick to notice the strained silence.

"Mr. Tyler, no excuses; sorry for no notice and us for barging into your office unannounced, but I have some information that you need to hear. Chief Brody's lieutenant and my assistant are special federal agents working on corruption in our respective departments," he said professionally. "Because of our ongoing investigations we have not been able to keep you in the loop of information. As you well know from past experience, private investigators are not trusted with inside information in capital punishment cases."

I remained silent and looked out at my beloved Indian River. Turning my back on them was not lost on them.

"We still need your help, Rock. There is still a murderer of little girls still out there, Rock. We have learned that there are one or more terrorists in our county, and you and your unknown friends have been working outside the box. Tell us what you know, Rock," he demanded.

When I concentrated on a south bound sailboat passing a smaller rowboat, my mind went to multilevel as it sometimes does in investigations. First, I remembered my last day with Natasha near this same spot on the river. Second, I remembered Gus, my friend and Jonathan, my fowl waterside assistant here in River Front Park. Both dead from eating *my* pizza. Third, I was brought back to a vibrating phone in my pocket, mumbling voices behind me, and a large man waving at me from the sailboat. He had a large Irish grin and a bikini clad first mate sunning on the deck.

"Does your ignoring us mean you will not help with the child murders and locating of terrorists?" I turned to face Chief Brody and his questioning face.

"You know why we had to lock you out? We have witnesses that say they saw you with another man at the fish camp and that both of you were in the boat headed north close behind the boat that was lost in the explosion. Who was that man and who were the two murdered men in the other airboat?" Sheriff Woodall asked, but his face was not expecting an answer, it was for the benefit of the other officers.

"Chief Brody and these two special agents know you have information that we desperately need, Mr. Tyler," the formal address reassured me that the sheriff knew I could not give them the information.

Chief Brody changed from authority to personal friend mode, "Now you know we are all on the same page you can trust us, Rock. Your information will go no further than us four."

I pointed toward his pocket with the recorder and motioned for him to bring it out. He shrugged his shoulders like he didn't know what I meant. I removed my phone, then he removed his cell phone from the other pocket, then I shook my head and pointed at the recorder bulging in his other pocket. He shrugged and removed it. I held out my hand. He was reluctant, but handed it over when the sheriff motioned for him to surrender it. I hit rewind and played their entire conversation up to his last words. He had continued to record every word spoken by the sheriff and including my arrest. Then, I motioned for the two special agents to lift their shirts.

They refused. I turned my back to them, watched the receding sailboat, and read my text from Zany while the fuzz returned to their marked and unmarked vehicles.

She wanted to know if I was okay, and if I could meet her in our favorite place for Q. My shrink had called her twice and left a message for me to call. The sheriff wanted to see me, too.

I do not text, but I did return her call. She did not answer, so I left her a message that I would be delighted to meet her at the Dairy Queen. I was off the hook on suspicion of murder, but no need to give phone tappers my next whereabouts. My stomach was already grumbling for Kay's Q.

On the off chance that someone would show, I did a stake out on the Dairy Queen. In the thirty minutes that I watched from an abandoned house, there appeared no less than three known department and agency representatives with an insatiable desire for a cone with a curl on top. I called Zany and asked her to bring my second lunch to our office. She texted back that she was there and would see me at the Q for raspberry ripple ice cream.

Clever girl. She would lose anyone tailing her and meet me at Ashley's in Rockledge, an upstairs private room. It was our agreed upon fall back place. We had actually joked about using yellow chalk as a countersign. On one of our non-date nights, we watched "Smiley's People" on a computer in her office, ate pizza from Ryan's, and designated Ashley's as Q in deep conspiracy.

I went back to my apartment and noticed that there had been visitors. The CPD was nice enough to announce a warrant even if they didn't show me one. Jack had discovered surveillance equipment and other evidence that I had no privacy. I had ignored it and refused to answer my phone even if another call came from the real killer. There had been no more missing girl reports, nor any calls according to the sheriff. Even the pimps and drug dealers appeared to be on vacation from violence. The protesters of all stripes were out of sight. I changed clothes.

The stakes on my life had gone up. I added my S&W J frame 38 special to my inside left boot holster and my combat knife to the other one. The lightweight vest under my pullover shirt was there as well, along with extra magazines for the Colt 1911 in my pockets. I am ready for Q.

As I drove north to the ACE hardware store, I have company. Another one parked. Inside and working my way around the plumbing section until the hall leading to the back door appears on my right. One of my Dairy Queen visitors soon strolls through the front door. I make sure he sees me before I duck around the floor to ceiling paint display, into the hall, and out the back door. In short order, I cross a narrow clearing behind the store. These are familiar woods, where we played cowboy and Indians on trails that run all the way to the Indian River. I am playing hide and seek today.

An old high school friend still lives in a riverside house that we all knew was haunted. More importantly, he rides his ten-speed bicycle every evening to get his beer and a slice at Ryan's. I sometimes take it for a spin.

I dial the combination lock, unlock it, and put the lock with chain in my pocket. Making good time all the way down Indian

River Drive to the Burger King in Rockledge, I chain the ride to a hitching post and walk to nearby Ashley's in Rockledge.

Zany, trying to hide her excitement to see me and to bring me up to date on her clients delights me. Especially, how she alluded to be aiding an attorney for the captured kid in Orlando and learned that he had been hired anonymously to dress in old clothes, act homeless, and drive the white van. He claimed to know nothing about the shotgun or drugs hidden in the back.

Iris's attorney father had not made contact, but Zany's source inside the CPD assured her his office would be in touch after the police worked the case for a few more days.

I filled her in on most of what had happened on my adventures in the swamp and on the river, leaving Jack out. I told her the CPD no longer was interested in me, but the feds were because of the terrorist's threats and shoot outs on the Saint John's River outside Titusville.

We enjoyed our meals and each other. Zany had the baked salmon and I the New York strip steak. The Caesar salads and sweet potato fries never tasted better. Throwing our calorie count to the wind, we both had raspberry ripple ice cream, two scoops.

"Shall I put the chip back in my phone and let our Fibbies know where I am when you leave?" I asked her.

"The Sheriff and the Chief have filled them in no doubt. The Chief thinks I am withholding information and holding a grudge against him, and the Sheriff knows I cannot share information involving others that are not supposed to be here. I could tell the FBI it's classified or I'm working on an ongoing investigation, and therefore cannot comment but that's their line," I told her.

We thanked our host and hostess for use of their office and left our waitress a large tip. Outside, Zany opened her car door and handed me a large doggy bag that smelled heavenly even after a wonderful meal. My Q! The thought that Ethel Allen had spent part of her last night in this very building crossed my mind. I am still not asked to help with the latest King Street case.

History has a way of staying with you–good or bad. Iris had been treated the same way except her body drifted to my River Front Park gazebo instead of a park near Rockledge.

I am careful to stick to the back streets on my way to return my friend's bicycle. The idea of walking back through the palmetto brush without a light did not appeal to me. Also, I do not want to be seen with friends that could also be put in danger from those who wanted me room temperature. My feet and legs keep telling me they have had a long day. So, I put the chip back into Zany's smart phone and called the Sheriff. As it turned out, he was near and would be delighted to pick me up within mere minutes.

"You have become a quintessential liar, Sheriff Woodall. You were not nearby, it's been over an hour, and you are not delighted to be with me instead of your family tonight," I chided him.

"Sheriff is still an elected office, Mr. Tyler. You're not a politician," he responded sarcastically.

He told me all he could about the children's murder cases and that the special agents had been called off from powers on high, most likely from the Director himself. They would not question me. Word was that Director Lawson had similar personnel problems to the Sheriff and Chief.

He accepted the fact that I had to remain silent on the adventure in the swamp west of Titusville. He does not know about the swamp east of Titusville nor will he learn of it from me. I owe Jack that much. I am relieved that he is alive and hope to hear from him again, but you never know about those guys. He said he has two guests which means the two they found were the ones he killed before explosion. Knowing the *Ghost*, he took out the snipers first, captured the two "guests," and blew the dead tangos and all evidence of his presence sky high.

In so many words, he told me a certain city police lieutenant and sergeant would be the least of my worries in the future. They had plenty to keep them occupied in the county jail. Both of them had been caught in their own illegal wiretapping by the FBI after a NSA sweep of foreign calls. There were connections to withholding vital evidence in several cases including murders. He was not specific, but hinted that they knew more than they had reveled about the murder of Natasha.

I am at once relieved and surprised; relieved that the desire to rush to cause bodily harm to those two was not present, and surprised that I could smile and not feel guilty about doing so. The good doctor will be pleased to hear about this when she is no longer in danger. Also, my emotions are in check when even a hint of finding anything remotely connected to the murder of my wife had previously caused my mind confusion. Now, my wife's murder investigation can join the two little girls with clarity. "Serena "Rene" Jones and Sabrina Moore, you are not forgotten, and you are loved," I whispered to them. It was true. I can feel them in my heart.

Time to get back to the *Village Voice* and my Cocoa. I will get caught up on the outside world. Read a few papers and watch a little TV. Hit my fav eateries. Maybe contact some old classmates.

CHAPTER 15

As I skimmed the papers, I learned a lot was being said about terrorists as a result of the St. John's River attack.

"Only the dead know the end of wars," said Plato. "I say, the wars are not over because the President declares them to be; the press, and thinking people know we remain at war with terrorists." To her credit, Sen. Hurwitz (D NY) was not afraid to identify the threat, nor did she try to downplay or diminish Islamic jihadist's involvement in the terrorist's hideout on the St. John's River. She warned that the source of the "huge malevolence out there" came from the "jihadist, Islamic community" that is dedicated to "Islamic Sharia law and the concept of the caliphate." The senator from New York added that she saw "more jihadists more determined to kill in Florida to get what they want like they did in Syria. So, it's not an isolated phenomenon. They are targeting Jews and Christians primarily like Nero did in Roam."

Her counterpart in the house agreed, "As the civil war in Syria rages on, the persecution of Christians at the hands of

Islamic jihadists continues unabated. Just days ago, twelve nuns were kidnapped from a Greek Orthodox monastery. Meanwhile, hundreds of thousands of Christians have fled to neighboring countries."

A former State Department spokesman added, "There is no question that Islamic jihadists are evil. Now there is an eye for an eye movement calling itself Christ's Crusaders that are waging terrorist attacks against Islamic targets. Neither group has the official backing of their religion. However, the threat of the Crusaders was given credit for a lull in bombing of Church buildings by announcing the revenge bombing of the Islamic Great Mosque of Aleppo. I believe it is a matter of when, not if there will be a war based solely on religion."

Back home, two officers were brought up on corruption charges in the Cocoa Police Department. Chief Brody of the CPD spoke to the press, "We recognized that the actions of the two officers reflect on the entire department. Officer Rammer's pulling a woman from her burning car last week and saving her life also reflects on this department. The misguided actions of two in no way reflect on the professionalism, dedication, and integrity of the rest of our department," he concluded at the press conference.

I continue reading the morning papers. "The new stealth destroyer DD 1000 Zumwalt; her two advanced guns on the forward deck can hit a basketball with a 155mm Howitzer-sized artillery shell from 63 miles away." *That is not your grand-father's tin can Navy mate.*

Back on the Cocoa *Village* beat and it feels great!

I am not so naïve as to believe that we can return to our native hometown and find it as it was, or to see again the joys that came to us free from adult conviction that life is absurd, and human beings with their flawed lives are meaningless. We took our favorite date to the outdoor movies and watched Hemingway's core hero choose his own values in the 1950s. Few, if any knew or understood the movies message was *Atheistic Existentialism*. Matter exists–God does not.

We loved the old movie's *action*, while Hollywood raved about Albert Camus'"*The Plague.*"

Later, these old movie re-runs were a big hit on college campuses as more professors took control of classes and teaching their brand of Socialism. Brainwashing students is nothing new. Indoctrinating us to "feel" guilt and self-loathing, mingled with hatred of capitalism, and religion as the "opiate of the masses" is our New Freedom. All the "intellectuals say so."

It is interesting if not a surprise to watch as otherwise intelligent people are duped into believing children taught to hate others to the point of terrorism is isolated to a few radicals over there.

Selective amnesia is so convenient when college professors skip the brown shirts, product of Hitler's National Socialism in Germany. Professors teach anti-Americanism, deny anti-Semitism, and ignore anti-Christians teaching routinely.

"Hatred and hate speech have been going on since Cain slew Abel," so said Natasha one day after reading about a new law.

The law increased punishment against convicted people guilty of crime against "special" people who suffered from hateful speech against them.

"Some animals are more equal than others," my little Orwellian bride chided.

This research and remembrance are moving me in the right direction. I experience a sense of well-being. The healing process is definitely in full gear.

"Hitting on all eight cylinders," as Gus would say.

Terrorism so close to home is trumping the murder of innocence. The public attention span is short. A condition that serves the politicians and their press so well.

My stolen smart phone is still locked away in the Cocoa Police Department's evidence locker with "other" vital material related to the last child murder case. Cleared by irrefutable proof that I could not have made the calls and was in fact on FBI and HS surveillance film in different location when the calls were made. It has been months since the last attempt on my life. The Iranian Colonel is confirmed to be in Iran. My heart is in such a forgiving mood that I am overruling my "other" nature. I will not press charges against the Cocoa Police Department for the *false arrest and holding a helpless, innocent, smart phone against her will.*

The NO CONTACT order from any law enforcement is working. In truth, it is a blessing. After a string of months where the only news was bad, no news is a relief.

Cocoa weather has a hint of coolness in the evenings and merchants are displaying their Halloween items. Most likely from storage. Sales have been off and events cancelled over the last two years.

Circulation of our *Village Voice* has dropped since Gus is no longer with us. My new assistant, a young, work horse, true believer, and all-around proponent of THE PEOPLE HAVE A RIGHT TO KNOW, says, "The drop is normal and a good thingy. It shows respect."

As we head into 2015, the country is divided almost evenly between right and left.

CHAPTER 16

WITH A GREAT deal of effort, I walk into King Street Community Church and sit in the pew that Gus and I have used so many times before. It is like attending my own funeral. In all honesty, there is not much spiritual presence coming from me. I miss Gus more that I want to admit or even realized. Hard to believe he is gone. Serena "Rene" Jones and Sabrina Moore's funerals come to mind as I sit here again.

The same people greeted me and expressed how sad they were to not see Gus with me. Their sympathy was genuine and it should have comforted me, but it doesn't doubtless due to my lack of forgiveness. I'm sure Beverly would say the same if I was still seeing her for counseling.

It didn't take long for the preacher to locate me and give me a nod of recognition. He too expressed mutual sympathy in his look. The congregation stood for opening remarks, a song, reading from the Bible, and prayer before being seated. It's like I'm in a trance.

Not familiar with the hymn, I am not in the mood to sing. Everyone else sings and their singing comforts me more than I thought possible. The ushers came and one prayed. When the offering plate came to me, I put in double my normal amount, then my heart began to loosen up a bit as I knew the other amount was what Gus usually gave. Oh God, how I miss Gus.

One of the ladies of the church that sang at both of the little girl's funerals sang, "What a Friend We Have in Jesus," as only she can sing it with all her soul. I was afraid to look to my left. It was like Gus was there and he would be smiling and keeping time to the music by moving his old gray head. It occurred to me that I had never told my friend that I loved him. He knew, but now I wished I had told him. I didn't get a chance to say goodbye either.

It might be grief that is overwhelming me. I am catching only some of what preacher Jerimiah is saying. He used the illustration that certain men crept in unawares to abuse and take the lives of Cocoa's children like the ungodly men came to church to rob God's teaching and His children.

My mind wandered to the history Natasha read to me while I rowed our boat on our last day together. I'm sure B.C. Willard and the first settlers in Cocoa had great expatiations when he built the first building, his general store in 1881. Then the Delmonico Restaurant that became the Cocoa House followed in nothing more than scrub palmetto surroundings.

Pastor Jerimiah's deep voice lifted to proclaim, "Men are proud of the work of their hands; proud of their city, as some name the city after themselves as Titusville for its founder Titus. Many do not give their name, but say I'm from Cocoa the home of champions!"

"We can no longer claim to be the trout capitol of the world. We dare not look at the spoil banks and pollution at the hands of man. Cocoa has become a monster that devours our children and senior citizens. King Street Community Church bears witness! We are a people that came from our representative fathers."

He waited for that to sink in before continuing.

"Bearing false witness, thievery, and murder is bound up in our hearts from birth. If you have desired a woman in your heart, you have committed adultery with her. Have you lied, have you committed thievery in your heart?

There were several who shouted Amen while others whispered, "God help us!"

In my mind, I saw myself putting a 38 special to a man's head that had been tormenting me in a bar. I told him I was going to blow sawdust all over the County. I pulled the trigger in my heart.

He asked the congregation to turn in our Bibles to Revelation Chapter 20. The messages ended with the soon to be fulfilled prophesy of the holy city, New Jerusalem, coming down from God out of heaven. The city prepared for those who have received Christ Jesus as their Savior.

While a deacon prayed the benediction Pastor Jerimiah walked quietly to the door to shake hands and speak to everyone as they left the building. After the prayer, I followed a stooped lady that might have been one of the mothers of the murdered girls. I didn't see her face, but her voice sounded familiar.

She said, "Pastor, my faith is strong, and I am getting along with my Jesus."

It was difficult to look him in the face as I shook his big hand. Strong hands grip mine. His are cool, mine hot.

Before he could ask a question, I didn't want to answer, or sense my guilt, I said, "I miss Gus and I'm doing pretty well."

He held on a few seconds and shook his head in a knowing way.

"Let sister Beverly or me know if we can be of help to you. It takes prayer, forgiveness, and time."

"I will," I remember the promise made while letting go of his hand and stepping outside.

Then it was like stepping into a new world. The sun was shining bright as a line of pelicans flew over in perfect formation. I looked up passed the tall Palm fans waving down toward the courtyard parking lot. A low beep sounded from a passing black SUV easing into King Street. The dark tinted windows prevented me from seeing inside. There was no need, though, I knew the driver was John Henry. Following close behind without tinted glass was his sister in her black BMW.

My car was in the back and as I bent to unlock the door, I keeled or was knocked down to my knees in the Bermuda grass parking area. It was there that something supernatural happened. I understand that I am to confess to the murder of the man in the bar. Then I confessed to things that I had thought were justified, but God saw as judgmental and wrong. I was overcome with the idea of people seeing me on my knees in public even with my eyes closed. I confessed pride as a sin, forgave whoever killed the children, Gus, Jonathan my sea gull, and then I saw the path that I was to follow and all was forgiven, even those who had taken the life of my wife.

On the cross, all sin is forgiven. Mine, theirs, everybody is forgiven. We are responsible for our actions and there is punishment, but we are not to punish ourselves through unforgiving others.

"But we who belong to Christ Jesus are forgiven and are to forgive completely in honor of Him."

When I stood up on shaking knees and wiped the tears from my face, I discovered I was all alone in the parking area though many cars were parked there. Dr. King, "Free at last!"

To this day, I smile inside when I remember the drive back to my apartment on Brevard Avenue. It was like I was weightless. The child and the man had come back home to Cocoa.

The memories were there but they were not painful. A new clarity made everything past and present crystal clear. I do not believe in paranormal power, but this was as close to clairvoyance as I have ever experienced. Past difficult ideas were presented to my mind without the previous doubts and hindrances. I know for a fact there is spiritual power inside and out of humans.

No morning early fog, my clear mind is still working as I sit in the gazebo on River Front Park. The pink clouds reflected on the glass smooth river interrupted only by the moored sail boats. A man is attempting to capture the beauty of this majestic morning with a time camera on tripod. He pitched left over bread from a breakfast burrito behind him to a small flock of birds.

A sudden shriek and rapid fluttering of wings drives the smaller sparrows away. Has Jonathan returned, I wonder? No, this seagull has different markings and a damaged right foot. Maybe from a bull shark attack or Kung Fu fighting, I can't help smiling as I accept my new friend named Steven Seagull.

Something Jack said before he disappeared keeps my mind on edge. "All Americans do not forget the troops who died or were mutilated at the hands of traitors. There are no traitors in Iran, Rock, they are all in our midst. All three branches of the government."

Then, he had lifted a coke in the air boat shack off route 50 and said, "A toast to the sniper." He loaded our gear into the boat while I paid, and we headed north up the Saint John's river.

He held up a pistol with silencer in a waterproof bag, and a hand grenade in the other. In Iran, he had done the same thing and said, "Where would the Mafia be without stealth, and the Irish without a potato. Death to the Great Ayatollah! Long live the BLOODY IRISH!" The S.E.A.L signals were used for "See You" as he sank under the black water. "See You." I signed back to his goggled eyes. I might have smiles. Yes …yes, I'm sure I did. The grim cruel smile is the last thing I remember and his haunting words.

CHAPTER 17

TWO PISTOL SHOTS echoed between the buildings on Brevard Avenue, swept down the alley across the two parks past the gazebo, and carried across the Indian River. It was just past midnight when I rounded the corner with pistol in hand. I placed a call to Sheriff Woodall and reported the shots and that I was headed toward the scene of the shooting. A meeting had been set up for me to meet with someone at midnight alone in my riverside office.

The sheriff was on a stake out across the Indian River on Merritt Island with high powered telephoto binoculars. The gazebo was wired with the latest equipment. I was beginning to wish I was.

The only place open at this hour was a part-time gay bar, the Ultra Lounge. Sidewalk benches had emptied and a strong arm was pulling a reluctant Bernie, my homeless friend, inside. I squeezed inside just as the barkeeper closed the door and locked it behind me.

"Anyone see what happened?" I wheezed.

I knew some of the patrons and wondered why even those I knew were staring at me.

Bernie asked, "Did you shoot somebody, Mr. Frosty?"

I backed up against the wall and shook my head no. Then it occurred to me that my 1911 Colt was still in my hand.

"No, I was down by the river when I heard the shots," I answered.

I placed the pistol in my belly holster and watched relief begin to register on each face. Karaoke music was still playing while everyone resumed their seating or standing at the bar.

"I'm going to see if I can learn what happened," I told him.

Bernie asked, "Can you spare a couple bucks, Mr. Frosty?"

There were a few that laughed and some groaned. They all knew I was a teetotaler and only bought Bernie food.

At the corner of Oleander and Brevard a voice said, "Don't turn around. Get note inside."

I slipped my hand on the Colt and walked toward my apartment building. At the door, I slipped the pistol out and entered quickly. The light was on over the stairwell. An envelope was taped to the inside door. I pulled it off and read the note inside.

"You are being watched by Sheriff and office is bugged. Cops are on the way. Meet me by the elevator of your old condo – 5 minutes."

Oleander was empty as I walked away from flashing blue lights on Brevard Avenue. I arrived at the elevator with a minute to spare, and found another note saying, "Your Floor, Old Room."

The door was open. I walked in and was surprised to see three people with mouths taped and bound to three kitchen chairs all back-to-back. I checked the other rooms and closets. The four of us were alone. I returned to the living room. A familiar note post it note stuck on each forehead. They were numbered # 1, #2, and #3, reporter, politician, and lastly preacher.

I don't want to speculate, but the woman was #1 and was I to believe in ladies first at this point? Her eyes were red, and terror seemed to seep from her face. The other two were men and shared her expression. All were looking at the 1911 with real dread. I put it away locked the door and sat down on the couch facing the woman.

Strong odor of Gauloise cigarettes filled the room. It grew stronger as I moved toward the three-bound people. I walked around them and each set of blood shot eyes followed the pistol in its holster as though they were soon to come to their murder. None had the will to make eye contact.

I have seen preliminary interrogations of terrorists in the service, but not the rough stuff of the CIA. Tape marks still indicated that they had been blindfolded, and their mouths were covered with gray duct tape. They were bound to chairs and each other with ordinary nylon rope from any hardware store. The stench of defiled clothing mingled with the Gauloise.

My mind was racing around trying to make connections. Was the cigarette odor a message? Gauloise cigarettes are French. A favorite smoke of the General in John le Carre' book "Smiley's People," and one of my all-time favorite spy novels. All my military and law enforcement friends know that. Of course, Bruce Willis had smoked Gauloise in the movie "Die Hard," also.

I slowly removed the tape from the woman's swollen lips. She began to weep and nod her head. A full five minutes passed before she looked at me.

"Listen to the tape," she moved her head to her left toward a small end table near the window that I knew overlooked the Indian River north of the bridge to Merritt Island. This had been our living room, Natasha's and mine.

The voice from the recorder got my full attention. It was the same as the one on the scramble phone, I was positive. "Sorry for the mix up. I got the wrong Jack. Not sorry for your pain. You earned it in Iran." I turned the recorder off.

"Please listen to all of it. He said he would kill you and us if you did not follow his instructions to the letter. Go to the bedroom, please." She was weeping again, and her black face glistening.

I carried the recorder into the bedroom and locked the door before plugging the machine back in to listen. Old memories from the best years of my life were trying to surface and I smelled the strawberry shampoo from Natasha's golden hair. It haunted me.

"A Morella mushroom grows best in the dark and turns real situations into major manure, and then meets the media with polluted political talking points. The best one grows by the river in northern Virginia. Look for useful produce to be clipped and shipped to you soon. Richard."

I do not believe the recorded voice misspelled the morel mushroom. A Michael Morell is the only name I know from the Company that resembles Morella. He was on board when the Iran operation was blown. Could this be Jack, the man of many faces and voices talking?

As I listened to the tape, several seemingly disjointed subjects began to come together in my mind. Whoever put this tape together had access to high security files, foreign or domestic.

Truth or fiction as the actual names were not given to my knowledge, but it seems that an angry hacker was into the very computers that held our nation's closest secrets. His or her anger was hinted at as the best defense for two notorious hackers was to get married and that the top law enforcement officer out of country be the best man.

Of course, "Richard" was a reference to our lifeline contact at Langley. None of us knew who he or she was at the Company. Also, "Mother knows" in the sentence with "who has loosed the hounds on you" was plain. The code name "Mother" was a name given one of the TV CIA operatives in the 2007 series, "The Company." He was the one who found the mole in the CIA, but no one would believe him. I switched the tape off and returned to the living room.

I learned enough from the tape to know the three captives were not likely to attack me if I set them free, but I was instructed to listen to each one separately in order. I was not to allow more than one to talk at a time. Number 1 nodded yes when I approached her with tape for her mouth.

The politician was #2 and he anticipated it was his turn to speak by looking me straight in the eye and nodding yes as I reached for his taped mouth. "I did not do what I was told. That is why I'm in this place and in this condition. He told me to tell you that. There were five of us to start with." He caught his breath and gave a deep sigh. "The policeman #4 and the pedophile #5 are dead," he said. "We three are here because we can be useful to you against the terrorists. Please tape my mouth and proceed to number 3."

I taped his mouth and untapped #3. He was different from the other two. He was a black man as was the woman, but there was fire in his eyes. They seemed to protrude as he stared at me.

"I was a Muslim before the World Trade Center was attacked. Numbers 1 and 2 joined after 9/11. The other two would not admit to being Muslim which led to their deaths, I believe. Both were shown to all of us as being involved in the 9/11 attack by association with the Saudi pilots down south. They were caught on video tape. Someone beheaded the pedophile and shot the policeman in front of us. It is on video and will become public knowledge soon. We have been told what happened to your wife and the little girls. We three agreed to help you find the Iranian through our Muslim contacts. That agreement alone saved our lives."

"And if you do not do as you promised, or if you work to bring harm to America, what will follow?" I asked.

I watched as none wanted to speak.

"This is also a requirement from the tape. Do you know all that is on this tape?" I asked as I held up the recorder.

All three stared at it like they had seen the Devil. Each in their way showed great fear.

The woman's lips began to quiver, and a thin line of perspiration beaded on her upper lip. Her eyes began to tear, and she looked toward the door as an avenue of escape or the fear her tormentor would return.

Number two, the politician, became totally withdrawn. He reminded me of our training on the *farm* when we were captured and interrogated to within an inch of our lives. Had Jack and I not escaped, the Iranians would have done worse.

The preacher of Islam looked at me with sad eyes. There was no hatred, but he knew that the man they promised was capable of anything and would carry out the penalty he had promised.

He said, "We are to recite to you the penalty for our failure. The man showed us a club and a red blood-stained building brick. Then he made us complete this rhyme."

He nodded to the other two and they began.

"Stick and stone _will_ break my bones," they all repeated in unison. The preacher continued, "He told us that the groups who are called 'Christian Crusaders' are radicalized groups. They are fed up with the ambivalence of our government and the press toward radicalized Islam. They intend to duplicate the violence in the name of Christ. None are true Christians like none of the terrorists are real peace-loving Muslims.

"His hatred of me as a reporter was almost beyond control," the woman blurted. "He had an article written by me after 9/11 that supported the event as getting even from all the repression and interference into Arab countries by America." She started sobbing. "He taped my eyelids open and forced me to watch people jumping from the World Trade Center."

"He also showed all of us a DVD with each of us in our places of residence, even in the showers." The lawyer had recovered from his trauma. "I defended a Muslim who was charged with the murder of a family who owed a corner grocery. The evidence against the man was overwhelming. The arresting officers made mistakes and the jury had no choice but to render him not guilty. The DVD showed my client committing another murder of a Christian couple in their home after Church one Sunday shortly after his trial." His gaze returned to the recorder. "He said I was not to worry about my wife and children while I'm away. He has located the man and hired him to look after my devout Christian family."

"My conversion to Islam had nothing to do with those who call themselves Muslims but are not. The DVD showed me preaching to a group that included the flyers training here in Florida. I too had my eyelids taped open and forced to watch the airplanes crashing into the buildings over and over." He too looked at the recorded as something holding his fate. "I withheld information concerning the murders of the two little girls and maybe the third. I swear I know nothing about who murdered your wife."

"The sheriff will be here very soon. Is there anything you wish to tell me before he arrives?"

"You can release us now, if you wish, his words not mine." The lawyer pleaded more than asked.

"I was instructed by Mr. Law on the tape to record this session. I have done so. If any of you wish to change what you have said, now is the time to do so. This recording must be mailed to Mr. Law on penalty of *our* lives. I believe him." All three said they had said exactly what Mr. Law had instructed them to say.

"I will make a call and then release you all to get cleaned up and get you something to eat and drink." I went back into the bedroom and called the sheriff on the secure scramble phone. He said they had found nothing near the site where shots were fired.

He promised to bring food and clothing for the three people in my old condo. I had left the door cracked and listened in on the captives. They were still scared but agreed to carry out their agreement. They were not terrorists and did not believe they were betraying their faith in helping find a fellow Muslim that was.

I placed the taped session in the envelope provided, placed it in my jacket pocket with the tape recorder and went back into the bedroom that faced the river.

There I dropped the package down the laundry chute to the basement as instructed. We waited what seemed like two eternities, but were more like thirty minutes before the sheriff and his posse arrived. The three still tied.

The Sheriff arrived with his normal deputy and an attractive woman in plain clothes. She is his wife, we learn, and takes charge of helping the captive reporter get a shower and dressed. The men took turns in the other bathroom and were soon dressed and eating the best all-night Wal-Mart has to offer. They each gave their statements to a deputy as the sheriff listened.

The sheriff had asked, "Where is the tape and recorder," just as his rookie FBI assistant and the Cocoa Police Chief entered the room. As they shook hands and made nice, I positioned myself near the door that led to the balcony and the outside door back into a hallway. They didn't notice me slip outside to the elevator, as a photographer began snapping the crime scene, and a discussion between the three agencies ensued over which had jurisdiction of the case.

The street is empty as far as I can see each way. I cross it walking as fast as I can without attracting attention from the unseen. None of the cars parked in the lot or on Brevard Avenue have any sign of life. Under the first table on the right as I entered the outdoor patio of the Black Tulip I loosen the taped envelope that my former instructions provided. The long way around to my car behind my apartment seemed the most prudent route. My watch showed it was 3 A.M. My lodgings were bugged by two agencies that I knew of, and now the buggers are bugging the buggers no doubt.

Here I sit, with new instructions in what promises to be another long night.

CHAPTER 18

"Nice of you to drop by old boy, on short notice," Jack was back to his English impersonation.

Unlike the visit to my apartment on Brevard Avenue, the old spy was less talkative.

"There are a lot of missing bits ole' boy," I commented as close to his cockney dialect as possible. "Like revealing a few classified activities between old friends, especially when they point to the topping of your oldest chum?"

Facing me without expression, Jack was a different man. It was apparent he had not escaped the explosion on the Saint John's River unharmed.

He called on the secure phone and directed me to lose anything that could be traced and meet him in the first comfort station north of Titusville on I95 as soon as possible. From there I drove north to the first exit and then back south to route 50 west toward Orlando. There was little traffic, yet Jack checked every vehicle we came near for a possible enemy. He had me pull over a few times and let a car or truck pass. At last, just before the small town of Christmas, he directed me to park behind a white van and a small church on the left. We went into the building so quickly I could not tell if he had a key or the door was open. It was still dark and I followed his trail by pen light through the church to a small windowless room near the rear. After closing the door behind me, he turned on a small floor lamp, and we sat facing each other on wooden chairs.

We exchanged envelopes. Mine held the tape recorder and new tape from under the Black Tulip table. I opened the flap on the large manila envelope Jack handed me. He looked at the recorder still in the envelope and closed it without explanation.

The reports I read through were classified top secret and had the seal of the C.I.A. Langley stamped on the top. The first was our covert operation into Iran. Not exactly new to us because it was our mission to extract a double agent out, until the last page that froze me to the core.

Agent signals that extraction is known to intelligence in Iran. Plan is to capture Americans and exploit as international incident at the extraction location. SEAL team to proceed as directed.

The next report, also with the agency seal, covered the Iranian agent's escape as planned. A footnote explained the collateral damage and eventual escape of surviving SEAL team members.

Last in the line of stolen reports was a detailed description of a rogue C.I.A. operative believed to be a causality of the World Trade Center 9/11 attack, but was likely a survivor. Forensics done on murdered people found in a New York warehouse indicated torture and DNA evidence of a former agent's specialty for obtaining information. Black Ops in more "undisclosed" locations.

"Freddie the ferrite, from the Company owed me his life. These copies for you may cost me my life he told me last week." Jack shrugged, "They did. Little ferrite is dead of apparent suicide."

"The big question; who knew our mission was compromised and sent us anyway, Jack?"

"When I know that, Rock, there will be another Agency suicide. What does this tape tell us?" he asked as he handed my envelope back. His hand still had burn marks from the hut explosion in the swamp. A trace of torture scars from Iran and infection scabs showed through his stubble beard. His former nondescript face was now pocked and gaunt.

I filled him in on all that had happened since we were together. I did not mention all I knew. He was at the Hubert Humphrey Bridge when someone took a shot at me. I said nothing about Zany or seeing a counselor about flashbacks of Iran and Natasha's murder. If he was surprised by our old friends from Ireland and Israel contacting me, he didn't show it.

The events leading up to and including everyone involved in the three captives in my old condo held his attention. He had me go over what had been on the tape I heard, and the one I recorded before I fastened them under the table at the Black Tulip. Then I told him what was on the new tape I found under the table.

"It is Double D. Remember David no middle name Dawson from the team in Iran?" Jack said as recognition formed and I nodded. "He lost his family on 9/11. Got his hands on film and watched his family jump. Agency wrote him off as being with his family. He snapped and is a one-man terror to anything Iranian or Saudi. Company has a terminate notice on him."

"He was the best interrogator the agency had. Is he connected with the Christian Crusaders?" I asked.

"Doubt it. Double D always works alone," Jack said, "He liked you, told me you were the only man that ever called him David. You never judged him for his work or how he looked. You know the man he called 'Mother' at the agency?"

"No. Wait, maybe, I do. It's not a man, 'Mother' is a mother, in records. She is the Iranian desk," I answered.

He got that far away look again, then leaned forward with his hands on his knees and shut his eyes.

After a long minute, Jack leaned back to ram rod straight, opened his eyes and said, "Let's go."

Arriving at the front door of the church, I learned someone had left the door open, or Jack had picked it earlier. He pushed the button in the middle of the lock and the door clicked locked when it closed. In the car, he lifted his shirt and showed me two matching Glock 19 pistols. I lifted mine and he came as close to a smile as I had seen on his lips in a long time. My 1911 was closer to him than any human had ever been. That is what he had said years ago at the farm.

We crossed U S Route 50 and soon entered a path through the palmetto brush under some scattered long leaf pines. My pen light followed the back of his black Nikes. He could either see in the dark or had travelled this path before. We were angling northeast toward the trailer park. The calls of bull alligators are nerve wracking at any time. The alligator attraction center was nearby, but in Florida you never know. Gator Land has hundreds on gators of all sizes. I'm sure the same is true for diamond-backed rattlesnakes in these very woods. *Perish the thoughts.*

Soon, the small wire fence around the trailer park was a welcome sight. We were quickly over it and standing near a square canvas on the ground. A mound of sand, decayed pine needles, and small twigs about two feet high and six feet in diameter reflected my small light. It appeared to be natural construction, while the other items resembled left over construction materials.

Jack took my light in his left hand and loosened the tie down cord around the canvas. He flipped it back to reveal two bodies bound, blindfolded, and their mouths taped. They were filthy in old swamp mud and their own body waste staked to the ground. The heavy morning air stank of leaf-mold and perpetual damp. I gave an involuntary shiver as a chill swept over my body.

Their captor ripped them from their clothing and poured water on them from two five-gallon paint cans. They began to move arms and legs in slow twitches. Jack roughly pulled them into clean clothes and placed old tennis shoes on their feet. He rebound their hands but left their legs free. The cramps became evident as they attempted to stand. Kneeling over the pile of sand, their eyes blinked rapidly as Jack took a long palmetto frond and poked the mound. Fire ants began to roll out. Each were bitten a few times before Jack knocked the ants off and splashed water on them. He pointed to the swarm and asked something in Arabic. They reacted by shaking their heads violently sideways. He wiped them off and applied Cortizone 10 to their wounds.

Jack produced a rope with a noose on both ends. He slipped each opening over a head and cinched the knot tight. One had the face of the Iranian Colonel but not the body.

They had about five feet of free rope between them as they followed Jack to the fence. We helped them over and retraced our earlier steps toward my car. The last leg our prisoners had a black bag tied over their heads as day light started to slant through the tall trees.

Back inside the church each man was given some dried fruit and water one at a time. Jack had me watch the other man while he took his "guest" as he called them to the restroom. The bags stayed over their faces the whole time. Hand cuffs and manacles replaced the duct tape. Their mouths were duct taped again, bags placed over their heads, and they were chained to the chairs inside the small room we had visited earlier.

He motioned for me to leave and close the door with some force. A minute passed before I heard a loud smack and a chair overturned. Some scraping and the same sound repeated. The door opened silently, and Jack motioned for me to follow him. He was in combat mode and dress.

We stepped outside and the door closed again without sound. The car could not be seen from the main road, but a side road ran along the Orlando side of the church. We were visible again.

"What now secret agent man?" I asked and pointed back toward the church.

"We go forth and conquer the world for democracy," he said. "Our guests have spilled their guts to me, but I want to interrogate them again for your tape recorder. They tried the silent treatment again when they saw I had a witness. I doubt they can identify you in the dark. Let's roll."

He transferred them into a very used white van equipped with U-bolts for chaining prisoners. The law prohibiting chaining during transport of prisoners had not reached Jack's understanding. The tape recorder captured every word of the blindfolded men in the windowless white van.

"If you change what you have told me or lie, I will know, and you will die," he had told them.

Like high officials in our country today, you enforce the laws you believe in and ignore the rest.

Like I said before, some men do not care about being nice to those who try to kill them, and the unlawful restraints did not cross Jack's mind. I followed his van back to the interstate rest stop.

These men are in America to kill as many people as they can. Jack put that on tape for my benefit. One of the Iranians was a double for the Colonel from Iran that lost his wife and oversaw the killing and torture of our SEAL team members. We were able to bring our bodies back, proof positive of the savage abuse from our captures still haunts us.

We also learned that our blown Iran covert operation was doomed to failure from the get-go by a mole in the C.I.A. The man we were to extract was a double agent and escaped with the aid of a trailing team unknown to our mission. They confirmed Sean and Ben's report that the Iranians' network bought faulty information that led to the murder of my Natasha. They were told she was Jack's wife, and the Iranian Colonel ordered a hit on her because Jack accidently killed his wife during our fire fight with the Iranian Army.

Jack's guests were part of a sleeper cell. The big explosion in the swamp, courtesy of the *Ghost*, destroyed Russian grade c4 that was headed to cities in Florida. Miami, Orlando, and Jacksonville were known targets. Others were possible. Location of Colonel, unknown.

How much our different agencies know about all this is anybody's guess. As usual, they were not sharing all their information. Jack had that distant look while he brought me up to date. He did not reveal who, if anyone, he had shared his "guests" or interrogation answers with.

He also confessed to me that he had been hidden on stakeout when I met Gator and Straight under the bridge, and that it was he who fired the warning shots when a sniper appeared. I knew that was truth because Jack would not have missed me once let alone twice.

"We have more like these in country, Rock," he said as he flicked his eyes toward the van. "They did not slip in. Most have been welcomed by visa and our new government open borders. We can trust no one, especially our close American 'friends.' Gang leaders like Marcus D. Roberts from New York, convicted police killers, are joining the Islamic jihad. The Feds continue their *catch and release.*"

He gave the sign for watch your six. Silently opening the driver side of the white windowless on the sides van, the *Ghost* drove into the north bound traffic on Interstate 95.

I hear what I think to be a cardinal's call from a nearby palm in the rest area. Immediately, I remember Natasha's love of her home state of West Virginia's official state bird. She had drawings from her elementary efforts up to adult oil paintings. There was even her red bird feeder in our back yard in Georgia. Natasha would motion for me to join her in watching the West Virginia state birds in their feeding. The bright red male and the reddish buff female were our exact opposites. She was the one that stood out. I could never experience the joy that bubbled up from her heart or the light that came from her smile as we watched.

"Toby, see how happy they are together… they use strips of bark from wild grape to build nests."

All I ever wanted was to be with her and make her happy. Our relationship was what held me together. Still does.

A heavy shiny black SUV with tinted glass all around pulled into the rest area. White U S government plates left no doubt about tax-payer ownership. It circled behind the buildings. I decide it's a good time to head north as well. Now, a combination of bird songs hit me.

The chirping bird came into view. It was a gray mockingbird, a complete phony...*figures.*

I drive north to the first exit and then do a U-turn back toward Titusville. This section of I95 is under heavy construction. There was every type of vehicle known to highway contractors along the corridor. Behind a long-necked crane, I see a van that is identical to the one Jack and his "guests" departed the rest area in ten minutes earlier. I slowed to make sure it is the same van. There is no one around except two highway patrol cars are coming up fast with lights flashing. I pull over in the only place I can to let them pass. They don't.

Behind the Florida Patrol, the government SUV forms a caravan which stops behind the white nondescript van. Armed men in black and white are swarming over the van like angry hornets.

I ease back onto the remaining two lanes of concrete and continue to the Titusville exit for U S 50. There, at an A T & T store across from Wal-Mart I buy a couple throwaway telephones.

I purchase two like the sales guy suggests. "They are cheap." He is friendly but no doubt working on a commission. Some things remain the same. Outside I remove the SIMS card from both and slip them into my billfold. A chirping starts, but I can't find the phone. It is not coming from the two phones that are supposed to be secure, one from the sheriff and the other from Jack.

Finally, I lift the cushion in the front seat. There, another little throwaway chirps. It is like the ones I bought. My mind says…*JACK!*

"Hello."

"Time to play telephone tag; do not use the secure I gave you. Use this one then one of the two you bought. Things are going to get hot. You should be fine. They all want me and my "guests.""

I look carefully around the large parking lot. Silly me, the *Ghost* did not wish to be seen. Neither do the *Ghost* busters.

"There are mops from the middle east in our neighborhood. Our friends from your *office* and my past want to share. Ain't goanna happen, we trust no one. Call this number in one hour."

"Headed to my apartment for a shower and a few winks, but I'll call in one hour."

The sheriff's scramble phone buzzed. I didn't think it prudent to answer. That thought was immediately confirmed when Jack's high-tech starlight began to twinkle. I was nineteen miles north of my bugged apartment. A hot shower and change of clothes would take off the jungle of Christmas, Florida. Like Jack said, they had no need of me. This is now a Federal case.

The Iranian connection still bothers me. The murder of Cocoa children still enters my mind on a regular basis. I put in a call from my apartment phone to the Sheriff's office. Then, I grabbed a long hot shower and changed into polo shirt and slacks. It feels good to be home.

My order for a Lady Zola gourmet cheeseburger, sweet potato fries, and Sprite at Murdock's was placed by nodding to Chris. I thought of Gus and went from pleased to the distant past. It was in Iran that all my hopes for a military career began to unravel. Now, I know our covert operation was a set up from the get-go. We were to be sacrificed; "traded" would be the tradecraft word for an Iranian informant. Good men died that day, but the plans of rats sometimes go astray. The informant, Jack, and a few of the Dirty Dozen lived to tell the tale. The big rat mole was on Jack's trail and desperately needed to rescue his prize double agent. The trap in the swamp along the Saint John's River off U S 50 had failed because they once again underestimated the ability of one well-trained man. I still shudder to think of the damage to egos that the *Ghost* caused there.

It is very nice to be home safe and sound on a Saturday afternoon.

Gus was the first person to befriend me when I returned to Cocoa. He recommended the Gorgonzola cheeseburger with sweet potato fries and Sprite. The waitress was new since then, but the meal in honor of Gus was consistently great.

That same day he took me into his business as a features writer for his pride and joy, the *Village Voice*. I lifted my plastic tumbler of Sprite to no one in particular as a toast, "To Gus, the dad I never had and to life."

I found it refreshing that the sheriff had not returned my call when I returned to the apartment. There were no messages in fact. One hour later, I called Jack on the cheap phone; no answer. I undress, stretch out on my old bed, and fall into a deep sleep within one minute.

I'm dreaming a crazy dream, a flashback to the old SEAL outfit. After Jack, came 8-Ball our Delta sniper as most respected and feared. 8-Ball had a photographic memory to boot. We all had nicknames. Most were in some way connected to events within the unit.

"Hey! Look at that shinny head, slick as a Q-Ball." Our medic whispered on the Iran mission.

"I resent that SLICK! You racist! Q-Balls bees' *white*."

"Yo, you bee's righteous," our Navy medic whispered back. "Yo, is the *shiny, sweaty, black 8-Ball!*"

Both men spoke three languages fluently in addition to English, 8-Ball with a Kentucky dialect.

The sniper who punched holes in people from a mile away and the medic who patched up bullet holes in our outfit became close and the names stuck in our unit for eternity.

"Sir, may I speak frankly?" 8-Ball asked.

"Certainly, sergeant, you know that," I answered.

8-Ball said, "There is a covert operation being played out in Cocoa. It ain't over till it's over."

Then there was the brief smell of a chemical. My dream raced back to the Iranian covert operation. There he was, the Iranian Colonel, with the smile of a serpent holding up an old spy glass and pointing out all our locations. Then the subject of our mission was running toward us and shouting in Farsi, "It's a trap." He made it to our western position just as what looked like the whole Iranian army came over the ridge above us.

I ordered our men back as Jack and 8-Ball gave covering fire. The colonel drove straight toward Jack, who stood up and fired double zero buck shot at his command vehicle. He shattered the glass and the driver turned sharply to the right behind some shrubs. I saw the colonel pull a woman from the truck cab and heard him screaming into his hand-held radio.

Airborne support arrived behind us. It was theirs. We were captured but our Iranian defector escaped. I smelled the blood and gore as the torture began. We were tied to hastily made crosses.

Stateside, debriefing by the Navy comes back in waves. I resigned my commission.

CHAPTER 19

TURNS OUT IT was not a dream. It was a premonition.

"What difference does it make, at this point?" I looked at the man who had asked.

The question came from a man that spoke English well for being Iranian. He was in no hurry, so I too waited, bound to my metal kitchen chair with duct tape over my mouth left little opportunity for a reply.

I shrugged my shoulders as much to relieve the tension as to answer his question. The smell of foreign cigarettes had brought me awake and then the chemical cloth over my mouth and nose. The next thing I remembered was the cold metal of the chair above my tight white boxers.

The last time I had seen this particular man was the night before Jack and I escaped from our Iranian hosts. He had hidden under the loose soil and some dead foliage near where we were staked out. My hope of being set free by the one we came to take out of Iran soon vanished when he slithered away and did not return.

After Jack pulled his Houdini act and set us free the following evening as our "pig roast and prairie oyster" fire was being built and praises were being made to Allah, we were told this man had been found with his throat slit. He healed remarkably well if that were the case. No sign of a scar on his throat.

There was no scar tissue around his throat, but the big smile was still in place. The smile grew as he looked from one scar to another on my body.

"You have a saying here in the west, 'Never send boys to do men's work'." His face went serious, "This has been proved twice. The Colonel let the boys have their fun with you and your friends in my homeland. Then he hired the worst of informants to track down our missing Jack Frost, the man who murdered the Colonel's first wife. They were told he was you, Jack Frost, now a writer in Cocoa, Florida."

He ripped off the duct tape from my mouth. The perspiration had softened the adhesive, so no skin came with its removal. I kept my breathing shallow even when my lungs wanted to expand.

I do not have the extensive training of the C.I.A. operatives, but I am determined to say or do nothing to aid this terrorist or his big daddy in the Company. My land line phone rang. He let it go to answer.

"Mr. Tyler, the sheriff has important information. Please return his calls." He walked over to the machine and erased the call.

Interesting, Gentleman Johnny (J. B. Woodall) had never asked anyone to relay a message to me. Was this an effort to let me know they were listening?

"You do not know who or what you are dealing with my infidel friend. I am Shi'ite from Iran. We believe Imam Mahdi in the Prophet's prophesy is near to return. It has been 1,000 years. The Battle of Damascus has begun as prophesied. Imam Mahdi will lead the faithful in establishing Islamic global rule before the end of this world. It is promised."

"Lebanon, Syria, Iran with the aid of our friend Russia will bring it to pass. A few in your country know this to be true. Crimea was the first step."

"Care to relay my other calls?" I asked, my breathing has returned to normal, but the perspiration continued and I have a splitting headache from the chemicals inhaled. "I was expecting a call from Langley. It seems two of your fellow countrymen have fallen into dangerous hands."

"The story we were not supposed to live to tell; the caper in Iran did not go so well."

My hands were tapped together at the wrist, but the strip holding them to the chair was soggy and stretched. Each leg was secured to a leg of the chair. I wanted to buy some time and get him to talk. Hopefully, one of the alphabet agencies was listening.

I may have pushed the envelope too much because he spun around holding a sax dagger. He knelt in front of me and cut the tape from my legs. The circulation began to restore the blood flow with a tingling sensation. It was then I noticed he had been wearing an ear bud. Someone must have given him new instructions.

He went out my door and down the steps in less than one minute because Jack was standing there in one minute.

His k-bar cut through the wrist tape, and I stood up, grabbed my weapons, and found out how the *Ghost* was getting in and out of my apartment unseen. We were closing the door to the room at the end of the hall as boots came thundering up the stairs. Jack led me to an open window. We shimmied through it to a high roof that had an old air vent. He lifted it off and I crawled in, followed by Jack, the chimney sweep, who fastened the vent top shut from inside.

He squeezed by and led me to an old ply board covering. The piece slid silently as Jack looked into an old storage room full of cobwebs and assorted cardboard boxes. One set of tracks lead in and out from the door to this opening.

Once inside with the board back over the opening, I said, "They will have a hard time finding us here. What's going on?"

"The Company has a burn notice out on me. Your Iranian friend has great connections within. He was going to try to work a trade. Our Lt. Commander for their Iranian colonel. Now that's funny, I took his queen, and he wants a lowly rookie in exchange. Some chess player he is," Jack smirked.

"Have you found your Company mole?" I asked.

"Not exactly, I know who he/she is not," he answered.

He looked at me a long time before saying anything.

"It is time to get you to a safe house and bring you in on this covert operation. Let's go," he said.

"Aren't we safe inside this abandoned museum?" I asked.

"Until they bring the heat seekers and spy two bodies behind the bricks. This operation allows that and a whole lot more. They have people close and high up all near to the POTUS," he said.

We put on City of Cocoa Water Department coveralls and baseball caps. Outside was the truck. We slipped out a seldom if ever used back door and were soon headed up Oleander out of town.

Jack took Forrest Ave north to U S 1 and caught the light green. A Cocoa black and white was headed south with lights flashing. The city truck attracted absolutely no attention as a green and white sheriff's cruiser passed us and headed into the construction area headed toward where we had departed.

We caught another green and turned left onto Michigan Ave., crossed Clearlake RD, and .5 mile on the left, and turned into the Brevard Museum and Natural Sciences. The sign said: **Hours of operation: Wednesday - Saturday 10:00-4:00 - Year-round.**

I glanced at the dive watch. Time: 3:30 P.M. The Cocoa Water Department truck flashed emergency lights and we drove through without paying the $12.00 fee for two adults.

Perspiration that had been building up under the coveralls was now saturating my underarms, brim of the official water department cap, and beading across my upper lip. Neither of us had said a word on this short trip.

Jack pulled right in front of the crowded gift shop, killed the lights, turned off the engine, picked up the toolbox, slid out, and locked the truck.

We walked to the lobby, entered the restroom, and got out of the coveralls. We put them in the toolbox and returned them to the truck and locked it inside with windows up and the keys inside.

A black SUV with government tags and dark tinted windows pulled into the entrance. Jack grabbed my arm and we started walking around the building. The SUV arrived beside us in less than one minute. We got into the open back door. I could not make out the driver behind the wheel in the tall driver's seat. He flashed the lights at the exit. I looked at Jack, no comment. I checked my watch. It read 3:35 P.M. The Dirty Dozen was back in business.

We were soon headed west on Rt. 528, and I was thankful we were not going back to the secret hideout for the President of the United States. We no longer had the same friends.

Near Port Canaveral, Jack pointed to a TV News Van, "Those BASTARDS!"

"General Giap of North Vietnam is correct, 'One or two more days of bombing Hanoi and we would have surrendered. We were defeated at TET. But we were elated to notice your media was helping us. They were causing more disruption in America than we could on the battlefields. We were ready to surrender. You had won!'"

A black shiny face looked around from the driver's seat and said, "A truism worthy of note: Do not fear the enemy, for they can take only your life, **fear the Media**, for they will distort your grasp of reality and destroy your honor."

The driver continued, "See that ride beside the Crown Vic with all the aerials? That is a civil forfeiture. It used to belong to a motel owner who was not wealthy enough to beat the case of enabling drug dealers and pimps. He was not a Russell Caswell. Caswell still has his $1.5 million Caswell Motel in Tewksbury, Mass."

"The taking of civilian property by law enforcement is a legal process known as civil forfeiture. According to AP reports, in 1985, the U.S. Department of Justice created its Asset Forfeiture Fund.

One year later, the fund, which holds the proceeds from seized property and is available to be divvied out to law enforcement agencies, brought in $93.7 million. In 2008, the amount had ballooned to $1.6 billion. In 2013, it reached $6.3 billion. On the bright side, this ride is one of theirs, courtesy of the civilian beside you, Commander," all of this was rattled off by rote.

8-Ball is simply amazing.

"Where is our friend Slick?" I asked.

"That squid is squirting black ink on paper in some little place called Fort Bragg, last I heard. Got hitched last year and expecting a little sea horse around Christmas," 8-Ball answered.

We pulled into a compound that normally has security on the gate. There are private sailing vessels with one yacht anchored one hundred yards from the wooden dock. Jack and 8-Ball slip on ski masks. Jack hands me one and a bullet proof vest. We put on vests and from the back of the SUV, we choose our weapons of choice from a large black box that holds several types.

8-Ball starts the motor on a small boat. Once the three of us are in, he moves us silently alongside the 100-foot yacht. Jack goes first, then me, followed by 8-Ball after he secures the boat. Walking up the ladder to the main deck, I get an eerie feeling. There are no signs of life anywhere.

This is one impressive yacht. Everything is immaculate and screams expensive. We enter the main cabinet and face five other masked men seated around the mahogany table. There are no greetings or offer of beverages. One man stands up. He is stocky built and wears a charcoal grey suit that is custom made, probably from Italy. Extra-large white silk shirt open at the collar and Italian shoes complete his power wardrobe.

"Any covert operation we undertake now and in the future is going to be joint, interagency, and multinational," he said, seemingly directing that toward us, especially the *Ghost*.

"We are faced with the likelihood of one or more terrorist attacks here in our homeland. As has been painfully demonstrated by one of our group, not all of our home boys are loyal. We are *interagency* and *multinational*. Everyone in this group has been vetted by that member or you would not be here. We trust no one outside this group until the threat has been completely identified and eliminated," he stated and sat down.

The man beside him could have been his twin in dress and stature. When he spoke, I get that eerie feeling, again. When you become a hunter of wildlife or men, you develop a sense of the presence of predator or prey in every situation. I am borderline, fight or flight.

This guy would be very comfortable, if one could ever be at ease, in a set down with the Godfather of Mafia central. Even with his face covered, danger seeped out of this man.

"We have located most if not all the bastards who plan to blow up our cities and kill our wives and children," he was reading from a paper with a heavy Italian accent. "We have learned today that they have sent disease as well as assassins to our cities. Orlando, Fla.: Our medical people have confirmed hospital officials in Orlando diagnosed a Saudi resident that flew in yesterday has MERS in the early stages. Others on the flight have begun showing symptoms. Hundreds have been infected."

"Doctors say the Saudi resident has a fever but is in good spirits!" The last was read more with a primeval growl than a human voice.

The first man stood and gave each of us a communication device that I have never seen before. It has the standard ear bud and wire, but the case looks to be something a member of the Starship Enterprise would wear on their belt. He pointed at each of us around the room and called out our number beginning with him. Jack is number six, me seven, and ironically 8-Ball is eight.

"Each of us has a separate code under the tape. Remove the tape now and memorize your code. Now, destroy the code with this lighter and ashtray." He waited until we had complied and then called our numbers to make sure all the devises worked. "Because of past operations, some of you may have recognized me or my companions. Forget it. This is the only way you are to contact a member. We are under the gun to seek and destroy. Consider all of your cell phones, and secure radios compromised due to our discovered Company rat. If you are caught, the red button will send out that message to each of us and the devise will self-destruct. Numbers six, seven, and eight are working as a unit. The rest of us are independent. Let's Roll!"

8-Ball left first, followed by me, while Jack brought up the rear. It was beginning to rain with gusts of wind and distant seagulls shrieked beyond the jetties. I was wet inside the battle dress and mask and now the outside dripped. We took our previously assigned seats after securing the boat at the dock. Our SUV soon fogged up from our body heat, but was quickly eliminated when the A/C kicked in. Jack held his communication devise out so 8-Ball could see it and we all turned them off.

"Who is number two?" I looked at Jack.

"He's the Italian Devil," 8-Ball answered.

The windshield wipers were working full time as a near whiteout rain fell along route 528 headed west toward Orlando. These heavy rains disappear about as soon as they arrive in central Florida. Often, the sun pops out and fifteen minutes later the sand has soaked up the water and it is as if it never rained.

We changed back to normal clothes, arrived back at my car, and Jack walked with me out of sight of anyone. He placed his vice like grip on my arm. We walked into the edge of the woods.

"We are being watched. We are on our own and we can trust no one number seven," he said.

"Did you know those people on the yacht?" I asked.

"All but one, but might know him if I heard him talk in a normal voice. The man you asked about is what Joseph Dominick Pistone, alias Donnie Brasco, was to the Bonanno crime family. He was a 'made man' by the time he reached age twenty. He infiltrated the FBI and continued to work both sides until the Mafia mistook his whole family, father, mother, and sister as informants by mistake. Number two found them with their throats cut. He didn't like that," he explained.

"The hit was made by a Saudi immigrant to make it look like the Italians had nothing to do with killing a 'made man's' family. Number two tracked the Saudi down and made him talk. He learned about the plans for attacking America and passed it on. It is rumored the Mafia has a 'hands off' order on him because of the mistake, also said the Saudi sleeps with the fishes," he continued.

"He is called *Biscotti*, or Biscoe from the Italian *biskotti*, but it is not from the cookie that is "bis" – twice and "cotto" cooked, that he gets his moniker. The FBI calls him a double agent, the mob calls him double trouble. His hits are twice as vicious even by Mafia standards," he warned.

"How do you know him?" I asked.

"He found me when he learned I had captured two Iranians in our St. John's River adventure. I almost shot him on sight. I first thought he was sent from one of my colleagues in the Company. His story checked out and we were invited to today's meeting. He too is off the books," h answered.

8-Ball handed me two items he found attached to my car. A tracking devise disguised as a bolt and a bug from inside found under the dash.

"Standard CIA equipment," he said with a shrug. "There is nothing extra in our ride number six."

"It is getting near impossible to tell the angels from the devils my numbered friends," I shook hands with 8-Ball and Jack, got in my electronic swept car and headed up Oleander.

The Cocoa *Village Voice* is still being run by my volunteer staff writer, Zany is still perusing her second-choice career in investigations, and my counselor is happy counseling. The normal contact places are staked out no doubt. All law enforcement has been advised to stay off my case. Still, I need to let those women know I'm alive. As far as I can tell, the Sheriff and Cocoa Chief of Police are back as friends. To what extent they are informed of the potential terrorist's attacks, and to what depth they have been compromised, I don't know.

I drove to Orlando on old route 50 and filled up at a gas station. The slim Jims were not as good as I remembered, but the coffee was surprisingly tasty. I scribbled a note and placed it in an envelope marked, SHERIFF – PERSONAL! The black baseball cap pulled down to hide my face was a sure sign that I was up to no good as the camera followed me to the pigeonhole window inside the Orange County Sheriff's office. I slipped the note through the bullet proof window and made my escape without being arrested. I called Sheriff Woodall and left a message to contact Zany.

The Sheriff of Orange will tell Zany and she will pass it on that I am alive and working a case.

Jack said we are being watched and I'm sure he knows. The Company has known for three hours that they have lost the sound and location from my car. I did not see a tail on route 50 when I pulled into the alligator tourist attraction and parked behind the dumpster. They might have traced me from the Sheriff's office if the note was delivered right away. I pulled behind a Waffle House restaurant near Kissimmee and waited for visitors from out of town. There were none. I went inside and freshened up a bit, then had scrambled eggs with cheese, smothered and covered, with raisin toast, apple butter, and coffee. The Slim Jims never had such good company.

In Kissimmee, I found a strip mall and backed up to the wall between two other cars. I spotted and avoided the camera. No need to assist the digital tracking network. A few people were walking to and from cars in the parking lot between stores. I donned my black baseball cap and joined them. When we came to a sports bar, I walked in with a couple. They were seated and I sat at the bar and ordered my sprite and an order of onion rings. All the TV programs were broadcasting one sports or another except a small one in the corner. It was local metropolitan news. The week's weather was highs in the mid-80s with overnight lows in the low 70s with a chance of afternoon showers. All of this I read as it ran across the bottom of the screen.

The couple that came in with me were standing at the bar waiting for a takeout order. The woman was dark complexioned as was the man who held his hand over his mouth. He had a full black beard. They paid and walked to the door. The man cleared his throat and the woman coughed. She opened the door, and he carried a large bag in each hand outside ahead of her.

A News Alert popped up and under the picture of a man in a hospital gown the words "MERS patient missing and considered dangerous – Middle East Respiratory Virus Contagious – Please contact local officials if you see this person – do not make contact with this individual!"

My new devise vibrated on my belt. I held up a $5 for the bar keep; seeing it, he nodded, and I walked outside. I clicked the accept option. "MERS threat in our possession may be others."

The words were like on a scramble phone or as if the altered voice was coming from a speaker phone in a deep cave. Message delivered and my phone went back to off.

Some days you get the feeling that all things work together for good. I spotted the couple as they entered a white Ford van. I memorized the Florida license plate number and hurried to my car. On the way, I used my out of space devise to report; "possible more MERS threats, bags of food, coughing, white Ford van, license number, my location, I will follow the vehicle."

Much to my surprise, the Orange County Sheriff was leaning against the side of my car. His car had me blocked. I had met him once when Zany introduced us at Kay's Bar B Q outside Cocoa, as the Sheriff of Orange. We had a nice meal and conversation. He and Zany were spending Father's Day together. Zany was dressed to the nines. Hard to tell if she was tempting a lover or going all out to harass her father who could not use his considerable weight to get her on his sheriff's department. She often referred to him as the *Sheriff of Nottingham*.

I pulled the phone off my belt. I Texted, "Delay, not in pursuit," Hit send and reattached the devise. Zany's father watched all this with a thin smile.

"I see you have replaced the flamingo pink cell since we last met," he said as he held out his hand.

We shook hands and he motioned me into his unmarked car.

"This is an unexpected pleasure sheriff. What brings you away from the castle to this section of Sherwood Forest?" I asked.

"Not what, where, when, how, but *who* my friend, good things come to those who wait," he answered.

CHAPTER 20

SHERRIFF ADAMS DIDN'T say anything, and I remained silent as well. The radio was normal dispatch back and forth with long pauses. He sat up a little straighter and squinted at an approaching taxi.

A small figure with long blond hair was barely visible in the back seat of the cab that stopped beside our unmarked.

The person with dark sunglasses leaned forward handing up a twenty, then opened the back door and stepped out, jerked our back door, and slipped into the back seat, and slammed the door shut.

"Hello Daddy," she said.

Zany wore her all-business black pants suit. Neither the sheriff nor I said anything. There was a slight suppressed smile forming on Orange County's chief law enforcement officer's face, as he eyed his daughter in his previously adjusted rearview mirror. Zany sat out of my sight directly behind me. The sheriff knew his daughter.

She opened an old newspaper. I could not read the mast head or the date. Then, she began to read.

"We are at greater risk of being attacked than we were on 9/11." General Keith Alexander testified. In a May 15, 2014 "New Yorker" interview with Mattathias Schwartz, the General said, "It's easy to stir up public emotion by saying: They're listening to your phone calls. They're reading your e-mails. And the answer is; if they're doing that, they should be punished."

"The number of terrorist's attacks globally in 2012, 'six thousand seven hundred and seventy-one. Over ten thousand people killed. In 2013, it would grow to over ten thousand terrorist attacks and over twenty thousand people killed.' Now, how did we do in the United States and Europe? How do you feel here? I feel pretty safe."

"Well, **I don't**!" Zany exclaimed short of a shout.

We in the front seat relied on the old adage, "Silence is the better part of valor."

Zany was on a tear. "The International Space Station cost $160 billion, with the U.S. of A paying $100 billion and Canada, Japan, Europe, and Russia paying the rest. We pay $3 billion a year to keep it going. Russia threatens to ban U S access to the International Space Station."

"The Russians are not our friends! The Russians are not coming – they **are here** – The enemy is not "at the gate" – **The Islamic Terrorists Are Within!**"

She leaned forward and squeezed my left shoulder with her childlike fingers and asked, "Is Uncle Sam's child still going forth to save the Arab world for Democracy?"

"Hello, Zany. I've come home," I told her.

"Home is the hunter, home from the hills of Iran, and the sailor home from the sea?" her whisper was more of a hiss than a statement.

My flamingo pink replacement phone or whatever they call it began to buzz.

"I have to take this call," I said and slipped out of the unmarked.

I noticed the waiting cab driver was leaned back with his head on the rest with his eyes shut. His face was between humor and panic as his long fingers tapped nervously on the top of the steering wheel. Humor at the actions of his customer, panic at the sight of two gentle giants in an unmarked police car, or the black suited mini ninja was hard to read.

"Do not pursue. Good work. Go back to normal in Cocoa."

The phone went dead before I could reply. I looked to see Zany in tears, standing up, leaning to hug her father from the back seat.

I continued to walk around holding the gizmo phone to my ear for about five minutes until Zany was seated again behind the passenger side.

A small piece of tissue stuck near the private eye's left eye and her crinkled nose. Her mascara had been blotted sans mirror. I noticed all this after a coward's slight glance as I regained my seat. The atmosphere had changed considerably.

"My lovely and talented daughter has news for you," Sheriff Adams said.

"The case of the murdered girls has taken a turn for the better. You have an appointment with west Cocoa's wise man, Mr. Solomon, tomorrow at 10 P.M., on his porch, directions to follow."

She did not apologize. We both knew there was no need.

"The call came to my office answering machine after midnight and the voice had a slight accent, but I could not determine the race," she said.

"How is your high-profile case coming along?" I asked.

"I still haven't talked with, let alone had a face to face, with the lawyer father. Because of what you are wrapped up in, I'm not even hearing from my boys in blue or green," she pouted.

"I am planning on returning to Cocoa this evening. Maybe we can have some Q at Kay's," I suggested.

I turned to see her slight smile, nod, and she started to cry again as she hurried to her waiting cab.

The sheriff was smiling, too, as we waved her a goodbye. He placed a bud in his right ear, fiddled with a dial under the dash, and then removed the bud.

"Honey, Rock is more than your partner. He is more than a retired deputy sheriff, or even an owner/publisher of the *Village Voice*," he said.

"I know that entirely, daddy, but he does not have to go away for long periods of time without letting me know he's going, or when he'll be back," she whined.

"Sometimes he does, and one of those times is now. There is a hand's off notice to every law enforcement agency in America. Nobody is to approach Toby Rockwell Tyler – **period!**"

The crying started and the recording ended by a turn of the dial.

"From Georgia, we have a mutual friend who informs me that you too are not fond of the Fibbies. He calls them 'pie-in-the sky amateurs' as detectives. Rock is the best case-man ever. Even my family is not exempt from invasion of privacy. There is no recording of you saying anything. You were never here, and this tape will self-destruct as soon as you leave. Be safe."

My trip across the old bee-line was uneventful and there were no calls. Some of my old patriotism seeped up from the depts. A visit with Zany and her dad was like a tonic.

They loved each other and their country. Many in our country have lost their will to fight for our freedom. One percent of our citizens put their very lives on the line to serve in the military to protect from foreign powers. Another few risk their lives in dangerous positions to protect and serve the ninety-eight percent who take freedom for granted. Some pay taxes.

My mind, for whatever reason, seemed to be free. My car had been out of sight while I was in the restaurant. The Company or outer-buggers may have paid it a visit. The Five, as my new group called itself, had my back, or so they said. Jack and 8-Ball had on many occasions, the Three.

In Cocoa, I called Zany after a short nap and a shower. Everything was in place just like I left it with Jack. I tidied up the bedroom and kitchen from my Iranian's visit and left the bugs in place for the listeners. I checked the private stash of cash and other essentials, they were untouched.

Comfortable black running shoes, black socks, gray pants, dark blue tee-shirt, and navy-blue sports coat with shiny gold buttons replaced with black. Wheel gun in left ankle holster, k-Bar knife and trusty old 1911 auto in the belly holster, and I'm ready for some Q with Zany and an interesting meeting in west Cocoa after dark. Still have room on the belt for my new gizmo.

There were no interesting new faces in Kay's when I called Zany. The clientele had changed from some law enforcement to none. Physical laborers and small business owners filled the building. I sat with my back to the wall next to the corner booth. She informed me she was on her way. I ordered non-sweet tea with lemon and requested another menu even though I knew what we would have. If it's not broke–don't try to fix it; Kay's Q in not broke.

My partner entered without her usual grand entrance. She had that woman on a mission look. She still wore her power black striped pant suit. The waiter staff pretended not to see her, just another child having dinner with her father. I decided to not tell her my meeting had been moved up.

My back was to the wall and only one chair faced me across the table. Yet, my eyes are opened to a new beginning since we were here last time. Our world is being turned upside down. Then, I was so upset with another child murder that I thought it doesn't get any worse than this. I had thought the same way when they murdered my wife. I was wrong both times. This time, I know things are going to get worse. I only hope I get to play a small part in making it happen.

Zany had called the meeting with her father the moment he passed the word. She had the message from Solomon, but he had a message that trumped even that. I was off the books.

Evidently, someone high on the food chain had decided that a covert operation was called for even in our own country.

There was no evidence that any of the five plus three were in the employ of the U S government. I know that I am not in the CIA. I honestly can't confirm or deny that the other seven are or are not. I'm sure Jack and 8-Ball requested me.

Our waitress appeared, "I'm having what Mr. Tyler is having. Medium pulled pork, fries, tea."

The waitress departed.

"AWOL forgiven, let's try to have a nice normal meal before Armageddon," she requested.

Zany brought me up to date on the happenings in Cocoa Village since she last saw me. The city had held concerts in the park, the merchants had participated in an old-fashioned Bar B Q. "None as good as Kay's" she was quick to say. A few of her friends asked about me and the article in the *Village Voice* promoting the play, "*The Ghost of Ethel Allen.*" Odd that a similar murder would pop up shortly after that play, then she admitted those friends were slightly inebriated at those times. The *Village Voice* was humming along under new management. She did not mention our old friend Gus, but we both nodded our respect.

"Where are all your law enforcement buds having lunch these days? No city, no county," I asked.

"I have asked that same question. They shrug, purse their fat lips, and look away. I believe there was too much bickering over the turf, and finger pointing to even be seen together in Kay's," she answered.

"Thank you for bringing me the message to see Solomon tonight," I said.

"I was of two minds on that. All of Cocoa is not safe now. West Cocoa especially is still reeling about the unsolved murders of those little girls. Old race baiters have re-surfaced, and no white man is welcome in the hood, especially after dark. Dad said you needed to know," she said.

"You're still Dad's little girl. That was very evident recently," I said with a smile.

A slight smile creased her lips before she could pout and narrow the eyes.

"He told me a little bit about what you all are doing. Don't tell him I told you," she said.

"Your secret is safe with me," I assured her.

She held up her right arm as high as she could. Even then, her frantically waving right hand was barely being seen over the other booths. I caught a glimpse of Kay. She was trying hard to suppress a laugh. Our waitress frowned at her, and then followed her head nod to see the commotion. The waving continued even when our serious waitress arrived. She topped off our teas.

"Does Miss Adams and Mr. Tyler care for dessert?" she asked.

"Miss Adams cares for a slice of hot Dutch Apple Pie and one scoop of cold vanilla ice cream," Zany answered.

The two women appeared to be complete strangers.

"Red Velvet cake please," I, too, held a very serious pose.

"One cannot be too friendly with one's servants," Zany whispered within her friend's hearing.

CHAPTER 21

A TEXT MESSAGE arrived, don't ask me how, on my new and improved secure devise—the GIZMO. A message that gave specific directions for my meeting with Solomon. I am to come alone. Ten P.M. tonight. So, here I am sitting in the shadows on a cane backed chair on a dim lit porch, facing the great man himself, who is in a wheelchair.

Solomon is the kind of person whose face is ageless in appearance. I soon found him to be wise in all that he said, and all that he retained. No doubt these contributed to his long life in his hostile neighborhood. In short, Solomon was not average in any way. His physical features were between black and Indian or Spanish. He lives in an old shack between unpaved paths. He has no street address.

One of his remarks about the church funerals for the murdered children stays with me, "The very poor like the very rich have few mourners."

"Why do you believe this to be so?" I asked.

"The poor are unknown. The rich have no true friends. They are as the queen of Sheba," he answered.

"The children had a church full of mourners," I stated.

State, County, and City officials were all there.

Solomon appeared to nod off with his chin on his chest, then said, "Children are loved for their youth and the pleasure they bring. Who was not there?"

"I did not see you at either funeral," I answered.

"Your journey has begun. Some keep the Sabbath going to Church. I keep it, staying at home," he said.

He nodded again and a beautiful young woman that seemed vaguely familiar came out on the porch. She laid a thin wrap over Solomon's narrow shoulders and wheeled him inside.

"Thank Solomon for me," I said it to her back as the screen door closed, but she gave no reply.

I am not alone as I walk back to my car parked in the weeds along the lane. Working in the life I have chosen, a sense of being watched day and night develops as a law of the jungle for survival, no doubt inbred by my species. The colt 1911 with safety off in hand is also a creature comfort as I attempt to stay in the shadows of scattered palm trees and abandoned buildings. The area between Solomon's porch and my car is the perfect killing field. I pray for no flashbacks. I see no one, but they are there. The watched is watching. My primal instinct has never failed me.

In my car's rearview mirror, I see a pin light flash briefly twice. I turn to face Solomon's porch in time to see two brief flashes in return. A quick turn catches the outline of a dark SUV exiting the lane a hundred yards off. Whether it is civilian or government I cannot tell. I catch another glimpse of it or its twin headed west on King Street toward I-95 as I drive the lane east; parallel we are both in a hurry to our relative safety.

"The Five" springs to mind again. Where have I heard this and why is my subconscious flirting with me? Five from my wife's Bible days is the number of God's grace. "The Five" is a group of reporters on the Fox News Network. Neither of these receives a light coming on in my psychic.

There is no need to pursue the SUV. So, now I'm driving east on King Street when I spot a black Chevy with U S government plates in front of me. "The night has a thousand eyes" – that's it, "The Five Eyes."

Jack shared with me some intelligence that could help our operation in Iran that was being withheld. A Joint SigInt Activity (JSA) revealed that the NSA and BND facility in Bad Aibling, Bavaria, had intercepted intelligence, but was unable to reveal it because it also involved the US. JSA Restrictions states that investigations cannot be made against citizens within the "Five Eyes" countries: Australia, New Zealand, Canada, Britain, and the US. The BND is a foreign intelligence agency, and like the CIA, is not allowed to spy on German citizens.

This information came from a high official within the CIA and caused a very hard agent to become extremely hardened toward certain members, who he labeled, "licensed lunatics." On another occasion after he had received a private communiqué, he exclaimed, "There is no room in an intelligence agency for politicians. Intelligent politician is an oxymoron for morons!"

The delayed flashback arrived. It was Iran when I was captured with the seat of my jeans cut out and stripped of briefs so that my buttocks were exposed. When asked about it, the report said, "Rock looked them in the eyes and hissed, 'Keeps the gnats out of my eyes.'" After the interoperation, they smashed his private parts between two stones. So reads part of debrief by Jack that we were now allowed to read in part for confirmation. I confirmed.

Painful then and another troubling memory to add to my growing collection, as my troubled past continues to deal from the bottom of the deck. Conversations keep coming back.

"I want to become a P. I.," the middle-aged scraggy musician stated to Gus through a twisted mouth as he squinted his dilated bloodshot eyes.

He wore flip-flops, ragged blue jeans, and a sweatshirt with the long sleeves ripped off. A faded logo had once proclaimed "Grateful Dead."

Gus peered over his wireless half glasses and pointed toward me, "There's your P.I."

"Why do you want to become a private investigator?" I asked.

He looked at me like I had asked a trick question.

After an unusually long pause, he mumbled, "I don't."

The three of us continued to exchange glances.

He screwed up his courage and blurted, "I am a paid informant. I want to be paid as your informant. It's my girl's idea. The band needs the scratch."

He handed me a business card with his phone number on the back, and the name Richard. The front was Zany's. He turned and walked to the door.

"We don't buy gossip. We report news," Gus reported in his charming way.

Then the door slammed, both charming expressions, in their very different worlds.

I met Richard later under the Hubert Humphrey Bridge after calling the number. The number turned out to be Ryan's Pizza. He worked there part time as a delivery guy. The night air seemed to clear his head from whatever had its grip on his mind earlier. Still the wise guy, though.

"You got a big nose. That why you are in the newspaper work?" he asked sarcastically.

"Yeah, a nose for news, what do you have for me?" I asked.

"I sell info to the Cocoa man. He's getting rough. No more pay. He's threatening me with jail time. I was a witness for the County on a murder a few years back, Dude been on me since," he responded.

"Who is the Dude? What info do you have for sale?" I asked.

"No can do on the Dude. He would put me in jail or hurt me. The info concerns drugs and trafficking. I call him Dude and he calls me Dick. Can we deal?" he asked.

"Sure, but there is no connection to the *Village Voice*; this is strictly between you and me. Where did you get the business card?" I asked.

"One of the waitresses gave it to my girl," he said.

"Our deal has nothing to do with the front of this card. No contact ever, we clear?" I told him.

He bunched his fingers of his right hand. I took the position to block a jab from reflex. Then he drew his fingers across his lips in a jagged zipping fashion. Old habits live on.

We agreed I would order a pizza when I wanted to talk with him. It would be delivered to my gazebo unless otherwise indicated. He would deliver a Ryan's handbill to me either at the *Village Voice*, if Gus was not present, or my apartment. I agreed to pay the going rate for information. We cut Richard's asking price in half which he seemed to know in advance.

"Dude is into everything. Even with foreigners, Arabs even. No charge," he said after we made the deal.

That was the last time I saw Richard in person. Word on the street was his so called "band" got a gig in Miami and became the band that never returned.

My overactive mind placed Dude in the hole shaped in a certain Lieutenant's form in the puzzle. Pity it didn't register earlier.

Why now, what is the connection, the tipping point?

My wise man Solomon had been telling me the truth, but he was telling it from a slant. I suspect he knew I would pick up on his quote from Emily Dickinson.

CHAPTER 22

The Village Voice
April 1, 2015

TALK OF THE TOWN:

AUDEN'S CRUELEST MONTH and April's Fool Day finds Cocoa in a festive mood. Our River Front Park is the gathering place for Cocoa's Marathon Race. Marathon course started in the one and only Indian River Lagoon completion swim, followed by biking, and a sprint finish. Now–the AFTERGLOW.

PUBLIC NOTICE:

Brevard County Sheriff's Office reports the daring escape yesterday of an inmate while being treated for cuts and lacerations to his face and neck. Former Lieutenant Gillard of the Cocoa Police Department is suspected to have had inside assistance. Gillard overpowered a guard in the infirmary, stole his uniform and the keys to a Brevard County Sheriff's cruiser. Considered to be armed and dangerous. Public is encouraged to call the police with any information concerning this escapee. Do not try to confront or otherwise make contact with Gillard.

COCOA MAYOR'S CRIME COMMISSION CONFERENCE:

Report on our Mayor's excellent Crime Commission meeting in the Civic Center. Now is a great time to put into practice the Mayor's words to Cocoa. "Let's refuse to accept crime in our neighborhood!"

Our City Manager placed his finger on the chart. "We know the problems. *HIGHS & LOWS* - We have a high crime rate. We have low median income. We have high poverty rate. We have low education rate." He continued to stress – "We are working on these and other problems. Cost of crime to Cocoa is SIX point SIX MILLION DOLLARS. Law enforcement and concerned citizens have brought crime DOWN SEVENTEEN (17) PERCENT.

Cocoa Chief of Police. "Citizens groups are making a difference. Fifty Faith-Based Groups and projects like Crosswind, and Diamond Square are paving the way to keeping down crime. We will soon have a body camera on each officer. We are working to overcome mistrust and misplaced fear in our city. Citizens must get involved and become our eyes and ears. Parents, it's time to be parents."

Brevard County Sheriff. "Our main focus is to get citizens involved in crime prevention. Get to kids BEFORE they get into crime. I echo the Chief – Get kids under control of parents.

Enroll your children in one or more of our city and county safety and recreation programs."

Other state and federal officials spoke at the Mayor's Crime Commission Conference. There are programs to get employment for individuals coming out of our penal systems.

No man is an island as the saying goes. Even an island is connected to other land if you dive deep enough. King Street Community Church is one of the groups mentioned in the conference. "Churches and other groups are making a huge difference and bringing down crime as members serve by becoming mentors to our youth and adults. Citizens helping citizens." That was the consensus of the faith-based representatives that commented.

"Ting-a-ling" announces Zany entering the *Village Voice* office utilizing her latest contribution.

"Thank you for Gus' antique doorbell Zany," I said with a smile.

"You don't like it. I can tell. I see it on your smug face," she observed.

There comes a time for smug smiles. This is such a time.

"It's just that there are no back rooms here for a bell to summons an absent newspaper employee. Only a back door," I explained.

"It just might keep you from getting a *"Surprise"* visitor. Don't you read your own editorials?" she asked.

Sometimes, it is difficult to read Zany. This is definitely one of those times.

"There is an escaped CPD officer who assaulted you in this very office, Rock. While you sit there cool as a cucumber, I, at least, installed a warning device. What do you plan to do?" she asked.

"Lt. Gillard is a trained police officer. He is also armed and dangerous after assaulting a deputy sheriff, stealing his side arm and cruiser. Most law enforcement officers are on the lookout for one of their own. The Lt. has more important worries than me," I responded.

"You never told me why he made a false arrest in the first place. We both know he did not suspect you of robbing the bank. He had a reputation of being first and right on arrests," she asked with the insight of s good P.I.

"Ting-a-ling." Saved by the bell.

"Hello, Chief, how may the *Village Voice* serve the Cocoa Police Department this fine day?" I asked.

"Hello, Editor–In–Chief," he said, then glanced side-ways toward Zany. "Lo, Zany."

"Not here to arrest me?" I asked with a smirk.

"No," he answered, revealing no sense of humor this morning.

"Collecting for the Policeman's Ball? Collecting loose cannons?" I asked.

Zany's partial suppressed shrieking laughter exploded making it more piercing than usual.

"We have new information on an old case that calls for your assistance," he said, ignoring both Zany's outburst and my attempts at humor.

"How quaint," I said as I turned toward Zany. "The all-powerful CPD needs assistance from a lowly private investigator. Have you ever in your life heard of such a thing, Zany? Fire up the advanced crystal ball."

"Seriously, Rock, I believe you will be interested in the information going back to your wife's murder. Two or maybe all three of the girls murdered may have a connection," the Chief said, trying once again to cut through all the foolishness.

"You have my attention Chief. Would this information have anything to do with the arrest and interrogation of your trusted former employees?" I asked.

"I'm not at liberty to say. That is an ongoing investigation," he answered.

"My Gosh! You sound like a FIBBIE!" Zany exclaimed. "The whole city knows your Lt. and Sergeant were crooked as a dog's hind leg. Drugs, prostitution, extortion, God knows what else!"

"Zany, Zany the Chief's outstanding officers are innocent until proven guilty and let off by a judge. It's the 'new' law of the land," I pretended to chide her. "Has the Lt. been tracked down by any chance?"

"Does this line of questioning mean you are not going to assist my department?" the Chief finally asked.

"It means, it depends. Are you going to hide what you have like before, and then demand we share information that we deem detrimental to a client?" I asked as I turned again to address my partner. "Zany, will you get the Private Investigator's Handbook, please?"

"Alright, alright I get it. The Department treated you unfairly by jumping the gun on the bank robbery. There was some unnecessary harassment and bending the rules by some former employees while you were conducting lawful investigations. What do you want from me?" he asked.

"An apology. In writing from you on Department letterhead stating what you just said for starters. Accountability Chief. I'll make sure the Mayor and other interested persons see your confession and apology to my ROCK!" Zany said, with that fox in the henhouse smile.

CHAPTER 23

Jack removed a gray bag from under his London Fog black raincoat, and said,. "Compliments of the Admiralty, or should I say your Navy ole' boy. Your standard burn jettison bag. It is suitable for setting paper documents on fire or weighted for deep sixing into Davie Jones' Locker if the bloody pirates have you by the throat, or some other bodily part."

A rather long statement for a man of few words and an abundance of action, mostly of the silent service persuasion. When I made no comment, he continued.

"This particular bag was rescued from the deep sewer that runs below Pennsylvania Avenue in our smelly seat of power by a clever aid-de-camp to a Senator that has the morals of an alley cat. I share this background because there is a strong possibility an assignment of long duration awaits."

He unlaced the heavy bag and placed a tall stack of documents on the table.

"No need to guard these with your life, there are copies in several locations, but do read them and be careful, they have caused the death of several friends," he warned.

That was the last time I saw Jack. He continued to let me know he was alive in his unique ways, but his location was never revealed in those brief notices. The documents that were to be destroyed by the Senator's clerk were smoking gun evidence that tied US agencies with foreign powers listed as enemies by our government. It explained how groups listed as terrorists also received foreign aid directly and indirectly from our Congress and approved by the President and Secretary of State. Russia and Iran were involved in the takeover of the Middle East and were working with terrorists like Hamas and Hezbollah against Israel, Jordan, and Egypt.

After Zany returned to her office, I opened the Navy for burning sack. I was not ready for this. The Cocoa Police Department had found material containing all my transcripts on the Atlanta and Savanah child murders and my medical retirement in Lt. Gillard's safe. Proof positive that the lieutenant had connections in high places. So much for sharing information from the CPD.

Gillard had this confidential information since shortly after Natasha and I arrived back in Cocoa to live in the condo Uncle Rob willed us. That explains his "arrest of me for bank robbery." He saw me as competition. He also knew the details of the medical examiner on every young person.

Last page: Iranian Desk – Top Secret!

This document is susceptible and for your eyes only – Crypto Clearance. Destroy after reading. Our secondary team for extraction is on the station. The "Ghost" and group? They captured. Our asset is ready for pickup.

My departure is imminent.

Jack told me about the Last Page. So does our "Richard" at the Agency have another well-connected Dirty Dozen member? It seems to be so. I know about David (Double D aka Mr. Law), and there is a termination notice from the CIA on David and maybe Jack. Not Jack. Not David. Then who?

It is time to drop another dime to Uncle Richard. I will use the same payphone, but I will not hire African American boy or see a drug peddling Gator. This killer is cautious and well-informed. So far, no one has rattled their chain. It is past time to shake their tree and gather the leaves.

My last caller had said on tape, "WE" and was specific about "killing another thirteen-year-old girl" an "My intent is to get even then die." "I am not alone. WE are not confused or sick."

CHAPTER 24

"Every child needs a mother and a father. Who can't see that? Only the disillusioned," said the Reverend Jerimiah then relayed a true story of a boy with no father and an absent mother.

"The boy was taken by a kind old couple and provided everything but meaningful love. A black and white long-haired dog followed the boy home one day. His caretakers allowed him to keep it. He named her Oreo. Cleaned her up, fed her, and made a place for her under the old wooden porch. A love began between the two. They went for long walks every day the first week. The boy reported that she tired easily and sneezed a lot. Oreo developed fatal distemper a week later.

The couple explained that Oreo was going to suffer more as the end neared. The boy, being curious as all ten-year-old boys can be, knew where the old man had a loaded pistol.

Oreo followed the boy to their favorite place near an old, abandoned garden. She whined as tears dropped from the boy's eyes on her runny nose. The distemper sneezing and look of apology he knew was not for her, but for him. Sick as she could be, she loved him.

He shot her between those loving eyes because he experienced love for the very first time. The grave was deep. Deeper than necessary because he could not quit weeping and digging."

Looking around, I saw there was not a dry eye in the congregation.

"The boy grew and visited me until he saved enough money to leave town. He was still sad. He didn't have to be, he chose to be," Pastor Jerimiah said as he concluded the story.

After church, I went to my "sanctuary."

"Here we are again," I said, talking to my "*Rock*," the Indian River, serving as my mother all these years.

Unlike the human one, she has never left me or forsaken me when the going gets rough. So many times, I have stared into the depths of her. A mother loses the natural closeness over a long period of absence from her child. I never knew the love of a father and mother for each other or for their child. I can relate to the preacher's follow-up on the lad and his dog. Neighbors near the now electrical fence around the old, abandoned garden witnessed a young man wrap bacon around the wire while the power was off. A dog that had been digging near Oreo's burial plot broke the wire in his yelping retreat after receiving an electrifying experience as the young man hit the on-off switch.

Reverend Jerimiah never revealed the young man's name, but it could have been me. Here am I digging up the painful past based on new evidence on the murder of my wife and two if not three young girls.

Pastor Jerimiah went on to make it clear that what the Prophet Daniel predicted would come to pass. Daniel prophesied the Middle East and Europe would explode in our time.

He pointed out that their Babylon is our Iraq, Persia is Iran, and Syria is still Syria on a smaller scale. Ten nations from the European Union complete Daniel's end time prophesy. "His Colossus lives!"

Monday, when I sat across from hm in his office, Reverend Jerimiah opened our conversation with these words from Psalm 90:4.

"Our world has entered into a very dark place and the children of light have been placed on 'A watch in the night,'" he said. "It has been rightly stated, the Church, instead of being the light, has grown accustomed to the dark."

Looking out the window onto King Street, his broad shoulders shrugged, his head shook, and the sigh that escaped his lips was between a snort and a cough. I looked out to see a well-heeled politician's convoy passing.

Reverend Jerimiah has made it clear to all, especially his congregation and the press, that he is one black Preacher wearing a "NOT FOR SALE" sign to the law or to the unlawful. Black President notwithstanding, politicians of every stripe are highly offended. I liked that about him.

"Things have lost their meaning purposely. Words are twisted to confuse and to conceal. My sermon yesterday was clear to my mind. The subject was the coming Antichrist. Today, I get word that many in our Church family did not understand that *anti* is a preposition. It can and does stand for two different meanings. The first meaning is 'over against,' and the second is 'in place of'," said Dr. Jerimiah and sighed again toward the outside view from his office window.

"That is clear enough," I said as I offered my encouragement.

"A dear sister emailed me a note: 'What did you mean – *anti* can be different AND the same?'" he told me, shaking his head sadly.

"I thought you illustrated it well when you said, 'Any written or spoken words or any person or group that denies the deity of Christ Jesus is antichrist. The person writing or speaking that there is another person that claims to be the Christ is against and is substituting in place of our Christ'," I quoted back to him.

"I'm glad you got it, Toby. Maybe you can explain it to our congregation, over half of whom believe the Muslim and Jewish teachings that the Christ of the Bible is not who the Bible says He is." A serious face turned to me as he continued, "The unfilled prophesy of Revelation is unfolding before our very eyes, and the people either cannot or will not accept the truth. The Middle East is about to explode."

"The Muslims are on the march. That much cannot be denied. Millions are pouring into neighboring countries. Conflict of cultures is certain to produce violence," he declared.

We looked at each other and then nodded in silent agreement.

"Pastor, I had flashbacks during your sermon from Iraq and the murdering of my wife. They stopped, and a new film played in my mind connecting to the Savannah girls' murders. However, I understood your message even with these distractions."

"You have a great mind, Toby. It can discern and separate facts and connections, but your emotions crowd out the conclusions. You know what you need to do," Reverend Jerimiah said.

"Yes. I need to pay a visit to our mutual counselor friend," I responded

Pastor Jerimiah removed his cell phone from his pocket, touched a key, and said, "Hello, Beverly. Give me a call when you get a chance."

"I will bring her up to date and collaborate with her and you. Church business has slowed to the point that I can help with counseling," he said.

"Thank you, Pastor Jerimiah, as our old friend Gus would say. I cannot tell you how much I miss Gus. He was the father I never had," I said sadly.

His cell phone chimed the beginning of a hymn, "Hello, Beverly. I am fine. Our friend Toby is here with me, and he is having flashbacks of the murder cases and his involvement in his military past. Yes. He wants to continue with you, and I have offered to team up with you against him."

Toby held out his hand, took the phone, and said, "Hello, Beverly."

After a minute, I said, "Sure, I can come to the office now. Zany will mind the store."

I handed the phone back to the Pastor and said, "Thank you. Beverly said for me to come over while everything is fresh in my mind."

We shook hands and I left. I stopped by Kay's B.B.Q. and got two take-outs for Zany and myself. I dropped hers off at the Village Voice and switched incoming calls to her office answering machine. I retrieved the files concerning the murders and the notes I had written from the newspapers, microfilm, and videos courtesy of our Cocoa Library. Fifteen minutes later, I was finished with my lunch and parked in front of Dr. Beverly's office.

"Hello, My Tyler. I will let the doctor know you are here," the receptionist said with a smile. "She is expecting you. Please take a seat."

Five minutes passed until Beverly opened the door and motioned me into her office. I sat down in front of her desk and laid down the notes and files.

"I have a lot of things I need to talk with you about the military assignments, murders, and separating my emotional thoughts concerning them," I stated firmly.

CHAPTER 25

"I WAS ON the phone with Pastor Jerimiah," she said. "He will pick up where we leave off, and I will collaborate with him as the lead counselor. Toby, I am going to do an intake interview again. Enough new memory has come to light to warrant a thorough counseling session. I have your childhood and history up to your marriage to Natasha. We will meditate on all that has come to light in your mind, dreams, and activities. Then we will tie all the evidence and clues together and separate your emotional responses from realities."

"That is what I need, Doctor. My mind is clear on events during my military assignment in Iran. I received new memory facts on the mission recently, written material from a mole in the C.I.A. who set my task up to fail," I told her as I patted the files in my lap. "I also have uncovered new information on my wife's and the two thirteen-year-old girls' murders. I have less on the third girl, but much of the confusion about the possible connection to the driver of the white lookalike van in Orlando is gone."

"Thank you, Toby, for clarifying your reason for this session. You want to tie all this together and separate them from your emotional hindrances. Is that correct?" she asked.

"Yes. I have also had attempts on my life other than the poison pizza that killed Gus. I believe all this is somehow connected. Your counseling helped me get over the nightmares and depression about my wife and Iran's failed mission. We need to handle the emotions again in light of this new information," I told her.

"Neurotic behavior is common to all people. We differ in degrees. In your case, we determined it was high due to your many threats. Depression over the loss of your wife, disappointment in the slow progress in solving the murders, trying to prevent others from occurring, and mood swings after the nightmares," she recapped.

"Like two-thirds of people we treat, you have recovered and did not go into clinical depression. You told me earlier that your overwhelming desire to find, seek, and destroy the killer of innocence is gone. That emotion is no longer a problem, correct?" she asked.

"Yes, the fear of what I might do to the killer of my wife and the two little girls is gone. All nightmare fears are history. They are gone like the nightmares. All fear is gone except the natural kind. I sense there is an honorable fear to warn of danger, but I know the killer or killers are human, too. I will obey the law and not kill them when I find them," I told her sincerely.

"Toby, to what extent are new emotions interfering with your life? We are looking first to identify them, give them a name, and regain control without coping mechanisms. I was hoping you could close your eyes and let your thoughts rest for a few minutes if a thought comes. Ignore it."

I glanced at my watch. It was noon. I closed my eyes, and a thought came, "Time stands still for no man." I ignored it. There was no follow-up thought. Several minutes passed, and I opened my eyes and yawned. Dr. Beverly still had her eyes shut. She was waiting for me. I suddenly sensed a warmness in my heart for her kindness.

"My mind is clear, Doctor. It is ready for whatever is to come next," I told her.

"I want you to close your eyes again while I pray out loud," she said. "Remember, any emotion or action that has prevented you from finishing your analysis. Remember everything no matter how trivial it may seem."

"Okay," I agreed and closed my eyes.

"Lord, we thank You for searching our body, soul, and spirit from our past tragedies. Now we ask for the identity of all that is troubling Toby. Grant his search for truth and hindrances in his life. We know that our stated reasons are often not the real issues we need to identify and gain control over. Amen."

"Doctor Beverly, I got thoughts of fear, depression, and anxiety. I thought I was over those. Oh, and frustration was there also," I told her.

"Excellent. Those feelings of worry, guilt, doubts, and fears concerning family, work, etc. are all products of your soul or your personality. Feelings of worry, guilt, doubts, and fears concerning family, work, etc."

"Let's us take one at a time, and you identify the place it finds in your life, past or present. First, what has or is worrying you? Take your time," she instructed.

"My main worry is that somebody will not catch the killer of my Natasha, Serena, Sabrina, and the third unidentified girl before they kill again," I answered. "This worry is in my past and present life **every day**."

"Good, what about guilt?" she asked.

"I feel guilty for being distracted while driving and not seeing the white van swerving into my left lane in time to prevent Natasha from being murdered. I thought I was the target. Every day I try to see what else I missed that day. Natasha was upset about the kid hitting the manatee on purpose. My mind keeps trying to show me something, but I get emotional, and a deep sense of guilt flows all over me. It shuts me down," I shared.

"Doctor Beverly, this is helping. I can't remember ever being able to think this clearly on more than one subject," I continued. "I have proof that we have corruption in every law enforcement agency connected with Iran and these murders. I have doubts about our solving these murders that have been tormenting me and identifying those who have killed others and are attempting to kill me."

"Excellent!" Doctor Beverly said. "Now, deal with your biggest fear."

"My biggest fear is that one or more people will be killed or injured because of me. I know the killer of Serena and Sabrina knows that is a fear that I shared while investigating the murders of children in Atlanta and Savanah. It was a quote in the *Today Newspaper* then and in the files recently found in Cocoa police officer's safe," I answered, then asked her. "What was the last one?"

Dr. Beverly said, "Frustration to the point of distraction from putting things in their proper perspective."

"Frustration is an everyday occurrence. I work a lead on a case every day," I said. "At the same time, I try to keep up with the *Village Voice* editing and production, not to mention all the things friend Zany conjures up to involve me in community affairs and her P. I. business."

Dr. Beverly laughed. "I heard she roped you into speaking to her women's group for Thanksgiving dinner instead of the mayor again."

"Doctor Beverly, there were many things I have not revealed because I can't, and I will not put you in danger. Pastor Jerimiah can paraphrase all the confidential information you need to continue counseling with him. It's just that many of the clues and past involvements are too dangerous for you to know. I have not been able to give you all the information you need to connect emotions with reality."

"We have identified the emotions, so how do we separate them from realities? The clues are just below the surface of my mind. All my surviving team members from the failed mission suffered post-traumatic stress syndrome and underwent testing. Because of the nature of our mission, I was not allowed to see the test results. We were all sworn to secrecy, and the threat against our lives continues from foreign and domestic sources," I shared.

"Toby, you are having trouble mentally because your central focus is dominant. It is self-preservation. It is a built-in response. Every person constantly seeks to fulfill their needs in this world. It starts with birth and continues until death," Dr. Beverly explained. "William Glasser, MD gives us this: 'In our lives, we must have at least one other person who cares about us and whom we care for ourselves'."[2]

"I don't know what to do next," I confessed.

"You go to Pastor Jerimiah," she answered firmly.

---

[2] *REALITY THERAPY* (Harper & Row)

"Thank you. We have come a long way toward reality since you started helping me," I told her. "I don't have nightmares and obsessive thoughts about killing the ones who murdered my wife and the children. I haven't woken up with cold sweats and shaking for a long time thanks to you."

"I need to get back to the *Village Voice*. That other person you spoke of was our friend Gus until they poisoned him instead of me. You are right, of course. Pastor Jerimiah is the only one I can trust with everything. He was there for Gus, and he is there for me," I said.

"We will continue as a team, but Pastor Jerimiah is your lead now. I will call him and update him on our visit. Pastor Jerimiah is the main one, but you have others who care for you very much. Zany and I will always be there for you. I am calling him back," she said as she dialed her cell phone.

"Hello, Pastor. Toby and I will give you a written report this evening. I am turning him over to you as the lead. Yes, he is still here. I'll ask him. He wants to know if you can continue in his study," she said turning to me.

I shook my head yes but showed her the *Village Voice* I was holding in my hand.

Shaking her head in acknowledgment, she told Pastor Jerimiah, "He is going to the *Village Voice* but will join you shortly."

When she hung up, I said, "Thanks again, D. Beverly. I will see you at Zany's women's club luncheon."

"I heard you, Mr. Tyler, as you opened the door. I plan to be at that luncheon also. That Zany is something. She even invited me, a lowly secretary. Have a good day," the receptionist said as I left the office.

As I walked to my car, I called Zany, "Hello, Zany. I am on my way to the *Village Voice*, you can switch my office phone back, and thanks. Dr. Beverly and her secretary are looking forward to your luncheon. I am turning my borrowed cell phone on and can receive any saved voicemail call."

My office phone greeted me as I entered the paper's office along with Zany's overhead tinkling bells. My cell phone joined the ringing office phone.

"Hello. Yes, I can come by this evening, Pastor. Around six will be fine. We had a great session, and I remember helpful events. Thanks, bye," I told him.

"Hello. Mr. Solomon's daughter? Sure, I can come to your house after dark again," click, click. "Hello. Hello."

Several messages about Thanksgiving advertisements. A few were about the *Thanksgiving in Cocoa* event and others in the surrounding areas of Brevard County. That took care of the saved messages on the answering machine.

The cell phone was a different matter. "Greeting from Uncle Dick. New Intelligence. I am in your neighborhood. See you soon." It had to be one of the dirty dozen's survivors.

I got the *Village Voice* ready for the press, then headed for a quick stop by Murdock's for my deluxe burger with sweet potato fries. Then headed for my other office with Zany in the upstairs of the Porcher House. My next stop was to finish my counseling session with Pastor Jerimiah at six.

───────────────

"Hello, again, Pastor Jerimiah. Several things are starting to come together in my mind and information from different sources," I answered when he asked me to fill in the gaps from my session with Dr. Beverly. "I received a sealed envelope from Chief Brody on my desk, marked PERSONAL TO TOBY TYLER. It read, 'The Sargent friend of Lt. Gillard has been arrested. The bugged office and telephone provided enough evidence to charge him as an accessory to murder and drug trafficking, and possible human trafficking.' The Chief wants to meet at my convenience. Also, Mr. Solomon's daughter called and invited me over after dark tonight. Apparently, one of my former associates is in town as well."

"My, my, I trust all these things are working together for good," Pastor Jerimiah said, shaking his head. "Dr. Beverly has filled me in on your good session. She is very optimistic about your progress and believes you are close to the clarity of thought both past and present."

"Toby, when you completed the intake interview with me, you said you were ready to accept the results and do what the Bible verses say. Are you still open to accepting and doing all that is required?" he asked me.

"I am ready for whatever comes, Pastor. I know that you and Dr. Beverly have brought me this far, and I am anxious to complete the counseling," I assured him.

"We established the chief problem that you presented was not nightmares from the past or your overwhelming desire to murder the ones who murdered your wife and the two children, but that they were symptoms of a deeper problem," he recounted. "You had been developing coping mechanisms to treat the symptoms. They helped relieve the pain, but the symptoms returned stronger the next time. The chief problem was self. Gus sent you to me, and we discovered you had been trying to overcome self with self. You discovered that you could never defeat self alone."

"That is correct," I confirmed. "So, that brings us to my dream about going through Iran on our mission. I recalled seeing evidence of the torture and murder of two little girls in an abandoned apartment that Christian families had occupied in a small town. One of our twelve-man team was especially disturbed, David (N) Dawson, who had children and was experiencing nightmares. Also, there was writing on the walls that appeared in the abandoned orange packing shed here south of Cocoa."

"Jerimiah, it was as clear as day," I mused. "Then the video I studied in the library gave me a voice and how the person walked in the Smokey Bear costume. It is Lt. Gillard, and I plan to show it to our little girl witness that heard the abductor on the playground. Sabrina was standing next to her as the parade passed. I believe she will be able to ID the voice and maybe how Mokey walked. Gillard may not be the murderer, but he is the abductor, I believe."

CHAPTER 26

INTERESTINGLY, MR. SOLOMON has me come to him by night. He is a member of Jerimiah's Church, yet he does not attend. I parked in the same place I was instructed to park on my last visit. It was an excellent hide and almost total darkness. Again, I carried my 1911 in my right hand, and pin light in my left as I cross from the palm tree to palm tree. There was no light on the front porch, but soft light filtered through a window, allowing me to make out Solomon in his wheelchair wrapped in a blanket and a four-legged straight back chair. I turned off the pin light and holstered my 1911.

"Good evening, and thank you for coming, Mr. Tyler," he greeted me from his wheelchair on the porch. "Your code name is Nicodemus. Jerimiah recommended you."

"Thank you for inviting me. Jerimiah is a great friend," I answered.

"You have new evidence concerning my two friends that died. I have current information as well. News travels fast concerning those two. Tell me what you can," Solomon said.

"I found a video of the parade and watched a costumed character, Smokey the Bear, growl at two small girls standing on the sidewalk in front of Trafford Real-estate Office. Rene was holding the hand of a small girl. I believe she was witnessing Rene's abduction. I hope to have her listen to the character's voice and watch him walk."

"It is as I have heard. We would like for you to come in, and then you and I will return here to finish your visit."

There was a slight buzzing. The front door opened, and his daughter unlocked the wheelchair, and I followed them inside. She turned off the lamp. The room went black. We passed through the small living room into a sitting room. The two rooms were surprisingly well furnished with antique wall hangings. There were no windows.

His daughter parked Mr. Solomon close to a couch facing the overstuffed chair she offered to me. Facing me was Mr. Solomon, his daughter, the mothers of the two murdered girls, and a small girl sitting on a woman's lap with a doll. There were no signs of refreshments being served. This was serious business.

"You have seen Mr. Tyler in Church, and you know he is trying to help the Chief and the Sheriff who took our girls. He believes the identity of a parade character will be a significant help. He also believes she heard the same voice at the playground when Rene was abducted," Solomon told them.

"I did not bring the video. I am sorry," I apologized.

Mr. Solomon nodded to his daughter, and she went into an adjoining room. I was surprised again to see John Henry wheeling in a cart with a video player. He moved a small seat to face the screen and motioned the little girl be seated. She grinned when the video of the parade started. The video stopped as soon as Smokey the Bear growled at her and Rene.

"Three things are here, Mr. Tyler. She has been evaluated and has the gift of perfect pitch. Her mother is my sister. She was in the parade and knows who Smokey was. She has the video as a parade worker," he told me.

"Is the voice on the video the same as she heard on the day Rene disappeared?" I asked.

"She said it is the same. The bear character was played that day by Lieutenant Gillard. Standing behind Rene is a foreigner of Iranian descent. Notice the Iranian is nodding his head affirmative," Solomon pointed out.

Solomon waved his hand, and the daughter and John Henry departed with the video and cart.

"Thank you, Mr. Tyler, for your help. We know of your great loss as well. We knew of your work in Atlanta and Savannah long before the easts Cocoa did. We have relatives, and there were black children murdered," Rene's mother said.

I was fighting my emotions again. The pain in her eyes was like mine when I saw them in the mirror while shaving. She was beautiful in her sadness. My heart went out to her, and her heart came to mine at that moment. We sufferer together. I noticed Mr. Solomon saw the pain we shared.

"This has meant more to me personally than I can say, and the evidence we can produce will advance our investigation immensely. If I can assist any of you or your families, please do not hesitate to contact me through Mr. Solomon. I have an answering machine at the *Village Voice*, leave me a message and I will get back to you as soon as possible."

There was a slight buzz, and the daughter returned, escorting Mr. Solomon and me outside.

"Goodnight, Mr. Tyler," Rene's mother said softly.

"Goodnight, Mr. Tyler," said the other mother.

"Goodnight, Mr. Tyler," a little voice echoed, peeking out behind a standing woman's dress. She was beautiful.

Seated in our original places, Mr. Solomon said, "The information I am about to share is personal, private, and painful. I know you will use it wisely and confidentially. Both of those women are close relatives. Both have husbands that are brothers and send support occasionally. The men were golden Glove youngsters and admirers of Cassius Clay. When he changed his name to Mohammed Ali, they became Muslim and changed their names, and studied Arabic. We also have friends in high places. Now, go in peace, my friend."

I changed my 1911 to my right and penlight in my left.

"Good night my friend," I said as I retraced my steps to my car and departed in darkness. Near the street parallel to King Street, I turned on the lights. There were no cars in sight.

My gizmo buzzed. "Office. Back door in fifteen. I am watching."

I am greeted at the unlit *Village Voice* back door by a smiling Q-Ball. He gave me the silent sign as I opened the door. He followed me in with a tape recorder-type machine.

Still smiling, he plugged it in and said, "Good evening, Commander."

The device using my voice, said, "Good evening. It is good to see you." Still the silent sign, and he leads me back outside.

I follow him south to the old, abandoned orange packing shed. He parks his prominent federal car with multiple aerials and motions to join him. I slide into the passenger seat and give him a firm handshake. A full minute passes before either of us says a word. Both of us grinned like high school kids and nodded our heads up and down.

He pushes a button and says, "V.I.P. on board and the station."

He stopped at the old Oleander Hotel in what used to be Eau Gallie, Florida. Childhood memories flooded back. The hotel and the royal palms with the sky-blue light shining are not there now. The City Pier where I caught fish is also gone.

The Eau Gallie pier was the scene of my most enjoyable fishing trips. Speckled trout and mangrove snappers went home with me most days. It is a wonder I didn't get sunstroke carrying them home in a bucket of water.

"A penny for your thoughts, Commander. I know this is your old hometown," Q-Ball said.

"I was overwhelmed by the beauty of the Indian River Lagoon, the vegetation, and the fishing. I was eight years old, and I had escaped the West Virginia Winter. I still have photos from a camera and those taken in my mind," I answered. "Is this our meeting place Q-Ball or are we playing cat and mouse?"

He gave the silent signal and turned all his gizmos on his car, belt, and hand-held scramble phone. There was a two-click reply on the car phone and hand-held phone.

We sat there in silence, five minutes, with the windows down, listening to the gentle breeze rustling the live oak leaves and watching Spanish moss sway back and forth. The sulfur smell of an artesian well was watering nearby landscapes. It was strong enough that I could taste it. I gave an involuntary shiver. Then two clicks on three devices.

My designated driver shut everything down and started his Company-owned confiscated vehicle, and we headed back north toward Cocoa.

"Yes, we are cats attempting to catch a mouse or two. If they are in Cocoa and think we are in your old hometown, it is the old bait and switch trap. Our bugged devices show we are in a meeting in your *Village Voice*, and some of us are in Melbourne."

We arrived and parked behind the Cara Mia Riverside Grill facing the river. A light rain was falling as we ran to the back door. Q-Ball opened it with a key. We hurried up the stairs. It was pitch black, and I followed his penlight trail. He opened the door to each room with a 1911 pistol silenced in hand. One room showed my Riverfront Gazebo and the lights across the bridge to Merritt Island.

A no windows storage room was our apparent meeting room. Q-Ball turned on a dimly lighted lamp. Much to my surprise, Jack Frost and Q-Ball's old friend 8-Ball makes four of our returning twelve black ops team assembled. Q-Ball gave the all equipment off signal. Everyone checked and gave the thumbs-up signal. A minute passed before anyone spoke. We were all stunned.

"This is a pleasant surprise," I said, breaking the silence. "I had given up hope that we would see each other as a group in person. Is there still a burn notice on you Ghost and Double D from our beloved C.I.A. and the Iranian Colonel knows I am not you."

"I say, ole' boy, you look chipper for a surviving poisoned shot at British imposter. The mole in the C.I.A. and the F.B.I. double special agent is identified and located. Country-wise but not their mailing address as far as I know. So, the Agency is not pressing my demise at present," Ghost replied

"Your friends in high places know this, and are they back on board with helping you? Both C.I.A. and F.B.I. Directors are on your side during my last contact. That puts all of us except

David, a.k.a. Double D and Mr. Law, in the clear with law enforcement. The foreign and domestic enemies are the Iranian Colonel and the murders of my wife and the Cocoa children," I told them.

All the meeting members were seated on supply boxes. Q-Ball stood up and handed each member a legal pad and pencil. There was writing on each pad. "These are the facts as far as we know them. I received them from each of you recently. Notice the Department of State Iranian mole, and the C.I.A. and F.B.I. double agents are also listed as enemies."

I read the fact sheets. "I am sure we all have something to add to this list of facts and clues. I recently listened to a Cocoa parade video and have positive proof that L.T. Gillard of the Cocoa P.D. is involved in the abduction of Rene, one of the murdered girls. An Iranian pointed them out to Gillard, and he growled at the girl. He was in Smokey the Bear costume, and one of her relatives was also in the parade. A little girl with perfect pitch hearing identified the voice of "Mokey" as she called him, as the voice she heard as the abductor of Rene."

Jack said, "Q-Ball is still in the good graces with the Company, and my friends are back as well, Ole boy. The F.B.I. has an arrest warrant out for our Double D. He is confirmed with severe mental problems and convicting evidence of murder. The two murders in New York and the false imprisonment of the ones in your old condo establishment. There is suspicion that he is connected to the girl's murders as well."

Q-Ball added, "Double D is in his right mind rarely. Your David died the day he witnessed his wife and children plunge to their deaths at the Twin Towers Osama Muslim attack, Commander. You are the only one he remembers as a friend.

The Agency believes he is back in Iran and fighting ISIS in his mind. Especially the tortures of Christian girls."

"Thank you, Q-Ball. That ties in with the wives of Muslim husbands who also lost their daughters to torture murders. That could be Double D if he traced the Muslim husbands. They changed their names to Muslim like Mohammed Ali and went to Iran to study Farsi. He is reliving the torture murders of Christian girls in the Iranian village by ISIS. Double D, or Mr. Law as he calls himself now, is still able to hack into any secret computer or phone system."

8-Ball punched his friend the Squid lightly on the shoulder and asked, "What do you have for us, you Navy Brat?"

"I have been out of the loop on all the things you have mentioned. I do have a bit of news, though. Remember our Too Tall Ted, our recon guy? He is six feet and seven inches tall, but he is also double-jointed and rated the best recon man in any branch of service. We couldn't nickname him Double T or 2TT because it might be misunderstood as our Commander Toby Tyler. He contacted me to let us know he is alive and well. Too Tall could slither like a snake into places no one could imagine."

"That is great news. Did Too Tall tell you where he is living and married? He was shy even when he gave me his recon report. I hope he will contact me," I asked.

"No, Commander," 8-Ball responded. "I invited him to our meeting, but he didn't reply. He, too, was caught and tortured by the Iranian Colonel. That makes six of our team that has returned from that fiasco mission in Iran."

"This has been a wonderful reunion and crucial meeting. As Q-Ball has labeled our murderers and attempted murders, the bad actors are much closer to being brought to justice. The bad apples in our law enforcement and C.I.A. have been identified, and the good apples are working to capture the criminals," I concluded the meeting with an offer to entertain any or all that could remain.

"I can't speak for Q-Ball and the Squid, but I plan to stay near to assist you in the capture of the murder of Natasha. She was a dear friend of mine. I can't say any of the listed ones will be brought to justice, ole' boy, especially if Double D gets to them first," Jack said.

"I, the loveable Q-Ball, am still on assignment with my present employer, who lives on the slippery slope of truth and a complete lie, who often slide down butt first into the political swamp. However, I get to drive a shiny black confiscated ride and the Ghost knows how to reach me."

"Where are the Sheriff and the Chief of Police on these cases, Commander," Jack asked.

"There is an all-points bulletin out for information concerning who cuffed Lt. Gillard nude to the back of his cruiser with his handcuffs, and he is an escaped fugitive. His Sergeant is jailed on some of the same charges. The rest of the force is helping," I said.

"The Sheriff has handled his bad apples, and a Lieutenant and Sargent detectives are working the two black girls' cases. They are the ones who got the conviction of a young woman that floated up behind a judge's house on the Indian River Lagoon. A young Cocoa detective has the white girl case. He is also working on the joint human trafficking task force. Natasha's case is considered a cold case, but the detective there is working with me. All are working together in spite of the Federal and political posturing," I answered.

"I can't tell you all how much this means to me. Seeing you all again and working with each of you is special ops. Each of you is special, and I hope you will keep in contact. We will leave five minutes apart. Best of luck and happy Thanksgiving," I told them sincerely.

I was the last to leave. I shook hands with each one and thanked them again.

It was a short walk back to the *Village Voice*. I opened the door and found out the recorder machine had been removed. Q-Ball didn't need a key. I drove back to my upstairs bugged apartment. I fully intended to let the buggers hear me snoring.

CHAPTER 27

I DO NOT remember putting in a 6 A.M. wake-up call and I can't find the widget that is buzzing. With one-half of the dirty dozen in town, nothing will surprise me.

I am surprised, though. The signal is different and appears to be a Farsi translation.

> "State Department Underground Rodent home address found. Extradition is not possible. Two black Muslim men paid for the torture of our children. I, Double D, found the home address. I do not believe I will complete our mission, Commander. The enemies, foreign and domestic, are moving in from all sides. My life expectancy is short. Difficulties. David."

David is a genius, but it is clear he is not in his right mind and is still on our terminated mission. Double D learned that two Muslim ISIS men had murdered children in Cocoa. He is still the best hacker despite his insanity.

A little light is slanting through the live oaks in front of my window. My bed blocks the door, and I snore into a bug we found. Confusion still reigns in our cases. Iran's colonel hit my wife because Lt. Gillard told him she was Jack Frost's wife. Now, David hit two innocent children because he thinks he is still on the failed Iranian mission. The light is beginning to shine in dark places.

The third girl murdered has not been publicly identified because Lt. Gillard was the case officer who withheld the D.N.A. identity. She is Iris Anne Silverman. Still, evidence points toward a copycat murder of Ethel Allen and a more recent murder of a girl placed in the river. Her bound and bloated body floated to a judge's dock in Merritt Island.

A text message on my standard phone says, "Don't forget. You are escorting Miss Zany to the Cocoa Women's Club Thanksgiving luncheon this Wednesday at 11:30." Great. That is today. I, as an escort is new to me, typical Zany. I will dress in my Sunday go-to-meeting clothing and head to the office. Early morning light indicates it will be a beautiful day in Cocoa.

Memory floods me as I order two sausage and egg croissants, French roast coffee, and a prune Danish. My dear departed boss/friend Gus Bellows, you are greatly missed. My order was ready through the serving window, and I headed down the street toward the *Village Voice* office. The roads are already decorated with lights and Christmas wreaths of green and sizeable red ribbon bows. Apart from law enforcement and terrorist threats, the City is ready to celebrate the holidays.

"Mr. Tyler. I am Billy from the boat rental. Remember me?" a young man says as I turn from the Black Tulip Restaurant and head for the *Village Voice* on King Street.

"Sure do, Billy. How is the boating business? I have noticed our winter snowbirds are arriving right on schedule," I answer him.

"It is fine. I read in your paper about the policeman that was arrested and escaped. He and another policeman came in and talked to the Silverman kid and pointed toward your wife while you were in the boat watching the wounded manatee. Silverman was upset and crushed his empty beer can in the paper bag. The police left, and the kid in his stinking wet Nikes with red laces marched back to their expensive speed boat," he said. "I thought you should know. I am so sorry about your wife."

"Thank you, Billy. That is helpful, and I wish you and your family a great Thanksgiving and Merry Christmas. May the New Year find your boats running circles around the Indian River Queen," I said with a smile.

"Thank you, sir," he said as he turned to walk away.

I opened the office door and was greeted with overhead jingle bells courtesy of Zany. I do not know what has come over me. I never give lengthy season's greetings. My emotions are in check even with the new ID of Lt. Gillard and his sergeant connecting them to Silverman's kid, and the murder of Iris Anne. The change in me is welcome, and I am thankful.

I plan on reviewing my notes for my presentation at the luncheon, but my widget is paging me and my office phone on the answering machine is flashing red light. Decisions. Decisions. Mr. Widget is a priority.

Text message: "We are in recon mode and are watching your six. We need a four-eyes meeting soon. New information like your young friend Billy passed on."

That is interesting. Is my body bugged now? No, but my handheld widget is picking up my conversations, no doubt. My sniper, 8-Ball, is in full recon mode. He probably has the Lady's Club meeting room bugged, too.

The croissants and coffee did not taste as good with Gus and Jonathan Livingston Seagull missing. My phone messages from the answering machine were routine. I started working on my presentation for the Cocoa Lady's Club meeting. I will complete it upon my return later today. Writing seems the best way to get the paper out without Gus. Good thing it is weekly. I would not be able to get the *Village Voice* out alone.

Once I was all caught up, I dressed for the Cocoa Lady's Club meeting. A quick look in the restroom mirror and I feel Zany will not have anything to straighten. I look so sharp I might cut myself. My senses are hitting on all cylinders today. Outside, the village is beginning to come alive with the hustle and bustle of merchants and early diners and shoppers.

I decided to walk to our P.I. office and escort Zany to the Community Women's Club on Rosa L. Jones Drive. The daughter of the Black Tulip was dressed to the nines and waved to me as she changed the outside menu.

It is Chamber of Commerce Day. Bright sunshine glittering the dark green, orange tree leaves twinkling like diamonds on the dark blue Indian River. Yet, there is a foreboding feeling in the pit of my stomach. I know one or more team members are watching my every move and surroundings.

I do not have the new information 8-Ball has, but he is on high alert. I am changing my usual route to the Porcher House office. 8-Ball has my six and his C.I.A. mobile computer/eye in the sky Company car. I am in the clear because my C.I.A. widget has not buzzed. The Brevard County Sheriff's Office and the Cocoa Police Department are silent also. It is good to be back in their good graces. I am ready for Zany's inspection.

A lady lawyer on the first-floor office wished me a Happy Thanksgiving on my way up the stairs. I thanked her and returned the greeting. That is the fifth person to greet me today that I do not remember meeting.

"Hello, handsome," Zany greeted me. "I see you dressed fitting to escort the senior private eye to the Cocoa Community Women's Club, Inc. Thanksgiving lunching. I understand it is a sellout crowd. It was nice of you to accept their invitation. They do a wonderful job for charity and education for Cocoa and Brevard County communities. You will be a smash hit, Rock."

"Is that a new cowgirl outfit?" I asked with a smile.

Denim bibbed overalls with a long-sleeved pink western jacket?

"I'll have you know Toby Rockwell Tyler, this is the latest fashion. Zany Investigations must be in top form in the presence of the most important women in Brevard County," Zany proclaimed, looking down her nose at me again. "Your chariot or mine, Sir Lancelot?"

"I walked. It is a beautiful day for escorting royalty on foot. The loyal subjects will have longer to pay homage," I answered.

"As you wish, trusted bodyguard," she said taking my arm.

I noticed the same woman in the law office pretending she didn't see us leave and head toward Rosa Jones Drive.

Two tall orange trees had been pruned and were sparkling in the sun by the Women's Club building.

"Look, Rock. That oversize bright orange on top escaped the pickers. The angle of the sun is perfect for a postcard photograph," she said as she quickly snapped a picture.

I glanced at my widget, scramble phone, and cell next to my concealed 1911 pistol. I turned the gadget and phones off. We entered the building, and the Club's president greeted us and her husband, the mayor. We exchanged pleasantries. Zany was seated in one of the front row tables, and I to the speaker's table. Much to my surprise Chief Brody and his wife were sitting with Sheriff J.B. Woodall and his wife center front. Rowena Simpson, SUNSHINE NEWS ~ COCOA was there with her photographer and other news people at a table in the back of the large room.

I recognized several waiters and waitresses from the Black Tulip, Cara Mia Riverside Grill (man and wife owners were serving), and Murdock's. There were others that I could not place. The president seated beside me stood and asked the Pastor of the First Christian Church to lead us in prayer. We exchanged pleasantries as the shrimp cocktail appetizers came. I was surprised to see twice roasted ducking from the Black Tulip. Of course, I ordered the duckling with Brazilian cashews topping. Someone had done their homework.

I glanced at Zany. She had that fox in the hen house look.

I still had that something is amidst feeling. I scanned the audience one by one. A couple of news people are scowling, but that is normal. To my right, a door to the parking lot opened, and waiters carry in a cloth-covered table.

After dessert, the president stood and recognized the dignitaries and other Brevard County women's clubs as guests. She thanked the restaurants and their chefs, waiters, and waitresses for the outstanding luncheon. Then she introduced me as the guest speaker of the annual Thanksgiving County-Wide luncheon.

I stood and walked to the podium.

"Thank you for inviting me. It is indeed an honor to share and give thanks in Cocoa, our beloved City. The village is ready, our winter visitors are arriving, and the weather is perfect. I am the second *Village Voice* guest speaker to be honored to speak at your Thanksgiving luncheon. The first was Gus Bellows, Founder, and Editor of the *Village Voice*. Gus, you are greatly missed by our village of Cocoa and surrounding counties."

I paused for a moment of silence. I spoke for twenty minutes covering some personal history as a boy who fell in love with Eau Gallie first and then Cocoa. I complimented the work done by the Mayor, Cocoa Police Department, and the Sheriff's Office. I concluded with several Cocoa Community Women's Club, Inc. in Brevard County. I thanked them again for inviting me. Zany is no longer seated front and center. She was standing in the back next to the lady from the Porcher House law office. I took my seat after the applause.

The Club's president stood and presented me with the beautiful centerpiece bowl of dried flowers. After the applause, she said, "Thank you, Mr. Tyler. You and the *Village Voice* are appreciated.

One of the scowling out-of-town news people stood and asked loudly, "Isn't it true, Mr. Tyler, that you have been a suspect in the murder of innocent children here in Cocoa and that you sleep with Zany Adams in the historic Porcher House?"

The lady from the Porcher House immediately had the "Reporter" by the lapel with his arm held high behind his back. She quickly escorted him out the front door.

Zany is following close behind them. The audience is in shock. Both Chief Brody and Sheriff Woodall are making their way through the tables.

A young girl at the front door shouting, "Come quick! Miss Zany hung herself!"

I exit through the door to the parking lot with pistol 1911 in hand and turn on my phone and widget. As I round the corner, I see Zany hanging from an orange tree on a pruned limb with the sizeable naval orange in one hand. The other is desperately trying to reach the limb that has her dangling three feet off the ground. I climb up the pruned stems and reach out to her. A flash of light causes me to draw the pistol. Rewena's photographer snapped a photo of us.

"Are you hurt?" I asked.

"No," she answered angrily. "But the stub ruined my jacket. I can't reach the darn thing to get unhooked."

I moved closer, wrapped my arms around her legs, and lifted her off the tree stub. Then I carried her to the ground. The camera flashed again.

We were now surrounded by the Chief of police and several plain-clothed officers. I nodded to Detective Romano from the Human Trafficking Task Force I volunteer on. My widget buzzed with a text, "Lady with us. We have the false reporter identified. Recommend you two return the way you came. We have you covered."

I clicked twice. The building emptied, and I waved to the mayor and his wife as we dropped out of sight. Zany was shaking, but still gripping her prize naval orange.

I walked fast, holding her arm. She practically ran to keep up.

"What was all that about, Rock? Who were the reporter and the woman that arrested him?"

"I don't know, Zany. The woman was in the lawyer's office when we left for the luncheon," I told her. "Do you know her?"

"I do not, but I am glad the woman was there. The man attacked our reputations as well as our innocence. It looks like Lt. Gillard's underhanded work," Zany declared angrily.

I arrived at the *Village Voice* without further incident.

Time to make some calls.

CHAPTER 28

My FIRST CALL was to 8-Ball asking him who was that false reporter and the woman from the lawyer's office in the Porcher House? Then, when is our meeting?

Gadget text came immediately, "All will be clear tonight. Bring all notes and recordings. The gang will be available with foreign and domestic information."

My office phone is ringing. The machine is showing Zany Adams Investigations, "Hello, Zany."

"This is not Zany; I am her answering service. Test question: What name did she call you when you arrived to escort her today?" "Handsome," I answered. "Correct. Zany said to make sure I told only you. The woman in the law office downstairs did not see her in their office. Also, she met for information from her C.P.D. source and thanks for rescuing her from hanging tree."

The line went dead before I could say thank you.

Another call came in, "Hello, Sheriff Woodall. Zany and I are safely in our respective offices, it was good to see you, Chief Brody, and your wives. I wish we could have talked some."

"Hello, Rock. We are seated in the backroom of Cara Mia and would like to do just that. Will you join us?" he asked.

"I will. There seems to be a new spirit of cooperation among agencies. I hope we can share and pool all our resources finally," I said sincerely.

"I believe we can. I told the Chief you are a sworn deputy, and he is more than ready to get back to working together," Sheriff Woodall said.

"Great. I will be there as soon as I pick up my car at the apartment," I told him.

I hung up with another incoming call from Zany, "Hello. I just hung up talking with Sheriff, and I am meeting him and the Chief at Cara Mia. Care to join us?"

"No can do, handsome," Zany said. "We are going to the Silverman enclave at 3 P.M. It seems he and his son are ready to talk. We are about to start earning our $1,000 retainer. Also, Lt. Gillard's Sargent is singing like a canary after he learned his Lt. set him up to take the fall for murder."

"Okay, Zany. I will meet you at our office at 2:30," I agreed.

I cleared the answering machine and turned it off, saying the office was closed. I arrived behind the apartment building to find my car as I left it days ago. I'm sure 8-Ball has debugged and checked for bombs regularly. I meet with local law enforcement now, the Silverman boys at 3 P.M., and the national team reps tonight.

There is a parking place behind the Sheriff's cruiser in front of Cara Mia, proving that things have changed. The water fountain is spouting, and the Italian chef statue is welcoming with today's menu. I head down the narrow hall to the back meeting room. The owner's wife asked me to give an impromptu talk to her mother's book club in here once. Woodalls and Brodys are sitting by the window.

They are the only persons present. I smell strawberry shampoo and remember Natasha.

"Greeting, Rock. We were saying how sorry we were about the outburst of the out-of-town reporter. He ruined a perfect Thanksgiving luncheon," Sheriff J. B. Woodall said, shaking his head.

"Is Zany okay?" his wife asked.

"Yes, Zany is fine and working, or she would have come with me. The reporter was a plant, of that, I am sure. Was the mystery woman that took him into custody one of yours?"

"You gave a good talk, Rock. Several women asked us to tell you how much they appreciated the talk and your *Village Voice* paper. The president asked me to express her thanks and apology to Zany for the attack against her," the Chief's wife said.

"I will pass that on to Zany. She took it in stride. Zany is a lot tougher than she looks. A Sheriff's daughter," I said as I sat down at the round table.

Chief Brody said, "No, to answer your question. The woman disappeared with the reporter, and they are not known to our departments."

Our hostess entered and closed the sliding door behind her. "Hello, Mr. Tyler. Would you or your guests like another dessert or perhaps orange juice?"

She was not successful in hiding her smile, "Thanks again for talking with my mother's Merritt Island book club. She said it was a delightful surprise, and they enjoyed the talk and Q & A afterward."

"You are most welcome. I enjoyed speaking with your mother's club. I also enjoyed our luncheon and appreciated you and your husband serving tables," I told her.

"We will join you in the dining room. Our husbands and Rock have a business to discuss," the Sheriff's wife said.

They followed her out, and she closed the sliding door.

"Are you two offering me a business proposition?" I asked.

"We would like to hire you, but the public will not allow it. I am happy to learn that you are a deputy, Rock. I understand why Johnny J. B. Woodall kept it to himself considering the bad apples in our departments," said the Chief.

"Thank you, Chief. You still have two bad apples. One in the jail and one on the run. Does this new relationship give me access to information on the murder of my wife and the girls?" I asked.

"You have all the privileges of a Brevard County Deputy. Will you and your higher authorities be sharing your information?" he asked.

"You will have all the need-to-know information that a Chief of Police is entitled to have. The Feds have not changed for the better. So, what do you have for me?" I asked.

"Sargent James is talking to save his hide. He has admitted to assisting Lieutenant Gillard in planting clues to help them solve cases. Abraham also said the Lt. has connections to federal agencies—F.B.I., C.I.A., and the State Department. He agreed to send the information on human trafficking, terrorists, and any most wanted on their posters. He was aware of the Iranian Colonel that was paying for information on the murderer of his wife by Jack Frost," Chief Brody said.

"Did he tell the Colonel that I was Jack Frost?" I asked.

Chief Brody paused and said, "He said he didn't, but no doubt he did for the money."

"Have you connected the reasons why your Lt. wants me arrested or dead? How well do you know his past, Chief?" I asked.

"Our department, with the help of the F.B.I. database in West Virginia, has run an in-depth background check. Nothing was indicating he was not qualified to serve in law enforcement. He is a Most Wanted now. He is also a suspect in the serial killing of the girls," he answered.

"The Company is searching for one of our doomed Iran mission teammates. He calls himself Mr. Law, but his real name is David (N) Dawson. He watched his wife, son, and daughter jump to their deaths from the Twin Towers on 9/11. He is the best hacker in the business when he is in his right mind," I shared with them. "He believes he is still in Iran somedays and is completing his mission. He rounded up several who assisted the Muslims in attacking America on 9/11. He extracted information and executed two of them, we believe. You know the rest from the captives he interrogated in my old condo. There is a termination notice on the teammate we call Double D because he had no middle name. However, he is close to locating the State Department mole that set up our doomed mission."

"Thank you, Rock," Chief said. "You have access to all that is allowed—our complete files on the murder of your wife and Iris Anne Silverman. Sheriff Woodall has the files on the two girls. We do not have access to federal files except where there is overlap."

"I will bring you up to date on all that we have, Rock. We have all been through a lot, but thankfully there have been no new terrorist attacks recently," Sheriff Woodall assured me.

"Zany and I have an appointment with our client Edward R. Silverman and his son Norman this afternoon. Do either of you have any background or suggestions?" I asked them.

"Silverman's total acreages is under electronic surveillance, his and ours. Even his yacht, cars, ski shed, and boat. If you wear a wire, it will be detected at the gate before you get past the guard," said Chief Brody.

Sheriff Woodall added, "We mean all."

"He is a defense lawyer. He is one of the best for getting the guilty off and innocent in jail. He has loads of money, which is not all from his law practice. Our department officers hate him, and he knows it. He has political connections," Brody shrugged.

"We will give you both the information he gives us, and you both will give what you have on him. Agreed?" I did my cold fisheyes stare at them. "He has client privileges with Zany Adams Private Investigations, Inc."

"The Cocoa Police Department has been swept clean of Lt. Gillard, all of his associates with their surveillance and false documentation. I want to meet again with you two in our secure location soon," Sheriff Woodall said.

"You are a sworn deputy, Toby. All our department is finally on your side. Lt. Gillard's charges and being on the most wanted list have left him with zero connection to us and our files," Chief Brody said. "Let's meet next week."

"Thank you, gentlemen. I will let you rejoin your ladies," I said as I prepared to leave. "The Tuxedo Bomb is excellent. I know they will love the second dessert."

We all stood up and shook hands. They returned to the dining room and me to my car. My scramble phone and belt gadget rang and buzzed as soon as I turned them on. My standard phone had a text from Zany. I am experiencing a new sense of freedom. For the first time, I feel confident that these cases will be closed, and all that is wrong about the Iran mission will be made right. The spring is back in my steps as I cross the street.

It is bumper-to-bumper back to the Porcher House. A tourist bus and cars have the historic house filled and surrounded. I work my way through the visitors. I escape to our upstairs office, unlock the door, and hear our phone ringing. It seems everyone must talk with me at the same time. There is a circular from Ryan's Pizza on my desk. I check the back. No note from my rock band P.I. Memories rush by, and a sense of loneliness is here for a moment.

"Zany Adams Investigations. How may we serve you?" Zany's trainee answered as instructed.

Then she handed me the phone, "Rock. Glad you are back. I have terrific news and will be there soon."

She hung up. It must be special news. Zany always waits for a response.

"I opened the scramble phone and the text messages: "The boys are back in town. There's Dancing Tonight." There was a shrimp boat symbol after the message.

I answered my belt gadget, and a familiar but long-absent voice said, "I say, ole boy, you are busy for a retired policeman."

"Hello, Sheriff. How are Chatham County and my favorite city dweller doing? Are you connected to my special gadget? I sure miss you, CCSO, and Savanah," I told him.

"Another ole friend patched me through and suggested the 'ole boy' bit. Let me get right to the point. All is well here, thank you," my former Sheriff said. "Our cold case officer turned up a missed connection to an unsolved child murder in Savanah. The man has three different legal names, but the slightly out of focus photo in the database is your Lieutenant Gillard in Cocoa Police Department."

"That is excellent! I just left Chief Brody and Sheriff Woodall. Their departments can finally pool their resources and work-force to find the scoundrel. The Company, the F.B.I., and State Department are not sharing, but we have friends with access," I shared with him. "A Company man is on our team. Jack is off the burn list. David (N) Dawson is still on the list, but he contacts me in his unique ways occasionally. Director Lewis Lawson is a friend, but limited by Agency rules."

"W.O.W.! Is this the young deputy detective Toby back on the job? Your mind is working on overdrive. I made a mistake letting you go on medical retirement. Our whole office misses you and speaks of you and Natasha often," he told me.

"Thank you and the department, and I will visit when all this murdering mess is over. I will treat you and the gang to a shrimp and grits lunch in Savanah. I have been in counseling with a pastor and counselor. My mind is right again," I told him confidently.

I was not surprised when another familiar voice chimed in, "I say, ole boy, you are sounding ducky," Jack said.

"An eavesdropper!" I said with a laugh. "Thank you, Sheriff. We will keep you informed."

"Great. So long, for now, you two," the Sheriff said.

"Will we be honored by Casper the Friendly Ghost tonight, or will this be our connection?" I asked.

"That depends on the recon at the time. The place is undetermined. We all have a bit to contribute. There is a seventh team member that may be a star on the wall at Langley but is really still among the living," he said.

Zany burst into the office and shouted, "GREAT NEWS!"

Then she noticed I was on the phone and said, "Sorry. It can wait."

She came close to blushing. She opened a desk drawer and put a recorder in her chartreuse bag.

"Tonight," then Jack was gone.

CHAPTER 29

As I HUNG up the phone, a message flashed across the screen: "The U.S. Navy seized three Iranian fast boats near the Strait of Hormuz today" reported the USA Today, news service. The Iranian boats were harassing a U.S. Ohio-class nuclear submarine violating international law. The undeclared war continues regardless of America's leadership failure to acknowledge that we are at war."

Our SEAL team did not go into Iran officially either. Officially, we are not at war, and our doomed mission never happened. Nevertheless, our team had realized we are still at war because of that unofficial mission in Iran. Thus, our rendezvous later this evening.

Zany had left while I was on the phone, so I called her cell and asked, "What is our great news?"

"Our interview with our wealthy client and his son is set up," Zany said. "Your business tower pantsuit will be perfect. Zany Adams Investigations will be well-represented. I'll pick you up outside the *Village Voice* back door."

Zany had received a $1000 retainer months ago. Why the delay in talking with us is one of the many unanswered questions for this afternoon.

"Yes, I'll be ready. Your candy apple corvette convertible is an appropriate ride to impress our wealthy client," I said.

I knew her corvette was not bugged like my car, so I grabbed the communication device 8-Ball had told me to use for him to be able to contact me. I did our agreed upon connection code and looked out the window before I headed for the back door of the *Village Voice*. Morse code says, "I have your six." That is comforting. I gave a thumbs up as I exited to wait for Zany's arrival.

"I am excited to be in on the big case," she said as I got into her car. "Aren't you?"

"No, I am not excited to be working with Cocoa's richest man who is a defense lawyer," I answered her. "Aren't we going to get there early for our appointment on the island? Do you want to grab a cup of coffee before we enter the inner sanctum of the Rich and Famous?"

"No, I want to catch Mr. Silverman off-guard if I can," she explained. "My source at the CPD has filled me in on the connections of the Fugitive Lieutenant Gillard to the Silverman family. I brought two tape recorders even though he will probably not agree to be recorded. His Mansion is wired for any electronic surveillance, and he has armed guards around the property. Our client has more reasons to be fearful of losing his money. He could lose his life."

"We also have another client at the same time," Zany said slyly. "His son Norman made an appointment with us earlier than his father."

"I have a good feeling about that interview, Zany. I believe Norman knows more about his sister than his father. Natasha and I met him and three of his friends at the boat rental place," I told her. "He was being an obnoxious show-off, purposely trying to run over an injured manatee with a 14-foot ski boat. Then he insulted my wife and tried to run over the manatee again, but I was able to get in front of her. The manatee was dead by the time the rescue team arrived."

"I called CPD and reported that killing and then my wife was murdered in front of the police station shortly after the manatee. Apparently, Lieutenant Gillard and his Sergeant talked with Norman privately after we left, according to Billy Payne, the boat rental attendant," I explained. "No charges were ever filed against Norman or his friends and my wife's case is still cold.

"Rock, you have total recall again," Zany commented as we approached the Silverman estate. "The information about Norman's connection with Gillard will be helpful when we interview them. Well, here we are."

After Zany pushed the call button, the unfriendly armed guard by the electric gate demanded, "Identify yourself and state your purpose."

"Zany Adams and Rock Tyler with Zany Adams Investigations," Zany answered businesslike with no friendliness in her voice either. "We have an appointment with Mr. Silverman and his son, Norman.

An irritated voice spoke through the gate speaker, "You are early, can you come back in an hour?"

Zany answered, "We are pressed for time today, Mr. Silverman.. We will wait here."

My gadget activated and 8-Ball said, "He is irritated and tossing papers into the fireplace."

I smiled knowing we have an eye in the sky and an ear in the room. There was no need for tape recorders.

Another minute passed and the voice said, "Very well, come in."

The gate slowly slid into its concrete hiding place. The guards showed no emotion as we passed in front of them and headed down the long curving driveway through beautiful flower gardens and tall, royal palm trees.

Zany parked in front of the steps to the lighthouse-style mansion. I pushed the door button and we heard chimes playing. A guard stands by as another one opens the door. We stepped in, and he closed and locked the vault-like door behind us. He spoke not a word as he led us to the large office where our client was seated behind a large mahogany desk by an open fireplace. A photograph of his deceased daughter Iris was angled toward him, and his son Norman sat beside him.

"Thank you for coming. Please be seated," Mr. Silverman said. "Would you care for something to drink?"

I looked at Zany who responded, "No, thank you. I am sorry for our early arrival. We had a client with an earlier appointment than yours. Have you met my investigator Rock Tyler" He is also the owner of the *Village Voice*."

"I have not had the pleasure, nice to meet you," he responded. "I did know Gus Bellows."

I did not say anything or mention that I had met Norman. His body language indicated he was being held against his will. He was leaning back in the padded chair with his arms resting and fingers interlace across the stomach. He had a deadpan face with blank eyes staring straight ahead. He was wearing the red bandana and white Nike tennis shoes with red laces he wore at the boat rental place. He was silently sending me a message that it was the Iranian who shot double-O buckshot through our first pickup windows, not him. It all flashes before my eyes. The body was dressed similarly found in the abandoned white van in Orlando. I gave a slight nod in acknowledgment of his silent message.

Zany took out our two tape recorders, one legal pad, and two ink pens, then asks Mr. Silverman, "For clarity, we record and take notes in all our interviews. Our clients have had the option to correct any comments after the interview and we have client privileges similar to yours and your clients."

"No recordings," Mr. Silverman declared. "You may take notes and I will approve them after the interview. Here's a check for your visit today. The reasons for the delay in seeing you have become apparently clear as Norman and I have received threats. They came from different channels. We know from whom in some cases, but have no idea who the others are."

"Perfectly understood, Mr. Silverman," Zany assured him. "Who are the known and have you reported them to the authorities?"

"The murder of my brilliant daughter is connected to and complicates revealing the who and some of the facts. I should have kept a closer eye on her, her friends, and their activities. As Norman knows, she had unlimited resources and the curiosity of a cat."

"Have Lieutenant Gillard and Sergeant James been involved, and did they threaten you and Norman?" Zany asked.

"Yes, Mr. Tyler knows I was threatened," Norman said, then took a deep breath and let it out slowly. "They both tried to frame me for the murder."

"Thank you, Norman. I was not aware of that," Zany said giving me a brief nod. "Mr. Silverman, do you have any other contacts who worked to harm you or your son? We know you have client-attorney confidential privileges just as Mr. Tyler and I do. What did Gillard and James have on you to force you to silence?"

"I have a respected law practice and a good record of successful results in defending my clients. I have been assigned to some unwanted cases by the judge.

I have made a lot of enemies by defending murderers, armed robbers, drug traffickers, human trafficking, and rapists," he answered. "There is prosecutable evidence against her friends also. Her closest friend is a senior in high school. Other girls in their group dared her and she accepted the dare. So yes, I have a lot of people who want to keep me from releasing this information and will harm us to keep us silent."

As I was thinking I want to get everything that he and Norman can give us, Zany jumped right in and said, "This may be our only chance to get all the evidence we need to prosecute murder suspects and accessories for all the murders. We are here to get leads to those responsible for the murder of your daughter and Norman, your sister."

Zany looked over at me, so I took my cue and said, "Accordingly, please give us anything you have on the murder of my wife and the two other girls that will help us bring the murders to justice. We have some evidence on the Iranian who posed as Norman and murdered my wife, Tasha. We have wiretapped evidence on Lieutenant Gillard. They were involved in a drug and sex trafficking operation. Many of the victims were from Iran. I believe CPD collected enough evidence to arrest the Lieutenant and Sergeant, but they may have had at least two other alias names and may have been involved in murders in the Savannah, Georgia area where I was a deputy sheriff."

"I did not have either as clients, so I am free to give you all I know," Mr. Silverman said as he picked up a file and read it silently. "Gillard also had a list of people he had contact with in drugs, human trafficking, and graphic photos. We also have the list of informants and victims he was using. Iris stumbled onto them when she hacked his computer and cell phones."

Norman broke his silence and said, "The curiosity of a cat got her killed. Lieutenant Gillard either killed Iris or hired it done. He copied the murder of another Merritt Island girl and placed her body in front of the gazebo you often visit Mr. Tyler. He also tied the murder of years ago to you as you wrote an article about the upcoming play titled after her name."

"Did he threaten you and your sister before she died?" I asked. "Did he threaten you that day my wife was murdered?"

"Yes," he said he knew she had illegally hacked the system of the police computer. He said you and the woman with you were undercover cops investigating the Silverman family. I didn't know until recently that he tried to frame me for the murder of your wife and frame you for the murder of my sister Iris."

For the first time, his lower lip quivered. Norman was still, and I knew he was still holding back some information. I hoped we would get to talk with him away from his father.

"I hired you to find the murderer of Iris Anne. I want the murderer tried, convicted, and in prison without parole. I would appreciate it if you concentrated on our murder case. You have all the information we have," said Edward Silverman.

He stood and asked for Zany's notepad. He looked through her notes, nodded, and handed the pad back and said, "Norman said he knows Gillard killed Iris Anne or hired it done, but we have no convicting evidence that will hold up in court."

"He did it, Dad!" Norman said angrily and stormed out of the room.

"Pardon my son, he is still very distraught over the loss of his sister. They fought like brothers and sisters do, but he was always protective," Silverman explained.

We shook hands and he said, "I am depending on you two to solve this case."

Zany nodded to him and said, "We will. With the evidence you have provided it is just a matter of time. We have no higher case to work on. I will keep you up to date."

She handed him our business card with a private number written on the card.

"Mr. Tyler, I know you are not fond of defense lawyers as a former deputy sheriff. However, the law is the law. As an officer of the court, I must provide the accused the best possible defense. Sometimes the guilty go free," he said. "I am also aware of the excellent work you did in Atlanta and Savanah on child abduction and murders. I am extremely pleased that you are on Iris Anne's case."

He must have some kind of silent signal because the same guard appeared and stepped through the door. Zany and I nodded to Attorney Silverman and followed the guard to the front door. We exited without a word. Zany fired up her corvette and we drove around a large flowering bush and there stood Norman, blocking the driveway. Zany stopped and Norman walked to my side of the car.

"My dear ole Daddy didn't give you all we have, and he doesn't know everything either," he said as he handed me a DVD disk and a girl's diary. "Daddy defended the murderer of my high school friend. I heard Dad in the client interview. The wealthy young man is a neighbor's son. The murderer said, 'My position is—I didn't do it.'"

Norman was obviously angry, "We were very happy he was convicted and is now in prison."

"Thank you, Norman," I said. "Everything you can tell us about Iris Anne and her friends and activities, even the smallest things, will help us find her killer. Sometimes, the seemingly unrelated information becomes the missing evidence needed to solve the case."

Zany held out her bag. I dropped the disk and diary into it, and she snapped it shut barely missing my fingers.

"Daddy didn't give you all he knows because Lt. Gillard had incriminating evidence and threatened him with disbarment. Also, you will see my sister was forced to do computer work illegally for Cocoa's Finest officer, Gillard. Her friend that posed nude was also forced to participate in a pornographic video in Ft. Lauderdale. Iris told me she gave up her virginity at one of her girlfriends' wild parties, but she didn't tell me who the guy was. Her girlfriends were juniors and seniors in high school. They are wild. You will find a lot more on the disk and in her diary."

I watched Norman closely while he spoke. It was clear that he disliked his father. He was turning his daddy in despite the possible disbarment from his law practice. I understand why he treated Natasha and me so rudely.

"This information is crucial. We will follow up with her friends and all the names we find," I assured him.

A guard appeared around the curve, but Norman was out of his sight. Zany started moving forward slowly.

"Beautiful flowers," she said as we passed the third guard.

The gate was opening as we arrived. The guard stood with his back to us as we departed.

Zany and I sighed and exchanged glances.

"You ready for that cup of coffee?" she asked.

"We have an appointment with Chief Brody at Kay's BBQ. We can kill two birds with one stone," I said. "I think he wants to tell us what we already know, but The Q will make it worth our time. He doesn't know about my inside police source. Then, we will study the disk and diary after the late luncheon, okay?"

She gave me that pouting down-the-nose look and said, "A girl's diary is private. No boys allowed."

We arrive at Kay's, and I saw Chief Brody seated, back to the wall, looking through the large outside window. Zany excused herself for the lady's room and I walked over and sat down next to the Chief.

We shook hands and I said, "Zany will join us shortly."

"How have you been, Toby?" he asked. "It is nice you are not on the most wanted list anymore. Lt. Gillard sure tried his best to keep you too busy to investigate him. He planted enough clues and doctored your phone and official records to frame you. He may have skipped the country by now."

"I would look in Iran for his choice of countries. He and his Colonel friend may be traveling together," I told him. "We have a witness that knows he set up Norman Silverman to take the fall for murdering my wife. He assisted the Iranian Colonel in the murder of my wife by lying to him. He said she was the wife of Jack Frost who murdered the colonel's wife. He did it to knock me off finding his connections to the murders in Savanah and in Cocoa."

Zany returned with that, "I have done something sneaky look." She had read Iris Anne's diary no doubt.

Misty, our usual waitress appeared and asked, "Will Miss Adams be joining these two gentlemen for lunch or dinner?"

"If the gentlemen use proper etiquette, and conduct themselves in a professional manner, Miss Adams will have lunch with them," Zany responded.

"Would one of you gentlemen care to place an order?" Misty asked, still carrying out the charade.

I studied the luncheon menu like it was a difficult decision and said, "I might recommend Kay's Bar B Q with sweet potato fries and raspberry tea for the lady and the same for myself."

Zany smiled and nodded yes.

Chief Brody said, "An excellent choice, I'll have the same."

We sat looking at each other for a minute before Zany said, "Well, that was a bit theatrical. We should apply at the Cocoa Playhouse to continue our new careers. How goes it, Chief Brody?"

Kay was back to busy, and she was working in the kitchen and glancing at the tables occasionally. Misty appeared with our three daily specials. She was still in the welcome first-time visitor's mode.

"How was your visit with Cocoa's most prosperous citizen? He has a lot of information about our criminal elements if it isn't confidential client protected," he asked as he took a big bite of Bar-B-Q and chewed hungrily.

Zany ignored his exaggeration and delicately took a small bite, blotting her small child-like mouth.

"We had a nice visit with our client and his son Norman. The staff was very professional," Zany answered.

"Chief, you say your ex-lieutenant has escaped the long arm of law and disappeared?" I asked. "But you have your ex-sergeant in chains, and he is singing like a parakeet, right?"

"Yes. James learned that his friend set him up and flew the coop. The sergeant is an angry bird. He has a lawyer but has given us enough hard evidence to convict Gillard on multiply counts of human trafficking, forced labor, and sex work, and an accomplice to all four of the murders you are working on Deputy Tyler," Chief answered. "Sheriff Woodall has all the information on the two girls, and I will share the information on our jurisdiction cases, Iris Anne and Natasha."

"We must admit Gillard and James had us tied up legally for a long time. With all his connections, he didn't know I was a sworn deputy, and under F.B.I. surveillance 24/7," I said. "They worked tirelessly planting clues and misdirection and falsifying your records. Gillard and James did not count on my old S.E.A. L. team coming to my aid."

I chewed my sandwich and fries and sipped my tea in a genteel manner, with Zany's approving nod.

I caught a hand wave from Drs, Jerimiah and Beverly. I waved for them to come over. Zany gave me a questioning look. She couldn't see anyone over the booths.

"It is Pastor Jerimiah and Beverly," I explained.

"Good afternoon, Pastor, Beverly," I greeted them and offered to have them sit with us, but they declined.

"Good afternoon. It is so nice to see Kay's is back to busy. I would like to offer you three a cordial invitation to our Thanksgiving services this Sunday. The pew you and Gus sat in is still available, Toby," Pastor Jerimiah said with a smile.

"Thank you, Pastor. I plan to be there," I told him.

"Count me in also," Zany replied. "We certainly have a lot to be thankful for this Thanksgiving."

"I am committed to my Church, but I appreciate the invitation," Chief Brody answered.

Dr. Beverly said, "Happy Thanksgiving everyone."

We all returned her greeting and waved goodbye. Misty returned with the bills. I took them and handed her the amount due plus a generous tip. She did a curtesy and said, "Thank you kindly. Do come again."

"You two haven't given me any new information, especially from your barrister Edward R. Silverman," Chief Brady said looking disappointed. "We are back to full disclosure after we collected all we needed to charge and arrest the two bad birds in our department."

"We took notes and were not allowed to record our visit. We will update you as soon as we study our findings," answered Zany, all business mode again.

"Okay. You have the means to investigate Iran, Toby. I know the team keeps in touch," Chief said. "The sheriff and I appreciate their help and understand why they keep a low profile. It is literally life and death out there for them."

He thanked me for lunch and said, "You two watch your six out there, it is a long way from over, and the threats foreign and domestic are real."

Zany whispered, "You will be delighted with the diary. She names people and their specific activities. I can't wait to watch the DVD disk," she said with her little girl giggle.

She drove us to the Porcher House office. She produced a DVD player and set two legal pads with pens on the table. The disk opened with a smiling Iris Anne Silverman and a grinning teddy bear in her bedroom. Then it focused on a large screen computer and a high school party which was in full swing. There was dancing and drinking of alcohol and soft drinks. One very attractive girl winked at the camera and led a boy out of the living room. Iris Anne held the video recorder to take a selfie. A boy handed Iris Anne a bottle of beer.

The next scene focused on her computer screen. The girl in the previous scene was posing for photographs and removing clothing. In the last scene, she was nude and holding a signed consent form and the nude boy beside her held five one-hundred-dollar bills. The girl was forcing a smile for the camera. The video came next and an outside shot of the welcome to Fort Lauderdale sign. An unmarked police car was parked nearby with the license plate fully exposed.

The DVD continued with the Cocoa City Police parking lot. The same unmarked car with a license plate showed Lt. Gillard getting in on the passenger side and Sargent James sliding behind the wheel.

The bedroom computer showed an offshore bank account number and weekly deposits of hundreds of dollars. The caption said, "Cocoa's Finest. Receiving income from Iran, Washington D. C., Savanah, Fort Lauderdale, and other unidentified places."

"That is amazing, Zany. Does the diary connect to any of these scenes?" I asked.

"It does and we have names of friends and associates as Iris Anne calls them," Zany answered. "She met with Gillard and James on several occasions just before her death. She was not specific, but she was definitely scared."

I read the diary. It was a treasure trove of information. She met with Lt. Gillard and hacked computers and bank accounts on many occasions. She sent compromising photos and recordings demanding blackmail payments and more groomed women and children for human trafficking, forced cheap labor, and sex workers. Zany made copies of the DVD and the diary and placed the originals in the safe.

I took them to the *Village Voice* office. I made another copy of the diary, but I do not have a DVD player. Our undisclosed location and meeting time are at hand. I cleared the answering machine and sent the appropriate responses. Thanksgiving in Cocoa is in full swing. All my advertisers were reporting record business. Some sent thank you messages to be printed the day after Thanksgiving.

"Night will fall over the sleepy wall again in about thirty minutes. Expect the four horsemen to attend in one form or another. All are invited through brother Richard." My gadget text again. 8-Ball no doubt. I grab my notebook, Iris Anne's diary, and DVD copies. Fifteen minutes passed until the gadget beeped again, "Meet me at our first meeting place." I text back, "On my way." It was the abandoned orange packing building south of Cocoa. The Sheriff may still have the area under surveillance, but 8-Ball knows all about it.

As I sat waiting where 8-Ball and I met the first time, I reviewed what we know now. The Iranian or someone he hired wrote the threatening notes on the wall thinking he was addressing Jack Frost, who killed his wife. We also know Lt. Gillard and Sgt. James were on his payroll. Gator and Straight were working with them as well.

Much to my surprise, 8-Ball tapped on my window. I rolled it down and he pulled up the lock and slid in the passenger seat. I rolled the window up electronically.

"Hello, Commander. I came through the back door. There is no one present, and the sheriff has called off surveillance."

8-Ball asked me to pull around behind the packing shed. "We are expecting others to join us."

Weeds as high as the car grew on each side of the narrow asphalt haul road. Two unmarked black confiscated Company cars were parked facing out. I circled around and parked beside them. We got out and entered one of them.

"I say, ole chap, you haven't changed. No worse for the wear," Jack Frost was in rare form. He shined a penlight on his face and then on mine. "Well, a little, perhaps."

"You are in the clear with your former employer I presume," I said, delighted to see my old friend the Ghost. "I am glad to see you alive and well."

A door opened silently and Too Tall slipped in the other side of me. Four of our team are present and accounted for. "This is great."

A buzzing caught our attention. 8-Ball held up his belt gadget.

The voice was loud and clear and unmistakable that of Q-Ball. "Greeting all." There was the sound of children in the background. "Anyone needs to be patched up?"

"All fit as a fiddle here, Squid. Sounds like you have the family with you tonight," said 8-Ball.

Our sniper and medical team member are still close friends, and it shows. The night air is cool, and the smell of rotting wood and dead vegetation meets us as we enter the old crime scene. The yellow police tape is still in place and so is the writing on the walls. Jack turned on a small blue light lantern. I am surprised to see the woman and man from the Cocoa Women's Club sitting on old orange crates. We joined them and sat facing each other on crates in a small circle. This is a scene out of a Halloween movie.

"Let me introduce Jane and John, our Company members and in the same employ as 8-Ball and yours truly," Jack spoke in his normal voice. "They assisted you Commander by ruining your talk to the ladies and official gentlemen. Jane and John are assigned to the real Iranian desk task force. The search for the rogue Gillard and his Iranian Colonel is in a full-court press, as you Yanks like to say."

"Why, may I ask was the disruption necessary?" Jane and John looked first to Jack and then to 8-Ball. Their faces showed no sign of hearing the question. "Need to know, I don't need to know?"

"Commander, there was at least one woman there who is or was under the control of our fugitive Gillard. We believe the scene got to him and we are tracking their communications. So far, they have made no other contact. He is in deep cover," Jack answered.

"I know you had Zany and I covered today at the lawyer's fort. Did you pick up the conversation between us and Norman on the driveway?" I directed the question to all of them.

Again, a minute passed before Q-Ball answered with a child crying in the background.

"Yes, we did Commander. We also heard you and Zany talking in her office. Yes, I am still employed. We all have a green light to assist you in the capture of the Iranian who murdered Natasha." He hesitated, then said, "Ghost has the code."

An involuntary shiver passed through my whole body at the mention of Natasha and the Company's all-out efforts to locate my wife's killer and his accomplice Gillard. The State Department is not involved, not trusted no doubt. Too much politics from the President's office down, all are making nice with China, Russia, and Iran. There is a lot of money to be made to those with political connections. Even my friend, F.B.I. Director Lawson is not in the loop.

"I am grateful," I told them.

"I made a copy of the diary and DVD. Sorry, I do not have a DVD player," I said, as I handed them to Jack who excused himself and departed our small circle of light.

"Any help from the East Coast Human Trafficking Taskforce you volunteered for last year, Commander? Gillard and James and the last victim Iris Anne were involved. Iris Anne was forced but she saw and did things that can convict them. Norman is blessed."

"Nothing yet, 8-Ball. I have passed on some of the information I received today, but I haven't heard back from our task force. When they meet the whole gang; Federal, State, County, and City representatives are present. I withheld info."

Jack Frost breezed in with DVD and diary in hand. He handed them to Jane. "My car," he said.

She took them and departed.

"These are Jane's area of expertise. If there is anything incriminating or vaguely apparent, she will find it." He paused, "By the way, Jane was the clean one on our doomed mission. She was in the chopper that took us in and brought us out. Jane is a communications expert. Yes, piloting is one of her many talents, and yes, Jane and John are fictitious."

A slight serpent's smile appeared. Jack is back.

"It seems we have enough to charge several with crimes and have evidence that will convict in a court of law. Brevard County Sheriff's Department and Cocoa City Police Department are working together finally. Both Woodall and Brody have trusted officers fully involved in the four murders and now human trafficking in Brevard County. I am a believer and know we will solve these cases and bring to justice the guilty," I said. "We are very close. Now that we have one-half of the dirty dozen plus two clean ones, Jane and John."

"There are only five of us here from our team Commander," 8-Ball corrected. "Double D is back from Iran but not with us. The Company still has a burn notice on him, and he is on the Most Wanted by the F.B.I."

"That is true, but he is still in his right mind occasionally and passes on the information we can't get otherwise," I said and waited for confirmation, but none came. "The big State Department Iranian mole in S. America is terminated. That came from Double D."

I am the only one that is not C.I.A., and I do not have the restrictions they do. Jane and John obviously have a vow of silence to protect their voice recognition. Jane came back in and returned the DVD and diary to Jack with notes attached. The serpent's smile returned.

"Iris Anne has opened a new window of opportunity for us. She truly was brilliant Jack said.

"Is this encrypted text legally submissive in a court of law?" I asked.

Jane nodded in the affirmative.

"Gentlemen, we have LIFTOFF!" Jack showed excitement. "Jane is a linguist expert and Iris has nailed Gillard and James with the crime of rape. The video shows the girl's signed consent to be filmed agreement. She gave her date of birth, and she is seventeen, not eighteen. Federally, any sex with a child is rape. In her text, she states that Gillard and James were in the studio and watched her being raped. They brought the girl and the video back to a Merritt Island motel and forced Iris Anne to make copies. Then Gillard and James raped her friend and Iris Anne."

"Is there anything on Serena and Sabrina, the two girls murdered before Iris Anne?" I asked hopefully. "We know that Double D is connected to those murders, but we do not know if he did the murders."

Jane shook her head no.

"Gillard dressed like Smokey the Bear in a Cocoa parade and pointed out Serena to an Iranian. We have it on tape and a little witness. She identified the voice, and the way Gillard walks. Double D reported the Muslim girls were murdered exactly like the Christian girls were murdered in Iran by ISIS," I them.

"We know Double D murdered two Muslim sympathizers in New York. He held them responsible for the murder of his wife, son, and daughter from the Twin Towers attack," 8-Ball said sadly. "He was the best hacker in the world."

Too Tall finally spoke, "It was Double D who hacked into the Iranian Colonel's radio transmissions and made our escape possible. I can't fault him unless he murdered the girls. I still don't believe he did." He gave his shy look around the circle. "I asked our Company director why we didn't have a burn notice on those two in New York and the Iranian Colonel. I am not popular with our director."

My scramble phone blinked. The text read, "I have escaped. Don't pay the ransom. DD." I am amazed. "Glory! The circle is unbroken."

I showed the text to Jack, he shrugged his shoulders and said, "Our sixth man is alive if not well."

I looked around our circle of blue light and asked, "Is there anything else we need to discuss or add to our gathering?"

I looked each one in the face, "Then again, let me say words cannot express my gratitude to each of you. I never expected to meet with all of you when I paid a young black hustler to call our Uncle Richard."

All around the circle nodded and even Too Tall, the human chameleon, smiled his shy grin. Jack killed the blue light. One by one we all departed to the Company cars. 8-Ball was behind the wheel and Jack in the jump seat. I sat in the back behind Jack. Da Ja Vue.

"Commander, the F.B.I. will not withdraw the arrest warrant and our Agency will not lift the terminate notice on Double D by direct order of the President. The powers-that-be are covering their behinds and fear offending Iran and their allies Russia and China. Russia is amassing troops along the Ukrainian border again and China has violated Taiwan's air space with several aircraft as we speak. It is clear they do not fear the politicians but the loss of billions of dollars in trade," Jack spoke in his nothing but the voice of the facts.

"We have not brought our evidence to a prosecuting attorney for that reason, and we do not want the defense to know what we have on the suspects. We do not want to tip off the suspects until we can arrest them," I paused before I mentioned, "Double D texted earlier that he has located 'Mother,' the baby mole, double agent, recently on Iranian desk State Department in Iran."

It was clear neither 8-Ball nor Jack knew and that means the C.I.A. didn't know either or was hiding it.

"We have had a long but very successful day. Iris Anne's disk and diary are the ANNE FRANK diary for our side. We must be more careful now than ever. I will try to interview Sgt. James now that the Chief knows I am a county deputy. Goodnight."

Jack and 8-Ball said goodnight in unison. I eased out of their car and into mine. The bed will feel great tonight.

CHAPTER 30

THANKSGIVING MORNING ARRIVED in a perfect setting for Cocoa, Florida. The sun forms its keyhole as it rises above my beautiful Indian River Lagoon. A southeastern breeze smells of salt spray and gently moves the limbs and Spanish moss on the live oak trees in my front windows. My bacon and eggs and grits are ready. A special breakfast to celebrate Thanksgiving and the excellent work on our cases yesterday by Zany and the remaining Dirty Dozen team members. My taste buds are singing. Bacon is crisp. Eggs over medium. Stone-ground grits need a little more butter and salt. Raisin bread toast with home-made apple butter courtesy of Prudence, my housekeeper. It has been a long time coming, but my spirits are soaring. I antici-pate closure for my wife and the three girls murdered in Cocoa, My Beloved.

"Good morning, Zany," I almost sing into the cell phone. "Yes, I am bright-eyed and bushy-tailed, as my Uncle Rob used to say."

Zany said, "Bushy-tailed?"

"Yes. We were squirrel hunters in season. Just the thought of going hunting in Pocahontas County, West Virginia, brought me wide-eyed awake," I explained.

"I am still buzzed from yesterday's success," Zany sounded excited more this morning than yesterday. "I am looking forward to going to Church with you. What time will you pick me up?"

"Services start at 11 A.M. so I will pick you up around 10:30 A.M.," I answered. "Most of the people dress modestly. Pastor Jerimiah said the pew Gus and I sat in is still available for us. I miss Gus. Happy Thanksgiving."

"Happy Thanksgiving, Rock," she said.

Immediately, my gadget and scramble phone buzzed, the belt gadget text said, "Beware of Greeks offering Gifts today. Suit up." My scramble phone voice said, "New information received. There is something up. Be Aware."

So much for dressing modestly. This navy-blue suit and white shirt will do nicely over the one-piece bullet-proof body shirt. 1911 pistol in belly holster, S&W pistol snug in the ankle holster, and my trusty K-Bar knife are all in place. My military patten leather shoes complete my Thanksgiving "Beware" outfit.

I text on my scramble phone and belt gadget: "Going to pick up Zany @ 10:30, and we are going to West Side Community Church. Should be out around noon." I close the window drapes and check the hall door to the fire escape. It is secure, and I am sure the team members still here are on station and ready for anything. There is something extra today my mind is saying. I feel no alarm.

It is 10:30 A.M. and as I park near the Porcher House rear entrance, a couple with a young girl are coming out of the back door. I will wait before I go in. The well-dressed couple walked by, and the girl opens my passenger door. ZANY!

She has on a light blue dress and shoulder-length blond hair. It must be a wig. She is wearing white stockings, matching black patent leather pump shoes, and a purse hanging from her shoulder. It is large enough for her lady's Smith and Weston thirty-eight special and other necessary stuff. It is not a disguise; it is a normal Zany.

"Hi, Rock," she says with her bouncy smile.

"Hi, Zany," I respond but can't get over how much she looks like a teenager.

I will not mention her modest dress, so she won't mention my well-padded modest best black suit. My mind flashes to the night I slipped into that back door soaking wet from my midnight swim after being shot at near the parking lot restroom door.

"I received some more information on our big case, but it can wait until after Church," Zany told me. "You look spiffy, I must say. The MAN IN BLACK."

She giggled as she buckled up for safety, and we were on our way to Thanksgiving Church service. Bumper-to-bumper traffic and the sidewalks were packed with pedestrians. Many were dressed in their Sunday best and headed to nearby Churches and the early lunch crowd. I had hoped to arrive early to sit in the pew that Gus and I sat in so many times.

Up to U.S. 1 through town and left on King Street West was congested with slow driving tourists. My mind flashes again as we slowly pass the spot where the Iranian Colonel murdered my Natasha. Also, the day Sgt. James tried to arrest me for speeding past the police station following Sheriff Woodall to the crime scene of our second murdered child, Sabrina More. I am lost in thought and wonder how the mothers of Serena and Sabrina are on this Thanksgiving Day. Zany is unusually quiet.

"This is my first time to this Church, Rock. You will have to tell me what to do; please whisper," she wrinkled her nose and made a full face. "I am nervous."

I found a place behind the Church between two business buildings. It is five minutes before 11 A.M. Oh well, we tried. A deacon welcomed Zany and me as we walked through the double doors.

He said politely, "Please follow me."

I received two surprises. Where Gus and I sat in the pew five rows was closed by a tasseled yellow visitor's ribbon near the middle aisle. The deacon removed the ribbon and ushered Zany and me into Gus's same seat. Seated near Zany was the small black boy who made my lifeline call to the C.I.A. at Starving Marvin's, and I met Gator. The child flashes the same toothy grin, but he is not wearing his one strap over the shoulder-bibbed overalls. He has a black suit. I did not know his name.

I see Pastor Jerimiah walk slowly down the center aisle, followed by the choir. He smiled at Zany and me as he passed by. He sat down in one of two cushioned chairs to the right of the pulpit on the raised platform. Fall arrangement flowers were on "The Lord's Table" in front of the pew. The choir took their places in rows behind the podium. The Church organ player began playing softly as other people filed in and was seated.

Glancing sideways at Zany, I see she is still unusually fidgetily with her fingers folding and unfolding on her lap. My heart goes out to her as the child Natasha and I never had. I am resolved to pay attention to this Thanksgiving service and be thankful.

I glance around at the people seated to the side and behind us. I see no one I recognize. I thought John Henry and his sister would be here, and maybe Solomon. I also hoped the mothers of Serena "Rene" and Sabrina would be here. I am not a regular attendee, but I have begun to accept these as my friends. I miss Natasha and Gus, especially today.

The overhead lights dimmed, and the organ music began a livelier hymn. Pastor Jerimiah moved behind the podium wearing a black college graduation robe.

"Welcome to West Side Church and especially our visitors on this fine Thanksgiving morning. Today is truly our Lord's Day. Let us rejoice and be glad in it."

He is making several announcements as I whisper to Zany, "We will stand for a congressional hymn or two and then be seated."

I picked a hymnal from the back of the pew in front of us and laid Gus' Bible between us.

"Please stand while we give praise to our Lord in singing," Pastor Jerimiah said as he raised his outstretched hands and the congregation rose. His choir director turned to face the choir.

Over his headset came, "Please turn to page 187." The two couples next to us put their hymnals back in the holder. I see why they did that when I turned to page 187 to the hymn by John Newton, "Amazing Grace." The auditorium is in full voice as only black people can sing. Zany and I were so amazed we forgot to sing. The atmosphere was charged with an electricity-like feeling. Zany is no longer fidgety, she is trance-like.

The choir director said, "Please be seated."

I placed the hymnal back in the holder, and we sat down.

"We have a special couple singing a special hymn of thanks," the choir director said.

Coming through a side door by the pastor, a handsome man and a beautiful woman picked up handheld mikes, and sang the hymn, "Thank You, Lord."

"Surely our Lord is in this place," the pastor said. "Let us pray."

"The enemy is the Devil! Working through his fallen angels, humans, and even animals," Jerimiah shouted.

There were several amens among the congregation.

"We watch while Satan tears down our government, our families, and our fellowship with our Lord," he continued. "But greater is He (he pointed straight up) in us than he, the Devil. The Devil brought sin and sickness into this world, and humanity is infected. We are born sinners, and all of us have sinned against God. But praise is unto God; He sent His Son into this sin-cursed world to pay the price for our redemption. Jesus the Christ died on the Cross of Calvary. That is the only remedy for our lost souls. Satan tempted Adam and Eve to willingly sinned against the known will of God. Jesus paid every human's price for redemption and making it possible to be saved. Hearing the Word of God brings this truth, and by believing Jesus died for our sin, and rose from the dead on the third day, and ascended back to His Father gets us found from being lost."

There is complete silence in the congregation. You could hear a pin drop. I do not remember any other West Side Church services like this one. My notebook is out, and I am taking notes. I don't know if I will print it in the *Village Voice* or keep it personal. Zany is looking up when the Pastor speaks, but she is reading a small paper in the hymnal.

Jerimiah is holding up his open Bible. He is walking back and forth as he reads it out loud. I didn't get the book of the Bible, but I wrote down, "For all have sinned, and come short of the glory of God. For the wages of sin is death, but the gift of God is eternal life through Jesus Christ our Lord." I missed some of what he said as I hear Zany crying. I noticed the lady next to her was praying, then it occurred to me this is the same feeling I had in our Church in West Virginia at the age of twelve. I received

Jesus Christ and received a believer's baptism. My heart leaped, and I am beginning to pray as well. I ask the Holy Spirit to save those lost by applying the faith He gives them to believe with all their heart that Jesus Christ cleanses from all sin by His blood shed on Calvary's Cross. He rose from the dead and saved all who put faith in Him for salvation.

Pastor Jerimiah continued, but I admit I didn't get much of what he said. Next to the little boy, the lady changed seats with him and had her arm around Zany's shoulders.

I believe fifteen or twenty minutes passed before I heard the Pastor say, "Some of you need our Savior for salvation. Come to the altar. We will assist you from the Word of God to receive Christ Jesus as your personal Savior. Everyone please stand as we sing 'Just as I am, Without One Plea'."

I heard the woman ask Zany if she wanted to go to the altar with her. Zany nodded yes, and I stepped out into the aisle and walked to the altar with them. There were others already there and more on their way. We all knelt, and the ones putting their God-given faith in Jesus the Son as Savior read salvation verses from the Bible. When the last one made their profession, we all stood with a beaming Pastor Jerimiah smiling broadly at all of us. Zany had changed tears of conviction to tears of joy for knowing she now has eternal life in Christ Jesus.

Pastor Jerimiah asked us to be seated on the front row of pews and asked the congregation to come by and give the new converts the right hand of fellowship. Each of the new Christians was given a tract by Charles R. Solomon entitled: "The Wheel & Line – A Guide to Freedom Through the Cross." Zany and I were the last ones to shake hands with the Pastor as we departed. He was near tears with joy and promised to be in touch with us soon.

CHAPTER 31

HEADING FOR THE car after we shook hands with Pastor Jerimiah, Zany bounced along beside me even more than normal.

"I am so happy, Rock. I never knew I needed a Savior. I thought if I treated everyone well, God would take me to Heaven when I died. It wasn't my fault that Eve ate the forbidden tree's fruit and gave it to Adam. You know, I prayed, Now I lay me down to sleep and trusted the Lord to keep my soul and take it if I died," Zany told me with a smile.

"Now you know we are all born into the sin nature of our parents, and you believed God's Word today, and what did Jesus do?" I said, as it all came back to me like when the Deacon in West Virginia led me to a believing faith in our Savior's death for all human sin and saves all who take their place as a lost sinner and receive Jesus as Savior by faith alone. "What did the Son of God do for you today, Zany?"

"Jesus saved me. I have eternal life in the Son of God. If I should die asleep or awake, my soul He will take. I am happy, Rock. So happy," she said with such joy I had to smile.

As we turned the corner and walked toward my car, a shot rang out. I shielded Zany and backed us around the nearest building of the used car dealership next door. We cautiously moved back to the Church and entered the double doors. The auditorium was now empty. I locked the doors and called 8-Ball on my scramble phone.

"Hello, somebody nearly shot Zany and me near my car. We are back in the Church with the doors locked. Did you get a visual on the shooter?" I asked.

8-Ball answered, "The shot was mine, Commander. I spotted a sniper rifle in the open window in the building across from your car. The Ghost is on it and entering the building. Will advise. Recommend you two stay there where you are safe."

Zany is as cool as a cucumber as if nothing has happened. For the first time, I notice the lady's pistol is in her hand like my 1911 is in mine. The Pastor's study and office are open, but no one is present. His side door is locked. There are no other doors, but a lot of windows in the building.

"Zany, I am going to check the other rooms. Don't open either door unless you hear me. Call my cell phone if you need me," I told her. "I am so sorry for this to happen on your most special day. I'll make it up to you with Kay's Q."

"It is special, Rock, and no matter what happens, I am happy inside and out. Be careful out there and watch you six," she said. "I got that from an old T.V. show."

"I will be back soon. Let's not call anyone about this just yet. 'The walls have ears' these days, and no phone is exempt. I will have the Pastor warned by one of my team. Lock both doors when I leave."

All the windows were locked, and a service door near the slanted sidewalk for casket entrance and exit was that is usually open was closed now. There may be somebody in here with Zany and me.

"Zany, it's me," I told her through the closed door.

She unlocked the door and locked it again after I entered.

"One door was open. We may not be alone," I told her as I moved the drapes a little and looked out. The window facing an alley is large enough for us to climb out. A slight knock on the office door brings us to the door with pistols in hand.

"Miss Zany, it's me," said a small voice that sounded familiar. "I sat beside you today."

Looking at Zany, I unlocked the door, pulled the child in, quickly closed the door, and locked it.

"Remember me? I made the not-so-good black man pay-phone call for you, and Gator stole my fiver," the boy asked me.

Zany frowned as I answered, "I remember. You did very well that day. It cost me another fiver when Gator snatched the first one from you. I didn't get your name that day, though."

"It's Leroy Lincoln Jones. We are related to Serena Jones' momma. My momma went with you down the aisle today, Miss Zany," Leroy told her. "I wanted to tell you, but I heard a shot and ran into the Church through the funeral door and hid in the broom closet."

"Thank you, Leroy, and thank your momma for me," said a teary-eyed Zany.

She put the lady's S&W back in her patent leather purse. Leroy was staring at the pistol.

"We are private investigators, and the self-defense weapons are legal, like police, Leroy," she explained.

"I know Detective Romano. He is our friend and is trying to find the man that murdered my cousin, Serena. He asked my momma about the 'traffic' one day."

He laughed and asked, "Did you shoot a while ago?"

"No. Someone else did, but no one was hurt," I answered and sensed Leroy knew more but didn't understand human trafficking.

I knew Detective Romano is on the human trafficking task force. I am a volunteer on the task force as well. Representatives from all law enforcement departments, federal to city, serve on the task force. There is another task force on the west coast based in Tampa.

"Did any other officer ask your momma questions about the trafficking?" I asked Leroy.

"Yeah. About a week later, but they were coppers and had police uniforms and pistols like yours," Leroy answered staring at my 1911. "I think they are silly. My momma doesn't know much about traffic. They asked about Serena's momma, too. They are sisters in the Lord and have the same Daddy. Rene played with me even though she was older. We all miss her."

"Did Rene ever mention the police in uniforms that visited your momma?" Zany asked him.

"Yeah. On the park merry-go-round. Rene called one a creepy copper, and he heard her. He called her a 'black dog baby bitch' and his partner laughed. Creep's neck got all red," Leroy told us.

My belt gadget reminded me that texting was incoming. "Ghost has sniper. The coast is clear."

"It's time to leave. Let us take you home, Leroy," I told him.

Leroy shook his head negatively and said, "I am staying with my aunt near the Church."

I let Leroy out and he went back out the funeral door. I locked it, and then Zany and I went out the front doors.

When we arrived at the Porcher House office, Zany said, "I am not in the mood for Kay's Q. I would really like to bring you up to date on our big case. My source in CPD gave me a written transcript just received stating the other identities of Lt. Gillard. We knew about the Texas Gillard being sexually abused by his stepfather, and Gillard is wanted for child and animal abuse. The other identity is new. Gillard is wanted in Laredo, Texas, and connected with human trafficking through Mexico. He received training in false identity and computer hacking from mafia traffickers. They gave him his 'three lives'."

"I apologize for not trusting your source. That fills in the background on our 'I led three lives' dirty copper reference from his phone call to me," I said.

"There is more. Norman Stanley Silverman is livid. He discovered his father's secret files connecting him to Lt. Gillard and Sgt. James and has been in human trafficking for years. He has names and proof of money received and dispersed from mafia families to defend their members charged with human trafficking and the pornographic work in Florida. Norman was crying when calling me. He said, 'My daddy got my sister Iris Anne killed and her girlfriend has gone missing now, too'."

"WOW! That is big, Zany," I said.

"I made an appointment to meet Norman at the boat rental where you first met him at 2 P.M. today. He is bringing all the files, and he is scared," Zany told me.

"Let's go now, Zany. He is in great danger," I said as I stood and prepared to leave. "The same thing that got his sister and her friend in a life-and-death blackmailing threat is now on

Norman's head. His fourteen-year-old sister and her seven-teen-year-old friend paid the price for all this."

We departed through the back door. I realized those files are what Lt. Gillard threatened to expose her father with and kept Iris Anne silent and compliant. The video we saw and her notes in the diary explained her older girlfriend was set up on a dare to apply for a "modeling" photoshoot in Fort Lauderdale. She lied about her age and residence on the consent form when she arrived. She used a fake I.D. Lt. Gillard is connected to the porno company and learned she was there. He called her and threatened to expose her boyfriend as his drug pusher on their high school campus. He is eighteen and would go to jail or prison. The girl agreed to do a full pornographic video to save her boyfriend.

We arrived at the boat rental at 1:30 P.M. As we entered the room where I called from to try and save the wounded manatee, Natasha and the child murderers' demon flashed the scenes to my mind. Now I know they tried to frame Norman dressing in the white Nike tennis shoes with red shoelaces. I know an Iranian Colonel murdered my Natasha that day. Zany and I ordered cokes and sat by the window looking at the Indian River Lagoon watching for Norman.

A small speed boat was racing toward the boat rental from the south.

"Maybe Norman," I whispered to Zany. "He used a ski boat the time Natasha and I met him."

We finished our cokes and walked out on the pier. The boat was coming into view when it exploded in a ball of fire.

"Oh, my God!" exclaimed a woman walking a poodle on a leash up the pier.

She took a cell phone from her purse and snapped a photo of the mushroom cloud rising from the river where the boat was and made a call.

"A terrible accident has just happened, dear. A small boat blew up on the river near the boat rental."

We continued to watch for five minutes or so. There were no visible survivors or debris from the boat. All was gone. I glanced at Zany and held up my wristwatch. It was five minutes until 2 P.M. We got in the car and heard a pecking on the back of the vehicle. I got out, and Norman was crouching behind the car.

"We must leave immediately," he said as he slipped into the back seat and laid down.

Zany handed me the keys to her car. I adjusted the seat and started her candy apple corvette. The top is up after our shooting event earlier. We decided to change cars and come to meet Norman. I adjusted the mirror and noticed Norman was under a Zany blanket she kept on the back seat. Smart on his part. I headed toward the abandoned orange packing shed and informed 8-Ball of my intentions. I did not tell him we had a passenger.

A crowd gathered around the boat rental building as we exit onto King Street West. My scramble phone and cell phone demand my attention simultaneously. I answer the scramble first. "Cherri-o, ole chum. The sniper is confessing his crime and connections. He is a 'Goodfellow' from a Chicago family. More later."

"Thanks, Casper. I have Zany and a V.I.P. with me heading to our first meeting location. Big break."

My cell was doing a missed call and buzzing again. I have two rings.

"Hello," I answered realizing 8-Ball has changed from text to call.

"Commander, the vultures are coming to Cocoa to roost. The boat explosion was not an accident, and the woman with the poodle is one of Lt. Gillard's contacts. She made you and Zany and all bad birds know the sniper was unsuccessful at the Church. I saw your passenger. You are safe in your location. Your old employer has news."

I clicked the phone twice, and the call ended. The other call was from the Sheriff of Chatham County, Georgia. I returned his call.

It is answered immediately, and I said, "Hello, Bossman."

"I wish Rock. Breaking news. I know you are up to date on Cocoa's man with three legal identities," the Sheriff said. "The information is that he was spotted in Mexico City yesterday. An intercept by F.B.I. from one of his two contacts in the Cocoa area led to the positive I.D. Fibbers is slow to share, but Director Lawson applied the pressure, and we received it over the secure wire today. The trouble is that the man and his many associates are also sure to know. He knows we know. Watch your six, my friend."

"I will, my friend, and my old friends are here as well. I would rather be in Savannah. Zany received Jesus as her Savior today, and we are happy," I told him.

"Tell Zany I am happy for her. Bring her with you when you want your old job back, and I will give you both the right hand of fellowship and a shrimp and grits dinner," he said.

"Sounds good. The fellowship and the Georgia shrimp and grits are as good as it gets. Zany is happy with Cocoa, and I still love my little slice of Savanah also. Thanks," I said.

Norman uncovered and sat up on the back seat of the corvette and handed Zany a large bundle of files tied with red shoelaces.

"I grabbed all that was out of his safe," Norman said as he looked around. "Where are we? Dear old daddy has two goons from N.Y. or Chicago here. One left early this morning after meeting with dad and the wise guy. He was carrying a shotgun or rifle in a case."

"How did you get to the boat rental from Merritt Island?" Zany asked while speed-reading the files and showing me a computer disk.

"I slipped out with the files and hitched a ride with a neighbor that was coming to Cocoa. My friend, Eric March, said he would join me here, but he didn't show. He was bringing our ski boat. I heard the explosion and saw the fire. I'm sure it was Eric in the boat. First my sister, now my friend, dead," said Norman sadly and teared up as he put his face in his hands.

8-Ball's call broke the long silence that followed Norman's conversation. "The Sheriff's office and the Florida Marine Patrol are searching for debris in the river where the boat exploded. Our eye-in-the sky picked up the boat, but we couldn't see who was in the boat. Ghost has secured his sniper and will join me. Headed your way."

CHAPTER 32

A CONFISCATED BLACK government sedan was winding through the tall weeds toward our packing shed hideout.

"On the station," my scramble phone said and received two clicks from me in reply.

Wearing a black mask, 8-Ball motioned for me to join him, then said, "I see you have the Silverman lad. Lucky for him he was not to be in the boat. His friend Eric is being held prisoner at the Silverman castle. I see the F.B.I. was able to intercept one of your Gillard contacts messages to Gillard in Mexico City yesterday."

I told him. "Norman escaped death in the boat and brought a treasure chest of files and a disk from his daddy's safe. Zany is reading them. Norman believes his friend Eric March is dead from the boat explosion. Zany has a disk player in the office."

Norman nods. He is listening with his earbud. A familiar white van is approaching. It is the one Jack used to haul his Muslim captives to the Church near Gatorland, west of Titusville.

"Bring the disk, Commander," 8-Ball said as he pointed at a disk player in the dashboard.

I nodded and motioned to Zany to roll down her window. I took the files and disk from Zany. Neither she nor Norman spoke. I slipped into the back seat of 8-Ball's car and handed him the files and the disk.

All three vehicles were now side by side facing toward the loading ramp and the access road. I can barely see Jack through the tinted passenger window. He is wearing a black cloth mask and appears to be alone. As he walked over to 8-Ball's car, he is talking on a handheld phone with a long antenna and carrying a rifle case.

"Lo, chaps," Jack quips, in rare form again.

He removed a 308 rifle with a scope from its case and said, "A mob hitman held this."

He pointed toward 8-Ball and continued, "But our hitman is better."

He rubbed 8-Ball's bald head as he got into the front seat, "You now have a camouflaged rifle to add to your confiscated car, my friend."

"It is great to see our dynamic duo back in business," I said with a smile. "Can you play the Silverman disk for us 8-Ball?"

"No. I am making a copy. It is not audio; it is a video. There is a video player in the trunk and a copy machine. I will copy those files also," he said as he got out and opened the trunk.

Jack and I joined Zany and Norman as we waited for 8-Ball to set up his equipment. I sat in the driver's seat of the corvette and Jack sat in the back next to Norman.

"Norman, did you read the files and watch the video disk?" I asked him.

"I read a page but didn't watch the video," Norman answered. "I knew it was written records of money transactions. I know the notes were in my father's handwriting. I saw Lieutenant Gillard's name. That's all I needed to grab the files and disk and run. I am so angry he did business with that murderer!"

"The good news is your friend Eric March is alive at your house. Do you have any idea who was driving the ski boat?" I asked him.

Norman was near tears and quiet for a minute before he said, "Eric is alive? I gave him the key to the boat. I asked him to meet me at the boat rental where we met you and the woman."

"Have you seen the two goons, as you called them, before Norman?" Zany asked. "Could one of the guards have been driving the boat?"

"Yes, I've seen those two and others like them. They have been coming for years. Our father kept Iris Anne, me, and my mother away from them before the divorce. We were not allowed to be in the office or talk with any of father's clients. No. The guards were not allowed to drive the ski boat, yacht, or sailboat," he answered, as he glanced sideways at Jack, wearing a black mask with a pistol on his belt.

Jack scribbled a note and handed it to Zany.

She read it aloud, "Did any Cocoa police officers ever visit your father at home or his Cocoa or Melbourne offices? Any people you recognized by name or photo will greatly help our capture of her murderer and our child pornography case against them."

"There were a lot of visitors in and out of our house and the offices. My father owns numerous buildings in those cities and other places overseas. The renters pay mostly by computer to bank accounts. My father's cocktail parties are famous for elected officials, bankers, insurance agents, police, and the like," said Norman as he tried to think of any he had recognized.

Jack scribbled another note for Zany.

She asked, "Were there ever any underaged boys and girls there?"

"Not at the cocktail parties which were for local business-people. Iris Anne didn't invite her friends to family outings, but sometimes they came anyway. Especially the seniors like her best friend and her boyfriend liked to crash the parties."

8-Ball beeped the car horn lightly.

"We will be right back," I told Zany and Norman as Jack and I headed over to the sedan.

8-Ball had the disk player set up. It started with a popular song as Sgt. James led a young girl into a well-known Merritt Island motel, followed by Lt. Gillard. She had a large backpack on her back, and she was crying.

The young girl entered a motel room. A brief selfie camera shoot showed a masked man behind a movie camera. Then Iris Anne entered the room, ran to her friend, and hugged her. The next shot showed the girl in a cheerleader's uniform and a ribbon in her hair sitting on the foot of a queen-size bed. Lt. Gillard sat beside her and slowly began to undress her and himself. They make a pornographic video with Sgt. James.

There was a pause, and then Iris Anne reluctantly takes off her school clothes and puts on a private Brevard County girl's elementary school uniform. There is brief nudity. The popular music begins playing softly. Then, Lt. Gillard undressed her from behind, turned her around, and laid her on her back. He raped her, and then Sgt. raped her. He put her uniform back on, and made her smile for the camera. Her fully dressed friend joined them, smiling. It is easy to see they were forced smiles. Iris Anne's tear-streaked face showed through the makeup.

The next scene showed Iris Anne making copies of the videos and handing them to Lt. Gillard. Grinning, he placed them into brown paper mailers. Then the filming continued with them leaving the motel, entering the white van, shooting through the front window, and finally heading down South Tropical Trail.

"Somebody should hang these two in the public square!" 8-Ball exclaimed.

"We have enough to charge and convict them on numerous counts. Rape, trafficking, unlawful sexual activity with minors, possession of child pornography, and distribution of child pornography, for starters," Jack said. "We must be careful with lawyers. The defense will undoubtedly try to get the videos thrown out because there was no court-issued search warrant to obtain the files and videos. Money is no problem for these people. They will hire the top barristers, ole boy, and get the most liberal judge possible."

"We need a safe place for our star witness," I said. "I do not trust Federal, State, or County protective custody. Does the Company have a 'black hole' in the states? I will stay with him until I can turn him over to someone you two bring."

Jack and 8-Ball exchanged glances, "The C.I.A. has such places, but can we hold an underaged child? I will show you a safe house, Commander. Our team will keep watch until we can make arrangements for the lad."

8-Ball looked at Jack, and each nodded.

Then he handed me a mask and said, "Ghost has guests."

Jack took us to the rear of the van. When Jack unlocked and slid the back door open, a poodle dog barked.

A man and a woman were bound with ski masks over their faces. I recognized the woman's dress from the boat rental pier. Jack slid the door shut and locked it. No one spoke.

We walked a short distance, and Jack said, "We have this, mate. 8-Ball and I will go over this with Jane and John. He held up the files and video disk. I would be surprised if we can't find a trail including terrorists from Iran money exchanged. Lawyer Edward R. Silverman may have been careless enough to get himself convicted if not killed. We will keep in touch."

We shook hands and returned to our respective automobiles. Zany was still on the passenger side, and Norman sat wide-eyed in the back. I started the car and headed out first. We came to the U.S. one, and I turned south toward Melbourne. I keep a room in what used to be the Oleander Hotel in Eau Gallie before Melbourne annexed it. I will place Norman there for a few hours. I know team members will be on the watch.

CHAPTER 33

THE HOTEL HADN'T changed much since I was a child fishing for speckled trout off the city of Eau Gallie pier. I registered at the front desk and went to my room as usual. Zany parked the corvette behind the building and entered Norman's new room without seeing anyone. She brought the files and disk and handed them to me.

"Make yourself at home, Norman," I told him. "The two men you saw earlier are undercover agents working on the case of your sister, my wife, and two other girls. They are employees of our government. Our lives are in danger. The names and actions of the persons in these files and the video are all we need to charge and convict them of serious crimes. Some of them would kill us to get these files. This room is secure for now. Our friends guard it, but I will move you to a safer location soon."

Norman broke his silence and asked, "How do you know my friend is alive at my house? I gave him the keys to the boat and asked him to meet me in Cocoa. Is my sister in those files and on that video? I want to see all that we have about her. We fought like brothers and sisters do, but we loved each other."

He walked to a chair and sat down with his face in his hands, "I miss Iris Anne and my mother. It would be best if you found my mother. She is in danger, I'm sure. I have no idea where she is, though."

"We will find Mrs. Silverman, Norman, but you must stay in this room with the door locked. No one is to know you are here. No contacts or phone calls until I get back, okay?" I warned him.

"Sure, Mr. Tyler. I understand. You and Miss Zany are the only ones I trust now. How long will you be gone?" Norman asked.

"About an hour," I answered. "I will bring you something from the kitchen and then I will be back in one hour. Please don't leave this room or let anyone in but me. Don't answer the phone if it rings or the red-light flashes a message. No one is to know you are here. Our enemies are well connected and have powerful friends in high positions."

I ordered a hamburger and fries from the kitchen on the room phone, "I'll pick it up at the front desk. Thanks."

The burger and fries were at the front desk five minutes later. I thanked the receptionist, signed it to have it charged to my room. I delivered the meal to Norman and went out the back door.

Zany was in the corvette on the driver's side.

"I'm almost tempted to ask, what's a nice Christian girl like you doing in a place like this," I said, smiling at her. "We need to get back to the office and act normally if that is possible."

"There is nothing normal about either of us, Rock," she said as she patted the folder containing files and video disk. "What do we do with these?"

"My associates made copies of the files and the disk. They are safer with them than being in a vault in Fort Knox," I said. "I can't say the same for us. Lt. Gillard is the worst of the worst criminals. He has so many contacts, it is just a matter of time before they know we have Norman and the files. They will kill to get them back."

"I am almost tempted to see how fast this corvette can run up I-95. We can get your car and disappear, but I guess that is not acting normal," Zany said as she turned north on I-95. "What about Norman?"

"Norman is safe. Look in your mirror at the black car two cars behind us. The driver is the best bodyguard there is in and out of government. We will make our appearance at Kay's for BBQ, and he will watch our backs. When asked, no one will have seen Norman with us. My other associate will have a safe place for Norman and us shortly. He will have all our evidence secured by now."

Scrabble phone texted, "Evidence secured. Two earlier subjects in Company housing. Will last subject accompany you two into new facilities?"

I text back. "Yes. We need to stick together until we have people identified who are a threat and suspects located. We are ten clicks out." I clicked twice. The sign said Cocoa 6 miles.

My belt gadget buzzed. "We hear you. Yes, I bugged the corvette. Ole boy—good news and bad. Lt. Gillard is in Brevard County. The bad is we don't know where. The Marine patrol found DNA of Edward R. Solomon in the river under the exploded boat. The second mob guy is still holding Eric March in the Silverman estate. We are watching and listening."

Zany parked beside my car in the back lot. It looks no worse, but it is bugged and watched by our team, I am sure.

Zany checked out our P. I. office and answered our answering machine. She brought us a change of clothes and a large bag of assorted things. We both drove to Kay's B-Q.

We parked side by side near a garbage dumpster in clear view from the windows to sit and eat as usual. We walked in together and received a hearty welcome from the waitresses. I look at every person and see nobody's body language to question. Our waitress is quick to bring our menus. One look at the smiling Zany and I ordered our Q and fries as usual. My back is to the wall, and I can watch the cars.

A familiar black sedan passed by. I glanced at a new car arriving and parking beside Zany and my vehicles. 8-Ball's sedan, I know, but I can't place the new car. The driver is sitting and making no effort to get out. I see the seat is high, and the sun visor is down, blocking the face. A black turtleneck shirt could be body armor. Our food arrived, and I asked for the check. There are three regular customers and no law enforcement present—a significant change from the old days. We finished our meals silently, and I paid the bill at the entrance.

Zany visited with Kay and the waitresses with her usual banter, and then she moves them back to the lady's room as we agreed beforehand. I called on the scrambled phone. "Do you have a visual on the car parked by Zany's corvette?"

"I have a scope on the driver. It is male with a Covid-19 black cloth mask. Could you give me the front tag state and number? I have the whole parking lot in view."

"Thanks, 8-Ball." I signaled Zany to stay with the waitresses and moved to peep out the window. "VICTOR ALPHA 19003, I can't see the smaller print. But it's Vets."

A minute passed, and 8-Ball texted, "It's Veterans Affairs." Another minute passed and, he texted, "Subject is on the move. He is headed inside and walks like a well-trained gorilla."

I watched him, and he seemed vaguely familiar when he entered the front door. He saw me and motioned me back to the table Zany and I shared. I can see the pistol on his belt.

He takes my place with his back to the brick wall, then said, "We met on the yacht and worked the terrorists' cases as a team. I'm still here. The others are gone. I am looking for your most wanted, the scum bag police officer, and a couple of good fellows. Your *ghost* has one, and the other is holed-up in Silverman's place."

"I didn't know you were here or working for the Department of Veterans Affairs. Are you connected?" I asked and watched him start to shake.

Then he let out a gravelly-voiced laugh, "Not anymore. I have wise guy status if you mean my former family. The ride is a loaner."

"I meant connected to my old team members, but it is nice to know you are on our side," I said.

I glanced at Zany. She winked. I nodded for her to head back to Norman.

Bisco, the off-the-books C.I.A. terminator, smiled and said, "I am still on terrorists' lookout, but I am a loner to your team. We communicate as needed. I know you have an asset and dynamite evidence. I wanted you to know how things stand. I hate the former dirty cops, Lt. Gillard, and his lackey, Sgt. James. I have a teenage daughter."

"It is nice to have you with us," I tell him as we shake hands, and I wave to the waitresses on the way out.

I fear he looks better with the mask. I catch Zany on I-95. 8-Ball is two cars behind, and we will be with Norman right on time if all goes well.

CHAPTER 34

Z ANY HEADED BACK to Norman and found him alive and well and sound asleep. She texted me she had left him a note and was on her way back to Cocoa. I thanked her and said I'd meet her in the morning before I interviewed Sgt. James. We had a busy day coming up and both needed some sleep as well. I, too, made it to the apartment and slept like a baby.

"Good morning, Deputy Tyler. Your full uniform is ready. Sheriff Woodall will meet you for breakfast at 9 A.M.," my answering machine in the *Village Voice* office greeted me. My large wall clock, courtesy of Zany Adams, struck 8 A.M.

Following that message, the machine said, "Deputy Tyler, your interview is set for 10 A.M. today in the Chief's office." There are several merchants' messages, mostly Christmas advertising.

My cell phone text came in saying: "Your 10 A.M. interview with Sgt. James moved from the Cocoa Police Department. The subject is under Witness Protection. New Location. Viera Office at Moore Justice Center (Viera Courthouse): 2825 Judge Fran Jamieson Way."

I had received the witnesses' statements courtesy of Chief Brody and Sheriff Woodall. Sgt. James was ready to come clean with his involvement with the former Lt. Gillard. His court-appointed lawyer was trying to get his charges reduced by the Prosecuting Attorney.

"Greetings, Deputy Tyler. Do you prefer to change your civilian P. I. clothing into our outstanding Deputy Sheriff's uniform in your office or the McDonald's restroom at 9 A.M.?" asked Sheriff Woodall, in rare form this morning.

"McDonald's is best. I promised Zany I would meet her in our lowly Private Investigator's office this morning. I'm on my way there now," I answered. "I will share with Zany the information I obtained recently in the Serena and Sabrina cases. The Brevard County Homicide Unit information is courtesy of detectives from Rockledge. The Sheriff's detectives were also very helpful with information on the copycat murder of a case they solved earlier."

"Good morning, Zany. I trust you got a good night's sleep. I slept like a log," I greeted her.

She was dressed to the nines, "You look especially well-dressed."

"I did sleep straight through the night and woke up in the same position I fell to sleep. The dress is the new me. I used some of Silverman's money," she said, as she giggled and struck a modeling pose.

"I'm on my way for breakfast with the Sheriff, then to get Sgt. James' statement. He is informing on Lt. Gillard. I have spreadsheets on the first two murdered girls. The detectives from the Sheriff's Department in Rockledge gave us all they have," I told her.

Zany handed me a suit bag with zipper pockets to change into the deputy sheriff uniform and our tape recorder and legal pad with pens, and said, "More Silverman money for my junior partner."

"Thank you, Senior Partner. You know this might be dirty laundered mafia or human trafficking money. He hired Zany Investigations for appearance. He knew who used his daughter to hack and make copies of pornographic videos. The straw that broke the camel's back was when he got the video of Lt. Gillard and Sgt. James, raping his fourteen-year-old daughter and her friend, Erica March," I said.

"I know our client is dirty, but his money spends all the same. He has a lot of it, and he will have the best legal defense possible. Sgt. James is lawyered up and will give you only a statement that does not incriminate him. I know you have interviewed high-profile witnesses before but be careful. You two have history," she warned me.

"The parameters have been set. Sgt. James' lawyer knows we will not discuss my prior contact with Sgt. James or Lt. Gillard. Someone will record the interview on tape and in a camcorder. I will write out the questions and answers. Sgt. James and his lawyer will read it and make changes or add more as needed. I will submit his statement, typed out, and signed for court-admissible evidence," I explained.

McDonald's for breakfast brings back memories of terrorist's days. The threat level is not as high, but it is still there.

Russia and China are saber-rattling again against Ukraine, Georgia, and Taiwan. Russia is demanding the prevention of Ukraine and Georgia's sovereign states from becoming members of NATO. China is repeatedly violating Taiwan's airspace.

I spot the Sheriff's very marked, unmarked car with a few dings and multiple aerials. I am parking my shiny auto beside it for comparison. The Sheriff and Chief Brody are sitting by the entrance door. The Sheriff hands me an official Sheriff's Department green suit bag. I take it into the bathroom and change into my deputy sheriff's uniform. Yes, I have a flashback to my days with Chatham County Sheriff's Department. The uniform is a perfect fit.

"Welcome to the real world of investigation, Deputy Toby Rockwell Tyler. My, he looks spiffy, wouldn't you say, Chief?" the Sheriff asked with a smile.

"Deputy Tyler does, indeed. A brand-new suit with a regulation sidearm. Spiffy!" Chief Brody laughed.

"Turn around for us, Deputy. As I suspected, 1911 backup. Lift your left trouser leg, Deputy. There is the S&W 38," Chief said, frowning.

"No K-Bar knife? How disappointing," the Sheriff added.

I lifted my right trouser leg to show the K-Bar.

"You will fill the basket at the Courthouse check-in," Sheriff commented. "Our court deputy is authorized to carry his weapons, and he will escort you to the interview room. He greets everyone with, 'Welcome to the Criminal Justice System and another day in paradise!'"

I arrived at the Courthouse thirty minutes early after a quick breakfast with Sheriff Woodall and Chief Brody. I unloaded all my metal in the car and removed my cuff key from the keyring and my pocket change. My tape recorder, pens, and wedding ring were placed in the basket, and I passed through with no problem.

Sure enough, I was greeted by an armed deputy who said, "Welcome to the Criminal Justice System and another day in paradise."

"Thank you and hello from the retired deputy, Sam, who worked with you here in the Courthouse," I said.

He frowned and then said, "Yes, I remember Sam."

We walked down the long corridor to the interview room. I took a seat in front of the room assigned for the lawyer, Sgt. James, and me. Fifteen minutes passed and he returned with Sgt. James cuffed and ankles chained. His lawyer was escorted by two more armed deputies. I followed them into the room and watched the deputies chain Sgt. James to bolts on the concrete floor. His lawyer sat beside him facing my chair across the long table and the camcorder. I took my seat and turned on my recorder and the camcorder.

"Good morning. This interview will be recorded, and Sgt. James' statement will be typed and signed for official use in the court of law. We are all familiar with this procedure, so I will ask Sgt. James to state his full name, date of birth, if he is making his statement of his one free will, etc. Sergeant, you and your attorney will have the opportunity to read the paper statement, listen to the recordings, and make any corrections or additions if necessary," I explained.

"I did not know you were a deputy, Mr. Tyler," Sgt. James said.

"Sgt. James, we are not to discuss prior contacts. We will obtain your written statement for future court appearances only. Are you comfortable with that?" I asked.

Sgt. James looked at his attorney and nodded yes.

"You must answer all the questions with your voice. You are encouraged to volunteer information at any time during the interview. You have agreed to testify against former Lieutenant Gillard. He will stand trial under several charges. So be as specific as you can," I instructed.

"We understand deputy Tyler. My client said, yes," his attorney said, showing negative body language and a defensive posture.

"Sgt. James, what can you tell the court about your relationship with Lt. Gillard? Please report all details no matter how small they may appear," I said.

The interview lasted for over an hour. Sgt. James' attorney struck a few comments that might incriminate his client. However, the former policeman provided detailed information that would convince any jury of the former Lt. Gillard raping two juveniles, receiving money from human traffickers both foreign and domestic, and his association with known criminals including the mafia in N.Y., Chicago, Mexico, and Iran. His attorney had coached him well.

CHAPTER 35

"SUBJECT IN YOUR room is on the balcony with a female. Moving to intercept any visitors other than our team." The phone clicked twice.

"We are near my room. Zany and one team member are in our caravan." I am texting our Ghost. "Do you have a safe place for two males and two females?"

"I have prepared places for all parties, ole boy. All government officers focus on capturing suspects and do not want to share the glory. But we have better toys than they have. Lt. Gillard is most wanted. Lawyer Edward R. Silverman was next wanted because he was the money man for Gillard's human trafficking and the NY Mafia."

"Gillard is here in Brevard County. We thought he was in Iran with the Colonel, the murderer of Natasha. We believe Double D eliminated the State Department mole that sold us out to the Iranian Colonel. He may be in Iran after said, Colonel. Your Company man, Bisco, has joined us and hates

Gillard and James. We are at our destination and will be ready for transport soon."

"Roger that, Commander. Let's hope we get to Lt. Gillard before the Italian Bisco does. He may have killed the Muslim captives Double D, aka Mr. Law, was holding in NY. The victims were savagely slain, like "twice baked" hits. He was with the same NY family Gillard and the Silverman wise guys. He has inside information and friends."

"We are on location. I will pick up Norman and his female friend. Zany, 8-Ball, and I will be a party of five in separate cars." He clicked on the phone twice.

8-Ball took up a position on the roof of the new building built near our hotel. I miss my old Oleander Hotel. Zany and I found Norman and his girlfriend on the balcony overlooking the river and causeway.

"I trusted you two, he shouted!" Norman put his arm around his friend. "Neither of you told me my father is dead, and the police raped Iris Anne!" he yelled like the old Norman that Natasha and I met at the boat rental. "This is Erica March, Iris Anne's friend. She has come out of hiding from the police. She told me everything you two didn't."

"You did a brave thing, Norman. Giving us the files and video was the right thing, but they contain evidence that many people would kill you for doing it. Erica, you, too, are in great danger, and they will kill you on sight. You are a prime witness and target. Let's get inside," Zany took her by the arm and led her inside.

Norman had his back to me and gripped the railing facing the Indian River. Belt gadget texting. "Get inside, sniper rifle under causeway spotted."

Norman resisted as I forced him inside.

"There is a sniper zeroing in on us," I snarled at him as a piece of plaster exploded above his head.

I locked the door. Norman began to shake as Zany led him to the couch beside Erica.

Belt gadget again. "That was close. New news, Edward R. Silverman is not dead. The boat had nobody in it when it exploded. Somebody planted the DNA. We are closing in on the sniper."

"Erica. Norman. Listen carefully to me. We are in a life-or-death time. You two are material witnesses in coming rape and murder court cases. Your safety is our priority. There will be plenty of time to review the files, video, and all those involved in those cases. Consider yourselves in protective custody."

Erica nodded affirmative, and Norman frowned. He is still rubbing the arm I used to drag him to safety.

"Norman, your father is alive," I told him.

"That's a lie!" Norman jumped up from the couch. "Erica saw the boat explode, and police found his DNA."

"Surveillance cameras picked him up at your house five minutes ago. Your brother is still alive in the house, Erica. We didn't know Eric was your brother," I paused for her response.

There was only a shrug of her shoulders as she watched Norman pacing the room.

"Unfortunately, the mob guy and at least four guards are there as well."

Zany is unusually silent. I glanced at her, and she moved her head sideways toward Erica. I nodded back.

"Erica, let's visit the little girl's room," she suggested.

"You and your spook friends have the power. Why can't you ride in on white horses and rescue my friend and father?" he asked.

"Norman, you must do as I tell you for the safety of Erica and yourself. You are in over your head and Gillard is in Brevard County. He wants your father, you, Eric, and his sister dead. Do you understand?" I told him firmly.

He shrugged his shoulders.

"We have a safe house, and the four of us are leaving under armed federal agents' protection," I said as Zany returned with Erica.

Both women showed signs of crying. Zany sat on the couch with Erica and Norman.

I texted on the scrambled phone, "We are ready for departure."

Jack texted back, "We are in two black cars in front of the building. Our sniper is still under the Eau Gallie causeway. 8-Ball has him located unless he has a submersible."

"We are headed to you," I responded.

As we started down the stairs, my mind flashed warning, precisely like it had done in my apartment in Cocoa. Something was not correct. I turned and shoved the three back into the room.

Norman almost whined, "Are we going or staying?"

I ignore him and Zany gives him her pouty down-the-nose look.

I texted, "Inside this building is not secure."

"Sit tight. We have assets inside," was the immediate return text. One minute later, "Threat neutralized, let Jane and John in."

A light tap on our door. I held 1911 in hand and turned the key. Jane and John, on either side, bring a hooded older woman wearing a print dress and large patten leather pumps with knee-high white socks.

I texted, "Assets inside with hooded woman captive." The phone clicked twice.

Our captive is bound head to toe. John practically drags the woman to a wooden chair and secures her to it quickly. He produces a K-Bar knife and slits her dress down the back. Underneath is a wetsuit, still wet. He cut away the front and found a 1911 pistol and a sniper rifle in a dripping waterproof case. A waterproof radio is beeping. John pushed the receive button. A foreign voice asks, "Mission accomplished?" John pushed talk two clicks.

Jane yanked the ski mask straight up.

Facing us is the hammer-head shark-eyed, red-necked gagged Lieutenant Gillard. Norman jumps from the couch and spits on our captive. I grab him before he can start slugging him with both doubled-up fists. Erica is shaking and begins to cry again.

I hear whirring blades of a helicopter growing more robust, and then my gadget says, "Secured. Bring the subject up." As our door opened, I have one hand over Norman's mouth and the other around his chest. Two prominent, black-masked men enter. Jane and John cut the tape and lift their masked captive. In seconds, the five are gone. I released Norman and he took a swing at me. He started cussing, so I taped his mouth shut and bound his wrists behind him.

"Zany, is Erica ready?" I asked.

When she nodded yes, I texted on the gadget, "Subjects ready for transport. We are coming through the front door." I have my 1911 in hand, and the other is holding the wrists of Norman as we walk out and enter the first black car. I see Zany has Erica in the second car. We rolled east across the Eau Gallie causeway in moments.

Norman is mumbling something. I shake my head no and grip his neck until he is quiet. Jack is the driver, and I believe

Bisco is in the passenger seat. I look back and see no black car following. My belt gadget texts, "Commander Tyler, we have your Iranian Colonel." There is static breaking up noise, then, "DD."

I texted back, "Good job, DD." My spirits soared, and I loosened my grip on Norman's neck. "Your Irish and Israeli friends are with me." The gadget clicked twice and went dead.

Before I can ask, Jack shakes his right fist in the air that tells me he also got the news. Bisco is looking first at Jack and them me. He is not a gadget member. We are on Merritt Island, headed towards Mather's Bridge and South Tropical Trail.

I remove the binding on Norman's wrists and the tape from his mouth. Norman just sat still, looking out his side window.

"Are you masked men taking me home?" he asks.

There is no reply. Norman is a subject, nothing more.

"Hey, guys, I'm on your side," he said.

A minute passed, and he shrugs.

Jack turned down a narrow trail, and we see a speed boat idling by an old abandoned wooden boat ramp. Two muscular masked men are men in black waiting in a cigar boat. I get out and open Norman's door, and he walks out the pier ahead of me. Neither man offers to help Norman get into the boat and sat down on the middle of the three seats. The man behind him provides a hand to me, and we sit together behind Norman. There is a medium chop to the river and a wind out of the southeast. I wonder if we are headed to the Presidential under-water shelter again. There are few houses along this stretch of the Banana River before it rejoins the Indian River. Our boat slows and enters a well-hidden cove. We dismount and join Zany and Erica in our underground bunker. They arrived minutes before we did.

This bunker is like the Presidential escape facilities near Cape Canaveral. It is not a command center, but it has steel vault doors and a prison-type restroom in each bedroom. May have been constructed by the same builders. Then again, this is C.I.A. and the other is Secret Service. There is no phone but a push-to-talk intercom. The door is opened from the outside. I push the talk button and ask to use a room with cell phone access. The door clicks and I open it to be greeted by one of the muscular masked men. He leads me to a small room and closes the door behind me. It has an air vent and a handle inside the door. Immediately, my cell phone and scramble phone demand my attention.

Sheriff Woodall is on my cell phone. Jack is on my scramble phone. "Hello, Casper. Nice facilities."

"Taxpayers Hideaway. The F.B.I. and the Sheriff's Department do not know we have Gillard and the Iranian Colonel. We are interviewing them as our special guests."

"The Sheriff is on my cell phone waiting for me to answer. I will not tell anyone of the captures. Everything will go through you unless you tell me personally. Our guests are high risk and Zany and I are as well. You have a wise guy and a Gillard informant woman as guests. Eric March is being held prisoner in the Silverman mansion. I will tell the Sheriff and ask him to be careful if they go in to arrest Silverman and the wise guy from N.Y." There were two clicks, and the line went dead.

"Hello, Sheriff." There was no answer.

Then a pleasant voice said, "The Sheriff has been expecting a call from you. I will put you through."

"Hello, Deputy Tyler. I am home with my significant other," there is a woman's laughter in the background. "You and Zany are in immediate danger. We have a deputy stationed outside the

Silverman residence and on the waterway in front. A mafia-connected man has been identified and is in the Silverman house. We picked up some chatter and you and Zany were mentioned. Also, fugitive Gillard is still on the loose. I am concerned for your safety. The Sgt. James statement you collected is excellent and will put Gillard away for life when we catch him."

"Thank you. Zany and I have taken precautions and are in a safe lodging. If you go into the Silverman compound be sure to get their hostage Eric March, Norman's friend. Sgt. James gave enough evidence to justify Edward R. Silverman's arrest and the threat is high enough to place him under protective custody. He will be cooperative, but the mafia man may try to kill him. I still have friends here that are watching out for Zany and me."

"That is a relief. I will keep you posted as events develop. Give my best to Zany. Goodbye," the sheriff said.

Two weeks later, Jack is visiting me in my cozy bunker room. He hands me a Ryan's pepperoni pizza and a cup of espresso. The crooked grin is back.

"I should collect $10.00 from you, but the taxpayers covered the bill. We are not in your apartment looking down on the lowly peasants scurrying like ants in their entertainment and we miss Natasha. The Gillard trial is set for next week. Security is so tight that even we do not know where it will be held. Maybe Fort Knox."

"I am surprised that the feds have not forced your Company to release Gillard into their custody. Human trafficking and sexual assault on minors are federal crimes," I muse as I take a bite of the pizza.

"Oh, they are trying, but possession is still nine-tenths of the law. Our director reminded their directors that they had bad apples in their Agencies recently and the accused was connected to them. End of discussion, so far."

CHAPTER 36

SHERIFF WOODALL'S TEAM entered the Silverman enclave from all sides and from the air. The loudspeaker blasted: "Come out with your hands in the air, and no harm will come to you. Everyone present is under arrest."

The Sheriff's unmarked car is parked in front of the house. At least twenty deputies are converging on the house and other buildings.

Two armed guards are coming out of the building with their hands over their heads. Two deputies quickly disarm them and cuff their hands behind them. Mr. Silverman leads Eric March out with one hand over his head and the other around the boy's shoulders. Four deputies find the N.Y. hitman hiding in the Silverman's yacht. He is disarmed and cuffed. The garage doors slide up, and the last guards come out unarmed and are cuffed.

The Sheriff approached Silverman and said firmly, "Mr. Silverman, I have a warrant to search all of your premises."

After Sheriff Woodall reads them all their rights, they are placed separately in waiting vans. I can see and hear everything from the helicopter circling overhead. Sheriff Woodall had sent a message to Mr. Silverman and told him Lt. Gillard was back in Brevard County and his life was in danger. Silverman agreed to surrender peacefully.

Jack Frost informed me all the bad guys and gals are bagged and 8-Ball is taking Zany, Norman, and me back to Cocoa when the chopper drops me off near the underground bunker.

8-Ball is wearing a mask, and Norman is cuffed and blindfolded like he was on the boat ride to the safe underground housing. He requested to see his father who was being held in the County jail. Norman has been a model teenager, but we all know Norman is Norman. He and Erica had been separated and in isolation in the bunker. Neither one knows the location. Erica has been transported separately as she is a key witness. Zany sat in front, and Norman and I are in the back. 8-Ball takes the long way around Merritt Island before crossing the Indian River into Cocoa.

"You two are a sight for bloodshot eyes," Sheriff Woodall said. "I will take our star witness now. Thanks for keeping Norman safe."

Not surprisingly, our cars had been brought up from the Eau Gallie causeway and parked side by side waiting for us.

"Thanks for everything, my friend. Our team did us proud again," I said as I shook hands with 8-Ball.

Zany and I got out, and 8-Ball waved goodbye.

After being sequestered in the bunker, it felt great to be outside.

"Zany, would you like to walk to Ryan's for a pizza on their upstairs patio?" I asked her. "It appears a perfect day weather-wise awaits us."

"I would love to walk the Avenue with you, Rock. I love to sit upstairs and watch the boats on the river and the children playing in the park," she answered with her bounce back in her step.

As we walk the Avenue, I realize why November is my favorite month in Cocoa. The ocean breeze gently moves the Spanish moss in the live oak trees. The temperature is near a perfect seventy-two degrees every day. Even on rainy days, the bright sun dries up everything, and you can't tell it was cloudy, or it rained. Several people waved to Zany and me as we passed by.

Just ahead is 406 Delannoy Ave. We turn left to walk up the two flights of stairs to the open-air rooftop of Ryan's Pizza. Monday appears to be tourists' day. I don't see anyone we know. An umbrella table with high bar stools is open near the railing. Even Zany can see everything in Riverside Park and along the Indian River Lagoon. After all, she has been through, Zany still looks terrific.

"Hello, Zany. Hello Mr. Tyler, or shall I address you as Deputy Tyler?" our waitress greets us,

She is a part-time waitress and a full-time Brevard college student who has waited on us many times.

"Someone left these on the table before you," she said as she handed me a *Village Voice* and a *Sunshine News - Cocoa.* "What can I get you to drink?"

Zany looked at me and smiled.

"We will have two raspberry teas please," I answered.

She handed me two menus, and I gave one to Zany as our waitress left to get our drinks.

"Thank you, a gallant gentleman. It's Monday Madness so any daily special on the menu or a slice of one-topping pizza, small salad, and a fountain drink are the 'specials'," she sighed. "What's a girl to do?"

"For the first time in a long time, I feel like celebrating, Zany. What do you say? Shall we have the pizza with pepperoni, salad with chunky blue cheese, and two raspberry teas?"

Zany's laughter rolled across the park and the Indian River. People looked at us from nearby, from the Riverside Park below, and I'm sure from the boats, too.

"Rock, we think alike, and we are predictable. What's a girl to say?"

My heart leaped as I reached into my pocket just as our teas arrived.

"Thank you, I told our waitress. "We will have the pizza with pepperoni and salads with chunky blue cheese."

I placed Zany's glass closer and put the small box next to the tea. Zany leaned back and then forward. She opened the box. For once in her life, she was speechless.

"A girl could say, yes," I whispered.

Zany went from smiling to tearing and back to smiling.

"Zany Adams, will you marry me?" I asked, now, I am near tears.

A full minute went by before she whispered, "Toby Rockwell Tyler, yes, I will."

I took the diamond engagement ring from the box and slipped it on her finger.

Zany came back from wherever she was in shock and began dancing around and showing everyone her ring as she shouted, "I said, YES!"

The waitress returned with our lunch. Zany grabbed her as soon as she set the food down. She shook the diamond ring before the girl's eyes, and they held hands as they twirled between tables.

The women in the restaurant were near tears shouting, "Congratulations, honey."

All were clapping, some men were stamping their feet, and two sailboats blew their foghorns.

"This is the Happiest Day of My Life," she exclaimed. "I am the future, Mrs. Toby Rockwell Tyler!"

There was great joy as Mr. and Mrs. Ryan joined us. She hugged Zany, and he shook my hand.

"Champagne for everyone!" he said, as he began to sing, "Shrimp boats are a-coming, there's dancing tonight."

An older man with a great baritone voice shouted and sang, "Bartender, put the champagne on my tab."

The bar is in the middle of the outside deck. The bartender lifted two bottles and nodded yes.

Mr. Ryan shook his head no to the bartender and the gentleman and said, "Champagne is on the house. Congratulations on your forthcoming marriage."

Mrs. Ryan took the lunch bill and tore it up while hugging Zany.

Zany sat back down, and the festivities subsided. I asked the waitress for take-out bags. We nibbled until she returned. I placed the meals and newspapers in the Ryan's Pizza and Pub bag. We said thank you to several well-wishing customers as we walked across and down the stairs. At the bottom, we were met with loud clapping and cheers from the dining room and pub.

I put my arm around Zany on the Avenue as we walked through the village. News travels fast in this little Savanah. Well-wishers met us in front of the Porcher House.

The two lawyers next door to our office congratulated us as we entered our upstairs office. Inside, I locked the door and gave Zany a lengthy kiss. I released her, and she almost fell backward into her chair. I have never seen her so lit up.

I sat at my desk and took out our lunches and the newspapers. The *Sunshine News ~ Cocoa* had a feature titled, "Sargent James, formerly with our Cocoa Police Department and a partner of the infamous former Lieutenant Gillard who escaped from the county jail. Our competitor, the *Village Voice* owner, interviewed Sgt. James. Toby Tyler is a sworn Brevard County undercover deputy. Tyler is a man wearing several hats. Deputy Tyler is a private investigator with Zany Adams Investigative Service, Inc. James is a material witness against Gillard and is under protective custody because of numerous death threats. The James trial is this week. The location is unannounced. We hope the unsolved grisly murders of our three local teenage girls, as reported in *The Sunshine News ~ Cocoa*, are now solved."

The *Village Voice* reported:

"Iran's Allies, Russia and China are on the verge of annexing countries under the premise of 'Liberating' their citizens from illegal rebels. It is the same old story.

When Russian forces attacked U.S. troops in Syria, we smashed Russia's forces. We sent lethal weapons to Ukraine and Russia backed off. That was then.

Today, our government keeps making concessions to Communist China and Iran. Can another take over like Crimea be far away? Our liberal non-vetting of Chinese and Russian, and Iranian college students and illegals crossing our southern border ensures more terrorist attacks in the future."

"On another note, our village merchants are in full swing for Christmas. Despite high unemployment in many states, our tourists return in record numbers. Our Mayor and City Council have authorized Christmas decorations on all our streets. Our merchants supply the electricity for lighting the Christmas wreaths and angels."

"Former Sargent James of our police department is going on trial this week. He and fugitive former Lieutenant Gillard are charged with multiple crimes, including connections to the murder of Natasha Tyler and three teenagers: Serena 'Rene' Jones, Sabrina Moore, and Iris Anne Silverman."

Zany is busy answering her cell phone and the office phone. She finally switched the office phone to the answering machine. She is shaking her head and making funny faces at me. She calls her father, the Sheriff of Orange County.

"Hello, Daddy! Rock asked me to marry him in front of a crowd at Ryan's Pizza and Pub just now. I said, YES!!"

After a short pause, she said, "Daddy, I have always been an honest woman. Yes, I will still be your little Zany. Okay, I will tell him. I love you, Daddy Bear." She laughed. "Daddy said he will give me away, but there is no dowery or hope chest."

My belt gadget buzzed twice: "Congratulations, Commander. I wish you and Zany a happy marriage and many children." - Q-Ball.

"You are one lucky guy Toby Tyler. Zany is perfect for you. A child bride, but perfect, ole' boy."

My cell phone chimed. "Wonderful news. My wife and I could not be happier for you two. Congrats," Sheriff Woodall.

It chimed again.

"Congratulations to you and Zany. You broke a lot of my single officer's hearts," said Chief Brody.

The scramble phone is flashing: "Message from F.B.I. Director Lewis L. Lawson. Congratulations to Zany and you, Toby. Natasha would be pleased. We have dropped the charges against David (D) Dawson, and the C.I.A. has dropped their termination notice against him. We have proof he did not murder those in N.Y. Also, we are opening two cases per day on Chinese spies in the U S., mostly students on college or work visas."

CHAPTER 37

WE ARE ONE week closer to Christmas, and tensions are high. Nationally, we are back to high terrorist alert. Assets in Iran picked up chatter that another 9/11 attack is planned for the Great Satan on Christmas. Many in our government dismissed the threat as "idle gossip." However, Security Agencies were able to raise the alert level after private meetings. Florida is on high alert because it trained the terrorists to fly the airplanes into the Twin Towers. One crashed in Pennsylvania and one into the Pentagon. Brevard County and Orange County remain alert because terrorists used our waterways for hideouts.

Law enforcement is excited that former Lieutenant Gillard has been captured and will stand trial this month. There are Federal, State, County, and City charges against Cocoa's dirty cop. Every jurisdiction is making their case to try him first. Politicians and the press are running over each other to get in front of the T.V. cameras and on talk shows. N.Y. mafia is interested in their former associate, "Nothing personal, just business."

I received a text from Syria, "Greetings Commander. Our Iranian Colonel has become cooperative. I leaked his connections to the human trafficking of Iranian women and children to his fellow believers. He is most wanted on the Aitolia's Most Wanted list and that he is in Satan America awaiting trial for the murder of Natasha Tyler and trafficking with Lt. Gillard. D.D."

I texted back, "Great News, D.D. Also, that you are in the clear with our Agencies."

"The Iranian 'student' spy hit man confessed to killing the couple in N.Y. and made it look like me or Bisco did it. The two were rounded up in Florida. See you soon."

Though we are still living in troublesome times with evil men seeking to fulfill their different degrees of so-called mental illness, at least Gillard and James are in confinement in secure locations.

With the threat to my safety reduced, my team members are returning to their previous status. 8-Ball and Jack are staying in the loop for our wedding which is planned for Christmas eve.

My cell phone rings. It's Zany. I smile to myself. My heart starts beating faster as I see her picture appear on the cell's screen. At least for now, my world is at peace this Christmas. My journey through all the death and tragedy has taught me much about the importance of justice, true friends, love, and ultimately about the real meaning of Peace...making peace with myself, others, and most of with God. I'm running late... time to rush over to pick up Zany. Merry Christmas to us.

CPSIA information can be obtained
at www.ICGtesting.com
Printed in the USA
LVHW080728010622
720059LV00014B/356